THE
LANTERN'S
EMBER

BOOKS BY COLLEEN HOUCK

THE REAWAKENED SERIES

Reawakened

Recreated

Reunited

THE TIGER'S CURSE SERIES

Tiger's Curse

Tiger's Quest

Tiger's Voyage

Tiger's Destiny

Tiger's Dream

The Lantern's Ember

THE LANTERN'S EMBER

COLLEEN HOUCK

EMBER

Text copyright © 2018 by Colleen Houck
Cover art copyright © 2018 by Billelis

All rights reserved. Published in the United States by Ember, an imprint
of Random House Children's Books, a division of Penguin Random House LLC, New York.
Originally published in hardcover in the United States by Delacorte Press, an imprint of
Random House Children's Books, a division of Penguin Random House LLC, New York, in 2018.

Ember and the E colophon are registered trademarks of Penguin Random House LLC.

Visit us on the Web! GetUnderlined.com

Educators and librarians, for a variety of teaching tools,
visit us at RHTeachersLibrarians.com

The Library of Congress has cataloged the hardcover edition of the work as follows:
Name: Houck, Colleen, author.
Title: The Lantern's Ember / Colleen Houck.
Description: First edition. | New York : Delacorte Press, [2018] | Summary: When
seventeen-year-old Ember, a witch living in the quiet New England town of Hallowell,
crosses into the Otherworld, Jack the gatekeeper sets out to find her before the
supernatural and mortal worlds descend into chaos.
Identifiers: LCCN 2017045632 | ISBN 978-0-399-55572-5 (hc) | ISBN 978-0-399-55574-9 (el)
Subjects: | CYAC: Supernatural—Fiction. | Magic—Fiction. | Witches—Fiction. | Love—Fiction.
Classification: LCC PZ7.H81143 Lan 2018 | DDC [Fic]—dc23

ISBN 978-0-399-55575-6 (pbk)

Printed in the United States of America
10 9 8 7 6 5 4 3 2 1
First Ember Edition 2019

For Daniel and Mitchell,

who still love my Scooby-Doo cartoons,

even though the monsters

give them nightmares

I spot the hills
With yellow balls in autumn.
I light the prairie cornfields
Orange and tawny gold clusters
And I am called pumpkins.
On the last of October
When dusk is fallen
Children join hands
And circle round me
Singing ghost songs
And love to the harvest moon;
I am a jack-o'-lantern
With terrible teeth
And the children know
I am fooling.

       –Carl Sandburg,
         "Theme in Yellow"

CHAPTER 1

CROSSROADS

Jack sat on top of the covered bridge in his favorite spot, his arm draped over his carved pumpkin. The gourd wasn't his first choice to house the ember of his immortality, but then again, he'd never really been given a choice.

It wasn't the first time he'd heard of foolish men who'd made deals with the devil. During every scary story he'd been told as a child on long winter nights, he'd clutched his covers to his throat imagining frightening specters, red demons, or wicked-clawed ghouls looming out of swaying shadows, ready to snatch up unmindful children and trick them with beguiling words. His imagination never came close to the truth. And he'd certainly never envisioned those devils walking earth as mere men, dressed as pirates, storing stolen souls in harvest vegetables.

The devil who'd conscripted him five hundred years ago was named Rune. Jack barely remembered the town he was attempting to save by negotiating with Rune, or the boy he'd been when he'd done it. Now all the villagers were long dead. But not Jack. He

1

wasn't so lucky. Instead, Jack was stuck in a monotonous job, the same job Rune once had. And Jack had the pleasure of looking forward to another five hundred years of doing exactly the same thing day in and day out.

It wasn't like the job was too difficult. It was mostly quiet, but when it wasn't, he did everything from exporting entire herds of gremlins, to clearing caves full of werewolves, to capturing a flock of Otherworld bats. Jack had even done the highly dangerous job of evicting a nest of half-breed vampires from an underground necropolis, entirely on his own.

Admittedly, the swaggering pirate Rune had come to Jack's aid a time or two, helping him avert what could have been disasters. But Jack quickly learned he didn't appreciate how Rune handled mortals. Too many of them died or went insane under his care.

Eventually, Jack ended up at his current assignment, a quiet New England town called Hallowell that butted up against one of the most boring, sleepy crossroads in the entirety of the Otherworld. Rune had probably thought Jack would complain about the placement, but the town was pretty, if small. There were plenty of large oaks and maples, elms and dogwood trees to offer him shade during the day. And in the fall the colors were beautiful. There was something to be said for a quiet life.

It was lonely, but Jack was used to being alone.

He was about to summon his horse so he could ride through the forest while the red, orange, and yellow fall leaves rained down upon his head, when he heard a noise.

"Must you sit all the way up there?" Rune groused, emerging from the covered bridge and looking up at him. Smoke trailed in after the large man, pooling around his polished boots and caressing his ankles with long fingers. Stepping forward, Rune peeled off black leather gloves and stroked his short, boxed beard, shaved in thin lines and curls. "Someone could get past you before you could intervene. Besides, I hate craning my neck to have a conversation."

Jack shrugged. "I like keeping my pumpkin far from the road, so there's no risk it could get trampled on. Besides, I'd hear someone long before they got close." Jack's pumpkin never aged or decomposed, but it could be broken, and that made his soul vulnerable.

"Yes." Rune fingered his firefly-shaped earring, a far better choice of vessels for a lantern to hide his ember than a fat orange gourd. He smiled up at Jack. The shaggy hair that slipped from his careless queue hung down to his shoulders, dark, except for a white streak that fell across his eyes. "I suppose, then, that's a wise choice."

"What do you want, Rune?" Jack asked.

"There's been a rumor."

"About?"

"Your town. It would seem a witch wind is blowing and it's coming from your crossroad."

"My crossroad?" Jack said, leaping down with his pumpkin and landing easily next to Rune, feeling thin and pale next to Rune's sun-kissed tan and deep-V silk shirt. "Are you certain?"

All the lanterns were apprised when a witch wind blew. The Lord of the Otherworld gathered winds from the mortal world in a great funnel. Most of the time, the winds blowing through the crossroads were normal, but every so often, a special wind blew, indicating that a witch had grown strong enough not only to enter the Otherworld but to undo it completely. Unless the witch was captured and his or her energy contained, the Otherworld as they knew it could be destroyed. Only one witch was permitted in the Otherworld. She was trusted not just to avoid destroying it, but also to run it. She was the high witch, the Lord's wife, and provider of all the magical energy in that realm. All others were a dreadful danger.

"There are whispers," Rune insisted. "Whispers in the wind of a powerful witch. One much more skillful than any you or I have dealt with before." Rune's own light glowed brighter, his earring winking as his dark skin brightened showing the skeleton lying beneath.

Jack sighed. "You must be mistaken," he said. "I've peered beneath the skin of every citizen of this town. There's not a drop of witch blood among them." He was relieved to be able to tell Rune the absolute truth for once. Hallowell was full of very content, happy mortals.

"It's not that I'm doubting your abilities, Jack," Rune said, giving him a meaningful look that made Jack wince. "I just need to verify it for myself. You understand."

Jack waved his hand in resignation and Rune sent his firefly high above the town. It zipped back and forth, pausing occasionally while the lantern himself stared into space, seeing through the eye of his light. His eyes glowed with a silver sheen and then finally dimmed.

"Told you," Jack said. "Do you think it's possible she got the location wrong? You could tell the high witch to look again."

"If a witch wind is blowing, you can be sure there's a witch or warlock out there. Look, I'm just asking you to watch. Be on your guard. And, if you see something, let me know." He clapped Jack on the back. "Don't worry, son; if you can't finish the job, I've always got your back."

Jack frowned, bristling at the slight. "Fine. I'll send word if I find any trace of a witch," Jack said.

"You do that."

Rune left and Jack was too distracted to head off on his morning ride after all. Jack sat thinking about how strange it was for a witch wind to blow in his territory three times. Most lanterns never even had it happen once, but he'd been there when witches were detected at both Roanoke and Salem. It didn't make sense. Perhaps he was just terribly unlucky.

He was thinking about it all day as he walked the borders of the town, and into the evening as he settled down for the night on top of his bridge. The light flickered in his pumpkin and he turned it so he could trace the eyes with his fingertip. He'd long ago hollowed out the orange globe and carved a smiling face. His only companion on long days and even longer nights. It comforted him to see his ember's glow in the pumpkin's expression. The light warmed him, giving him hope that somehow, somewhere, there was a spark of freedom waiting for him, even if it was at the end of a very long, weary road.

Jack had just fallen asleep when he heard the thunder of hooves on the road leading to town. Summoning his black stallion, he leapt off the bridge and onto the monstrous horse's back as it material- ized from the Otherworld, nostrils steaming and eyes glowing with fire. The horse reared and Jack, with the pumpkin tucked beneath his arm, kicked the horse's sides, and they galloped toward the road.

He stopped on the hill and saw a carriage, shiny and new, a fine pair of horses pulling it quickly down the path. Jack chose not to show himself, but sent a moaning wind that frightened the driver who glanced right and left and cracked his whip to make the team run faster.

Jack, the lantern, sat and watched as the carriage made its way to town. Just as it passed him, the curtain moved and a small, white face was lit by a moonbeam. It was a wide-eyed little girl, her brown hair curled in ringlets. She pressed her hands against the glass and her pink mouth opened in a circle as she stared right at him.

CHAPTER 2

ROANOKE

She was, of course, a young witch. The high witch had been right after all.

Ember O'Dare was the only witch in the village; and with no one to teach her, Ember made a lot of mistakes. Once, she turned her great-aunt's kittens into piglets and only managed to turn two of them back. When her aunt asked about the litter, Ember simply handed her great-aunt the same kitten twice and the old woman was none the wiser.

Another time she singed off her own eyebrows in an attempt to cut her hair with magic. Jack, who had decided to keep an eye on the young witch instead of reporting her, had disguised his form with leaves and laughed from his perch in a tree as he watched the smoke rise, and she yelled at the sky that it wasn't funny.

She quickly became adept at using little spells such as snapping her fingers to finish her chores, or wriggling her nose to make a basket of freshly harvested corn cobs shuck themselves, or blowing a kiss to inveigle the boys in school to carry her books to and fro.

Jack often trailed along behind her, remaining hidden by disguising himself as the wind, creeping fog, or a ray of sunshine, and watched her carefully.

Even as Ember grew into a lovely young woman and a powerful witch, he never turned her in to Rune or the Lord of the Otherworld. He'd seen what they could do firsthand.

A witch wind first blew through his territory when Jack was guarding Roanoke in 1587. He was watching over the small colony that had set up their town a bit too close to his crossroad. The local witch's name was Eleanor Dare. She was powerful, Jack knew, but she was also good. Eleanor often wandered into the woods, looking for herbs and plants, singing all the while. While he glared suspiciously, the witch addressed Jack politely, nodding to him but leaving him alone.

Sometimes he'd point her in the right direction of various flora, and, in exchange, he accepted her offerings of fresh loaves of bread or small baskets filled with berries. Jack didn't need to eat, but he liked to and he appreciated her small gestures and the kindness she showed him. She asked about the Otherworld once, mentioning that she had heard that the Lord of the Otherworld hunted witches.

Jack shifted uncomfortably. "Only the dangerous ones," he'd said.

No one had told Jack that he couldn't befriend a witch, at least not directly. Three months passed with no indication that the Lord of the Otherworld was hunting a witch. Eleanor had a baby, a sweet girl with a loud cry and dark hair. Jack settled into a comfortable routine and even took to watching Eleanor from time to time while she foraged.

One day, everything was going fine. Then the call came. The witch wind was blowing. Eleanor and her baby went missing. A week later, strange things began happening.

Men screamed and tore at their hair as they transformed into wolfish monsters in the light of the moon. Others became as still as death and were buried, but rose in the night to hunt their neighbors and drink their blood. Some turned into shrinking beasts with humped backs and warty faces. They ran into the trees and lived in hollowed-out logs. All the mortals phased into Otherworld creatures.

Jack knew what was happening: The two realms were blending. He knew this only happened when a witch crossed over, but he was certain Eleanor hadn't gone to the other realm through his crossroad. He would have felt it. Still, Jack summoned Rune to help, but it was too late. The entire village had either been consumed or disappeared into the forest, becoming something altogether unhuman. It would have to be destroyed.

The two of them rounded up the monsters they could find that still lurked in the area. They killed the ones that wouldn't cooperate and sent the ones that did back to the Otherworld.

Before they left, Jack wandered over to the witch's cabin and checked to see if there were any signs of Eleanor or her daughter, but they were gone. Sadly, Jack stood, whispering words to the wind. The light in Jack's pumpkin flickered and a powerful gust dismantled the village.

As he headed back to Rune after flattening the town, he caught sight of a witch's spell. He raised his lantern and cast light upon the spot. Hidden behind the spell was a skeleton and a dead tree with letters carved into it. It was a strange word that meant nothing in any language he knew. It said CROATOAN.

Jack thought he should probably tell Rune about what he'd seen, but after the two lanterns stepped through the barrier and were safely through the crossroad, Jack concentrated on steeling himself for what he knew was coming, his final death. An ember must be extinguished to close the route.

"There's another way," Rune said quietly.

"Another way?" Jack asked. "Why weren't we told?"

"Honestly, most lanterns are to blame for the failure of their crossroad and deserve to have their lives end. I can see, however, that in this case it wasn't your fault. The witch crossed over without your knowledge."

Jack watched as Rune pulled a tiny clockwork ball from his pocket and swung back the hinged opening. He held it out to Jack who took it.

"Now toss it into the breach," Rune said.

Peering inside the container, Jack's breath caught as he saw a tiny, smoking ember dancing inside. "Whose is it?" he asked in wonder.

"Doesn't matter," Rune said. "Be happy I have an extra so your light isn't forfeit."

Deciding it was better to live and have questions than die and know answers, Jack tossed it beyond the barrier and there was a boom that rocked the land so hard, Jack stumbled and nearly fell. The light exploded and then quickly collapsed, taking the crossroad with it. There was a scent of ozone and sulfur in the air but the sweet smell of magic was gone. The crossroad was closed.

When he asked Rune about the technology, all Rune would say was that the Lord of the Otherworld's mysterious benefactor had invented it. But all Jack could think about was who had died so that he could live.

That was his first witch wind.

The next time Jack saw his boss was when he was summoned to help Rune in 1692. The devilish pirate had been sent to a crossroad in a town called Salem and once again the witch wind blew. All the work order had said was that Jack was to help Rune "contain the situation."

By the time Jack got there, many villagers had already been hanged as witches. The local lantern was nowhere to be found and Rune took seemingly great delight in stirring up the pious town reverends and magistrates. When Jack arrived, the entire town was haunted by visions of demons and witches. Jack asked Rune who among the townspeople was the witch and Rune shrugged as if it didn't matter.

Strangely, Jack was never able to find a witch, and he wondered if Rune was keeping secrets. Regardless, he never forgot Rune's callousness in either situation. He pledged to never again ask for the devil's aid, if he could help it.

Now here he was in Hallowell, watching Ember O'Dare grow up and hoping that no one else would discover his deception.

CHAPTER 3

SLEEPY HOLLOW

J ack remained vigilant where Ember was concerned and had watched over her since she was a little girl. The orphan who blew into town and was adopted by her distant great-aunt, a woman so blind and deaf she could barely tell her charge from the black cat who hissed at Jack every time he came near.

When Ember discovered the magical barrier of his crossroad, she didn't attempt to pass through the breach. Instead, she turned in a circle, her fists on her hips, and stared right at Jack's hiding place as if she could see him in his tree form. After an hour, she gave up and headed back to town.

Jack set up warnings at the cobblestone entry to the bridge but it didn't matter to Ember. She bravely wandered over to the bridge at least once a month and listened carefully as Jack set off every trigger he could think of to frighten her away. He'd tried the standards first—ghostly moans, creaking wood, echoing hoof beats, hooting owls, and chilling fog that wrapped cold hands around a mortal's body—but nothing worked.

Every time she visited, he added more tricks, bells, and whistles. After a few years, the road leading up to the bridge housed a graveyard with creepy stone gargoyles; dead trees that creaked, groaned, and snapped; cawing ravens; and spiderwebs so thick they could trap a horse.

Running out of ideas, he decided to use his horse, the giant black stallion with the fiery eyes that he'd named Shadow, to scare the girl.

The great horse galloped out of the breach, steam from his nostrils blanketing the ground, his hooves stamping great furrows in the soft black earth. Jack told Shadow to run the girl down but warned him not to harm her. The stallion pawed the air, spun, and took off down the road in a flurry of mane and tail.

Hours later, satisfied that he hadn't seen Ember in some time, Jack heard a giggle and an unmistakable snort from his frightening mount. Appalled, he followed the sound to find his horse trotting behind the seventeen-year-old girl, nudging her shoulder and smacking his lips as she held out an apple. She was bewitching, and looked as innocent and pure as a crisp fall morning—a bit windtousled and russet-lipped. Then his mouth fell open when Shadow lowered himself to the ground so she could climb on his back for a ride. Ember slipped onto his back—for she wore breeches under a half skirt—and kicked her practical black boots gently into Shadow's side, grinning as the gigantic horse delicately rose to his feet and trotted toward the meadow.

When she finally slid off and headed back to the village, Ember called out to the dark forest with a flirtatious and, dare he say it, victorious toss of her hair, "Thanks for letting me ride your horse!"

Jack stalked back to the bridge, furious. The light in his pumpkin crackled and spat. When Shadow, head hanging guiltily, clomped closer, Jack said, "That was about the most pathetic thing I've ever seen. You should be ashamed to call yourself a great and feared stallion of the Otherworld. Get on home and think about what you've done." He slapped the horse's rump.

Shadow nickered and shook his head, then headed back into the breach and disappeared while Jack shouted after him, "And no dinner tonight either! You already made a pig of yourself!"

· · ·

Ember cast the spell again, asking the whispering leaves to tell her the name of her watcher, but the only answer she heard on the wind was "Sleepy Hollow." She didn't know what it meant or why it was important, but she began carving the phrase into the old fallen tree anyway, and lit a fat tallow candle when the meadow dimmed with oncoming night so she could finish the job.

She never felt frightened in the western woods. Even at night, she'd occasionally sleep in the glade alone, wrapped in her cloak. There was nothing of the nefarious in her fellow townspeople so she never worried about being caught there unawares. Long ago, she'd developed the ability to read minds. In most cases, the villagers had nothing to hide other than the occasional husband imbibing in secret to avoid lectures from his wife, or a slight misrepresentation on the quality of produce sold or traded. The townsfolk were good at heart.

As for wild beasts, she knew wolves roamed the woods, but Ember didn't fear animals. All the forest creatures she'd come across had been strangely interested in her, but not because they wanted to devour her. Even the unruliest horses quieted beneath her hands.

Besides, there were plenty of sheep, cows, geese, and chickens roaming around and they'd be much more tempting a dinner for a pack of wolves than a human.

Wandering strangers would normally pose a threat, she'd admit, but Ember was nowhere near the roads leading to town and she knew she was never really alone, not truly. Her invisible protector was always near.

She'd only seen him once.

When she was young, she'd caught a glimpse of him on his horse. All she could recall was wild, unkempt hair as white as a moonbeam, a dark coat hugging a long, lean form, and silver eyes that pierced the darkness. Even then she hadn't been afraid of him. Only curious.

She'd felt his presence often since then. Sometimes she dreamed of him. As a child, he seemed to her like an older brother. A guardian and a friend. Someone who knew what she was, who understood her power. Ember sensed him watching and honed her skills with magic, hoping he approved and was impressed by her abilities.

When Ember grew older and the young men of the village began seeking her out, hoping to engage her romantically, her dreams of her invisible sentinel changed. Her breath hitched when she sensed him near and she sought more opportunities to walk the paths he guarded.

None of the village boys she knew interested her. They were as easy to read as tea leaves at the bottom of a cup or the promising taste of rain in the sky. Ember didn't want easy. She wanted mysterious.

Above all else, she wanted him to reveal himself. To tell her why he'd been watching from the shadows all her life. When nothing she said out loud worked well enough to get him to respond, she turned to spells, but no magic she conjured would show her what she most longed to see.

Exhausted from trying once again, she lay down in the grass near the fallen tree she'd just carved words into. She wriggled uncomfortably for a moment, her boots catching on the hem as she dragged the length of her skirts over her legs and then twirled her fingers in the air to loosen the stays of her corset, a trick she'd learned very quickly when she'd come of an age to wear one, and fell into a deep sleep.

When she woke to the sound of chittering squirrels, she found she was warmly wrapped though she knew she'd forgotten her cloak. Ember inhaled and caught the scent of leather, wood, and something rich and dark, like mulling spices. Rising, she shook out the greatcoat that unmistakably belonged to a man and studied it.

From the length of it she could tell he was taller than she, though most men she knew were. The coat was dark, a sort of blue-black, wide at the shoulders and draping straight through the waist only to flare out slightly at the bottom. The buttons were carved ivory or bone, very finely done and colored to look like leering grins and sunken eyes. She brushed the leaves off the fabric and slid her hand down the inner lining, reveling in the silky feeling.

Stretching out her senses, she didn't detect him near at the moment. As Ember chewed on her lip, her stomach rumbled with hunger. She remembered that Samhain began that evening. That meant the harvest celebration would soon be well under way and she had a lot to do since her school oversaw all the festivities. Her aunt would be missing her.

Ember cut through the apple orchard, waving to the men who were up early harvesting the ripe fruit and reminding them to save her a bushel for her winter stores. Her mouth watered as she thought of her aunt's famous apple cobbler served up with a warm mug of frothy milk topped with cream. Ember liked pouring the milk right on top of the bubbling cobbler so the sweet dough soaked up all the cream and the rich liquid filled all the crannies.

When Ember reached the now-familiar cobblestone path, she ducked between the overgrown bushes and skipped ahead quickly, ignoring the cawing ravens, the moaning wind, and the flickering lights meant to frighten her.

After Ember arrived at the bridge, she cleared her throat and said loudly, "Thank you for lending me your coat, good sir. It was much appreciated." Carefully, she folded it and placed it atop the stone wall. Then, kicking the toe of her boot in the dirt, added, "So, tonight the town is celebrating Samhain and the harvest. If you're of a mind, I'd be happy to offer you a cup of cider and a meal to repay you for the use of your coat. I heard that old Widow Mead is making currant bread pudding with sticky toffee sauce."

There was no answer except the stirring of leaves at her feet, but Ember knew he was near, listening.

"Well, do as you will, but know you are welcome." With that, Ember curtsied awkwardly, turned, and marched stiffly down the path toward home.

CHAPTER 4

SAMHAIN

She dressed carefully that night. Instead of her comfortable breeches and knee-high boots flecked with mud, she wore a full dress in a blue print with tatted lace at the elbows and collar. She paired the dress with a soft pair of white, silk stockings and black slippers. Her waist was cinched tightly, accentuating the soft curves of her body both above and below her corset. Ember ran a hand over a plump hip and sighed.

She would much rather be thin and small-chested like several of the girls in her class. A large bosom did nothing except to serve as a distraction. How many times had she been talking with a classmate about something serious, only to find his eyes had drifted down by degrees, settling somewhere between her chin and her navel and taking up residence?

Ember's dark brown hair hung down her back in soft ringlets, the sides pulled up and pinned back with a pair of jeweled combs that belonged to her great-aunt. One lone ringlet was positioned over her shoulder, the end of it just reaching the neckline of her gown and making the bare skin above it glow in contrast. She daubed on a splash of perfume she'd created using the skills her aunt taught her combined with a small spell meant to draw the eyes of the one she wanted to meet.

When Ember was ready, she took the arm of her great-aunt Florence, who tucked a delicate handkerchief into Ember's sleeve, and then Ember guided her to the festivities. The night was warm, and Ember settled her aunt in a chair next to her friends, then turned to watch the boys as they bobbed for apples, flicking back their sopping hair and shouting their success to the crowd as they tried to tempt unattached maidens to take the first bite.

Older women peeled apples in long strips and handed them to their unmarried daughters and granddaughters to toss over their shoulders. After doing so, the girls would turn with a squeal to examine the patterns the peels made, hoping to divine the first letter of their future husband's first name. Ember's aunt handed one to her.

Ember sighed. "You know this means nothing," she said loud enough so her aunt could hear. "It's just a silly game. There's no magic in it at all." According to Florence, Ember's great-great-great-grandmother had been a witch, so Ember's abilities didn't frighten her in the least. Ember had repeatedly offered to try to find a spell to give her aunt back her sight or her hearing or both, but her aunt had opted not to try. "There's a price to pay for all magic," she'd said. "And I'm not sure I'd want to pay something so heavy."

Now Florence responded, patting Ember's hand. "I know, dear. I know. But oblige an old woman. There's a bit of magic in hope, and I'd like to entertain the notion that you won't end up alone in your later years like me."

Squeezing her aunt's hand, Ember said, "Fine. I'll throw the apple peel. But only because I love you."

"What?" Ember's aunt asked.

"I said I'll throw it!" Ember said next to her aunt's ear. Then she closed her eyes and tossed the peel over her shoulder. It landed in a long line with a tiny curl at the bottom. "There, you see? It makes no letter at all."

"It matters not in the least," Florence said. "It's all part of the fun."

"Right. Fun," Ember said.

"Looks like an 'I' to me," a bushy-browed man sitting near her aunt said into her ear trumpet.

"Oh, Ignatius," said Florence as she threw a peel in his direction. "Ember's much too young for an old man like you."

Ignatius, the town magistrate, waggled his eyebrows at Ember as he adjusted his slipping wig and loosened his cravat.

"He's far too handsome a lad for me, you mean," Ember said with a wink. "Besides, what would his wife say?" As Ignatius sputtered, and Florence asked loudly, "Where's your wife? Is she here?" Ember took her leave to find the food.

The air smelled of apples, smoke, pumpkins, and cinnamon. Young people crowded around the bonfire and filled their plates from the fare placed on long tables by the women of the town. Betrothed couples tossed hazelnuts into the fire waiting to see if they would pop and separate or burn close together symbolizing a harmony and peace in their upcoming unions. Ember ignored them and loaded a plate with roasted corn, pigeon pie, steamy chicken and dumplings, fried hominy, a slice of fruit tart, pickles, and a fresh baked roll slathered with creamy butter and thick jam.

As Ember tucked into her food, she noted the abundance of lanterns lit with flickering candles. They graced porches and windows in an attempt to ward off evil spirits thought to wander the dark roads on Samhain. According to tradition, some folks thought they were also meant to welcome spirits of deceased loved ones.

Ember didn't know if ghosts were real. She'd never seen one though she'd looked. Ember knew there were things she couldn't see that were perfectly real, but she told her aunt that, in her opinion, ghosts and spirits probably had a lot more interesting things to do than haunt the living. Her aunt agreed. Even still, her aunt had set an extra place at the table that night for her late husband. Ember supposed it gave comfort to the living and, if the dead were given a peek, she thought they'd probably like to know they were still in someone's thoughts.

Something moved in the corner of her eye. She thought for a moment a lantern was dancing in the dark, but then, when she blinked, it was gone. She heard a plaintive meow and bent down, giving a stray cat her uneaten pigeon pie. When she stood, Ember stretched out her mind and felt the comforting presence of her silent watcher. Picking up the cleaned plate, she patted the cat on the head and strode outside the glow of the bonfire.

A hand touched her shoulder and everything in Ember stilled. "I believe you dropped this," a squeaky male voice said.

Ember frowned. In all her imaginings, her guardian's voice had never squeaked. She turned. "Oh, Finney. Thank you," she said, taking the handkerchief he held out.

The young man blushed when she tucked it into the décolletage of her dress. She'd done it hastily and a corner of the handkerchief stuck out the top of her neckline. "Yes, umm . . . well . . . you're welcome, Ember," he said, shifting nervously and scratching his head.

Then he took a deep breath and offered his arm. "Care to take a turn around the barn with me?"

"Why not?" Ember gifted her friend with a smile but the smile faded when she glanced behind at the dark road lit with lamps.

Later, after dinner, she played a game with the girls just to make everyone happy. They took turns pouring egg whites into a bowl to see if a letter formed. Again, the letter was supposed to indicate a future husband. Though she was hardly interested, she took the offered bowl of water, and poured in the stirred egg. Of course, hers moved very differently from everyone else's. At first, the egg swirled and swirled and then it straightened into a long line with a hook at the end, just as the apple peel had done before. Someone suggested it was a "J" and another hollered "I," which resulted in a hoot from Ignatius.

When the evening's festivities were over, the bonfire burned out, and the food put away, Ember put her aunt to bed and blew out all the candles except one. Taking a mug of cider and a small plate of delicacies, she went to her room and placed her offerings on the windowsill, covering the food with the handkerchief she pulled out of the bodice of her dress.

"This is for you," she called out softly. The night air had turned crisp and the full moon bathed her face in light as she looked out into the thicket surrounding her home. "I'm sorry you weren't comfortable enough to come to the party. I brought you a bit of cake though."

The air felt thin and bursting with life. It always seemed to Ember that on Samhain, the world sucked in a breath and held it, waiting for the chime of midnight to ring, and then it slowly exhaled, blowing all the unseen things far back, away from the world of the living.

She sensed it now. The world getting ready to inhale, leaving summer behind and plunging headfirst into winter. Ember turned her back to the window and sat in the small chair by her writing desk. She looked in the mirror to take the combs from her hair and felt the curls tumble around her shoulders. Picking up a brush, she began to run it through the long strands. The lone candle in her room wavered as if it would go out and then the flame turned icy blue. Her breath fogged the mirror and, when she looked up, a moonlight-haired boy with steely, silver eyes stood behind her shoulder, looking at her in the mirror.

Gasping softly, Ember dropped her brush and felt a soft breeze on her cheek as the candle went out.

CHAPTER 5

HARBINGER

Even without the benefit of the light, she could see him in the mirror behind her. His skin glowed as if lit from beneath. The world hung on the cusp of commutation as the midnight hour cast its spell. Nervously, Ember reached for her water pitcher and filled a cup. The water sloshed out over the sides as she pressed the cup to her lips. She said, "I'd hoped you'd come."

The young man behind her frowned and began to walk toward the window, lifting a lit pumpkin in his hand. Ember spun and stood abruptly. "Don't go!" she exclaimed. Her chair toppled and she reached for it, but missed. The striking apparition with the moonbeam eyes caught it for her and set it on its feet. "Please," she said. "Not yet. I have . . . I have so wanted to meet you."

She twisted her hands and her guardian looked down at them and then back at her face, then he took her hand, opened it, and placed her folded handkerchief in her palm. Ember's fingers tightened over the bit of cloth, catching his fingers in her own, and she gasped. "Your hands," she said. "They're warm. I didn't expect that from a ghost."

He snorted and pulled his hands away. "For a witch, you certainly don't know much about how hauntings work."

His voice was rich and resonant, with a timbre that lingered, caressing Ember's skin long after he'd finished speaking. Boldly, she assessed his appearance. He looked exactly how she remembered, though she'd just been a little girl. He was several inches taller than she was, and though she suspected he was older, he appeared to be only a year or two her senior. The young man's moonlight hair was still wild and unkempt, framing his head like a halo, and his silver wolf's eyes sparkled, gleaming in the dark.

"What's your name?" Ember asked.

The young man shrugged. "Does it matter?"

"Of course it matters. How else am I to address you? Manners dictate we should be properly introduced."

He laughed softly, placed his arm across his middle and gave her a formal bow, though he never took his eyes off hers. "In that case, since manners are so important, you can call me Jack."

"Jack." Ember clicked her tongue, considering his name, and found it suited him. "Very well, then. Hello, Mr. Jack. I am Ember O'Dare."

"There's no 'Mr.' Just Jack."

"Just Jack."

"Exactly. And I already know who you are. You're the town witch."

Ember placed her hands on her hips. "I am at a disadvantage. You know what I am, and yet I have no idea what you are."

A rumble echoed in the sky and drops of rain pinged on the

open windowsill. Ember headed over and looked outside. Sensing the storm, she shut the window tight, closing the curtains. Then she froze, remembering there was a man in her room. She turned her head to glance at him over her shoulder just as lightning struck. Jack's face was illuminated by the light, but instead of a chiseled jaw, wide nose, and angled cheekbones, she saw a grinning skeleton.

She started and let out a tiny gasp of alarm. When the light faded, his face looked as it had before. Ember had never seen such a thing.

Jack studied her and shifted, lifting his pumpkin closer to his face. "It's a trick of the light," he said. "The ember inside the gourd shows my true nature as well."

When he lifted the orange globe, the skeleton beneath his skin shone through once again.

Ember gulped. "So does that mean you're . . . you're . . ."

"Dead?" he answered, then shook his head. "No. I'm not dead. Though, technically, I'm not fully living either. I straddle the line between the two. That's what it means to be a lantern."

"A lantern?" Ember echoed, thinking of the still-winking lights outside meant to either summon or scare away the dead.

"Yes. I guard the crossroads between the mortal world and the Otherworld."

"Otherworld?"

"Yes."

Ember cocked her head, curious. "Would you like to sit down?"

Jack stiffened and glanced at her bed. "No. I don't think that would be appropriate," he answered. "But, thank you for the . . . invitation."

Mortified, Ember paced to her table, feeling a flush burn her cheeks. "No, I . . . no. Of course not. It's just that this is the first time you've shown yourself and spoken with me, and I have so many questions."

"Yes, I know."

Ember's brows knit together, suspicion gnawing at the corners of her mouth, turning them down. "Why tonight?" she asked.

"What do you mean?"

"Did you come because I invited you?"

"Yes and no."

"Well, which is it?"

"I . . . I follow you often."

"Yes, I'm aware of that."

Jack grimaced. "I didn't intend for you to see me."

"So you weren't planning on introducing yourself tonight?"

"No. Lanterns often struggle to cloak themselves from witches who have come of age," he explained. "The veil is thin on Samhain. The lines are blurred. I should have remembered that and avoided coming to town."

"Why?"

"Why is the veil thin?"

"No. Why have you hidden from me all these years?"

Jack sighed and set his pumpkin on the table. He swept back his greatcoat and put his hands on his lean hips. Ember found she was distracted by the waistcoat that hugged his form and the silver chain that adorned it, one end disappearing into a pocket on each side. The chain itself was lovely, each link was intricately designed with swirls and loops, and there was a pendant hanging below the button where the chain was attached. She could just make out the shape of a key.

"Is that for a pocket watch?" she asked.

"It is."

"What use does a ghost have for a pocket watch?"

"I'm not a ghost. I'm a lantern. And what I use a pocket watch for is my business."

"Can I see it?"

"No."

Ember stepped closer. "Why don't you just cram the chain inside the pocket along with the watch?"

Jack's mouth opened, as if appalled. "Because the chain would scratch the watch. It's an antique."

"All the more reason to show it off, then. Perhaps you should pin it to your waistcoat instead."

"And risk it getting rained on? I think not."

Her piqued interest extinguishing decorum, something she was far too often guilty of, Ember touched her fingertips to the watch chain and asked, "But why do you have a chain on both sides?"

"Because I carry two watches. One keeps time in the mortal realm and the second keeps time, as it were, in the Otherworld."

Ember's face took on an expression of sheer awe. Audaciously, she trailed a finger down one of the chains, but Jack immediately took hold of her hands and cupped them together, then took an obvious step back and dropped them.

"The Otherworld is filled with the devil's fire, young miss. It would behoove you to consider the consequences before you leap after it."

The wind scraped the shutters outside, causing them to thump against the house. Jack brushed aside the curtains. The sky was a tortured tint of roiling black and purple. It would be a long night for him. "I have to go," he said.

"Why?" Ember hated that she'd asked him that same simple

question more than once when her mind was absolutely brimming with things she wanted to know, things more complicated and wondrous than a simple "why."

"The first reason is that it's highly inappropriate for me to even enter a maiden's room, let alone linger in it." He didn't bother to mention that he'd been in her room multiple times over the years without her knowledge. "The second reason is that the veil is thin tonight, like I already said. I need to guard the paths, make sure creatures of the Otherworld don't sneak through."

"You mean like ghosts and goblins and such? They can do that?"

"Ghosts, as you call them, are not really what you need to worry about. Though I would watch out for goblins. They like to eat magic."

Ember blanched. "Eat . . . magic?"

"Oh, yes." Jack gave her a mischievous grin. "They especially like to nibble on the toes of young, impertinent witches."

Shoving open the window, Jack hopped up onto the sill and threw his legs over. Ember caught his arm. "Will I see you again?" she asked. "Say yes."

The lantern looked outside then back at the witch. His eyes softened and the corners of his mouth quirked into a small smile. He pushed her away gently, though she still clung to his arm, and summoned his pumpkin. It lifted off the desk and floated over to his outstretched hand. "It will be harder for me to hide from you now that you've set eyes upon my face," he answered. With that, Jack snapped his fingers and his body melted into fog and drifted outside, disappearing in the dark.

Ember stood there a long time. Long enough for the rain to soak the front of her dress and her hair to droop in wet lengths down her bodice. Finally, she ducked inside, closed the window, and sopped up the mess. When she climbed into bed that night, she couldn't sleep. Jack, and the magic surrounding him, filled her thoughts.

• • •

When Jack left Ember, he cursed. What the devil had he been thinking? He was no wet-behind-the-ears, new-to-the-Otherworld lantern. He knew what might happen, and that by visiting Ember he risked her seeing him. Then to speak to her? It was folly.

He knew how Rune handled witches. The more Ember came around, which she would, knowing her, the more certain the chances that Rune would notice her.

But hadn't a part of him wanted this? Why else would he have draped his coat over her as she slept? Jack didn't know what was wrong with him.

The rain beat down on his shoulders as he trudged up the cobblestone path, but Jack froze when he smelled something sweet and acrid: a troll. Trolls were not uncommon, even in the mortal realm, though most humans never even knew they were there.

Jack checked the barrier to the Otherworld, but there were no tracks, no scents emerging from his bridge, which meant the troll had wandered into Jack's territory through the forest. It had likely been born and raised in the mortal realm.

By the odor, he could tell it was a male, perhaps leaving the brood for the first time to forge out on his own and seek a mate. To gain the interest of a female, he'd have to occupy and secure a nesting area. Sadly for this troll, he'd chosen Jack's covered bridge while Jack had been in town.

Crouching down, Jack peered underneath the timbers. A gleaming pair of eyes flashed in the darkness. "I'd come out if I were you," Jack warned.

A voice hissed back, "Stay away or I'll eat ya."

"I don't think you'd find me very tasty."

"Who's ya ta tell me what's tasty?"

"I'm the lantern that guards this land. You've wandered into my territory. Now, are you coming out of your own free will or do I have to drag you out by the long hairs of your head?"

"Not comin'," the troll said. "Never heard o' no lantern. Go guard some other place. This here bridge is mine. Best move on now before I change me mind and gnaw your bones for dinner."

Never heard of a lantern? That was a new one. Most Otherworlders living in the mortal realm gave lanterns a wide berth. Any seen fraternizing with humans or coming near a village were immediately sent to Otherworld holding facilities.

Jack sighed. "Very well." He held up his pumpkin and the light inside brightened.

The troll beneath the bridge screamed as the light became brighter. He wailed, "It hurts! It burns! Douse your light! I'm beggin' ya!"

"Will you come out?" Jack asked.

"Yes. Yes," the troll said, his eyes streaming with tears. Quickly, he scrambled out from beneath the bridge, his long fingers digging handholds in the mud and clasping rocks as he pulled himself up.

Jack studied the trembling creature. His bald, craggy head sprouted only a few long, wiry hairs, and he had the skinny frame of youth. The troll's hunched back was covered in lichen and sprouting mushrooms, and the few clothes on his body were mildewed and half rotted away. The wide feet were bare and mud-caked and the nails were long, jagged, and blackened with fungus. But his arms were strong and elongated, giving him the ability to hold on to the underside of a bridge for an extended length of time.

Jack knew the longer the arms were, the better the odds of the troll choking his rivals to hold his bridge or grasping on to and holding a female captive during mating. Jack wrinkled his nose. The troll's odor would be attracting half the female trolls in the territory.

"I'm sorry," Jack said, "but you can't stay here."

"I knows. I knows. I'll move on."

"That's not enough now," Jack said. "I'll have to send you back."

"Back?" The troll's shining eyes widened in alarm. "Back? No! Please. I can't go ta the other place!"

"It's called the Otherworld. It's not a bad place, just different."

"Me great-gramperes escaped from there. They told me terrible stories. Trolls gots no freedoms there."

"Of course they do," Jack countered, though he really didn't know if they did. He'd only spent brief days in the Otherworld, staying only long enough to learn his duties, and then he'd been assigned to the mortal realm where he'd remained ever since. From what he remembered, the cities of the Otherworld were remarkable. Full of inventions the humans hadn't even considered yet. Still, a country-raised boy like Jack felt much more comfortable in quiet towns like Ember's. The Otherworld cities were much too wild and chaotic.

"I begs ya!" the troll cried, tugging on Jack's coat. "I'll go far away. Ya'll not see a hair o' me head or catch a whiff o' me hide."

"I wish I could let you go. I really do. But you've already marked my bridge. If I allow you to wander, you'll attract too many others—both males who want to battle and females who want to . . . er . . . wrestle with you in other ways. I'll be up to my ears in trolls." Jack's mouth twitched wryly as he considered the troll's long tapered ears, the centers tufted with hair, and the backs pocked with warts.

The troll puffed up his chest at the idea of females looking for him, but Jack could still see the fear on his wide face. "I warns ya," the troll said. "Ya sends me there ta me death. That other place is no home for a troll. The bridges are metal. They gives no life ta trolls. The sky's so full o' smog, the moss on me back will shrivel. What female will take me then?"

"I really couldn't say," Jack answered, blinking, as he pondered what a female troll would be attracted to. "But I'm sure you'll be fine. If you have a problem, contact my superior, Rune. He'll help you find a bridge to call home. Now close your eyes. It will hurt less that way."

Jack raised his pumpkin high and the smiling face he'd carved into it cast its light on the troll. The creature shook violently, steam rising from his body, and then there was a flash and he was gone. Setting down his pumpkin, Jack dusted his hands and sneezed.

• • •

The man, if you could call him that, stared into the orb watching Jack banish the troll. He waved his hand over the looking glass to cut off the precious witchlight and the image inside disappeared. The girl was nearly ripe for the plucking. He could almost taste her. The power she possessed would fuel him for five hundred years, perhaps longer. The last one hadn't been as strong. He'd only gotten a bit more than two hundred years from draining her. This one, though—he was certain she was the one he'd been looking for.

When the time was right, he'd draw her in. Bind her to himself with a witch's song. Something no witch could resist or escape. And then, when she walked in his door, he'd play the kind benefactor at first, ply her with riches, a seat of power, all the comforts she could ask for, in exchange for just a taste. She didn't need to know that once the door to her soul was open, he could take everything.

The girl could say no, of course. Fighting him would offer a different kind of pleasure, but it would, unfortunately, damage his prize. He'd lose some years that way, but he could afford to. After all, he'd done this for eons and the devil always got his due. He chuckled and rubbed his hands in anticipation.

There was a knock on the door. The high witch curtsied and asked if he was ready to join the celebration.

"Absolutely," he said, offering the old hag, her face painted with a spell, a simpering smile. "I wouldn't miss it for the world."

When he laughed, she joined him, but hers sounded more like a cackle.

CHAPTER 6

GRAVE CONSEQUENCES

Jack woke to the sound of someone calling his name. "Jack? Jack! Where are you?"

Groggy, he shifted to a sitting position and ran a hand through his hair, making it stand up on end. "What is it?" he asked, his eyes still closed.

"What are you doing up there? Were you sleeping on top of the bridge? It's late afternoon. I'd think you'd be up and about by now. I barely slept at all last night, thanks to you."

"Miss Ember?" Jack said, rubbing his eyes.

"Of course. Who else would it be? The boogeyman?"

Immediately, Jack leapt from his perch, landing softly in front of Ember. "Shhh," he said, pressing the tips of his fingers against her mouth. He looked left and right as if waiting for something. Her breath was warm and moist against his fingers and her lips were as soft as rose petals. "Don't invoke his name," Jack warned.

"Who? The b—"

Jack made a noise and covered her mouth entirely with his palm. "I'm serious," he said.

"Bit is jess a tory," Ember said against his hand.

"What?" he asked, moving his palm away.

"It's just a story," she repeated quietly.

"There's a reason for most stories," he replied. "Even lanterns are scared of the . . . you know who."

"So he's real?"

"As real as I am."

"Humph," Ember grunted.

"Look, a long time ago the Lord of the Otherworld banished the . . . the one we're talking about. It's part of the reason Otherworlders have kept the Lord in power for so long."

"How was he defeated?"

"No one really knows, but it's said one of his weaknesses is onyx. It's probably just an old wives' tale but even when I was a boy—a long, long time ago—there were stories. Once he was gone the Otherworld changed, for the better, most people think. Now, enough about that. What brings you here?" Jack said.

"I've decided I want to see this Otherworld," Ember declared with a deadpan expression.

Jack couldn't trust himself to speak for a moment. Only a squeak came out. Then he took hold of Ember's shoulders and pushed her away from the crossroad until her back hit a tree. "No," he said, looming over her, in a voice that brooked no argument. "In fact, I don't want you to come here ever again."

"But why not?" she asked.

"You don't need to know why. You only need to obey."

"Obey?" she echoed, aghast. Ember placed her hands on her hips. "I'm not your dog or your horse. Nor are you my master."

Jack flinched. The words he'd just said had been an echo of the way his father had spoken to his mother many hundreds of years before. The memory still fixed in his mind, he deliberately removed his hands from her shoulders, and said, "I'm not trying to subjugate you, I'm trying to protect you."

"Protect me from what?"

"Do you want a list?"

"It's a good place to start."

"Fine." He held up a hand. "Trolls, goblins, werewolves, vampires, gremlins." Raising his other, he continued. "Reanimated corpses, banshees, golems, succubae, incubi." When he ticked off all those fingers, he dropped his hands and, seeing her chin was still lifted defiantly, he pressed on. He had to make her understand. Panic filled him and his voice increased in volume as if he were trying to communicate with her practically-deaf aunt. "Dark witches, phantoms, specters, spooks, devils, a host of familiars and creatures enslaved to serve their masters, the one you mentioned that we don't name, and, oh, yes, especially lanterns such as myself!"

When he finished, he was panting, but, for all his agitation, Ember remained unaffected. "Is that all?" she asked quietly, attempting to fold her arms across her expansive chest, and failing.

"Isn't that enough?" Jack shouted despite his determination to remain calm. "Any one of those creatures would eat up a child like you for breakfast and still need a midmorning snack!"

Anger flared in Ember's eyes. "I am *not* a child," she said, enunciating each word.

Jack took in her flushed face. A becoming pink stained her cheeks and neck, but he grunted, threw up a hand, and turned away. "It doesn't matter," he said flatly. "You're not going."

"I'll find a way."

"I'll stop you."

"I'm not giving up."

"Ember, please." Jack took her hands and pressed them between his own. "You don't know what they'd do to you over there. They don't trust witches. In fact, once a witch is discovered, she's carted off to the capital, never to be heard from again, and I suspect that some . . . some have been destroyed.

"When you came to town, a witch wind blew. That means you are markedly interesting to the Otherworld. If they knew you were here, they'd take you away and I . . . I'd never see you again. Not even I know exactly what happens with these special witches. You must understand how dangerous this is. I haven't told them about you for just this reason. Not anyone. Even my superior doesn't know you exist. I've been very careful to keep him far away from the village and you in particular."

"But why?" she asked. "Why do they hate witches so much?"

"They don't hate them. It's more like they fear them. At least, that's what I've been told. Who knows how much of it is true." Sighing, Jack sat down on the stone wall, crossing one long booted leg over the other at the ankles.

"Please, Jack?" Ember said, putting her hand on his arm.

He almost couldn't help himself. He began talking. "Long ago," he said, "witches ran the Otherworld. Then the high witch married a man and gave him the power to rule. He called himself the Lord of the Otherworld. Other witches protested his right to reign but stayed, even as they worried he was pushing for automation too quickly. Now the entire realm operates by witch power."

"Witch power?"

"Yes. Instead of candles, Otherworlders use witch lamps that turn on with the push of a button. There are tall buildings, some five levels high, with steam-powered boxes that lift people to the top. And there are machines that do everything from bringing in the harvest to controlling the weather to producing fabric. Witchlight heats homes and cauldron steam fuels air transports, boats, and steel wagons large enough to move a dozen people or more over tracks that connect cities."

Ember slowly sank down beside him. "We can do that?" she asked in wonder.

"Your power can. Your innate witchlight in particular is very powerful, especially for one so young and virtually untrained." He paused, collecting his thoughts. "But for the Otherworld to advance so far beyond humans unbalanced the realms. The mortal realm and the Otherworld sit on a precarious scale, only separated by crossroads in fixed positions like mine. They teeter back and forth a bit naturally, but the witches believed that if one shifts the balance too much, the realms would bleed together and entire cities disappear on both sides, vanishing into the ether. So the witches were not pleased, and they protested, loudly, wanting to evict the Lord of the Otherworld from his lofty perch. They even did something unthinkable. They called upon the one we never summon, the . . ."

"The boogeyman?"

"Shhh! Yes, *him*, for help." He sighed. "It didn't work. And so, the witches saw no other choice but to leave. They left the Otherworld, taking their power with them, sneaking into the mortal realm and settling there in quiet places."

A cat wound itself between Jack's legs. He nudged it away with his boot and then pressed on with increased resolve. "Without witchlight to fuel the Otherworld, power was rationed. Only the high witch, the wife of the Lord of the Otherworld, remained. Many of the machines stopped running. Everyday living became . . .

difficult. Some Otherworlders snuck through the divide, looking for a better life."

"Good for them." Ember nodded.

"Not so fast. Too many were leaving, and the Otherworld couldn't function without workers. A new law was passed to criminalize those who fled. So now lanterns send Otherworlders back when we find them, and if they refuse to go, they are destroyed."

"You mean . . . you . . ." Ember's words trailed off and she swallowed, her pulse pounding when Jack nodded.

"Yes. Me. Witches are the exception," he added reluctantly. "We are to report any witches, never destroy them ourselves."

"I see," Ember said quietly. "But . . . you haven't reported me?"

"No."

"Why not? I mean, that's your job, isn't it?"

"It is," Jack admitted. "But, you're just coming into your power anyway. You were only a child when the witch wind blew and, after I got to know you, I just couldn't put your fate in their hands. I work for them, but I don't trust them."

"Oh."

Ember knotted her fingers in her lap and Jack had a strong desire to reach across, take her hands in his and loosen them, weaving them with his own. Instead, he asked, "Do you understand now why it's dangerous for you to be here, so near the crossroad? To even consider going into the Otherworld is reckless."

"Yes," Ember replied. "I see your point."

"Good." He hopped down, clasped his hands behind him, and stretched out the kinks in his back, then cracked his neck loudly.

"I'm still going though."

Jack spun around. "Did you not hear a single thing I said?" he asked incredulously.

"I did. It's just that I feel . . . I feel drawn to it. I can't explain it fully. Not exactly. It's like I'm being called to it." Ember reached down automatically when she felt the brush of a tail against her leg and patted the head of the meowing cat. She wasn't sure how they always found her, but cats had followed her for most of her life.

"You have to understand that I'm wasting my life away here, Jack. I need to explore, to see the world. The people in my village are sweet, but they just want me to pick a husband and have babies. I know I'm not ready for that. I'm not even sure if that's what I want for myself. There's so much I want to see and do, I'm practically bursting with the tension of it."

"Then . . ." Jack worked the muscles in his jaw. "Then take a trip. Migrate south with the birds. Go visit a big town with your aunt. Even visit the next town over, but don't set your sights on the Other-world. It's too dangerous."

"Maybe . . . maybe if you went with me, it wouldn't be." Her eyes begged him to consider it. "Please? I'm sure the pull will go away if I just see it once. You'll keep me safe. I know you will."

Strangely, he found he wanted to go with her. Not to the Other-world necessarily, but somewhere, anywhere. He'd be proud to escort a young lady like Ember on his arm. After a beat, he answered, "I can't. I'm not allowed to leave my post."

"Fine." She lifted her chin stubbornly. "I'll bring Finney, then."

"No, you won't bring Finney." Jack chafed at the thought that she might take her red-headed, coltish friend over him. "You can't cross over, Ember. I won't allow it," he finished, slashing his hand down in a there-will-be-no-further-discussion-on-the-matter way.

"There's something you need to learn about me," Ember said, sauntering closer and poking him in the chest. "No one, not even a devilishly handsome, pumpkin-carrying lantern, tells me what to do."

Ember stood on tiptoe but she still only came up to Jack's nose. She was close enough, though, for him to catch a whiff of her hair. Ember smelled like fresh baked spiced apples. Taking hold of her shoulders again, Jack leaned down, ignoring the warning hiss of the cat. He heard Ember catch her breath. When his mouth was a few inches from hers, he lingered there for a heartbeat and then moved his lips to her ear.

"You'll never get past me," he promised.

Stiffening, Ember stepped back, eyes flashing. "We'll see about that," she said.

CHAPTER 7

I PUT A SPELL ON YOU

Jack had to give it to her. Ember was determined. Never in his long life had he had to guard a crossroad so carefully. She tried every trick she could think of to get past him. Some of her ideas bordered on the ridiculous, such as when she tried to trap him with a knife planted upside down in the ground. Such a thing might work on a wandering spirit who would become fascinated with their own reflection, but Jack was no simple wandering spirit.

Then she tried sneaking up on him wearing all her clothes inside out. He laughed so hard that she yelled at him for a good half hour before stomping home. Many a human had lost their life trying to fool the undead or werewolves by doing so. Those creatures relied on scent to guide them anyway. They couldn't care less about what the humans wore.

She tried a handful of spells and potions, but they were just irritating. One covered his bridge in fog for an entire week, but he was a lantern and could see her familiar soul coming the moment she stepped onto his path. He stopped her easily and turned her back home with a firm kick. If he wasn't so worried about Ember being discovered, he wouldn't have minded her attempts to best him.

When winter came, and the nip in the air bit sharper than a newborn vampire's teeth, Ember's efforts to get past him dwindled. When he found he missed her and, more important, suspected she was up to something she shouldn't be, he drifted to her house in the shape of fog and knocked softly on her window.

It was a cold, moonlit night and she pulled back the curtains, regarding him with glacial silence before finally letting him in. Jack streamed inside her home in a blanket of freezing mist and allowed his body to coalesce slowly. By the light of his lambent pumpkin that drifted in next to him, he could see her desk was littered with bottles and potions, and there was a heavy tome open to a spell.

With a twist of his hand, the pumpkin floated about the room, revealing all the dark, hidden corners. There was a small black cauldron propped over her hearth, steam billowing in her room and filling the air with a noxious odor. Damp tendrils of curled hair stuck to Ember's forehead and cheeks, and when she turned away, he had the strong impulse to touch his lips to the back of her warm neck and the curved arch of her shoulder. He didn't, of course, and berated himself strongly for even thinking such a thing about a girl he was supposed to be watching over. He corrected himself: watching *for*.

Peering at the book, he asked, "Where did you get that?"

"It was among my mother's things. At least, that's what my aunt tells me. I've been playing with her recipes a bit." Ember reached down and stroked the back of the cat twining about her legs. Its green eyes looked upon her steadily, and she swore she could almost feel a ghostly pair of arms wrap around her. Whatever or whoever her mother was, Ember liked to think she'd been loved by a parent once.

Jack frowned, ran his finger across the warm rim of the cauldron, and wrinkled his nose. "I'll say," he muttered. "What's this
one?" Jack grimaced at the smell as he stirred the concoction. "If
your intention is to run me out of town with stink, you might just
have something here."

"Hush," Ember warned. "Flossie just went to bed."

"Flossie? Is that the name of your new kitten?"

"No. I just found out that my late uncle used to call my aunt
Flossie instead of her given name, Florence. It was a pet name, and
I like the way she smiles when I use it."

"Flossie," Jack echoed, and wondered if he should call Ember
something other than her given name. As hard as he tried to come
up with something different, Ember suited her. "You still haven't answered my question," he said more quietly. "What are you so busy
making?"

"That's none of your business."

Jack leaned closer to her, close enough to hear her catch her
breath, which he hoped was a good reaction to his nearness, and
picked up the leather belt on the table behind her. It was far too
long to fit around Ember's small waist. If he had to guess, with the
number of large loops on the belt, he'd say it looked more like a
bandolier, though what kind of projectiles might fit into the thick
loops, he didn't know.

Then he glanced over at the cauldron again and saw a row of
tiny glass bottles, each one the size of his thumb, all stoppered.
Some were filled with different-colored liquids, extracts, and tinc-
tures, some held only a gaseous substance, while others appeared
empty. Though, with his lantern eyes, he saw a glow or a slight tinge
of color in each one. Taking the belt over to the hearth, he knelt,

picked up a vial, and tucked it snugly into a loop. It settled in place like a bullet.

Picking up a second, he let the light of his pumpkin fall upon it. "A sleeping spell?" he said. "Ember, I hate to tell you this, but a vampire or a werewolf would take you down long before you got close enough to throw it accurately. I commend your ingenuity but—"

"I don't have to get close," Ember said.

Jack set down the glass vial carefully. "What do you mean?" he asked. When she didn't answer, but shifted slightly to cover a drawer with her skirt, he nudged her out of the way and opened it. Nestled inside, wrapped in red velvet cloth, was a pair of blunderbuss pistols with wide muzzles. They were heavy, the barrels and grips made of polished brass. He'd never seen their like before. "Where did you get these?"

"Finney made them for me."

"Finney," Jack said.

"Yes."

"And does Finney know what you are, then? What you intend to do?"

"He knows I'm a witch," she said proudly. "Other than that, he's in the dark."

"Right. So what happens when you load this weapon with one of your glass vials and the spell explodes all over you instead of your enemy?"

"The vials don't get stuffed down the barrel. They're inserted here and here," she said, taking the weapons and clicking not one but two different vials into each wide-mouthed, sawed-off muzzle. The glass protruded from the bottom next to the trigger. "You can pick which spell you want to use by flipping this switch to the right or the left."

"The glass could still break in a close fight," Jack said.

"It did once," Ember admitted. "Luckily, we were just using stink bombs. They're supposed to scare off vampires. Finney had to bathe five times to get it off."

At least that news made Jack feel better.

"Since then, I've magicked the glass. It won't break. Not even if you slammed the vial with a rock." Ember opened another drawer and took out a leather belt. This one was double-holstered, and she put it on. It fit snugly around her curvy hips. As she dropped one of the guns into place, Jack noticed the hand-tooled leather detail on the side. It was a rearing horse. Its rider had a grinning pumpkin for a head.

He raised an eyebrow. "Ember," Jack said, taking her hand as she attempted to snatch the other gun back, "I don't think you've thought this through. In the Otherworld, even the citizens not intent on your demise would turn you in. If you went in guns blazing, you'd last only five minutes."

"I think I'd last longer than that. First of all, I don't intend to go in guns blazing or announcing to the world that I'm a witch."

"Really?" Jack said, folding his arms.

"Yes. Really. I know there's a way to hide my presence. You've somehow managed to protect me from interested parties over the years. I've seen your salt circles, and I'm sure you have a few tricks up your sleeve that you haven't been sharing. But since you won't help, we've watched how you cloak yourself, and Finney thinks he's just a few weeks away from devising something that will work for me."

Jack swallowed, his Adam's apple bobbing in his throat the only sign that he was worried things were getting out of control.

Ember continued. "Regarding my guns, what you don't know is that my ammunition will last much longer than you think. You see," she said, pointing to the vials, "only enough potion to knock out one victim is drawn up. Each vial contains enough potion for six to eight shots, depending on the spell. I have my bandolier with more vials and then a pocketed cloak and bag with room for extras. If I happen to run out, I can make more with my dried packets of supplies. I can also scrounge up more ingredients if they exist in the Otherworld."

With a flourish, she pulled a knot and unrolled a clever little pack full of pockets. They were stuffed with empty vials, a small mortar and pestle, various sizes of lancets, bags of dried herbs, squishy and pungent pouches, scoops, a chisel, a tiny hammer, pipettes, tweezers, knives, scissors, pincers, brushes, and powders. Everything was meticulously organized.

"You've been busy." Jack lifted a gun to study it. "So how does it fire?" he asked, his interest crushing his instinct to lecture her on the dangers of the Otherworld. Besides, there was always time for that. He twisted the gun, sighting along the barrel and cocking the hammer. There was no pan, powder, flint, or ramrod that he could see. Only a dark, shiny plate where the hammer would strike.

"That's the beauty of it. Only a witch can use this weapon. I fire it using witch power, or witchlight, or whatever you call it."

Jack froze. "What do you mean?"

"You know, witch power. You're the one who told me that everything in the Otherworld runs on it. I just figured out how it works. Instead of flint or a fire, I press my thumb on the plate, and when I pull the trigger and the hammer hits, boom!" Ember saw Jack's openmouthed expression and sighed. "It's really too easy. Come on. I'll show you."

Ember gathered her cloak and a couple of vials of potion, then lifted her skirts and kicked her leg over the windowsill. The moon was hidden behind the clouds as she snuck across a well-worn path through the thicket of trees. Jack followed, wondering what he could have said or done differently to steer her in a safer direction. She took him over to the old cemetery. Not the one he'd fashioned to keep people away, but the other one, the real one near the cornfields.

Kneeling behind a gravestone, Ember placed her arm on top of it and then centered her weapon on her arm. Carefully, she sighted along the barrel, using an old scarecrow as a target, and flicked the lever to the right. Jack glanced down and saw that the vial contained a nebulous green gas.

"What's in there?" Jack asked, his voice creaking with nerves like a weathered rocking chair left out in the rain.

"A sort of acid cloud" was her response.

"Acid?" Jack hissed. "I think we should pick something less toxic."

"Too late," Ember said with a smile. She'd touched her thumb to the strip of metal and it turned red-hot. Then the hammer went down with a click and there was a *thwomp*, like a cork being pulled out of a wine bottle. A green jet soared across the field, and when it hit, the scarecrow burst into a cloud. Not a moment later there was a sizzle as the pumpkin face melted into a pile of goo and plopped onto the ground next to a smoking pile of discarded clothing, steaming hay, and a blackening wood frame.

Swallowing and jerking his suddenly tight collar away from his neck, Jack sputtered and glanced at his own grinning pumpkin. "That's . . . that's—"

"Incredible? Amazing?" Ember filled in proudly.

"Terrible!" Jack said.

"Uh, no. I believe the word you're searching for is 'ingenious.' "

Jack was about to tell Ember how this exercise in witchy weapon-making was ill-conceived at best, when he cocked his head. A familiar scent tickled his nose. "Vampires," he muttered under his breath.

"Really?" Ember stood straight up, looking around the field, absolutely unafraid.

"Get down!" Jack yelled, taking her hand and tugging until she was down next to him. "Do you want to be killed?"

"Maybe I need to meet another Otherworlder and get a second opinion," she said. "Besides, shouldn't he be more afraid of you than you are of him?"

"Engaging a vampire is foolish," Jack said, ignoring Ember's question. She wasn't wrong, and that bothered him. "Stay here. I'll take care of it and then we can finish this discussion."

"Jack, you don't understand. It hurts." She blinked, a sheen filling her eyes as she rubbed her stomach. "I have to . . . I—"

Taking her face in his hands, Jack touched his thumbs to the soft curves of her cheeks, tracing over them gently. "Please, Ember. Will you stay here?"

Ember's heartbeat escalated and she nodded woodenly, still feeling his touch on her cheeks even after he left, which made the incessant pull in her gut, the one drawing her to Jack's bridge, lessen to a tolerable level. Jack's foggy form and his pumpkin disappeared into the trees.

With her back to the gravestone, she kicked a furrow in the dirt, frustrated that she'd let him distract her so easily. She heard a noise and spun around. As quietly as she could, she lifted her head just far enough so she could peek over the edge of the stone and then gasped.

A man lounged nearby. He sat on a stone bench, his arm draped carelessly across the next headstone over while a leg dangled over the arm of the bench. As he kicked his leg languidly back and forth, he watched her with glittering eyes. She hadn't heard him approach, and when she looked down, she didn't see any footprints except her own and Jack's.

The man's lips twitched in a slow smile that built until it turned almost into a leer. It made Ember very uncomfortable.

"Hello there," the man said.

"Hello," Ember said, grasping the gravestone and pulling herself up. She lifted the gun at the same time and cocked the hammer. To her consternation, the man seemed completely unperturbed to have a weapon pointed in his direction.

"Ah. How disappointing," he said. "I was rather hoping you were going to be a good little hostess and offer me a drink."

CHAPTER 8

SOMETHING WICKED THIS WAY COMES

Deverell Christopher Blackbourne studied the slip of a girl staring him down from the barrel of a small gun as he tapped his shiny black cane on his even shinier black boot. If he hadn't already been taken in by her heady scent of apple blossoms and cinnamon, he would certainly have been drawn by her spunk. The gun matched the young witch's diminutive form, and he thought the weapon almost as handsome as she was. He wanted to pull the wisp of a girl onto his lap and sink his teeth into her lovely neck.

As he was pondering the possibilities, the girl pulled the trigger and Deverell's world erupted in pain.

His flesh sizzled as her spell went to work. He hadn't expected her gun, as delicate as it was, to have anything inside it other than pellets or bullets, neither of which hindered a vampire at all. Instead, she'd concocted a potion that, though slapdash and amateurish, was still rather effective for a newly ripened witch.

He was no young vampire, and normally, he was powerful

enough that he would have recovered from the willful girl's attack within a day or two.

But he had no time for that. He did, however, have a charm of protection from the high witch herself. Closing his eyes, he called upon the accelerated healing power of the charm and felt his magical blood seep from his bones to the damaged places of his body. The injured tissues were quickly repaired, leaving new, fresh skin behind.

When the job was done, the blood returned to his hollowed bones. It filled his frame from his feet to his ribs, but left the rest of his skeleton—most important, his skull—as empty and ravaged as a newly made vampire's grave. The depleted stores triggered his hunting impulse, and his fangs throbbed with want.

Unfortunately, his white shirt and black trousers, still smoking, now hung from his frame in tatters. His cravat and jacket were ruined, and there were holes eaten away in his most comfortable pair of leather boots. One sleeve of his shirt was completely torn away, except for the cuff, which was still perfectly intact. His diamond-geared cuff link was even there.

Dev searched and found his black beaver hat lying unmolested behind the stone bench. "Thank the maker," he said, reaching down and grasping it with his long fingers.

Tucking the length of hair that had escaped from his braid behind his ear, he stood and blew the dust from the brim, studying the crown and the batwing hatband for damage. Last, he ran his fingertip over the lucky raven feathers and the high witch's token charm that he'd personally sewn onto the band. They appeared to be unspoiled.

Turning to the witch, he ran his tongue over his now sharp teeth. She squeaked at seeing his quick recovery and prepared to blast him again. "I think not," the vampire said, and stared deeply into her eyes. He knew his blue eyes were now as bright as icy stars, a side effect of using his vampiric power to mezmer. Dev saw the faint blue light on her cheeks as his abilities worked their magic. The gun trembled in her hand, and she blinked as if confused.

"Lower the gun," Deverell said, his voice sultry and commanding. She complied. "Very good. Now you will come with me."

He turned, placed the hat on his head, and retrieved his cane, gritting his teeth against hunger. The wanting had been bad enough before, but now that his stores had been depleted, he was practically starving for her. He'd been a fool to postpone refection.

Witch's blood was considered the most potent, the most delicious, the most sought-after blood, and was also, unfortunately, the rarest. Because of this, almost all vampires had left the Otherworld when the witches did, millennia ago. The vampires hoped that by allying with the witches, they'd be taken in and nourished by them. It hadn't worked. Only a few such relationships had come to be.

Long ago, too far back for most to remember, he'd been one of the first to leave the Otherworld, sneaking out with a young witch he'd charmed. She'd freely shared her blood with him until her untimely death.

Dev hadn't loved her, not in the way she loved him, but he was sorry to see her die. Especially as her death meant he was on his own. Still, he'd gained much power from the witch, enough to sustain himself for quite a long time—a millennium, in fact.

Dev sighed as he smoothed back his ash-brown hair and positioned his hat on his head. He thought about his long-time witch companion. He missed those days with her immensely. He'd had no choice but to return to the Otherworld. It was possible to work one's way back into the good graces of the powerful who ran the city. Dev in particular had done so, making himself invaluable to the high witch.

He managed to get just about anything she needed done, done. With just the right mix of mischief and mockery in his tone, Dever-ell drew others to him. Men trusted him. Women wanted him. He studied those who resisted, which were very few, with fascination. And he either charmed them until they fell into his arms, or he fi-nagled out their secrets like a pickpocket and blackmailed them until he was satisfied and moved on.

Thinking he would very much like to take some time to charm the little witch, he turned back to her, only to see her running away. Cursing, he raced after her, his booted feet barely touching the surface of the ground, and was blocking her path before she could get to the tree line.

That she'd made no sound startled him. He should have heard her, or at least felt his mezmer slipping.

"How did you break free?" he asked bluntly.

"That's none of your business, you diabolical rogue!"

Dev smiled. "I rather like the sound of that title." A gust of wind blew through the trees behind him, making the tatters of his shirt billow. "I should think I have more cause to be angry than you. Look what you've done to my favorite pair of boots." He angled his foot one way and another and raised an eyebrow in satisfaction as Ember glanced away from his face and down at his boot. Only a sympa-thetic girl would look. He could work with that.

The young witch pursed her lips but didn't lower the weapon. "Why are you here?" she asked. "Do you mean to raze my town?"

"Raze your . . ." Dev's mouth twitched and he laughed. "Not at all. I've been sent to fetch you."

"Fetch me for who?"

"Ah, that's the question, isn't it?" He gave her a conspiratorial wink. "Perhaps we could start again." He put his hand on his chest, flattening his shirt over the muscles of his chest. "Deverell Christopher Blackbourne, at your service." The vampire bowed, but his eyes never left hers. Nonplussed by the weapon aimed at him, he stood and said, "And may I ask your name?"

"My name's Ember."

"Ember. A lovely name for an even lovelier witch."

"Perhaps you should stop trying to flatter me and tell me what your purpose is."

"In short, my purpose here is to find you and then escort you to the Otherworld."

Ember's mouth fell open. Deverell thrilled to hear the racing of her heartbeat and see the quickening of her pulse in her delicate neck. He would benefit from making the effort to charm this witch. If she was powerful enough to toss off his mezmer so rapidly, then young Ember was a girl he wanted to know.

"I take it you know of it?" Dev asked.

Ember lifted her chin and straightened her back. She probably did it in an effort to look intimidating, but her figure was about as intimidating as a kitten's. "I do," she said.

"And are you interested in seeing it?"

"I am," she answered frankly, the strong tug of Jack's bridge rising again. "I'm just not sure you're a proper escort."

Deverell dug his cane into the dirt and twisted it casually, looking away from the girl. "I'll admit, I'm not attired with as much panache as I usually am, but I would remind you that my current state of dress is entirely your fault. Might I inquire as to who you think might serve as a better escort?"

"Jack," she replied instantly.

"Jack," Dev repeated, frowning. "Are you speaking of Jack the lantern?"

She hesitated. "Yes," she finally answered.

Dev chuckled and then placed his hand over his mouth as if embarrassed and apologized.

"What's so funny about that?" Ember asked.

"It's just amusing to me that you'd feel safer with Stingy Jack than with one of the most powerful vampires in the Otherworld."

"Why do you call him that?" She lowered the gun slightly and Deverell gave her a warm smile. It was disturbing to realize that the little witch already had a relationship with the lantern. The fact that the lantern hadn't turned her in meant that the girl was important to him for some reason. Dev knew there was no way the lantern, who had ringed the entire village with salt, had failed in his duties to such a degree that he'd never noticed the witch growing up practically beneath his nose. Luckily for Dev, it had rained the night before, so passing through the salt, while painful, wasn't deadly.

He'd been able to distract the lantern with a steam spinner that shot out a gallimaufry of scents, sounds, and signs while leaving a disturbing number of tracks in different directions. That the lantern hadn't figured out he was on a wild-goose chase yet surprised Dev, especially knowing Jack had been personally trained by Rune.

Right now, the lantern was probably baffled, wondering how a goblin, a whip jacket, a prigger, a vampire, and a colony of Otherworld, metal-enhanced bats had ended up in his forest. Even so, the lantern would be back soon. Dev had to get the witch past the barrier as quickly as possible. He couldn't take any chances, and he definitely didn't want to face the lantern. He'd probably win, but it would come at a cost.

Dev clucked his tongue. "I'd tell you his story, love, but I'm afraid

Stingy Jack will be along any moment now and he'll put a quick end to our enchanting meeting." Leaning forward, he said, "You do know what he will do to me if he finds me?"

Ember swallowed and lowered the gun even more. "What . . . what will he do?" she asked.

"He'll shine his light on me. It hurts something fierce. That power of his will debilitate me for quite some time. It banishes me back to the Otherworld, you see. I wouldn't be able to come back and fetch you for a long spell, if at all. I would imagine he'd be even more vigilant after that." The vampire scrubbed his jaw. "That one's very powerful. There's not much that gets past him."

"That's true," Ember said, and when Dev saw the longing look on her face, he knew he had her. "I'll have to go home and collect all my things first," she added finally.

"Of course. Shall I help?"

Ember bit her lip, looked the vampire up and down, and then shook her head. "I'd prefer to meet you at the crossroad, if you don't mind."

"I don't mind at all," the suave vampire replied. "Waiting on a beautiful woman whets anticipation, so the man appreciates her arrival all the more. Until then."

. . .

While Dev waited at the crossroad for the girl, he pulled a tiny clock-work owl and a letter from his cloak pocket and read the message from the high witch one more time. . . .

> I am entrusting you with a very dangerous assignment,
> one that needs to be completed with the utmost discretion
> and secrecy.

There is a young witch I've scryed who needs to be
escorted to the Otherworld.
   You may use any means to bring her, but you must not
damage her.
   I have included a charm for your own protection, as
well as half of your payment.
   It has already been deposited in your preferred
manner.
   The final payment will be delivered upon completion
of the task.

After retrieving a fresh piece of parchment and a pen from his cloak, Dev began writing a message of his own. . . .

I have located the witch and am bringing her directly.
   Assuming all goes well, we should arrive within
the week.
   The lantern is . . . an interested party, so steps will
need to be taken to avoid his notice.
   This may be my last communication until I arrive.

When he had finished, he attached the parchment to the beak of the owl. Satisfied, he wound up the owl then switched on the witchlight to power the device. The owl zoomed up in the air, its wings clicking, and then it sped down the bridge and disappeared into the mist.

CHAPTER 9

RUNNING LIKE CLOCKWORK

She stood frozen in the woods for a moment, wondering if she was doing the right thing. Then, feeling the painful tug in her gut pulling her toward the Otherworld, she decided not to ponder it too much and ran to her window, her breath fogging the air in front of her.

When she got back to her room, she changed into her warmest and most practical traveling clothes, donning her leather leggings and throwing another two dresses in her bag. Then she quickly packed the rest of her bag with vials, books, a small cauldron, and her pack of supplies. She added two flasks of water and a bag of dried fruit, dried meat, and biscuits. The fire in her belly grew even hotter, especially when Flossie's cats twined their bodies around her legs, meowing piteously.

Ember checked both guns in their holsters and then donned her cloak lined with pockets. Ready, she stole away from home for a second time that night. She wrote a note to Finney and hid it deep inside the Sleepy Hollow tree where they'd practiced with the blunderbusses, asking him to take care of her aunt and thanking him for helping her with her spells. She told him not to worry about her, though she knew he would.

As Ember made her way up the hill to Jack's bridge, she wondered if she should have left a note for Jack too, but she knew he would only try to follow her and bring her back. She wished she could say goodbye.

With her pack already weighing her down, Ember slogged through the snow and stopped just shy of the bridge. Deverell watched her, eyes gleaming, and studied her quietly for a moment, trying to determine the best approach to gaining the witch's trust. He stepped from the trees and was behind her in an instant. A trained witch would have sensed him already. That fact confirmed his suspicion that there had been no one around to teach this girl the art of witchcraft, and it explained her unique take on spell-making and potions.

"Are you ready, then?" Dev asked.

The girl whirled around. "Oh! You frightened me."

"I apologize. I didn't mean to do so. I've been . . . hiding from your lantern," he said, only partially lying.

"I don't think he'd hurt you," Ember said, defending Jack. "He's not cruel."

The vampire paused, choosing his words carefully. "Perhaps you don't know all there is to know about lanterns." Then he offered Ember his arm. "Shall we? I'm rather excited to show you the wonders of the Otherworld."

Ember wrung her hands instead of taking his arm. "You never told me who sent you to find me." The draw of the Otherworld was almost unbearable. A cat ran past them, darting onto the bridge and disappearing in the dark.

Dev blinked, considering the ramifications, and then answered, "The high witch sent me. She sensed a new witch, one powerful enough to cross over, and asked me to find you and then contact her. My guess is that she'd like to meet you."

"*The* high witch?" There was a gentleness, a soothing of her nerves, that washed through her. When she thought of the high witch, all Ember's doubt and hesitation fell away like autumn leaves in a brisk wind.

"Yes. Now, if you don't mind, I'd like to get safely away from here before your lantern returns. I promise to answer all your questions on the other side."

"Very well. I suppose meeting someone can't hurt," Ember said, almost as if in a trance. Threading her arm through Dev's, she declared, "I'm ready."

Dev wondered if that was true. The tender witch was so innocent. It almost made him feel guilty. Almost. "Now hold on tight," he said. "This might sting a bit."

The vampire stepped onto the bridge and kept going. Ember felt nothing at first; then her skin flushed hot and prickly bumps erupted all over her body. She trembled, and saw that the vampire's pale skin turned a sinister shade of red as well.

Ember paused, but the vampire tugged her forward. "You must press on!" he shouted as a hot wind whipped around them. "To stop is to languish in the hellfire."

"Hellfire?" Ember shouted back. She didn't like the sound of that. At some point, she felt the tendrils of her world loosen their grip, and something new began tugging her forward. Her heart thrilled as she pondered what lay ahead—surely the Otherworld was a place full of mystery and miracles—but she also felt a sort of melancholy for her longtime guardian left behind.

When they reached the other end of the bridge, Ember noticed that the creaking wood had become iron struts, beams, and bracings. The air smelled different too. Almost like fire mixed with dirt and ore. It left a metallic taste on her tongue.

They walked on toward a hillside, leaving the bridge behind. Before her stretched a wide city full of tall buildings. Each one had a chimney that puffed out billows of black clouds, which gathered together and hung in a gray mist over the city. The persistent tug hadn't left her, but it had settled somewhat. The feeling would lessen to a tolerable level when she was around Jack, but now that she was finally there, in the Otherworld, she felt right, centered, like she belonged. The great, yawning world lay at her feet, and she wanted to open her arms and embrace the whole of it.

"Welcome to Pennyport, one of the more . . . interesting towns in the Otherworld. Come along, then," he said, pulling her forward.

Ember's mind was full of questions. "So is Jack's crossroad connected to Pennyport specifically?"

Deverell made haste to get Ember far away from the crossroad, and the lantern. "There are as many cities, oceans, and continents in the Otherworld as there are in your world, but there are very few access points between them. Your lantern can access any one of five cities from his bridge. This is the one I chose. One simply needs to think of the desired city. The bridge reads your intention as you cross."

"Then I could have ended up anywhere if I'd tried to get here on my own."

"If you didn't have a city in mind, then, yes, the bridge would have selected a place for you."

"Amazing!" Ember heard a rumble and gasped as a large machine began harvesting grain in a field nearby. "What's that?"

"It's a cogwheel reaper," he answered.

"But where are the horses to pull it?"

"We don't need horses here, though we do breed them. Our machines run on witchlight."

"But how does it work?"

"It sensed your witchlight and turned on."

Ember gaped at him. "You mean I'm powering that contraption? Right now?"

"You are, my dear."

Ember looked out across the vast fields and saw a half-dozen people wandering through the waving grain. "Are you sure they aren't running it?"

"Who, the ghosts?"

"Ghosts?"

As Dev mentioned it, Ember realized she could see through the people to the grain behind, and that those who were reaping captured nothing in their hands. Almost as one, they turned to her and began slowly marching closer.

"They've noticed you," he said with a frown. "We'd best get going."

"Right. Well, I don't want to leave the machine running. So how do I turn it off?"

Dev considered her for a moment, blinking, and then murmured almost to himself, "Yes. I'll have to help you learn how to do that. But first, I'll need to get ahold of some dead-man's hand."

Ember gulped. "What is that? An ingredient for a spell?"

"Of a sort," he said, pulling her forward. "In your world, men say that the hand of a dead man hanged on the gallows has mystical powers, such as giving the wielder the ability to incapacitate others and open locked doors. But here, dead-man's hand is a root that grows in certain regions. It makes an infusion that cloaks a witch's light."

Dev had decided to take Ember the long way around to the capital city, where the Lord of the Otherworld lived with his high witch—not that the Lord of the Otherworld was aware of Ember. No. The high witch had been very explicit regarding just how and where he was to deliver the girl. Still, the Lord of the Otherworld had spies everywhere, which meant Ember was in danger of being discovered, even here in a faraway outpost. Dev would have to shield her to keep her from harm.

"Don't worry," he said. "I chose this town on purpose. I know just the place to find the infusion."

"You do?"

"It's a tavern called the Brass Compass. The owner owes me a favor. I'm sure he'll brew us up enough so you'll have the freedom to walk around for several days without being noticed."

"Perfect. Then let's go."

Dev caught Ember's hand and drew her back. "However, you will be obvious on the way into town. Every light, every bell and whistle, and every contraption from here to the pub is going to be announcing your presence, just like that reaper back there. And when I say a witch is valuable, I mean she is valuable as a captive. Not only is her blood worth a fortune, but her power can be siphoned off, or she can be sold to the highest bidder."

"Oh," Ember said softly. She glanced up. The machine was still chugging away, blowing clouds of steam from the pipe on top as it plowed down row after row of ripened corn. Biting her lip, Ember tried to sense the power it pulled from her to move, but other than a tickle in her abdomen, which was tiny when compared to the connection she had to the Otherworld itself, she felt nothing. "So what do we do? I don't want to be taken prisoner."

"I don't want that either," the vampire agreed as he stroked his chin and gave her a piercing look. "It's an easy-enough fix. Just need to drain about half of your blood."

CHAPTER 10

A VAMPIRE'S KISS

"It's the only way, Ember. Without taking your blood, you'll stand out like a horse wearing a hat. Don't worry about pain. A vampire's bite is as pleasurable as his kiss. Well, my kisses, at least."

Ember folded her arms across her chest. "What if I say no?"

"I cannot take a witch's blood without her express consent."

"What if you're lying about why you want it?"

"Tell you what, I'll give you a vampire's promise." He bit his wrist, the fangs puncturing the skin as if it was rice paper. Blood swelled from the two points as he held out his wrist to her.

"Vampire blood cannot lie. Touch your tongue to my wrist and you'll know my words ring true. Besides, vampires are honor-bound to keep the promises made with a blood oath."

Ember looked at him skeptically, but touched the tip of her tongue to a single droplet of blood. There was a rush of sweetness, like she'd just licked a spoonful of sugar.

"There," the vampire said. "Now listen carefully. I promise I will not kill you or turn you into a half-breed vampire. I only want to help you get to the city undetected."

Ember studied his face as he said the words, and her heart beat quickly. There was a ringing in her veins, a hot rush of confirmation. She knew he spoke the truth, just as she knew the sun was shining or that water was wet. But there was a tinge of murkiness in the water. There was something off, something he wasn't telling her.

Dev could have cursed himself for adding that last part. It was the "only" that caused a problem. He certainly wanted more from Ember than to "only" get her to the city. He could see on her face that she caught the deception, but she nodded anyway and told him he could proceed.

"Come with me," he said, and guided Ember to a small shed. A dim light went on overhead as she walked in. Glancing up, Ember marveled at the row of pendant lights made of pipe glass. The tubes were blown in such a way that the bottoms swelled like small, long-necked gourds. Steam shot out the top of each tube, and the filaments, which resembled thick strands of corn silk, grew hot and bright. In fact, the pipes began whistling and steam filled the room. Dev worried that the system would soon break if he didn't siphon off a bit of the witch's power.

"Try to temper your output," Dev said.

"How?"

"Think of it like banking a fire. Imagine you're dousing flames with water or kicking a layer of cold sand on top of hot coals."

Ember closed her eyes and concentrated on the tickling in her belly, trying to visualize drinking an entire bucketful of ice-cold water.

"That's better," Dev said as the whistling stopped and the lights, which had been approaching the brightness of the sun, dimmed to a normal level. "You're a quick study. Now, shall we begin?"

He guided a reluctant Ember over to a wooden table and wrapped his hands around her waist. When he deposited her on the tabletop, she squeaked in alarm and scooted back, away from him.

"Ember," he said gently, "I'll need you to come a bit closer for this to work."

Frowning and obviously uncomfortable with the idea, Ember shifted and held out her arm.

The corner of Dev's mouth twitched. "As pleasant as it would be to press my lips to your wrist, a vampire can drink blood more quickly when accessing the veins of your neck."

Ember touched her fingers to her throat, then pushed aside her hair with a stiff determination. She nodded that he should proceed and gritted her teeth, closing her eyes as if Dev was going to do surgery on her.

With the heady scent of her skin wafting around him, Dev moved his lips over her neck, barely touching his tongue to the skin, until he felt the telltale thrum of her pulse. Then, ever so gently, he pierced her flesh and sweet witch blood gushed into his mouth.

"Oh!" Ember said softly, sucking in a breath as the vampire drew blood from her vein. Dev's hair tickled her cheek, and her eyelashes fluttered, but she didn't open them. She fancied she could still see the yellow glow of the lights dancing across her eyelids as they flickered from the exchange of power. She heard Deverell moan faintly. One hand slid up into her hair to angle her head, while the one cupping her waist pulled her close.

His lips moved over her throat slowly, drawing, pulling, taking, but it didn't hurt. In fact, warmth shot through Ember's body, baking her from the inside out. It reminded her of lazy days when she lay in her meadow on a blanket, napping in the hot summer sun. At first, it was just nice. Then it became more than nice. A sort of urgency stole through her. The warm sun was no longer enough. She strained closer to it. The sun burned, but she didn't care. She wanted more.

She felt more than heard him mumble something against her throat, and then his arms tightened as light bloomed around her in an explosion so bright, she couldn't see, couldn't hear. The light slowly dissipated, and as it did, Ember's mind was set free. She rocked gently, drifting on the soft, gauzy layers of semiconsciousness, relishing the dark space between sleeping and waking.

It was a good place to be. Pleasant and worry-free. It was like all the nice things she loved wrapped into one feeling. It was her favorite comforter on a winter's eve, the petals of a rose tickling her hand, the taste of her aunt's fresh buttered rolls, the snap of a newly washed dress before it was hung on the line, and the warm body of a purring kitten snuggled in the space between her arm and a pillow.

The idyllic feeling retreated as a dim awareness dawned. Her head throbbed and she groaned for an altogether different reason than she had before. She was wrapped in her cloak as tightly as a newborn babe in a blanket. There were stars overhead, which meant she'd been out of commission for an embarrassingly long span of time. It took her a moment to realize she was being carried.

"Mr. . . . Deverell?" she said.

"I'm here, Ember. And, please, call me Dev."

"What . . . what happened? Did it work?"

"It worked. Too well. Your power is so strong, I've never seen the like. Even I couldn't absorb it all. I took as much as my body could handle and I'm still twitching like a live wire with the potency of it. You also blew a hole in the side of the shed and exploded all the lights in town, and probably most of the working machines. The good news is that the townsfolk will be too busy trying to figure out what happened to notice a witch in their midst." Dev laughed. "I suppose that's one way of going about undetected."

Ember wriggled in her cloak. "You can set me down now. I think I can walk."

"Are you sure?" Dev's grin was even more visible in the dark, his teeth gleaming in the light of the moon.

Ember could no longer see the sharp points of his now retracted fangs and thought that was probably a good thing.

"You've given me enough power to carry you around the Otherworld eight times," he added.

"That's . . . good, I suppose," Ember said.

He set her down gently, her booted feet striking the cobblestones. The city smelled cool and damp, with the bite of smoke tickling her nostrils. Carefully, Ember unwound the cloak, checking the deep pockets to make sure she still had all her vials.

"I've got everything, if that's what you're wondering," Deverell said. He pointed to her bag slung across his shoulder. "Your weapons are inside."

"Thank you. I can take it now."

"There's no need," the vampire replied. "Like I said, I have enough energy to fly to the moon and back. The least I can do is offer to carry your bag. Despite my . . . overtures, I do consider myself something of a gentleman." *Where did that come from?* he thought. Dev had said such things before, but with Ember, he meant it.

Ember's eyebrow rose. If Deverell, the vampire, was what passed for a gentleman in the Otherworld, then she was in trouble. He seemed totally unperturbed about the wide expanse of his chest on display. He still had on his poor ruined jacket, but its cut was purposely wide so as to reveal the lovely vest he'd once worn. Ember wondered where the remains of his shirt were and had the vague memory of her fingers ripping it.

Heat crept up her neck and she tossed him her cloak. "Here. You have more need of this right now than I do. You look like you've been robbed."

Dev smiled. "And so I have been. I'd be proud to share the tale of the witch—though, on reflection, I should perhaps change that to 'wench'—who held me immobile. She was lovely, yet merciless, as she waved her sawed-off musket in my direction, forcing me to remove my starched shirt and cravat so she could have her way with me."

Ember's mouth dropped open. "That's not what happened at all."

"Perhaps not," Dev said as he tossed the cloak around his shoulders with more flourish than Ember could ever muster. "But you have to admit, my version is much more exciting."

Ember cocked her head. "You're not at all what I expected a vampire to be like."

"Thank you, I think," he said, tucking a length of his brown hair behind his ear. "And you're quite different from the witches I know."

"Do you know a lot of them? Witches, I mean?"

"I've known a few," he said as they headed down the cobblestone path. "Stay close now. Most Otherworlders avoid vampires, and they'll likely assume you're one too."

A few townsfolk joined them on the road, and Ember couldn't help but gape at the wide assortment of beings. She saw a man so tall and thin, she could practically see through him. He lifted his bowler hat and gave her a skeleton smile. A short, stocky man came toward them. He wore an apron stained red and carried a leather satchel. When he looked up, she saw that his eyes glowed red. He hurried along, ignoring Ember's stare.

There was a large woman walking down the path that intersected with hers. Ember could only see her from the side at first. She was shaped like a barrel, with no discernable waist. Her dress fit like a potato sack, and her hair hung in long, droopy ropes. When she turned and Ember got a good look at her, Ember shuddered. The woman's nose was as big as one of her aunt's heavy zucchinis, and worse, there were warts all over it in varying sizes and shapes. She had sausage-fingered hands with curly hairs on her knuckles. Her eyes were small and squinty, and when she stared at Ember and Dev and hurried past, Ember could see only black stubs where teeth should have been. "Ugly" was too nice a word for her.

Then there was the smell. The woman reeked of brackish swamp and mildew.

She had a bag slung over her arm, and a little green head peeped out. It hissed at Ember and bared its teeth. "What . . . what . . . ?" Ember sputtered, not knowing how to politely ask what she wanted to know.

Dev leaned over and whispered, "She's a troll. The creature in her bag is a pet gremlin."

After the woman turned, heading down another street, a gang of young boys hooted at them from a dark alley and called out as they passed. Dev bared his teeth. His eyes glowed blue, and she heard their jeers become whines. When she peeped around Dev, she saw gleaming yellow eyes and heard a howl.

"Werewolves?" she asked.

Dev nodded.

Ember licked her lips. "Jack said I should be afraid of goblins. Are there any here?"

"Goblins exist in every city of the Otherworld. They're commonly the tinkers—the ones who create all the machines and gadgets you see. They have long, dexterous fingers, powerful eyesight, and a knack for figuring out where things go and how to make things run. They're part of the working class, and the best of them are sought out to fill positions in the capital."

"But do they nibble on witches' toes?"

"I'm sure if they caught one they would. They love nothing more than gnawing on bones, sucking the marrow out for a treat. Usually, they stick to animal bones, though, there are rumors of some hermits in the wild that would kill you as soon as talk to you. They're ugly, coarse, and mean, but for the most part they're harmless."

"Right. Harmless," Ember said.

"It's not the ones who look different from you that you should be careful around," Deverell said. "It's the ones who look human."

"Are there a lot of those?"

"Do I not look human?" he asked, throwing out his arms and pirouetting.

Ember's lip twitched. "I suppose you do."

"And am I not the most dangerous creature you've ever met?"

Ember didn't know how to answer his question. He was dangerous, certainly. But she didn't think he was dangerous in the way he meant. "I . . . I suppose so," she answered.

"The correct answer is yes. Vampires are extremely dangerous, but not so much to witches. What you need to be worried about are succubi and incubi."

"And those are?"

"They are of the same race. Succubi are female and incubi male. They . . . um . . . take nourishment from seduction."

"Really? How does that work, exactly?"

"Once they . . . mate, their chosen victim is under their thrall. There's no escape from it. The lucky ones end up as slaves."

"And the unlucky?"

"Their souls are slowly consumed, drawn out through a kiss until the body dies. It can be a slow process or a very, very long process."

"Isn't that the same thing?"

"The sad news is no. Most would rather take the slow death."

"Still, I could think of worse ways to die," Ember said, thinking of what she could remember of Dev's vampire kiss and wondering if Jack's kiss might be even better.

"You wouldn't say that if you saw one of their spellbound," Dev said. "And let's hope you don't."

The vampire rattled off several more facts about the Otherworld and pointed out the shops they passed along the way. They approached a signpost and Ember read a sign that said WELCOME TO PENNYPORT!

"It activates when you touch it," Dev said.

Ember found a black button, and when she pressed it, she heard a whirring and clicking as something rattled inside. A section of the box opened and a horn made of shiny, thin-pounded metal shifted out and angled downward in mechanical jolts. She turned to Deverell.

"Show us the Brass Compass," he said.

The horn retreated, disappearing back into the box. Then a large map wound down with a smooth shifting of gears. On it Ember could clearly make out the city, each building a raised bump.

"Amazing!" she exclaimed, turning to Deverell. "It's a map!" When Dev didn't look at it, she said, "You already know where it is, don't you?"

"I do. I just thought you might like to see the map."

They paused at a dressmaker's shop with a glass display window. Ember started when she saw a woman behind the window move. She was made of metal and turned one way and another, showing off the latest designs.

In front of a haberdashery, a copper man doffed his hat to every passerby and pointed to the clicking buttons on his vest, to the cuff links on his shirt, and then to his cane. Then, with a flourish, he bowed his head and gestured that they could find such wares inside the closed shop.

Dev paused and examined the vest on the humanlike machine. "I do like those buttons," he said. "I'll have to return later for a new vest."

Ember squinted in the darkness, moving closer as she tried to get a better look at the tiny moving buttons that rotated in and out of the buttonholes all on their own, and a light over the store suddenly turned on, encircling the metal man and glinting off his shiny head.

Looking up at the light, Dev said, "Looks like your power is coming back. We should press on."

"But, how does he work?" Ember asked, walking around the man in a circle.

"He's an automaton. A bit like a fancy pocket watch, only with larger gears. He's wound up through an opening in his back, hidden beneath his vest. He'll run for a week before he slows down and needs to be reset. We'll have more time to explore after we get some of that tea inside you," Dev added, taking her arm.

They passed an alchemist's shop; a tannery; a place with a sign that read SOUL COLLECTOR; a store that advertised the most accurate foretelling, card readings, and séances; and a millinery. She paused when she noticed a clock shop. Everything from grandfather clocks to devices that whirred and ticked across the shelf to pocket watches was waiting for her to discover it. The gleaming gold pocket watch resting in a bed of red velvet reminded her of Jack. She wondered if he was searching for her right now. Ember felt a little tinge of regret for not leaving him a note. Maybe he'd find the one she left Finney.

When they turned onto the next street, they were suddenly in a very different part of town. Each building had a thin coat of soot, and instead of the high-rise buildings with living space on top and shops beneath, smoking chimneys coughed their plumes over structures that sat next to mountains of metal, coal, or heaps of discarded refuse, creating a fantastic layer of smog that sat over the city like a filthy cloud. "There are bound to be cutpurses lurking in the shadows of the train yards. The mechanists have all headed home by now."

"What's a cutpurse?" Ember whispered.

"A man bent on stealing from you. Or worse."

Ember's eyes shifted to the dark spaces between buildings and she quickened her pace. Things started happening around them. Machines came to life. They rumbled and spat smoke in the air. One such contraption roared, bathing them in golden light.

"Is it me?" Ember whispered. "Do you need to take more blood?"

Dev shook his head. "Try to do what you did before. Tamp down on your power. We're almost there." Under his breath, he added, "We never should have come through the ironwork district."

Ember could tell the vampire was worried. He glanced nervously in nearly every direction. Finally, he pointed ahead to a building with wide doors and brightly lit windows. Apparently, the establishment was relatively unaffected by the power outage. Either that or they had the means to recover quickly.

It stood apart from the other businesses surrounding it. Ember caught the tang of salt and brine in the air and wondered if there was a river or ocean nearby. As they drew closer, Ember could hear music and laughter. More of those curious lighted globes swung back and forth as an evening breeze stirred, illuminating a moving sign.

A set of gears whirred and ticked over the shop. It was a giant metal compass complete with a moving needle. But unlike any compass Ember had ever heard of, the shifting needle pointed straight down, either to the ground or to the establishment it lent its name to. They approached the door, and Dev, giving her a nod of reassurance, pushed it open and tugged her inside behind him.

The music suddenly stopped and the laughter died as every patron turned to look at the pair.

A beautiful barmaid—very scantily dressed, Ember noted—sauntered up to Deverell, picked up the mug of ale on her tray, and tossed the contents in his face.

"Deverell Christopher Blackbourne. How dare you show your face here!" the woman exclaimed.

With ale dripping from the tip of his nose, Dev said, "Glad to see you still remember me, Serina."

CHAPTER 11

THE BRASS COMPASS

Jack searched in vain through the second city he'd traveled to in the Otherworld for a sign of Ember. He felt like a greenhorn having been taken in by a steam spinner. He should have known that it was impossible for that many creatures to pass over his bridge or enter his territory without his knowledge.

Still, the bats had been real. He'd had no choice but to follow the colony of metal-winged bats. It wouldn't do to have them mingling with the native bats in the human world. Jack had to wait until they found a nesting spot and settled down; then he had to angle his pumpkin just right to capture all of them in its light at once. He couldn't afford to miss a single fluttering creature. The shrieking they made when the light fell upon them was earsplitting.

The only other creature that had been real was the vampire. It didn't take a genius to deduce that it had been the vampire that had tricked him. Every other creature he sensed wouldn't have had access to a steam spinner.

Worried about Ember, Jack raced back to the cemetery where

he'd left her, only to find no trace of the girl. He did, however, find a smoking cravat, as well as a diamond cuff link that was unmistakably of Otherworld origin. She'd definitely fired on the vampire; had she scared him away? The alarm he felt quickened his pace. Vampires traveled fast. Once he got to the Otherworld with his prize, the game would be up. Rune would appear soon after, his face dark with fury, full of questions and demands.

With his pumpkin lighting the way, Jack changed into fog and streamed in through Ember's window. He hoped to see the diminutive girl bent over her cauldron or polishing her newly made pistols, a smug grin on her face. Instead, her room was empty and ransacked. Her cloak and vials were missing, as was her bag, and her chest of drawers stood open. Articles of clothing lay strewn about. A sort of horror gripped him.

What happened? Jack thought. *Was she taken against her will?* The evidence pointed to no. A vampire absconding with a witch was nearly impossible, and he wouldn't have thought to return her to her home and then stand by waiting patiently as she gathered her things.

Did she trade blood for passage to the Otherworld? That was certainly possible. Just the thought of such a thing made Jack sick. For a fraction of a second, he imagined his poor Ember caught in a vampire's embrace. His fists tightened, and the light in his pumpkin flared dangerously.

A vampire would certainly have escorted her past the crossroad in exchange for a commodity as valuable as a witch's blood. It was the only possibility that felt right.

He raced to the bridge and crossed over into one Otherworld city, shining his light in every nook and cranny, hoping he wasn't too late, and knowing that if another lantern saw his light, he'd be reported for abandoning his post.

Hours passed in the Otherworld as he searched meticulously. He drummed his fingers and pulled out his Otherworld pocket watch constantly to check the time as he searched this second city. Then night fell and his pumpkin sailed over the dark city like a tiny moon, casting its all-seeing eyes on building after building. He closed his own eyes, willing his light to find that familiar golden soul, the light as recognizable to him as his own, his Ember. Panicked, he left the second town and crossed over the bridge, turning his light onto the third metropolis.

· · ·

Deverell managed to find a small section of his damaged shirt intact and wrenched it from his body to sop up the mess on his chest and face.

"And who's this doxy hangin' on your arm, then? Awfully brassy of you, Dev, bringing her here."

"It's not what you think, Serina."

"Isn't it?" The girl came closer to Ember, looking her up and down with an expression of contempt, then declared loudly to all the patrons, "She's not even your type."

While Ember's face turned red, Dev placed his hand on the irate girl's neck, his thumb tracing little circles over the delicate blue vein. "Now, now," he said. "There's no need to go publicly checking me that way."

Her eyes drifted up to his face almost involuntarily, and Ember caught the sheen of blue on the girl's cheeks as Dev used his power to soothe her. Her mouth fell open slightly as he mezmered her.

"I apologize profusely for my ungentlemanly exit the last time

I was here. It couldn't be avoided. I was summoned away on urgent business. You won't hold that against me, now, will you?"

"Won't hold it against you," she echoed.

"There's a good girl. Now run off and tell your boss I have business with him." She turned to leave. "Oh, and bring us some refreshment, will you, my dear? I'm sure my traveling companion is famished."

"Yes, Dev. Of course," she said with a distrait smile on her face as she stumbled off.

Ember glared at him. "What sort of way is that to treat a young lady—"

He interrupted her with a laugh. "Serina? She's no young lady. She's one of those I warned you about. She's a succubus."

Ember's eyes widened. "You mean she . . . ? And you . . . ?"

"I'm not nearly that naïve. As lovely as she is, Serina does not hold me hostage to her will, as much as she'd like to."

After a few moments, a sulky Serina approached. She glared daggers at Deverell now that his mezmer had worn off. "Your dinner will be served in the back room." Leaning closer, she bit her lip seductively and grinned as if she'd just cornered her next victim. "Payne can't wait to see you again."

Dev sighed as she wandered off, then took Ember's hand. "Come on," he said. "The back room is this way."

Ember followed Dev through the swinging door, which was still swaying after Serina's entrance. They stepped into a very different section of the building. Instead of ale and the laughter of men, the back room smelled of cigars, perfume, and copper. The furniture was covered with plush red velvet, and men, women, and creatures Ember didn't recognize lounged on them drunkenly.

Scantily clad beautiful women stroked hair, brows, and various limbs as they filled glass flasks with blood from the veins of their chosen victims. She heard the plinking of blood as it filled the containers.

On settees, both men and women gave long, drugging kisses to those lying prostrate. When they pulled away, ghostly vapors were drawn from their victims' mouths and deposited in catchments that were promptly corked and handed off to others, who waited for the contents. Ember was scandalized, to say the least, but she was also morbidly curious.

A man she passed coughed violently enough to make Ember jump. He held a jar to his mouth and expelled a sticky phlegm that fell into it with a splat. He handed it off to a man who gave him copper coins in exchange, and then he wandered out the door, heading back into the pub side of the establishment.

"What is this place?" Ember asked Dev softly.

Before Dev could answer, a bald man wearing a leather apron with a gut the size of Ember's favorite cauldron took hold of Dev's shoulder and spun him around. "You black-hearted, earwiggin' conveyancer."

He slapped Deverell's cheek with his meaty palm hard enough to knock Dev aside, though Ember didn't sense any maliciousness in the gesture. In fact, the pudding-bellied man was all smiles.

"What're you after this time? Escapin' a catacomb? Or are you here ta take a break from the eternity box and sluice yer gob?" He leaned closer. "Jes got in a fresh batch o' lantern blood. You and I both know how rare that is. Only thing harder ta come by is the boogeyman's fingernail clipping. But I figure ya must have more than a few coins ta rub together, considerin' on how you skipped out on the last job I offered ya."

Ember was immensely curious about what one might do with the fingernail clipping of a boogeyman; or was it "the" boogeyman? Either way, she made a mental note to ask Dev later. She daren't ask this man himself. She heard the implied threat in his tone and her eyes fixated on his fingers rubbing together with a papery sound, ostensibly to demonstrate coins. She wondered if Dev owed the man money.

Deverell attempted to straighten his sorry jacket and tucked his hair behind an ear. "I assure you, Payne, once you are made aware of the reason I'm here, you will more than forgive my abandonment of before." The large man grunted as if nothing Dev could say would win back his favor. "However, as you can see, my companion and I have recently fallen upon hard times and we require your help as well as your . . . discretion, regarding our circumstances."

"Do ya, now?" Payne replied. "An' what in the bathysphere makes ya think I'd be willin' ta help the likes o' ya?"

"We have something very valuable to trade."

"Really?" Payne folded his arms across his chest, his thick black brows meeting in the middle of his forehead. "I very much doubt ya or yer little human girl, a creature what's mighty heavy baggage in these parts, have anything o' worth ta peddle ta the likes o' me."

Ember could see the steel trap hidden behind Payne's smile and the thought occurred to her that such a moniker fit him very well. A large, orange tabby cat stood on the bar and stretched languidly, then, before Payne could push it aside, it leapt into Ember's arms.

"Blasted creature," Payne said. "Hate those things."

Ember turned away, nuzzling the cat and then gently setting it on the floor. It ran quickly out the door and disappeared into the night.

Deverell leaned closer to the man—so close that his lips almost touched his ear. Ember couldn't hear what he whispered, but she saw Payne's eyes widen and the tavern owner looked her up and down with interest. There was a light in his eyes that wasn't there before.

"And here I am stompin' around in my surly boots when I shoulda laid out the red carpet." He turned and shouted, "Dorzin! Drakin! Get yer lazy limbs in here. Immediately!"

Two lumbering . . . somethings with green skin and beady eyes appeared from behind a curtain. "Yes, boss?" they chanted as one.

"Set up our best accommodations for these two." The creatures Ember suspected might be half troll, half gremlin looked at each other. "And if I catch wind o' either o' ya askin' ta nibble on the girl's toes or fingernails while yer servin' 'em, I'll be kickin' ya out without so much as a by your leave!

"Forgive me, my lady," the big man said to Ember. "We're not used ta having one so fancy in our midst." When she just shrugged, he turned to the vampire. "Whatever ya need, let me know. Sky's the limit. No. Not even the sky. Ask anything and if I can make it happen, I will." Then he leaned forward. "But if there's any skullduggery on your part or any uncooperatin' on hers, I'll lay waste ta ya both. You can be assured."

"I pledge we are in earnest," Dev said.

The two manservants returned and indicated all was ready. With a flourish, Payne personally escorted them upstairs. He stopped next to a large cylinder made of glass and twisted iron gates. Payne took hold of the metal and pushed. It folded back with a screech and Ember peeked inside. There was a long cable running through the center of the contraption that fed through both the roof and the floor.

"What is it?" Ember asked Dev.

"It's called a hoist. Go on. Step inside."

Dev rather liked the way Ember gripped his arm as she moved forward. When they were all aboard, Payne shut the gate and said, "You'll be stayin' in the penthouse tower. We jes completed construction so there may be a few kinks. But figured that would suit yer purposes. Now, seein' as she's a first-timer an' all, the lady should go ahead an' push the top button on the hoist. The one what says 'tower.' And then hold on."

Ember stuck out her finger and pushed. Payne took hold of a leather strap as the machine rumbled, coming to life, and he pointed to another strap above Ember's head. Warm, yellow light filled the tube and steam hissed overhead as the floor jerked upward suddenly and then steadied, taking them higher and higher at a grindingly slow clip.

Looking through the glass, Ember could see giant gears moving in synchronicity. They passed one open hallway filled with rooms and then a second and a third. She counted five, and then they exited through a hole in the roof. The tube ended, and now the hoist was dangling by cables in the open air, rising into the sky as Ember looked in awe out its windows.

Ember's stomach lurched, and she had the sudden feeling that she was a fish caught on a line, being reeled out of the comforting waters where she lived and thrust into the air. Her heartbeat quickened and the power overhead fluctuated. She closed her eyes, desperately trying not to be sick.

Both Dev and Payne looked up at the lights and then at each other as the hoist bobbed in the dark. "She needs that tea," Dev said quietly.

"Not till after she gives me what *I* need," Payne answered.

"What he needs?" a panicked Ember asked, the hoist lurching with her feelings.

Dev sensed her discomfort. He patted her hand in a reassuring manner. "He simply wants to siphon off some of your witchlight to fuel his business. Such a gift would save him quite a sum, a king's ransom as it were, since witch power is so carefully regulated and rationed."

Ember shivered, feeling Payne's eyes on her. She sidled closer to Dev, who wrapped an arm around her. It was strange how much she trusted the vampire. She'd only just met him, and yet she felt as comfortable with him at her side as she usually felt with Jack or Finney. Since her arrival, the persistent tug hadn't left her, but it had settled somewhat. Walking the paths of the Otherworld with Dev felt right, intuitively, even though her mind told her to be wary.

Ember knew Dev was keeping something from her, but when she gave serious thought to it, a calmness stole through her, and she ultimately decided he meant her no harm. She gave Dev a small smile and decided to trust her instincts. Up and up they went. Ember could see the roof of the building far below. "Is this tower in the clouds?" she asked. "We must be halfway to the moon by now."

"Most days it is surrounded by clouds. Had ta negotiate with the skyport for three years ta build onto one o' their tram stations. Then had ta commission a team o' tinkers ta make it, and the hoist. Cost me most o' me earnin's, but I'm fixin' ta make it all back within the first year. Got all the latest advancements, it does."

Ember peered into the dark through all the windows, but she saw nothing but sky. The city below them had started to regain power. Entire sections were now lit up. Ember thought it was a quite remarkable view. They were indeed technologically advanced. She couldn't wait to tell her aunt all about it when she returned.

Squinting as she peered out a window, Ember saw something moving over the town. It looked like a falling star, except for the fact that it seemed to stop in midair and then shine light down on the city below. When she pointed it out to Deverell, he sucked in a breath. "Will we make it?" he asked Payne.

The man glanced up. "Almost there. Just need to wait for the hoist to rotate a bit."

Dev didn't tell Ember what the object was, but both men seemed worried about it and followed its progress closely. She heard a grinding noise, and there was a lurch as the hoist stopped and then swung gently.

Overhead, there was a flat surface in the shape of a circle with a dark opening in the bottom. The opening drew closer, and something above them clamped onto the hoist and pulled them inside with wrenching clangs, finally stopping with a resounding clank.

"We're in," Payne said. "That light'll not penetrate the tower's windows. Even if her witchlight goes haywire."

Payne slid open the gate. Ember had to admit it was a relief to exit the hoist, but she felt as if she'd stepped into another world. She felt benighted when compared to Dev and Payne. They pushed buttons, pumped levers, checked valves, and wound cranks, revealing a panoramic view of the city through floor-to-ceiling curved windows. The view was punctured only by copper walls with sliding doors. She peeked into one and found the most exquisite bedroom she'd ever seen. Following the circular path, she found that the dome was at least four times larger than the home she shared with her aunt, and it hummed happily.

She nearly stumbled when she felt the rubber floor under her feet shift slightly and become bouncy. "Mind that," Payne said. "The floor's pneumatic. It's pressurizing as we speak."

Ember thought the two of them were speaking in another language as she listened to Payne tell Dev about the steamworks bath, warn him about the wraparound gangway, and teach him how to turn on the automatic furnace.

Finally, he promised that new clothing and a hot meal would be delivered on the next rotation, as well as a number of other items Dev requested. Then he gave Dev a box before he opened the sliding door and climbed back into the hoist.

Ember walked over to a table and found a large apple. She bit into it, catching the juice dripping from the corner of her mouth with her thumb. "If you'll give me my bag, I'll have a scrub and change my clothes."

"Very well." Dev handed over her bag and went into the room with her, adjusting valves and turning knobs until water, almost too hot for Ember to touch, poured out from a brass spigot into the largest claw-foot tub she had ever seen.

As Dev took the liberty of trickling in some scented oil, a powerful ray of light shone through the windows, illuminating Ember's face even through the steam. "What was that?" she squeaked. "Can anyone see in here?"

Dev's blue eyes burned icily as he frowned. "No one can see in. The windows have ectoplasm running between the panes."

"Ectoplasm?"

"Its origin is . . . well, do you remember the creature coughing into a cup?"

"Yes?" Ember replied in a small voice, not really wanting to know where he was going with his explanation.

"Basically, it's a substance that can block out mostly anything, even witchlight. If it's applied on only one side of glass, it prevents people from seeing in but allows those inside to see out."

Ember held up a hand. "Good enough for me. As much as I'd love to know more about a substance coughed up from the lungs of a . . . whatever that was, the water is growing cold. If you'll excuse me, I'd like to rid myself of the dust of the road."

"Of course." Dev stepped out and pulled the door closed.

The room was now full of steam, and as she pulled pins from her hair, her locks drooped around her shoulders. Ember called out, "And, Dev?"

"Yes?" He cracked the door open.

"Don't get any ideas about sharing that rather large bed with me."

The corner of Dev's mouth rose. "The thought never occurred to me," he said cheekily, in a way that let Ember know he'd definitely entertained such a notion.

"Thank you," she replied, turning her back to him and stumbling a bit as the dome rotated slowly on its axis.

As Dev shut the door a second time, he wondered if he was losing his touch. He never usually had to work so hard to get a woman to swoon into his arms. Particularly if he'd already sampled her blood. There was an intimacy that formed when blood was taken directly from the source.

Not only were those kissed by a vampire much more easily seduced, but they also developed an intense longing to be near him. And the vampire who returned to the same person repeatedly eventually grew fond, and occasionally protective, of them. Some vampires had even been known to fall in love, which was the ultimate in folly considering the life span of their race.

The question in his mind now was: Why didn't Ember feel the

same as the others? Usually, once he'd given a girl his vampire's kiss, she would enjoy the experience so much she couldn't wait for more. He very well knew that Ember had liked it at the time.

Perhaps it was rather roguish of him to think it, but he couldn't help wishing that the little witch was just the tiniest bit unladylike. He took a seat in the comfortable leather chair and decided if he couldn't enjoy the view of Ember soaking in her tub, then at least he could relish the splendid panoramic view from the tower dome, especially knowing that the searchlight that occasionally touched the tower with probing fingers was the thwarted lantern looking for his charge.

CHAPTER 12

FIRE BURN AND CAULDRON BUBBLE

Jack couldn't understand it. He'd checked each city. Granted, he'd passed over them quickly, but his pumpkin cast a powerful light. Every single soul in the metropolis lit up in its presence, powerless to shield their own inner lights against its glare. There wasn't a witch to be found in any of the five cities connected to his crossroad.

He paced on top of his bridge wondering what he should do. He couldn't just abandon his crossroad to search for her indefinitely. It was possible they'd kill him. But, then he realized that it was *also* his job to protect the Otherworld from witches. In fact, he'd be negligent *not* to abandon his bridge to seek her out. He went back and forth until he finally decided that whatever the consequence, he'd accept it. He had to find Ember.

Jack was a good tracker, but he wanted someone on his side. Someone he could trust, who would have Ember's best interests at heart. Someone Ember might listen to, since she wouldn't listen to him.

Jack materialized outside Finney's window, letting his pumpkin light dance over the sleeping boy. Red hair stuck out at all angles from beneath the blanket, and he could hear the boy snoring loudly even through the closed window.

Softly, he knocked, and the young man snorted, coughed, and rolled over onto his stomach, settling back into a light snore. Jack sighed and lifted his fingers. The window opened and snowflakes drifted inside, landing on top of the boy's bare arms and shoulders.

Finney groaned and jostled, sleepily trying and failing to yank the blanket over his body, to shield himself from the cold. Jack turned to mist and drifted inside, his pumpkin trailing behind. "Hello, Finney," he said, his voice quiet.

"'Ello," the young man said, smacking his lips and then falling asleep again with his mouth open.

"Finney," Jack said. "Ember needs your help. It's time to wake up."

"Ember?" he said, eyes still closed. Then his mouth turned up in a sappy smile. "Ember," he said, as if he'd conjured her in a dream.

"Finney!" Jack hissed. "Wake up." He shoved the boy's shoulder and, when that didn't work, took hold of Finney's blanket and yanked him from his bed, allowing him to fall to the floor with a thud.

Finney finally roused himself enough to look around, run a hand through his hair, making it stand on end, and attempt to climb back into bed, as if falling out of it was something that occurred nightly. Jack shifted irritably from one foot to the other, making the wooden floor creak. Finney jumped back, startled, finally noticing he had a nighttime visitor.

"Who's there?" Finney said, and reached for a pair of bifocals on the bedside table. He slid them up the bridge of his nose. Jack found

it interesting that he'd never noticed that the boy wore them before. He must have tried to hide his weak vision from Ember. When
Finney got a good look at Jack with his floating pumpkin, he gasped
and said, "What are you?"

"I'm Ember's lantern. You've been helping her with spells and
weapons. Did she tell you why?"

"She wanted to go on a trip. I was hoping if I helped her, she'd
take me with her."

"Well, it's too late for that. She's gone. Abducted by a vampire."

"A . . . a v-v-vampire?" the boy stammered.

"Yes. And you're going to help me get her back."

Finney swallowed and then reached behind him to pick up an
ocular device with different-colored pieces of glass connected to
a frame. He removed his bifocals and screwed in the device, then
flipped the colored lenses up and down, looking at Jack. "Fascinating!" he said. "There's a sort of vapor around you that my naked
eyes can't register."

"I'd wager there's a lot your naked eyes can't register."

The boy's face turned as red as his hair. "Tell me about Ember,"
the young man said boldly as he picked up his clothing and dressed.
Jack found himself impressed with the lad, even though he was
about the skinniest fellow Jack had ever seen.

"She's lost in the Otherworld," Jack explained. "I know you made
those weapons for her and have been helping her with spells. You're
going to help me track her." He glanced at the boy's worktable and
was surprised to see it littered with gadgets and parts and an interesting armature that resembled a crude version of an automaton.
He raised his eyebrows.

The boy was a tinker at heart, an inventor with rare talent in the mortal world. Then again, witches did tend to inspire humans to invent, and Finney had spent a good portion of his life trailing Ember's footsteps.

"Bring along whatever things you want," Jack said, "but know you'll have to carry your own bag. Humans aren't allowed in the Otherworld, so you'll have to stick close to me. My light will hide you, but only if you don't stray too far."

Finney filled his bag and asked if they'd be taking Jack's phaeton. The lantern snickered but then sobered. "I don't have a carriage." As he said it, he realized how badly Finney was going to slow him down. He hadn't thought of summoning his horse, but now that he did, he decided it was a good idea. "We'll take Shadow. Come along then."

He streamed out the window and Finney gasped again as Jack materialized on the other side. The boy leaned far away from the hovering pumpkin as it floated outside to join Jack. Finney threw one leg over the sill and leapt down, stumbling clumsily as his pack fell open and his inventions spilled out onto the snow.

"Hurry," Jack said, though he didn't bother to help Finney gather his things. When he was ready, Jack led him to the bridge, wincing at the noise the young man made as he walked.

Jack knew how stubborn Ember was. Surely even if she didn't care about the danger to herself, she'd be hesitant to put her friend in harm's way.

When they got to the crossroad, Shadow thundered across the bridge, leaping from the mist and rearing on his hind legs. Snorting and blowing smoke from his nostrils, the horse danced and shrieked, doing his job to frighten the young man away. "It's all right, Shadow," Jack said, stroking the horse's mane. "He's with me. We've got to find Ember on the other side."

At the mention of Ember, the horse nudged Jack's chest and looked around for the apples she usually brought him. When the horse quieted enough to mount, Jack said to Finney, "Up with you, then. Tie your bag around your chest. Hold tight to Shadow's reins. He doesn't take to new riders easily."

Jack cupped his hands, giving Finney a boost. Once the boy was astride, Jack called his pumpkin. It floated over, sitting on his palm. "Are you ready, lad?" he asked.

The boy nodded. He was nervous, but he was taking it all very well, considering.

Smiling almost as widely as his pumpkin, Jack whispered instructions to it. Then he tossed the globe up in the air a few times, drew back his arm, and threw the pumpkin as hard as he could inside the dark bridge. As the fiery ball sped past the horse, Shadow screamed and lunged after it. Finney turned back to see if Jack was following, but the man had turned into fog again. Finney shivered, and goose bumps erupted on his arms as Jack's fog passed over him.

Finney held on for dear life, his pack bouncing up and down noisily as the horse galloped at speeds no natural horse could travel. When Finney dared to look down, he saw sparks flying from Shadow's hooves and a trail of black smoke curling in their wake.

One moment they were on the bridge, and the next the horse's hooves met steel and they passed through a barrier into a new land, one Finney had never even conceived of. Night had turned to day. Wood turned to iron. A small farm town turned into a bustling city, much larger in scope than he'd ever dreamed possible.

And Finney felt like he had finally come home.

• • •

"Loren, you deceitful little witch," her husband said as he entered her chamber.

"How nice to have you grace my chambers, Melichor."

"Don't act innocent. You think I haven't noticed your blasted minions sneaking in at all hours of the day and night? You're up to something, and you're fooling yourself if you think I won't find out what it is."

The high witch shifted her thin gray hair over her shoulder. "As you know, my dear, I don't have the energy left to do anything. You hook me up to your machine at every opportunity. I can barely walk, let alone plan anything."

"Perhaps. But just to be certain, I'm instructing the doctors to take double your energy today."

A shiver ran down the witch's spine, but she bowed her head demurely. "As you wish, Melichor."

"I think I prefer hearing my formal title fall from your lips," he said.

"Of course, my lord."

When he left, the high witch's legs trembled and she fell back onto her bed. A tear leaked from her eye and was quickly lost in the papery wrinkles of her cheek.

• • •

Ember woke to the hum of the dome as it rotated slowly in the sky. She raised her arms above her head, stretched, and sighed contentedly before sinking back into the wide, luxurious bed.

When she'd finished her bath and combed out her hair the night before, she'd found a robe draped over a hot iron rod and a thick pair of slippers waiting for her. On the table beside her bed were two silver food domes with intricate designs on the edges, covering the most splendid feast she'd ever seen. Tiny sandwiches that smelled of mint, tea-boiled eggs, thin slices of pink fish with herbs on top, shepherd's pie, a round loaf of bread so dark it was black. Ember ripped off a chunk and nibbled, enjoying the sour, spicy taste. Beneath the smaller dome, she found a bowl of berries with clotted cream and bright green butter, triangular pastries shaped like gears with a whortleberry jam, and white puffs dusted with an orange powder that dissolved on her tongue and made her lips pucker from the sweet and sour flavors. She ate a little bit of everything except the green butter and set aside the pastries for her morning repast, then tucked no less than a half-dozen pillows around her body and fell asleep with her room bathed in starlight.

She had no idea how long she'd slept, but sunlight slanted into the room, the rays moving over her legs and toes as the tower dome spun on its axis. There was movement at the door.

Dev poked in his head. "Finally," he said. "I was thinking you'd sleep the entire day away."

"What time is it?" Ember said, sitting up with her back resting against the pillows.

Entering the room, Dev flipped back his jacket and pulled a pocket watch from his gray herringbone vest. The gesture reminded her of Jack. "It's nearly three," he said. "Payne has arranged our transportation on a skyship. The captain is discreet, which will work in our favor, but we'll have to get to the skyport with enough time to find the *Phantom*."

Ember chose to ignore all the strange words Dev was spouting and instead focused on his new clothes. His waistcoat was gray herringbone, and his cutaway coat and trousers were solid gray in a shade or two darker. His crisp white shirt made his skin look less pale, even though the necktie he wore was a bronze-rust color.

"Did Payne send those up?" Ember asked. "Or have you been down to the shops without me?"

"Despite the fact that you slept half the day away, no, I did not leave the tower. Payne sent these up. He also purchased some clothing for you. Would you like to see?"

"Yes."

Ember shifted to the edge of the bed, tightening her robe. When Dev set down a box secured with a red ribbon, Ember stood and headed to the end table.

"Open this one while I get the others," he said.

"The others?" Ember said. "You mean there's more than one?" Dev didn't reply and quickly disappeared, so Ember pulled the end of the ribbon. Underneath the lid, she found delicate paper so white and fine that she could see her hand through it. Carefully, she lifted the folds away and gasped, finding the most beautiful dress she'd ever seen. Lifting it out of the box, she held it up and prayed it was cut generously enough to fit her.

The color of the dress matched the tie Dev wore, a sort of burnt orange that reminded her of maple trees in the fall. The skirt was heavier than any she'd worn before. There was a steel-boned corset with a paisley pattern meant to fit on top of the dress, with thin gold chains tied to the ribbons so a woman could attach a watch or other small charms. The overskirt was cut to show off the black netting underskirt, and there were layers of fabric pulled up in flounces to form a bustle. The dress ended in a train that also had gold chains sewn in so it could be pinned up when traveling outdoors and let down when attending a party. It all seemed too complicated. Pretty, but complicated.

Another box Dev brought in held petticoats, stockings, and bloomers so finely made, Ember had never seen the like. Even the trim on the bloomers had adorable little ribbons interwoven with delicate lace, an extravagance unheard of in her small village. A third box contained shiny black boots with buttons, and the fourth had a lace parasol and gloves to match as well as a fitted jacket.

She put on the bloomers, stockings, and petticoat, then sat at a mirrored desk to work on her hair. Ember had never seen a mirror so large before and when she reached her hand out to touch it, light bloomed around the border.

When her dark tresses were tamed and drawn up in a loose chignon with a few cascading curls, she donned the dress, doing her best with the corset. Her aunt had always helped her with her corsets before, but this one was intricate, and she couldn't even figure out how to use her magic to connect the steel boning or the ruff. Cracking open the door, she summoned Dev, asking for his help. He entered, but was frowning at a letter. Distracted, he set it down and turned his attention to her.

"The boning is joined by gears," he said. "It works like my cuff links. Watch." He touched his finger to a cuff link and a tiny gear inside whirred. Then the two pieces disconnected. When he touched it a second time, they fastened together again. "They run on witch-light," he explained. "Just the tiniest bit. But even the drop of power used to fashion them comes at a very steep price. Your corset is worth a fortune. It's easily the most expensive piece Payne gave you."

Ember looked down at her dress and couldn't imagine how something as commonplace as a corset could be so valuable. The loose contraption slipped where she held it. She yanked it higher, pressing it against her body and tugging at the dress beneath, scowling when Dev seemed amused with her predicament.

He made as if to help her, and she deliberately took a step back and raised an eyebrow. He chuckled and held up his hands. "To fasten it, just get it in the proper position and then run your finger from the bottom of the corset, where it sits at your waist, to the top. It will tighten itself.

"But any time it becomes uncomfortable, or if you just want it looser, you trace your finger down the front from top to bottom, slowly, until it relaxes to a comfortable degree. Draw your fingertip down the entire way and it will disengage the corset gears so you can take it off."

Ember frowned. "It sounds like you have some personal experience."

The slow smile that lifted the corners of his mouth touched his eyes too, with a devilish gleam. Still, Ember followed his instructions and heard a tiny clicking noise as the corset she held in place began to tighten.

Ember was distracted by the ruff and her reflection in the mirror. Never in her life had she worn anything so fine. The top of the ruff stood straight up, framing her face in such a way that made her feel like a queen, and Ember wondered if it was lined with crinoline. Her aunt had a fancy petticoat made of the stuff, which she pulled out only on special occasions.

Dev knelt at her feet and attached her train to another chain that hung from the bottom of her corset, showing her that it also had gears that almost leapt toward one another as if by magic.

"There you are," Dev said, one knee still on the ground. "Pretty as a picture. In fact, you're only missing one thing."

Ember suddenly realized that Dev looked like a young man about to propose marriage. She coughed delicately and turned away. "My parasol?" she asked, picking it up along with her gloves.

"I was actually thinking of this." He stood and picked up another box. This one was round and had been placed on the plush chair since there'd been no more room on the end table. Inside the box, protected by the soft paper, was a jaunty little hat. It resembled Dev's, but it was much smaller.

"It's got a batwing hatband like mine," Dev said. "But yours also has owl feathers and a potent witch charm."

"A witch charm?" Ember took the hat from his hands. She pushed aside the netting and found a tiny bronze cauldron. "It's lovely," she said, stroking a feather.

"Yes. But it's a bit more than lovely."

"What do you mean?"

Dev put on a pair of gray gloves and a very stylish overcoat. "The cauldron can store some of your power. Enough to fuel a skyship."

Ember's mouth flew open. "But how? It's so small."

"Witch power doesn't take up space. It's not like a hairbrush or a broom. The witch charm is simply a container that can harness and hold power for you. Which reminds me . . ."

Dev picked up a bronze box and turned a key to open it. Inside was a pair of short rods with a mounted plate full of gears and knobs in between. "What is this?" Ember asked.

"It's called a voltameter. It's a much fancier version of your witch charm. This is the payment Payne requires in exchange for his help."

"What do we do with it?" she asked.

"You will hold on to the levers here and here, and it will siphon off a portion of your witchlight." Ember gave him a dubious look. Deverell explained, "Unlike taking your blood, which is a physical drain, powering a voltameter is a natural use of your power. You won't feel weakened afterward and it doesn't hurt, but you won't be able to use any of your natural witch abilities for a while.

"Powering a voltameter like this will give Payne the ability to run his business for the next fifty years without paying a single bronze coin to the establishment. In fact, it's such a valuable commodity that he's given me enough currency for the two of us to travel in style for the better part of a year as we explore the Otherworld together. You'll be able to afford the best of everything."

Ember bit her lip. She was happy to explore, but a year? What would happen to her aunt in that time? She started to protest that a week would be more than sufficient, when her stomach twisted again like it had before she'd come to the Otherworld. Going home felt wrong. Then something at the window drew her attention. A cloud in the shape of a cat hovered just beyond the dome, and as she watched, the cat appeared to wink at her.

Dev went on talking. "Of course, after this is done, you'll have to drink your tea. It will inhibit your witchlight even further, to the point where you can move about in the Otherworld undetected. In the meanwhile, I can teach you how to use your power, as well as how to tamp it down when you like. We'll even be able to wean you off the tea eventually. If you still want my help by then, that is."

"It's become quite clear to me that I absolutely need your help. If only there was something I could give you in exchange," she said, smiling as she turned away from the strange cloud outside her window.

"There is no need," Dev said gallantly as he inclined his head. "Thanks to your munificent generosity regarding Payne, my pockets are lined. And sampling your blood yesterday will sustain me for quite some time. Other than those two things, there's not much a vampire needs." He gave her his most charming smile and touched his gloved fingers to her chin, squeezing it gently. "There's something else I should tell you."

She pulled away from his hands, discomfited by the condescending gesture. "Oh? What is it?" she asked as she adjusted her hat.

"I've received a letter from the high witch. There's been a slight change of plans. We aren't going to meet with her in the capital just yet. Her schedule simply won't permit it. Instead, we are heading to an island first. There's an inventor of some note that I think you would enjoy meeting. But fear not. I shall keep her apprised of our whereabouts, and as soon as she's available, I'll introduce the two of you."

"Oh," Ember said. "Will it . . . will it be a long wait, do you think?"

"I can't imagine it will take too long. My guess is we won't be at the inventor's island for more than a week or so. Do you not wish to see more of the Otherworld?"

Ember did want to see more, but heading off on a journey by boat to a distant island and then back was a bit more than she'd planned on. She was about to say she'd rather stay in town and window-shop when her gut twisted painfully. Then Dev took her gloved hand, kissed it, and smiled warmly at her, and the twinge dissipated.

"Shall we get on with it, then?" he asked. "Our skyship awaits."

"Skyship? You mentioned that earlier. I thought we were going to an island."

"We are. Otherworlders can travel by conventional boat, but skyships are much faster."

Despite her reservations, the idea of a skyship was remarkably intriguing. She allowed Dev to lead her over to Payne's machine as he explained the concept. Ember thought of Jack as Dev droned on. She wondered if the lantern was missing her yet. A part of her hoped he was. As much as she wanted to explore the magic of the Otherworld, she would have much rather had Jack as a traveling companion.

"Right. Here we are," said Dev, indicating the contraption meant to collect her energy. "Witch lesson number one: Focus on the power in your core. Can you feel it?"

"Yes," Ember said, closing her eyes.

"Good. Now imagine that power is made up of thousands of tiny bubbles."

"Okay."

"Now you're going to allow just the top layer to burst and flow up and out toward your fingertips. The machine does the rest."

Ember shook out her hands and wrapped them around the grips. They grew warm, and she felt her arms and then fingers hum with energy. A blue light arched between the levers making a sizzling sound. "Is . . . is that normal?" Ember asked.

"It is. Watch the indicator in the device. It will rise as the box fills with energy."

The machine droned and shook. Ember saw the needle rise to ten, twenty, thirty. She felt the tingling in her stomach but focused on only the uppermost layer of bubbles, pushing them out into the machine. Then something slipped. Her belly turned to fire. There was a blinding flash and her world tilted. She heard Deverell calling her name and she blinked. She was lying on the ground but didn't remember falling.

"Try to calm down. Center yourself," Dev said smoothly as he stroked her arm in a soothing way. "Take deep breaths."

Ember did, and the dizziness left her. "I . . . I think I'm better now. What happened?" she asked.

There was a rumbling on the table, and Ember glanced up to see that the box she'd been touching was jumping up and down on the table as if it were alive. The needle banged against the top in the red zone, blue arcs sizzling up and down the levers.

"You overcharged it," he said. "Once it was full, your energy had nowhere to go but to the dome's centrifugal motion. It's slowing to normal now, though. We're going to have to get that tea in you and start regimented training as soon as possible. You're so powerful, you're dangerous."

Dev was smiling, but Ember sensed a seriousness to his words.

He lifted her to her feet as easily as if she weighed no more than a feather. Then he held out her hat and asked her to touch the cauldron charm. He told her not to even think about the power, to just let it flow naturally. Then he handed her a cup of dead-man's-hand tea and told her to drink it down while he took the liberty of pinning her hat on. Again she was reminded that Dev seemed to have a lot of experience in dressing—and undressing—ladies.

Picking up his hat and cane, Dev took her cup, set it down on the table, and gallantly offered his arm. "Shall we go, then? I believe our buoyant carriage awaits. I've taken the liberty of transferring all your belongings to this new leather satchel. If you'll allow me to carry it for you, we can be on our way. You can break your fast at the skyport."

CHAPTER 13

THE HAUNTED HORSEMAN

Jack led Shadow by the reins as young Finney walked ahead, scanning the ground while adjusting his strange spectacles. "She definitely came this way," Finney said without looking back at Jack. "Her trail is quite easy to follow when you know what to look for."

"Finally." Jack sighed. It was the third town connected to the crossroad they'd tried. But why Pennyport? He would have expected that any vampire, finding himself in the company of a witch, would have taken her directly to the capital to turn her in for a finder's fee. Pennyport was the most distant city from the capital that he could access from his crossroad. "Press on, then, lad. It's imperative that we find her."

"There are other tracks with her. They're red, like the color of fresh blood."

The vampire. That felt about right to Jack.

Looking around at the fields and the distant town, Jack considered Ember's disappearance. How had his light missed her?

If she'd only waited. Been a bit more careful. He might have found a way to let her explore a little. The thought of what might be happening to her at that very moment made him ill with worry. But all Jack could do was trudge along at a human's pace and hope the mortal boy could track her.

He'd been fortunate indeed when Finney told him he'd already isolated Ember's particular resonance. The boy reluctantly admitted he'd used it since Ember was thirteen. Like many, he'd been smitten with the young girl, but, unlike the others, he'd done something about it: He'd invented a clever device that showed her footsteps. Finney always knew where to find Ember, even when she secluded herself in the forest. He quickly learned that the fresher the print, the stronger the color. In Ember's case, her footprints glowed orange when Finney adjusted his spectacles a certain way. Normal tracks, those of mortals or earthly animals, had no color at all. Finney told Jack that when Jack's feet touched the ground, a rare thing for a lantern, the prints appeared white and there was a blue aura about Jack when he traveled as fog.

Jack was surprised to learn that he was trackable at all. He was also shocked to hear Finney say that he'd shared that secret long ago with Ember. He'd even offered to help track Jack to win Ember's favor, which was why he'd handled meeting the lantern more easily than Jack had expected. Ember had declined his offer, saying she wanted to meet her mysterious guardian on her own terms, but she did ask Finney to let her know when new tracks appeared in her hollow. Jack felt embarrassed to have been caught spying on her. Finney thought the whole thing a great adventure, and didn't blame Jack at all for invading their secret hideaway, which was fortunate for Jack. The boy was proving his merit.

Jack watched the skinny young man as he gazed at the ground intently. "You remind me a bit of Ichabod."

"Who's Ichabod?" the boy asked.

"He was a warlock who lived in Tarrytown. I had to keep him away from my bridge there, just like I did with Ember."

"Was he as difficult to deal with? I imagine he would have been a rather sneaky, ingenious sort of fellow."

Jack laughed. "Not at all. Protecting my bridge from him was almost too easy. Haunting Ichabod was fun. I'd never seen a man so frightened and superstitious." Jack launched into the tale of how he'd pursed his lips and puffed wind into the reeds of the river so they'd sing a frightening song, and then twitched his fingers to send frogs and bats to torment the warlock.

He told Finney about when he rode the man down holding his pumpkin in one arm and brandishing his sword in the other after Ichabod had attended a party, and of how the man screamed and cowered on his rather pathetic mount. Jack leapt on Shadow to show what he'd done. He galloped around Finney in circles, laughing maniacally. Just like with Ichabod, Jack raised the collar of his black greatcoat and allowed the darkness inside—the yawning emptiness where his soul should be—to be seen, and his skeleton became visible.

When Finney just stood there, staring up at him, not laughing at all, Jack slipped from Shadow's back and finished haltingly, "The man ran far away from the crossroad and Tarrytown and never came back. Later I heard the townsfolk gossiping about a headless horseman who haunted the stone bridge and, after that, not a soul, mortal or otherwise, dared cross my path."

"So you think me a coward, then?" Finney challenged with a frown.

"No . . . that's . . . that's not it at all."

"Ah. Then you think me a bumbler? Superstitious? Gullible?"

"No. I merely meant that you resemble him physically, and . . ."

"And?"

"And he was smart. Easily frightened but smart. He was a school-teacher, in fact, and had a lovely singing voice."

"I see. Well, if you don't mind, horseman, I'd like to get back to finding Ember."

Jack stumbled over his words, something he hadn't done in a long while. "Yes. Yes, of course." The boy had somehow managed to make him feel ashamed. Ashamed of being a lantern. Of using his abilities to frighten others. It made him feel small, and he didn't like it one bit. Had he intended to frighten Finney as he had Ichabod? Why else would he manifest one of his darkest powers? Perhaps he was just showing off. He didn't like the thought.

"They definitely went through here," Finney said, distracting Jack from his musings. Finney's goggled eyes were fixed to the ground.

Jack followed the boy for a short distance, ignoring the strange cluster of ghosts in the field staring in their direction. They arrived at a farmer's shed and took in the scene.

Finney whistled. "You should see the lights in here," he said. "Colors in every hue are splashed against the walls in layers, concentrating right there, where you see the hole."

Summoning his pumpkin closer, Jack crouched over a fallen table. The lit eyes focused on a tiny spot of dark brown. Jack wet his suddenly dry mouth. "Blood," he said quietly. "He must have fed on her."

"Fed on her?" Finney whipped up from where he was studying the blast. "Do you mean the vampire killed her?"

Standing slowly, Jack let out a breath. "No. At least, it's highly unlikely. A witch's blood is powerful. A tempting thing indeed for a vampire. But the only way he'd be able to take it is if she offered it freely."

Finney wrinkled his nose in disgust. "You mean . . . you mean she wanted him to bite her? But why?"

"Ember would stand out like a sore thumb in an Otherworld town like this. Every light she passed, every machine in range of her power, would hum to life. By taking a portion of her blood, he'd be able to hide her witchlight—innate power."

"But then how do you explain the destruction?" Finney asked. He bent down and turned over a twisted piece of metal.

Jack rubbed his jaw. "Those were Otherworld lamps. They run on witchlight. If Ember was frightened, her power would expand to protect her. It might explain the hole in the wall."

As Finney bent to pick up one of the broken lights, studying the mechanism inside the shattered glass, Jack asked, "Can you see her tracks leading out? They might be muted in comparison."

Finney shook his head. "Her tracks stop here. The vampire's tracks lead out though."

Jack kicked some glass. "He's our only lead. Let's trail him."

"Right. And once we find him, we'll work him over until he tells us where she is." Finney held up his hands in fists, jabbing the air.

Amusement twisted Jack's mouth for just a moment before worry over Ember crept back into his brain. "Let's go."

When they reached the outskirts of the city, Finney caught Jack's arm. "Her tracks are back. He must have been carrying her. They're weak, though."

"They would be, if he drank from her."

They kept going. Finney often stopped as they walked through the city, his eyes growing large as something in a shop window caught his attention. Jack's light stayed bright enough to discourage most citizens' interest. Lanterns weren't generally liked in the Otherworld. Not only had lanterns been human once, which was a good enough reason for dislike, but they were responsible for forcing self-exiles back. Otherworlders tended to give them a wide berth either way.

The light from the pumpkin, which drifted overhead, wrapped around the young human as well. Otherworlders might glimpse the shadow of another person with him, but for all they knew, Jack's traveling companion was a specter or a goblin or some other prisoner being escorted to town.

When they got to the tavern, they hid in the trees. "You're certain they went in there?" Jack asked.

"As certain as a crow in a cornfield."

"Why would she willingly enter such an establishment?" Jack asked, more to himself than to Finney.

"Don't know our Ember too well, do you? You're awfully sententious for a spook."

Jack sighed. "I am not a spook."

"Yeah? Even so, she went in. But I've been all around the building, and neither she nor the vampire ever came back out."

Jack closed his eyes and maneuvered his hands. His pumpkin leapt and wove a path through the air, traveling around the building, peering into each window, and casting its light into every dark space. Up and up it moved. Jack saw everything it did, though his eyes were closed. When it reached the dome, the light shone on the windows but could not penetrate them. Jack frowned and increased the intensity only to fail yet again.

The pumpkin orbited the structure like a moon and the light fell upon the tram. Understanding filled him. His eyes snapped open. "I know where he took her," Jack said. "Come with me."

CHAPTER 14

THE *PHANTOM AIRBUS*

The doctor knelt before one of the cats. He wasn't overly fond of the creatures, but they served their purpose. "Soon, my darling," he said to the blinking eyes of the white-and-black-spotted cat. "I've found the one who will fix everything. Just hold out a bit longer. I promise I'll find a way to save you."

His message sent, the doctor stood and cursed his popping knees. How he hated growing old. It was a terribly undignified thing. Perhaps some of his new elixir would soothe his aches. He glanced up at the sky and frowned at the circling ghosts before calling for his trusted servant and giving him instructions to prepare the house for guests.

...

Once Ember was settled into the compartment of Payne's private airtram, Dev pumped a lever and the door shut. He bolted it and took a seat as the tram began moving upward. Within a moment, they were soaring over the city, swaying to the tune of rhythmic thumps and clacks. They passed over what Dev called the warehouse district, and Ember could see long metal tracks branching off in every direction. A large contraption ran along them, moving fast, belching clouds of steam as it went.

"What's that?" she asked.

"The quicksilver train. The fastest way to get from one Otherworld city to another over land," he said.

She pressed her nose against the window and Dev sat back, unable to wipe the smile from his face.

He hadn't cared about much since his former witch died. He'd been drifting aimlessly since then, taking random jobs, engaging in all manner of fisticuffs and devilry. But it all felt like nothing next to his time with this unexpected witch. Each moment he spent with Ember increased his loathing of the idea of letting her go.

While she'd slept the night before, Dev had made plans. Now that they'd been diverted from the capital and were headed to the inventor's island, Dev wondered if there might be a way for the both of them to disappear. He knew the Lord of the Otherworld and the high witch could want Ember for only one reason, and it wasn't altruistic: They needed a replacement. The high witch was old and feeble, and Ember was young and full of power. The only reason he'd give up Ember now was if he had no other choice, and perhaps he wouldn't even then. Just the idea of what might happen to Ember should he turn her in sickened him.

He was going to find a safe haven for them, and now the path was open.

A wild zephyr nudged the tram, causing it to bounce, and Ember squeaked in alarm, but Dev laughed and assured her it was normal. They sped aloft, entering a thick bank of clouds, and the tram became dim. He struck his cane against the steel floor and the crystal bulb in the handle gleamed, brightening the inside of the tram. "Better?" he asked.

"Yes," Ember said. "Thank you. Is it powered by witchlight?" She held out her hand so he could pass her the cane for inspection.

"It is. Lesson number two: Can you tell if it is from a witch or a warlock?" he asked, curious to explore more of her innate ability. "When you touch the stone, let its power flow into you through your fingers, then use your mind to ask it your questions."

Ember's brows knit as she removed a glove and lightly touched the glowing top of the cane. "It's a . . . a witch, I think."

Dev was about to respond when Ember continued, "She had light hair, blue eyes, ruddy cheeks, and . . . and she loved you!" Her eyes flew up to meet Dev's.

"She did," he answered quietly.

"But how did I know that?" Ember asked.

"Each witch or warlock has a different tint to their power. It's a signature, if you will. I'll admit, it's rare for an untrained witch to see another so clearly. I suppose the fact that she's dead has made it easier. She's not around to block you from seeing."

"It's amazing." She stared into the orb of light as if trying to scry for the witch who'd powered it. "Oh," she said. "It's easy to see because she wanted you to remember her. This was a gift."

"It was," Dev admitted.

"She . . . she knew she'd be leaving you, and she wanted you to be safe."

Deverell stiffened. "You can sense that too?"

"Yes."

The vampire turned away, his blue eyes taking on a wet sheen.

"I never would have left Lizzie if I'd known. She sent me to fetch her some items two towns over. I'd have saved her if I'd been able." He closed his eyes. "She should have told me they were coming for her, that she'd seen her death in her scrying."

Ember shifted over to sit next to Dev and took his hands in hers. The tram rocked gently. "Don't immure yourself for something that wasn't your fault," Ember said. "She wanted you to live. Whatever her reasons for keeping you away, it was done out of love. I hope you believe that."

He shook his head. "I didn't deserve Elizabeth's love. My regard for her wasn't as deep as hers was for me. I cared for her in the way that vampires do, but it wasn't the same."

Ember said nothing for a moment, and Dev was afraid to look at the expression on her face. He feared what he'd find.

"Perhaps it doesn't matter," Ember said finally. "I think if she was powerful enough to gift you with this, then she was powerful enough to read your heart. Your sorrow over your lost witch is telling. A cold man—or vampire, in your case—would have only taken what they needed and went on their way. Perhaps your feelings for her were different in tone, but your bond with her was no less emotional. You miss her."

Ember sensed Dev was embarrassed by their discussion and decided to change the subject. "Dev?" she asked.

"Hmm?" he replied distractedly.

"Do you know much about the . . . about the boogeyman?"

Dev's brows knit. "What's got you hunting after that old wives' tale?"

"Jack told me a bit. Then Payne mentioned fingernail clippings."

"Ah. Well, most Otherworlders don't invoke his name. To do so, they believe, is to summon him; and when he comes, he's as likely to steal your soul as he is to help."

"But you don't believe in that?"

"Oh, I do. But he's gone missing. Has been out of commission, so to speak, for quite some time. The Lord of the Otherworld would have us believe that he's responsible. That we no longer need to fear the boogeyman because he's personally done away with him."

"Truly?"

"Who knows. But I can tell you there's been no sign of him for a long, long time. You can trust me on that, because I've lived for many centuries. Still, it's better to be safe than sorry, I suppose."

"I guess that's true. But can he really steal a soul?"

Dev shrugged. "Depends on who you ask. Some say he's a thief. Some call him a devil. Others say he's a collector. But most Otherworlders believe we are haunted by the ghosts of those the boogeyman has harvested over the millennia."

"So he just drops them here? Like a pirate's hoard? That's terrible! I assumed they were simply another race of beings who lived here. What an undignified ending."

He was saved from commenting when they emerged from the cloud bank. Smoothing back his hair, Dev put his hat back on his head and tapped his cane on the floor to shut off the witchlight. "There it is." He pointed to a large building floating in the air. Ember gasped. It resembled a small, mechanized moon.

They zoomed inside, and once again, Ember's face and hands were pressed against the glass.

Welding sparks crackled as blooms of witchlight framed workmen in a haunting visage. It glinted off their goggles as they hung from long ropes or walked along monstrous steel skeletons that looked like boats. Then she saw one, finished, with a net above it being filled with air. No. Not air. Witchlight! She felt the power as it flowed from a generator into a pliable, fine-wired metal net that caught and held it.

Dev looked out the window at what captured her attention. "That, my dear, is the latest in skyships. Something you won't find in the human world for at least another century."

"And we're going to fly on one of those?"

"We're flying on one of the best of those. Well, practically speaking, with the best crew. She's docked on the other side."

There was a shout as a coupling broke. It careened toward them, barely missing the tram; then it fell, the length of cable spiraling down like a loose thread. The man attached to it screamed as he was wrenched away from the side of the ship and plummeted through the open spaces, barely missing the thick steel frames that supported the various levels of the port. The noise of construction cut off, but only for a moment, and then the buzzing and sparks overpowered the shouts.

"Isn't someone going to do something?" Ember asked, aghast at the sight of the falling man.

Dev shrugged. "It's the risk of working up here."

Ember gripped the glass window as she looked down. She could definitely make out the blue light of the sky peeking through from time to time. Ember fell back against the seat, her stomach feeling leaden, as her enthusiasm for the wonders around her dimmed.

They remained silent as the tram continued until it reached the center of the skyport. The tram hub was full of people. Of course, "people" was a slight overstatement, since only about half of the citizens she saw milling about could even begin to pass as human. Ember caught sight of creatures she believed were trolls, and some very tall, almost diaphanous, beings she remembered as being specters.

When she asked Dev about the rest, he said the port would be filled with all sorts, but she would be the only witch. As far as the citizens of the Otherworld were concerned, the only witch in the entire realm was the high witch. It was she who provided all the power—well, she and the diminishing reserves controlled by the capital.

The tram docked, bumping gently against an air-filled mesh before settling flush against the side; Dev hopped out and then turned to offer his hand. Adjusting her hat, Ember set her feet on the metalwork deck and, swaying slightly, used her parasol to steady herself. At first, she thought her awkward balance was due to sitting in the tram for so long, but then she realized the entire skyport was shifting gently beneath her feet.

"How does the port remain in the air?" she asked Deverell. "Do the tram cables hold it up?"

"Not at all," he replied. "The skyport retains its position using incendiary propulsion, much like the dirigible balloons."

A strange yellow-skinned creature with a humped back shambled toward them, holding out a glowing flower. "Rose for the missus?" he chirped hopefully. "I trades for coin, candy, or clippings."

Dev turned glowing eyes on the creature and said simply, "Leave us."

The flower in its hand drooped as the Otherworld being fell under the influence of Dev's mezmer. He wandered off in a daze and headed over to another couple.

"Candy?" Ember asked.

"Otherworlders have notorious sweet tooths, or in my case, sweet fangs."

Dev cleared his throat when he saw her eyes drifting to a news-reel on the energy crisis and the high witch being near death. "Hungry? I've got the perfect place picked out."

"Famished," Ember answered with a smile.

He led Ember to a quaint dining establishment with cozy little outdoor tables. They lounged in the dining area sipping tea, Ember nibbling on shiny topped pastries she'd spread with butters and jellies, while Dev often checked the time on his pocket watch. He tried to explain the fifty-hour clock used in the Otherworld, but Ember couldn't wrap her head about it.

On the next level, Ember was amazed to see a bustling row of shops selling everything from clothing and accessories to books and maps. There was even one shop showcasing nothing but sweets and candies. Ember pulled Dev inside, and the most marvelous scents greeted her.

She happily leaned across the counter, her breath fogging the glass as she pointed to candies that looked like lemons or cherries and dark creamy confections Dev called chocolates. They gave her one to sample, and it melted on her tongue, igniting an unquench-able need to acquire at least a dozen or perhaps two.

Ember attempted to pull Dev into a shop boasting of witch spells and potions, but Dev stopped dead in his tracks. "We cannot, my dear. I am quite sorry to deny you such a thing, but there are often diviners keeping shops such as that one."

"Diviners?"

"Seers or weavers of fortune. They use their abilities to exploit their customers by peering beneath their skin, seeing who they really are."

"You mean like Jack?"

"Jack? Your lantern?" When Ember nodded, Dev felt a small tightening in his gut. He didn't like how she said his name, as if the two of them were on better-than-familiar terms. "In a way," he answered hesitantly. "They don't have the same power exactly, but they will see enough to know you are hiding something and they will be intrigued."

"Oh." Ember glanced at the shop window longingly but allowed Dev to pull her along. "Still, it would be nice to learn more. I'm very untrained for a . . . for one of my kind," she said, lowering her voice as she glanced at the passersby.

"Yes. And I promise I will help you with that to the best of my ability. But first, we need to get you on the ship and safely away from prying eyes."

"Right."

Dev guided Ember to a set of moving metal stairs that appeared to be wound with gears. New steps appeared before her feet and shifted upward, going higher and higher before twisting out of sight. "Don't be frightened," Dev said, seeing her hesitate. "They won't bite your boots. Do be careful of your dress hem, though. I've seen many a lady's train get caught in the gears."

Hearing that, Ember hiked up her skirts to a very unladylike and somewhat scandalous level, which Dev didn't mind at all, and set one shaky foot on the moving step. Her leg started to move and she squeaked in alarm as her appendage went ahead without the rest of her. Dev saved her by lifting her by the waist and setting her in front of him as he stepped behind her.

Once she was on the autostairs, she quite enjoyed the experience. She held on to the steel handrail and laughed as they went higher and higher, passing many levels in slow loops. Dev kept them on until they passed five levels, then indicated it was time to disembark.

Ember exited and adjusted her frock, and Dev led her from the central hub out to the far-distant edge of the skyport. Light filled the space, and Ember soon realized that this part of the port was open to the air. Wind whistled through the level, rustling her dress and making both her and Dev place hands on their hats to keep them from blowing away.

When they reached the edge, Ember saw a long metal ramp extending into midair. At the end was a large vessel made of iron. Round spheres with open slats hung below the ship; within the slats were thick, telescoping barrels that looked like guns large enough to shoot balls the size of Ember's head. There were four spheres on the side she could see and probably more on the other.

The front of the vessel came to a wicked point, while the back had metal pieces that looked more like fins. Oddly shaped witch lamps hung around the deck both above and below, and windows near the front glowed with flickering light, making the ship look like a great beast with lit eyes and a mouth. Heavy ropes and cables connected it to the skyport, as well as two large clamps that looked like great claws. She spied several men dangling over the side, sparks flying before their faces as they made repairs. On the side of the ship was a steel plate that read *Phantom Airbus*.

Dev hurried Ember forward, steering her toward the ramp. But before they could get there, a tall woman hopped out of the skyship and landed with a jostling thump in front of them.

The woman's long, dark hair was tied loosely at the nape of her neck and hung over one shoulder. She wore a white shirt with long tails; high leather boots, more scuffed and worn than shined; tight breeches; and a simple black corset. When she smiled, Ember was startled to see a sharp fang, which looked like it had been dipped in silver, on one side of her mouth. The other fang was missing.

"Well, well," the woman said, running her tongue over her fang and eyeing Ember and Dev with a predatory gleam in her eye. "You must be pretty desperate, to call in a favor from me, Dev. Why don't the two of you step into my parlor and tell me exactly what"—she eyed Ember up and down—"or who I'm about to be carting around as contraband."

Grabbing the wobbling cable, the woman leaned entirely too far over the ramp to err on the side of safety, which also served to give both Ember and Dev a glimpse of her very shapely derriere, and hollered in a very unladylike fashion, "Frank! Quit muckin' about and get your humpbacked, shock-brained self back on the ship and prepare to launch! The cargo has arrived!"

A man hanging precariously from two thick cables attached to his—Ember swallowed—his neck and nothing else looked up and removed his goggles. Ember gasped. Even from a distance, she could tell there was something very wrong with the man: His limbs were different sizes.

"Yes, boss!" the giant of a man replied. He detached the cables at his neck and wrapped them around his wrists; then he swung his booted feet against the side of the ship and Ember heard the smack of metal-soled shoes hitting a steel surface. The man then walked himself up the side of the ship, one boot clicking and then the next. It was almost as if they clung to the slick side on their own some-how. When he reached the top, he landed with a jarring thump that shook not only the ship, but the ramp they stood on.

"Amazing!" said Ember. Never in her life had she seen such a large, strong person. The man called Frank was more than twice her height. He wouldn't even need a horse to plow his fields. He could do it all on his own.

The woman raised an eyebrow, her mouth curling in a smirk. "Come on, then, Dev. Let's get you and . . ."

"Ember," Dev said.

"Emm-ber," the woman said, drawing out the girl's name with a smack of her red lips, "settled before we take off."

"Right behind you, Delia," Dev said.

The woman glanced back at Dev and Ember.

Don't say it, Del, Dev thought.

She said it anyway. "That's 'Captain' on board my ship, Dev-erell."

"We're not technically on your ship yet, are we?" Dev answered with a smirk.

Ember squeaked. "Perhaps it would be best not to irritate the captain," she said.

"Yes, Dev," the woman said, poking him in the chest. "Don't ir-ritate the captain."

Ignoring the woman's smug smile, Dev held out his hand, indicating Ember should go in first.

Ember paused for just a moment, wondering anew if she was making the right decision. She glanced back at the skyport and then at Dev's outstretched arm. When she laid her hand atop his arm, her indecision fled once again. Being there in the Otherworld, getting on the skyship was right. At least, it felt as if she was going in the right direction.

Besides, Dev was a trustworthy sort of vampire. And a hand-some one. Oh dear. Ember swayed on the ramp just a bit. She felt just the tiniest bit tipsy, or perhaps it was being so high in the air. Yes. It must be the altitude.

It wasn't until Ember was safely inside the *Phantom Airbus* that Dev finally felt like he could relax. His shoulders slumped and he took in a deep breath.

Delia led them into the captain's cabin and leaned against her desk. She offered Ember and Dev a seat, but only Ember accepted. "Now then," Delia said. "Don't you think you should tell me what I'm risking my neck, my crew, and, most of all, my ship for, Dev?"

CHAPTER 15

A HAUNTING TALE

Jack and Finney arrived at the bustling skyport quickly enough, but Jack didn't feel entirely comfortable with the looks they were getting. He increased the intensity of his light but was discouraged by the slow process of rediscovering Ember's trail. Finally, Finney picked up her tracks and they headed up the autostairs, running down the launch deck only to find an empty dock.

Jack sent his pumpkin into the sky once more, and it circled several ships until it found one with not one but two vampires. Still not catching even a hint of Ember's light, his pumpkin returned, and Jack looked forlornly at the boy who'd gotten him this far. Without Finney, Jack could change to fog and head off to the ship, but he couldn't leave the human boy behind. Not only was it illegal to bring a human into the Otherworld, but any human on his or her own was considered fair game. Finney would be killed before he could take a step.

"Well?" Finney said. "Where do we go from here?"

Jack looked around, and then an idea sprang to mind. "We'll take a screaming banshee."

The boy stammered, "A . . . a what?"

"A banshee. They're not terribly maneuverable, but they're fast. We should be able to catch up with the ship. Every port has at least one that is reserved in case of emergency or attack. They're located on the very top level of the skyport."

With that, Jack led the boy back to the central hub and took the autostairs up and up and up until there was nowhere left to go except through a steel door. Jack's pumpkin shone on the lock, and the inner gears moved of their own accord. Nothing could hide from a lantern's light. Every creature, every passage, every lock opened to it. Once his light did its work, they were able to turn the circular lock on the hatch and throw it open. Then they went up a set of normal stairs that led to the top level, open to the sky.

Wind buffeted them when they reached the roof. There, nesting in a launch pad, were a set of three screaming banshees. Jack removed the cables affixing the nearest one to the roof. When that was done, he shouted, "Climb in!" to Finney. He pulled a lever, opening the glass door, and Finney scrambled across the captain's chair to the other side.

Jack's pumpkin floated in, dropping into Finney's lap. When Jack was aboard, he told Finney to attach the harness to himself, showing him what to do by attaching his own. Technically, as a lantern, he didn't need to secure himself, since he couldn't die until his contract was fulfilled—not unless his pumpkin was destroyed.

Once they were ready, Jack waved his hand over the console and lights flickered on. The vehicle hummed and rumbled until steam floated out from beneath the bubble of glass. It grew in volume until Finney heard a high-pitched whistle, like that of a teapot.

The air filled with the scent of combustible fuels and propellant. Then the whole ship rumbled and they bounced off the ground, hovering for just a few seconds until the sound reached a feverish pitch.

"Hold on!" Jack shouted over the noise of the ship, just as Finney saw workers scrambling up through the hatch and circling the ship.

The steam billowed, fogging the windows until Finney could no longer see anything. Then it happened: The scream of the ship became so loud, Finney pressed his hands against his ears, and just as he did, they shot straight up toward the sun as fast as cannon fire.

The pumpkin plummeted to the floor and rolled around until Finney could catch it and hold on to it tightly. It might have been his imagination, but he thought the carved face looked irritated. The ship leveled off and slowed as Jack moved levers and wound knobs. The initial screaming caused by the noise of the engines firing died down just a fraction as they lost speed.

Jack glanced over at the frightened boy holding his pumpkin and chuckled. Then he rammed the throttle lever down and the ship shot forward, gaining momentum. As wind buffeted the banshee again, the terrible sounds of screaming metal grew even more horrible and Finney realized the tension was likely due to how the wind moved across the fluttering wings of the ship.

"You'll get used to it after a while!" Jack shouted as the boy tucked his head down, trying to cover his ears with his shoulders. "It's the sound of progress."

"I should think progress would be a bit quieter!" Finney hollered back.

"Best get used to it," Jack said, taking out a pocket watch and glancing at the time. "We won't be catching up to them for some time."

Finney sank back in his seat, miserable at the idea of having to endure the noise for long. Then he sat up and reached into his vest pocket for his pencil and notebook and busied himself sketching an idea for ear stoppers that would block outside noise while playing soft, replicated sounds when wound. It would have to be something soothing, like rustling leaves or a tinkling brook. If he used some of the marvelous clockwork metals he'd seen on display and came up with some kind of tiny winding mechanism, it might work. He'd call it a symphonium, or perhaps an ear stopper, since the little players would work like a cork in a bottle of wine. Soon he was so busy designing his new invention, he forgot all about the screaming banshee.

When he was done, Finney asked Jack if one was born a lantern or if one was made into a lantern.

"I was born human, like you," Jack replied.

"So then I could be a lantern?"

"You could. But I wouldn't wish it on my worst enemy."

"Why not?"

"It's rather complicated. One doesn't choose to become a lantern. Most of us are tricked into it."

"This happened to you?"

"Yes. The only reason I'm a lantern now is because of my love for a witch."

Finney's eyebrows rose and his mouth opened.

Jack adjusted a lever, leaned back, and shared his story. "I was born over five hundred years ago in a small Irish village called Harrowtown. My father was a drunk who crippled my sweet mother when he decided she was purposely beguiling the other men of the town. She was very beautiful, with white-blond hair, which I obviously inherited, and naturally drew attention, but she was faithful to him, though he never earned her loyalty. He was a jealous man, and his fists still found her face far too often.

"The only other woman I thought as beautiful as my mother was the town witch."

"Was she evil?" Finney asked.

"Not at all. You've seen Ember. Not all witches are hags who boil newts and frogs in black cauldrons and tempt children to their homes to fatten them up and suck the marrow from their bones. Many are good—white witches, who dabble in healing ointments, sleeping spells, and simple love potions that a young girl might use to catch the eye of the farmer's son she's interested in.

"Our witch was lovely. The prettiest sight to ever grace the market. She was pink-cheeked, with long red hair almost your color. It often escaped her cap in corkscrew curls. Though she was easily twice my age, as a young man I was half in love with her." Jack glanced at Finney, who nodded in understanding.

"One pleasant fall afternoon on market day, the witch—her name was Rebecca—appeared in the town square. I followed her around, noticing that the breeze lifted her heavy skirts and nipped her cheeks with the crisp bite of the coming winter. She wandered, perusing the carts full of hazelnuts and a farmer's bounty of carrots, cabbages, parsnips, and turnips. When she dropped her basketful of purchases and I helped her pick them up, she smiled and tossed me an apple.

"I was busy with the harvest, but I later learned that her beauty had captured the eye of a visiting lord who'd come to Harrowtown to collect taxes. The man inquired after her place of residence. That night, as the sleepy villagers dreamed of a bounteous harvest and the celebrations to come, he sought out the witch with a few of his compatriots. The next morning, the witch came to town accusing the lord of using her in a most vile way.

"When the people refused to come to her aid, the witch vowed vengeance not only on the lord and his men, but on all the cowardly residents of the town, declaring in her wrath that she would bring disease and famine upon us all.

"That night, the lord and his men choked during their evening meal, coughing up small animal bones. All four of them died in a very slow and painful way. Then the sickness came upon the village. Disease killed off the elderly and the young first. My father fell victim to the black boils and fever brought on by what the townsfolk labeled as the witch's black death.

"Then my mother passed, not of sickness, but of her grief over the demise of her abusive husband. Half the population of the town was gone within a month, and the harvest was eaten by rot. Flocks were torn apart by scavengers. Those who survived the plague suffered in other ways.

"The day I buried my mother, I set out to find the witch. I discovered her sitting dully in the corner of her small, well-kept cabin, her hair stringy and unwashed, her eyes haunted. I begged her to stop the curse.

"'It can't be stopped,' she answered listlessly. 'Once a curse such as this is inflicted, it must run its course. For what it's worth, I'm sorry for it. I thought it would ease my pain, but instead, I am doomed to suffer along with you.'

"Then her eyes brightened and she began speaking of a deal with a devil."

"So the devil made you into a lantern?" Finney asked.

"He's as close to a devil as I've ever met. In this case, the devil was the head lantern, Rune. Who also happens to be my boss."

"Interesting." Finney scribbled some notes on his pad. "Go on. What happened next?"

"The witch told me that if I sacrificed myself, the devil might heal our village of the plague. She said all I had to do was serve the Otherworld. She said I was a special soul who might be of interest to him."

"And what was it exactly that made you special?"

Jack shrugged. "All I know is that a potential human has a keen sense of things outside the bounds of the mortal world. Perhaps my relationship with the witch made me so, like your closeness to Ember enhances your abilities to invent."

For a moment, Finney appeared shocked. Then he mumbled "Fascinating," after which he wrote a full page while Jack waited.

When he was done, Jack continued, "The witch promised me that until I shook the devil's hand, nothing was set in stone. I decided it couldn't hurt to hear the devil's offer, so I waited for him in the alehouse. When he arrived, he was not at all what I expected."

"Go on," Finney said. "Describe him, if you would."

"Rune entered the building, smoke trailing in after him." Jack frowned at Finney's initial sketch. "He didn't have devil's horns or red skin. In fact, there was nothing about him that might brand him a child of Beelzebub, at least outwardly. His brown skin made me think he was a man who lived in a place of long, hot days, where the sun kissed his skin relentlessly. He had no pitchfork or tail, and his clothing was simple—black trousers, polished boots, and a brocade vest. If there was a devil to be found in the man, it was in his eyes. They were lined with black, as if they were rimmed with charcoal, and when he blinked, they pierced me to the core. I didn't realize at the time that he was looking at me with his lantern eyes."

Finney asked, "What does that mean?"

"When a lantern's eyes shine silver, we are using our lantern, the ember we carry with us, to see through the skin to the inner soul of a person."

Gulping, Finney asked, "Does it hurt?"

"It can if we wish it to. Rune keeps his ember in his earring."

"And where's yours?"

Jack glanced down at the pumpkin that shimmied on Finney's lap, turning toward him and offering him a wide grin.

"Oh," the boy said, swallowing so his Adam's apple bobbed.

Jack ignored Finney's discomfort and said, "When Rune studied all of us in turn, he said, 'I understand one of you pathetic mortals desires to trade in his soul to break a witch's curse. Now, which one of you is it? And speak up. For I can't abide time wasters who mewl like kittens.'

"I told him I was the pathetic soul he was looking for. He held out his hand and I reached for it automatically. When I asked about the terms of my service, he just laughed and said he'd already accepted my offer. The pumpkin was Rune's little joke. He thought it would keep me humble to have to carry around my pumpkin for a thousand years."

"A thou . . . a thousand years?" Finney squeaked. The pumpkin blinked at him and then looked at Jack, its grin turning to a grimace.

"That's right."

"I see," Finney said quietly. After a moment of staring into the sky, he licked the tip of his pencil and said, "Tell me more about Rune and your contract."

• • •

"First of all, she's a witch," Dev said.

"I gathered that much, Dev." The woman inhaled and closed her eyes. When she opened them, she said, "The scent of her blood is masked, but I can still smell it on your breath." Dev stiffened. "You've done a good job hiding her," the woman went on. "If I didn't know you well, I never would have guessed. She's clearly not from the Otherworld, though. Her eyes are far too . . . inexperienced for this place."

Ember folded her arms. "I'd appreciate it if the two of you wouldn't speak about me as if I were deaf. My aunt actually *is* deaf, and she hates nothing more than when people talk around her as if she's not even there."

The woman's lip twitched. "My apologies. Perhaps I should address my questions to you, instead of the tall, too-handsome-for-his-own-good, looks-for-trouble-even-when-he's-not-looking vampire who has brought you on board my ship, endangering us all."

Frowning and glancing at Dev, Ember rose and held out her hand. "My name is Ember. I am from the mortal world, and I'm also a witch."

Deverell slapped his face with his hands and drew them down slowly. While Ember did her best to ignore him, the woman laughed, pushed off from the desk, and took Ember's hand, pumping it up and down once. "Name's Captain to most. Delia Blackbourne to others. But you can call me Delia."

Ember's eyes widened as she glanced from the captain of the pirate airship to the vampire. She swallowed. "B-Blackbourne? Does that mean you and Dev—?" Ember's words cut off.

"Yes," Del answered, a gleam in her eyes. "You've caught us."

"She's your . . . your . . . ," Ember started.

Dev sighed. "My sister."

"Your sister?"

Delia laughed heartily. "Oh, Dev, how I love teasing your paramours."

Color heated Dev's cheeks. "Ember is not my inamorata," he said bluntly.

The captain grinned cheekily at Ember. A dimple appeared that made the lovely woman even more beautiful. "Perhaps not yet. But you have plans, don't you, brother dear?"

"That's none of your concern. You owe me, Del, and it's time to cash in on a favor."

Del's smile darkened. "Fine. Just don't expect me to roll out the red carpet. I'll take you where you want to go, but if you endanger my crew, all bets are off. If anyone's head is going to roll for this, it won't be mine, I assure you."

A thin black cat with yellow eyes stood in the window. It gracefully leapt onto the desk and stuck its face toward Ember. She stroked its head. "Who's this?" she asked.

"Ah, that's Edward. He's usually shy around strangers. Don't let him out of my office. I find him in the most dangerous places when he escapes." With that, Delia made for the door. "Wait here. I'll have Frank take you to your quarters and give your witch a tour of the ship."

There was a lurch as the ship left the dock. Just then, the door was thrust open with a bang and the large man, his skin slightly tinged green, ducked his head and entered the room. "I am supposed to give you a tour," he said, his voice rough as gravel.

"Yes. I should like that," Ember replied, deliberately threading her arm through the man's, though she had to reach up to do it. "Frank, is it? Might we be able to see the port from the deck of the ship? I've never flown on a skyship before, and I have a lot of questions."

The man wet his black lips and moved his mouth, baring his

teeth in the semblance of a smile. Though his gums were quite green, his large teeth were white, and she could now see that the area around his mouth had been damaged. The scars might account for the strange smile. Some might be frightened of a man as misshapen as him, but Ember felt more pity than fear. When she looked in his eyes, she saw kindness. In Ember's experience, eyes spoke the truth. He blinked and she heard the click of metal.

Frank, she learned, was named Victor Frankenstein von Grimm. He was Del's first mate and had been with her for as long as she'd been captain. He showed Ember to the deck, keeping his large hand on her back to steady her as the ship cleared the skyport and made for open air.

Once the ship leveled out, he showed her the great engines that ran on witchlight and the bellows that kept the balloon overhead inflated. Ember pressed a handkerchief to her nose. "It's quite, er, mephitic, isn't it?"

"I suppose it is," Frank replied. "My nose hasn't worked right since a ball removed my head."

Ember took hold of his arm, pulling him away from the noise of the bellows. "What did you say, Frank? I fear I misheard you."

"I said my nose hasn't worked properly since they reattached my head."

"Reattached your . . . your head?"

"That's right. I'm a lot like the ship in that way. See this seam here?" He pointed to a section of the hull that overlapped and seemed to be soldered with metal. "This piece came from the captain's first ship. Not much left of her now. Captain Del, ya see, she's a collector. We take down other skyships and harvest their parts. It's dangerous work and comes with side effects."

He opened a door and headed into the aft part of the ship, just beneath the bellows. It was extremely warm in the space, and the workers who maintained the engines wore very little and were sweating profusely. Her guide seemed unaffected.

"Side effects like losing your head?" she asked.

He guided her down a walkway that led to another section of the ship. "There's that, yes. But there's also the ghosts."

Ember swallowed. "Ghosts?"

"When you take down a ship like that, there's bound ta be deaths."

"I would think so."

"Those deaths haunt ya. Literally."

"I see."

"When we take a piece to patch our own, we get the ghosts too. Captain Del's one of the few who can live with the haunting. Others go mad."

"And will we see the ghosts?"

"I reckon you will. Don't be scared of them. They mean no harm. Just like to be seen. Long as there's no witch aboard ta stir 'em up, they won't get too excited."

Ember glanced at Dev and he shook his head the tiniest bit.

After they came to a door, Frank opened it and led them down steps to a lounge with large windows framed in metal. "This is the VIP lounge. Your rooms are off to the side. Captain didn't know if ya two wanted to bunk together or not so your things were left in the first room."

Dev's hands were pressed behind his back in a perfunctory sort of way and he gave no indication whatsoever as to his preferences on the subject at hand.

"We'll be sleeping in separate cabins," Ember said, more to clarify her position to Deverell than to Frank.

Her escort's noticeable limp as he climbed the stairs worried Ember. "Does your leg hurt much?" she asked, when they returned to the main deck.

Shrugging, Frank answered, "Not my leg. So no."

Ember's mouth fell open. "It's not your leg?"

"Naw. Captain never wants ta lose me. Every time I get injured in battle, she just picks up the pieces and has me put back together. Most of my parts are automaton now. We've an exceptional tinker on board. Like I said, he even reattached my head. Don't need to eat neither. Scottie just attaches charges ta my bolts when I run low on energy."

"Do you mean you're fueled by witch power?"

"I am. Getting so I'm pretty hard to kill. I reckon only twenty percent of me is still original parts. That's why I go by Frank now. Every time a piece of me is cut away, I shorten my name. Last year I was Frankie."

An apparition appeared behind him and passed through his body. Ember shivered seeing the man was without an arm. "Get off," Frank said as the ghost began pawing Frank's right arm. "How many times have I told ya, you'll get it back when the captain lets me pass on."

The moaning ghost gave a final frustrated tug and then held out a hand to Ember as if in supplication. Then he stopped and peered at her closely. He licked ghostly lips like he was tasting the air then came closer, wailing. Ember backed up, not stopping until she hit Dev's chest. He wrapped his arms around her as the ghost's wailing became louder. Frank gave him a little shock, the bolts in his neck brightening. The ghost's face burst into tiny particles and knit back together. Then, with a final howl and a sad look at Ember, he raced forward, passing through both Ember and Dev before disappearing through the wall behind him.

"Sorry about that," Frank said. "He's one of my personal ghosts. This arm used ta belong ta him, and he's not happy about my taking it."

Ember didn't know what to say about that, but she liked that Dev kept a hand on her waist as they headed back up to the main deck. It helped steady her as a new wave of dizziness made her stumble on the stairs. The wind blew her skirts and Ember noticed another ghost standing next to the side of the ship. It was a woman. She looked around, gritted her teeth, and climbed up onto the railing. Then, before Ember could even respond, she closed her eyes and leapt.

"Dev?" Ember said, grabbing his lapel and tugging. "Did you see her?"

"Yes, my dove." Dev swallowed, his eyes fixed on the ghost in such a way that Ember decided that moment wasn't the proper time to tell him she preferred he didn't call her a dove or any other type of bird. Birds ended up in cages. He pointed. "She's back again. Doing the same thing."

Shuddering, Ember turned and hurried along to catch up to Frank. When she looked back, she saw that the apparition had paused, her dark eyes following Ember. Instead of jumping, she climbed down and trailed slowly behind them. Ember supposed that if Frank could get used to being haunted in such a personal way, then she could try to accept it as well. She just hoped there wouldn't be any ghosts in the water closet.

As Frank took her over to where the captain stood, steering the ship, Captain Del shouted, "Adjust our course to thirty-nine west by eighty-two south."

"Aye-aye, Captain," a man replied, and pushed a series of buttons and then wound a handle until it came to a ratcheting stop. There was a groaning and creaking as the light filling the web above them flickered and the ship lurched and then steadied on the new course. "Course adjusted. Heading to the roustabout!" he shouted.

"Good." The captain turned to Frank. "Did you finish the grand tour?"

"All done," he answered.

"Excellent." Captain Del was about to continue, but then she paused, her ear trained to something Ember couldn't hear. "Is it what I think it is, Frank?"

The large man lifted his head, tilting it, and closed his eyes. "Sounds like it," he said.

The woman slapped her hand against the helm. "We've got a banshee on our tail." She pushed a red button and the ship exploded with power, thrusting them forward at double their previous speed. "Get us to the roustabout!" she shouted. "Now!"

Overhead, the thin strands of metal infused with witchlight began to burn red hot. Ember barely kept upright by grabbing on to a piece of decking as they shot forward. Dev wrapped one arm around Ember and the other around a rail. His grip was as tight as the steel bands of her corset.

"What's happening?" Ember shouted.

"We're being followed. If we can make it to the roustabout, we might lose them."

They sped upward. One moment they were in the clouds, and the next they were above them, headed toward something high in the sky. It looked like a giant metal platter with a large hole in the middle. The contraption rotated slightly, spewing steam from each of four engines.

"Angle it just right, Frank! We've got to enter her at top speed!"

A projectile shot from one of the forward guns. It burst in a crackle of sparks just before it reached the machine, exploding with light. The circle in the center flickered and then shimmered. It looked very similar to the barrier at the crossroad Ember had passed through, except that this one was still moving. Images coalesced and then, just before the nose of the ship touched it, the barrier snapped into place and the *Phantom Airbus* powered through.

The deck around her squeezed and reshaped, transmuting its form into a long barrel as they pierced the flexible barrier. Ember felt like she was being re-formed along with the ship. Her corset felt too tight. She couldn't breathe. Dev was crushing her. A ghost sped past, her openmouthed scream echoing in Ember's ears as her transparent body was crushed and pulled as if someone was yanking her arms apart like long ropes of puffy bread dough.

There was a sharp scent, redolent of metal and copper. Then the world around Ember spun and went white.

CHAPTER 16

SAID THE SPIDER TO THE FLY

Rune dismissed the heavily jowled creature. The beast shrugged and stood, then shook itself like a dog. Its jowls slapped its neck and drool splashed the wall and table.

The head lantern peered at his cup, still full to the brim with amber liquid, and pushed it aside with a grimace. The creature's arms and hands were matted with a copse of hair so thick, he wouldn't be surprised to see small animals making a home there, and he didn't want to risk any fallen hairs or spittle in his cup.

He had been tasked with the invidious job of locating a witch who had infiltrated the Otherworld, and so far, he'd been unsuccessful. Of course, it wasn't exactly Rune's fault. His boss, the Lord of the Otherworld, gave him nothing to go on except hearsay. None of his lanterns had reported in. Each one was especially tuned to his crossroad, and they knew better than to hide witches.

His first thought was to check the crossroad where the witch wind had last blown, but he had just scanned Jack's town not too long ago and had found nothing. Besides, Jack never lied to him, and he was the most faithful, dependable lantern he had. Jack's reputation was almost as fierce as his own when it came to enforcing Otherworld law. As far as Rune could tell, the only one who knew of the witch's presence was the man who'd sent him on the ridiculous witch hunt in the first place.

Rune's boss was becoming more unhinged as the years passed, nearly obsessed with finding the key to immortality. The Lord of the Otherworld had been sending Rune on wild goose chases for the better part of a hundred years. The head lantern, who had decidedly better things to do, in Rune's opinion, had wasted his time chasing down rumors of bespelled medallions, fabled golden cities with buried scepters that unspooled the lives of others then knitted the torn threads around the life of its wielder, hidden natural springs that granted years to those who drank from them, and tinkers who could supposedly give life to automatons.

This witch hunt reminded him of the time he'd been sent to Salem in the year 1692, according to the mortal calendar. There had been a rumor of a powerful witch living in the town, one strong enough to catch the attention of the Lord of the Otherworld, though how he knew, Rune truly didn't understand. What he'd found when he arrived was a town in a frenzy. He'd even had to summon Jack to help him contain the situation.

Many mortals were hanged as witches, and anyone with even a drop of power was carted off to the Otherworld. Even though he found no witches of note, the entire town was harangued by threats and warnings from the pulpits. To exact revenge on the pious town reverends and magistrates, Rune sent them visions of devils and ghosts and dark things that made them shake in horror.

After Jack arrived, he set the lad about cleaning up the town. To his credit, things began to settle down more quickly in Jack's care than his own. The boy managed to quell the violence and soothe the ruffled feathers while he checked in with the Lord of the Other-world, who, to Rune's surprise, had promptly drained each witch he'd brought, wringing every drop of power from them until the poor creatures lay shriveled and dead at his feet. Then he shouted that Rune had brought him no one of substance and if he wanted to remain the head lantern, he'd better find his lord someone worth his while.

The Lord of the Otherworld immediately sent Rune back to Salem on a fool's errand to find the witch his wife had assured him was there. When he still found nothing, Rune napped near the cross-road, letting Jack do all the work required by a lantern. Though they remained for many months, no other witch was ever found, and both lanterns were soon reassigned.

Most citizens avoided the Lord of the Otherworld now. Even the head metallurgist, one favored by the high witch, had run away. Rune had been sent after the man, but he never found him. The Lord of the Otherworld had added five hundred years to Rune's con-tract for that. He had to waste an entire year recruiting to bring that number down to a mere fifty.

Rune scowled into his ale. The Lord of the Otherworld should have been put out to pasture long ago. He was becoming desperate and maniacal. Desperate men made mistakes. Big ones. And Rune was paying close attention. It would be much simpler if he would abdicate. Then Rune could slip into his place as easily as a knife into a sheath. But the Lord of the Otherworld wouldn't abdicate.

Rune had seen it before. Even in the mortal world old men clutched power with an arthritic grasp, holding it covetously close to their chests. They were like failing dogs pathetically gumming bones, attempting vainly to hide them from view. They growled and whined and made a loud, obnoxious fuss, but ultimately they were past their prime, in need of putting down.

Rune was ready. He was primed. He was waiting. He was already a king in his own mind. He just needed a throne.

But before Rune could take his rightful place as leader of the Otherworld, he needed to find the blasted witch. Or, even better, proof that there was no such creature in all of the Otherworld. If he could do that, then he had grounds to prove that the leader of their realm was losing his mind.

Finally, he caught a break. It wasn't exactly the break he'd wanted, but at least it was something. A goblin had a cousin once removed who'd seen a lantern sneaking around his town. As far as Rune knew, none of his lanterns were on holiday or preferred vacationing in Pennyport. It was small and on the far outskirts of the Otherworld. Nearly backwoods compared to the comforts of the capital.

He left immediately and quickly located the tavern where the report had originated. Rune's eyes narrowed as he took in the flagrant waste of witchlight. The owner obviously had an excess of it. It was possible that he was trading in the black market, but even if he was, it wouldn't account for the man's brightly lit gambling hall, the long line of patrons demanding entrance, the extra guards, or the working compass on the outside of the establishment. When very few could even afford to power their homes with witchlight, the tavern stood out like a beacon in the darkness.

Ignoring the extremely large bouncer who growled at him, Rune flicked his earring, allowing his light to shine. All those waiting in line flinched, including the bouncer, who let him pass without saying a word.

Unfortunately, the tavern owner appeared uncooperative. Even when threatened by the head lantern, the man was cocky. He freely admitted that he dabbled in black-market items. He even offered such to Rune to sample, free of charge. The man called Payne said he'd seen no sign of a lantern except for him. As to the excess of witchlight, he said he'd traded for it. Rune's lanternlight shone into Payne's soul but found the man was telling the truth.

Frustrated at his waste of time, Rune shoved the man away and headed to the bar. He sank down at a table, ordered a drink, and kicked the feline skulking around the legs of his chair. It yowled and hissed before scampering off, its tail sticking straight up in the air. When a succubus slid into the chair across from him, he wasn't surprised. "You won't find what you're after here," he said. "Best brush off, and take those anodyne lips of yours with you."

"Now, now. Don't be so hasty, love. Serina's got something for you. Something you'll be mighty interested in," the woman purred as she reached for Rune's hand.

"Is that so?"

"It is."

He scoffed and tried to shoo her away.

"It's not your affection I'm after," the succubus assured him. "I have information." She glanced around before continuing, her voice lowered, "I know you're after a witch."

Rune sat up. He hadn't even mentioned as much to the tavern owner, though he'd hinted well enough. It wouldn't do to get people up in arms hunting a rumor. Even if the girl was blowing smoke, it couldn't hurt to listen. "And what do you want in return for this information?" he asked.

"Not much."

"Not much indeed." Rune twisted his earring and the creature across from him hissed as the winking light blinded her. He read her intent as clear as day. Her motivation was emotion. Usually that meant either love or revenge. Since she was a succubus, Rune was banking on love. He dialed up his power and saw the red tinge around her heart. So, she wanted to know the whereabouts of a vampire. Interesting.

"I see. So in exchange for a vampire's whereabouts, you'll tell me . . ."

"I'll tell you that my boss came into a shocking amount of witchlight very recently," she murmured, her red lips against Rune's ear. "This happened the same night my vampire came to town with a strange woman. She was petite, and far too pretty for my liking. It wouldn't bother me at all to see her taken away. Perhaps then my Dev will come back."

"Ah. So you don't really want to know where he is, you just want me to get rid of the competition."

The woman sat back, one eyebrow raised as she shrugged.

"You must be aware that if the girl turns out not to be a witch, you'll be punished."

The girl smiled. "Do you promise?"

Disgusted, Rune stood, overturning his chair. "Let's hope for your sake, you're telling the truth."

"One more thing," she said boldly as he made to leave. "Look for them at the skyport."

Rune nodded, then tossed the girl a bag of coins, which she quickly slipped down the front of her bodice. When he stepped outside, wind whipped his hair and wet droplets of rain peppered the ground. He flipped the collar of his greatcoat up and commanded his light to lead the way to the skyport. A gear shifted on his earring and the entire bulb detached and hummed.

Like a firefly, it darted overhead, circled, and then sped off. Just as fat drops of rain splashed his cheeks, wetting his hair, he transformed into a storm cloud of his own and zipped off to follow his light, eventually absorbing it. The light rolling inside the cloud shot lightning sparks as it led the way to the skyport.

CHAPTER 17

LIKE PULLING TEETH

Ember was fairly certain she hadn't swooned. It wouldn't do to have embarrassed herself in such a fashion. She'd merely fainted. She'd certainly experienced enough excitement in the last two days to justify fainting. Still, it wasn't like her. Dev helped steady her as her feet found the deck, while Frank passed a flask of something pungent beneath her nose.

Ember thrust her head away from it, smacking her skull into Dev's chest. "There's no need for smelling salts, Frank," Ember said. "Though I thank you for thinking of me. I believe my corset must be too tight."

Once she was standing, Ember took stock of her surroundings. The roustabout mechanism the captain had been racing toward was gone, and afternoon had become deepest night. They rode on an ocean of clouds and were surrounded by stars. "How . . . how long was I unconscious?" she asked.

"Only a moment," Dev assured her. "Del got us through the roustabout in time. Whoever was in the banshee would be hard-pressed to discover our location now. We're far out over the Saccadic Sea, a great distance from where we were just a few moments ago."

"The roustabout," Ember began. "Is it like the barrier at the crossroad? It leads us to another place?"

"It does. The roustabout works on principles of alchemy. The bismuth projectile triggers a destination based on the alignment of stars upon detonation. After this, the azimuth is determined and then a code . . ."

Ember held up a hand. "It's too much, Dev."

The vampire gave her a debonair smile and kissed her fingertips. "You did ask, my dove."

Pulling her fingers away and straightening her jacket with a frown, Ember headed over to the side of the ship. The wind, which blew wisps of hair into her face, carried with it the smell of salt and the tang of something metallic. As she peered down at the clouds, she fancied she could see the shimmer of black water far below them.

"It's dangerous," Dev said, joining her at the railing. "If we got shot down over the Saccadic Sea, we'd likely be swallowed up by sea monsters."

"Sea monsters?" Ember turned to him with a smirk and a glint in her eye. "Are you telling a story to frighten me so I'll fall shivering into your arms like the cooing dove you believe me to be?"

"Will it work?" Dev's answering grin told her he wouldn't mind such a thing.

"No."

"Well then, I'll just warn you that the Saccadic Sea is home to many creatures. There's a particularly pesky one that sneaks through the barrier and frequents a lake somewhere in the British Isles. It's something of a mystery—no one in the Otherworld can quite figure out his crossing point."

"I thought all crossing points were manned by lanterns."

"All the known ones, yes. But there are some who speculate that there are thousands of undiscovered junctions."

"And you're saying that the terrible monsters living in your sea can just cross over to our oceans and rivers willy-nilly?"

"Like in your world, we have only begun to explore the arcane seas and oceans of the Otherworld. There's a great deal that we just don't know. There are some who have tried to protect the mortal realm by controlling the animals rather than the crossroads. Unfortunately, the only successes were achieved via hobnailing them to the Otherworld by giving them a more ironclad nature."

"Do you mean they affixed metal permanently to living creatures?"

"I've seen it personally."

"Why, that's barbaric!"

"On occasion," Dev admitted. "You've seen my sister's tooth? The one covered in metal?"

"Now, now, brother. The story of my tooth is mine to tell."

Ember and Dev turned. Though Delia wore the same billowy shirt, tight breeches, and corset, she now also donned a warm, hooded cloak. Her eyes flashed a luminous blue in the starlight.

"It felt rude to ask, but I'll admit, I am curious," Ember said. "What happened to your other tooth?"

Delia took Ember's hand and patted it. "Perhaps it is a story best told over a meal. Would you care to dine with me?"

"I thought vampires didn't eat that often."

"We don't, usually. But when a witch is present, a vampire's appetite is whetted. Isn't that right, Deverell?" The vampiress grinned widely, showing her silver fang, but Dev ignored her and offered his arm to Ember. She took it, and they followed the captain to her private dining room. As Dev pulled out her chair, Ember noticed a shadow pass over his face. He either didn't want Ember around his sister or was nervous about what his sister would say. Which meant Ember was now insatiably eager to find out which was true.

A fine repast was brought in. When her plate was uncovered, Ember bent to inhale the fragrant steam of plump sausages, flaky fish, and caramelized root vegetables. When she looked up, she saw a ghost staring at her. It hung half in and half out of the wall. The young woman, if a ghost could be called a young woman, opened her mouth as if she wanted to speak, but then Dev turned his head to see what Ember was looking at and the entity vanished in a puff of smoke.

The server spooned a green vegetable onto Ember's plate, distracting her. She'd never seen it before and picked up a piece, nibbling it delicately. It was salty but tasty, with little crunchy bits on top. As she ate, she wondered what the ghost wanted to say.

It wasn't until she'd tasted everything that Dev told her she was dining on seaweed topped with crispy eel bladder, and that the fruit salad was dressed with something similar to frog's eyes. She didn't dare ask what the sausage was made of, and instead set down her fork and knife and asked the vampire captain for her story.

"I was in love," Delia started, her dimple flashing. "It was a scandalous affair, and one my parents highly disapproved of, which made it all the more exciting, in my opinion."

"Wait," Ember said. "Parents? I assumed the two of you were brother and sister because you'd been made by the same vampire."

"Darling," Delia said with a laugh, "vampires are only made

in the way you're thinking in the human world, and we consider them . . . what's the right word, Dev?"

"Half-breeds," he answered.

"Yes, half-breeds. They have certain limitations that we do not, such as the need to avoid sunlight."

"In our case, we were born vampires, just as you were born a witch," Dev explained.

"But you do live long lives. Or are you immortal?"

"By your standards, yes, we live a long time, but we are not immortal. Nor are we invincible. Though we are nearly so when engaged with a witch, such as Dev has been," Delia said with a cheeky smile.

"Del," Deverell warned. "I'll thank you to share your own stories and not mine."

She sighed. "Fine. You know you're nearly as fussy as Derrick."

"Derrick?" Ember asked.

"Our brother," Dev explained. "I am the eldest. Delia is fourth. Derrick is the fifth and youngest. Numbers two and three are Daxton and Dragan, who are twins."

"So Delia is the only girl?"

"I am. And the only skyship captain too. Mum and Dad are ever so proud."

"Well . . . shouldn't there be a Damon or a Dixie or a Dan or about a hundred more of you if vampires live so long?"

Delia laughed heartily and Ember's cheeks burned. "Are you asking about a vampire's reproductive cycles for educational reasons or personal ones?" She winked at Ember and waved a hand. "The answer is: Vampires can breed as much or as little as they like. Our parents wanted five, so they stopped when they filled the available positions." Delia cocked her head. "You're an interesting one," she said. "I can understand why Dev's trailing you like a puppy looking for a home. Love's a funny thing, isn't it?"

Glancing at Dev, Ember saw that the vampire's eyes were trained on her. He didn't look hungry, not exactly. He seemed to be . . . well, she really didn't know, did she? Was it concern she saw there? Fondness? Worry? Though she was fairly adept at reading the minds of mortals, Ember found the skill didn't seem to work on Otherworlders. But if there was one male emotion she knew well, it was worry. Jack wore that look constantly. Well, that and vexation.

Delia sighed heavily. Her features had gone soft. And not in the way of most women. Human women's faces sort of melted. Especially when it came to babies and weddings. Their expressions were like bowls of butter left out on a summer day.

With Delia, it was more of a slight tenderness behind the steel angles of her cheekbones. A gentling of her lips. An easing around the eyes. A relaxing of the shoulders. She spoke about the first ship she'd ever sailed on. It was a flexion class, though Ember didn't understand what that meant.

The captain who ran it was a pirate, a smuggler like Delia, and was the only one interested in taking her on as an apprentice. It seemed that vampires were rarely trusted. Even so, he made her do all the hard, menial jobs, hoping she'd give up and walk away at the next port. But Delia was smart, efficient. They grew to appreciate each other, and he frequently asked her opinion when it came to which ships to attack and which to avoid. She had an uncanny way of knowing whether a ship had a large payload based on the way it sat in the air.

Delia said, "Eventually, he made me his first mate. One night, when we were passing belowdecks, he stopped me, and when I asked what he needed, he kissed me. He was my captain, and he was my first and only love. He was quite rakish and dastardly, and I fell for him harder than I did for flying. Even though he was a werewolf, a natural enemy of vampires, and despite the fact that engaging in an intimate relationship with a fellow officer was a solecism of skyship code, we sought every clandestine opportunity to be together."

"So what happened? Did your families protest? Were you discovered?" Ember asked.

"Ha!" Delia barked. "It wouldn't have mattered to us if our families had found out. When we were on land, we shot convention out of our cannon and did as we pleased. But when we were on the ship, we were careful. It wouldn't do to spoil both of our reputations. For all the crew knew, we were simply first mate and captain. To keep our moving about at a minimum, he created a secret passageway from my bunk to his."

"Then I don't understand. What happened?"

Delia's face hardened. "He betrayed me. Me and his crew. We were thick in the throes of battle. Our ship was taking a beating. Part of the bulkhead had been destroyed, and we were running dangerously low on witchlight. We were after some highly dangerous cargo, something only rumored to be real—a doomsday device. The plan was to disable the ship, capture the device, and then sell it to the highest bidder."

Ember hated to ask but had to know. "Did you find it? What was it supposed to do?"

"Supposedly, the device was to be used at a certain crossroad. A pivotal one. The idea was that if enough witchlight was harnessed, the device would separate the Otherworld from the human world forever. Either that or collapse them. We were never told the truth.

And, no, we never found it, though we did find the ship supposedly carrying it."

The captain went on. "We lined our ships up, parallel to each other. The other ship was one of the best in the Otherworld fleet—the *Nautilus,* it was called. It still had plenty of witch power. The nets were practically bursting with it. We'd barely made a dent in its hull, though ours was tarnished with smoldering pits. We were hemorrhaging witchlight just to remain afloat.

"I told the captain he should signal the retreat. That we would be fools to stay and if he chose to do so I was desperate enough to call upon the boogeyman for help. I told him we were faster; we could hide in a cloud bank. He refused, and when I demanded to know why, he looked at me with such resignation, such sadness, I practically choked. I knew he was giving up. But I didn't yet know why.

"That's when I saw it. Another ship rising behind the *Nautilus*—one that was well matched to it. The two ships began to battle, and the *Nautilus* turned its attention on the much larger enemy. I knew immediately that we'd been used to provide distraction.

"The new ship was no pirate airship—at least, none I'd ever seen—but it didn't belong to the Lord of the Otherworld like the *Nautilus* either. It flew under no banner, and its technology was far superior to anything I'd seen. We needed to scramble out of there before we were captured and interrogated. And yet my captain gave the command to help the new ship and continue firing on the *Nautilus.* He was no pirate following a code. He was in league with someone. My captain, the man I loved, was a spy.

"At first, I just stood there, immobile. Then the crew started shouting, crying, 'Infiltrator!' 'Turncoat!' 'Code breaker!' and 'Toss him overboard!' As the first mate, I had to respond. I caught his shirt in my hands and thrust him against the balustrade. 'Do you admit you've betrayed your crew? Betrayed me?' I demanded, my heart breaking.

"He looked me in the eyes and nodded. 'I have.'

"'Then you leave me no choice,' I said. Baring my fangs, I sank my teeth into his neck. I'd fed from him before, countless times, and, for a moment, I was able to close my eyes and pretend that it wasn't happening. That my ship wasn't crippled. That the man I loved hadn't acted falsely. But he had. And now it was my duty to end his life.

"'Goodbye, Delia,' he said softly, whispering in my ear as he cupped the back of my head. One moment I was draining his blood, destroying the one thing I would have given my life for, and the next there was a painful wrenching, and he was gone. He'd slipped over the railing. My weakness showing, I cried out for him, stretching out my hand to catch his, but he fell fast, disappearing in the clouds.

"I called the retreat and we limped away as quickly as we could, leaving the *Nautilus* and the ship attacking her behind. It was quite obvious to me that the *Nautilus* was floundering. It was going to spiral into the sea any moment, just as surely as our captain. It wasn't until we were well away that I realized I'd left one of my fangs behind, embedded in the neck of the spy I loved."

Delia touched a fingertip to her one silver fang. "I had this one dipped in metal as a reminder. You see, when a vampire drinks, he experiences pleasure through the tooth. I can survive without the pleasure. This way, I'm not tempted to love again. Nothing, no one, will leave their mark on me like he did."

Just then, the ship rocked. A man appeared at the door.

"What is it?" Delia asked, rising quickly from her chair.

"It's been a mite blashy the last hour," the man said. "Weatherglass says we're headin' into a storm."

Delia smiled. "I suppose it's all hands on deck, then. Dev, if you wouldn't mind escorting our guest to her quarters? It looks like we're in for a bit of a ride." Before she exited, she turned. "Oh, and, Ember?"

"Yes?"

"Try not to cast up your accounts on my ship, eh? Won't be able to spare a deckhand to clean up after you for a while, if you do." With a cheeky wink and a flash of her dimple, the captain disappeared.

CHAPTER 18

BEWITCHED, BOTHERED, AND BEWILDERED

The lights flickered, and Ember stumbled against Dev as he guided her speedily through the corridors. When the ship lurched suddenly, Ember screamed, "This feels like more than a storm! Are you certain we aren't being attacked?"

"When it comes to my sister, I'm not certain of anything!" Dev replied.

Finally, they reached their section of the ship. Dev threw the lever securing the door to their quarters and quickly escorted her to her room. "If you'll excuse me, I'd like to check on my sister."

"Surely you're not planning on leaving me here," Ember said. "Just lend me some clothing a bit less cumbersome and I'll join you on the upper deck."

"Absolutely not. You'll be much safer here in your room. Besides," he added, tugging on the flounce of her now-drooping collar and daring to kiss her nose, "I rather like this dress. It suits you."

Ember frowned as he turned away.

"Drink some of your tea," he added over his shoulder. "I believe your witchlight is returning. You'll find it on the table."

"But, Dev—" Ember began.

He shut the door behind him, fastening the lock on the other side, effectively barring Ember in her room like a prisoner. Angry at his dismissal, and even more irritated at being sent to her bed as if she were a naughty child, she picked up the bag of tea and threw it at the door. Powder poofed in a golden cloud and settled onto the carpet. Ember stomped over to the fallen bag, scooped up what she could, and headed to the bath. Turning the spigot to hot, she ran the nearly boiling water into a mug and added a few pinches of tea powder into it.

It wasn't a proper tea at all. She didn't like its taste, its graininess, or the manner in which she'd been dismissed and commanded to drink it. After stirring it with her finger and sucking the excess drops from her fingertip, she prepared to down the liquid by pinching her nose, when a flash of light distracted her.

Setting down the cup, Ember strode over to the large windows of the shared sitting room. Ember's and Dev's rooms were located on the aft side of the ship. As such, she couldn't see where they were going, only where they'd been, and at that moment she couldn't see much of anything. A volley of rain pattered the glass, obscuring the view of the darkened sky.

As she stood there peering into the night, there was another discharge of light. She thought it was lightning at first, but the normal thunder that accompanied it was different. The boom was softer, sweeter, more like a song, and the light seemed to curl around the ship like a ribbon.

Pressing her nose against the glass, Ember wished, not for the first time, that she'd borrowed Finney's spy spectacles. She could just make out swirling shapes, and she longed to peruse them under one of the different spectrums of Finney's glasses. They appeared to her naked eyes as slightly darker shadows against the dim backdrop of the sky. They were illuminated every time the peculiar lightning struck.

She heard a scream pierce the sweet music of the song, and in response, something shifted belowdecks. At the bottom of the window, Ember could just make out the black barrel of a cannon as it maneuvered into position. They were firing on something! The skyship shook as it shot, but she heard no resounding blast. Whatever they were aiming for was safe for the moment.

Another boom sounded as the gunner shot again. This time the aim was true. The screaming noise faltered, sputtered, and stopped, and a distant craft caught on fire and hurtled toward them. A bright light grew and grew until Ember had to shield her eyes. Certainly, this was the other craft crashing into her part of the ship, but there was no time to get out of the way.

Ember screamed and covered her eyes with her arms.

When nothing happened, she lowered her arms and took a nervous step back, and, strangely, the light followed her. It wasn't rushing toward her at all. Then something bumped against the window, something familiar. *Jack's pumpkin!* She scanned the window to see if she could open it, but it was sealed on all sides.

The pumpkin shook its head at her, and she could swear it was gesturing her away, so she took a few steps back. The light grew brighter, so intense that Ember could only look through her fingers. The glass cracked, forming lines of damage like delicate spiderwebs. Then the window shattered. The debris, whipped by the storm, peppered her skirts and was sucked out into the night.

Flying in, the pumpkin did a little pirouette, but it was clearly weighted down. It had a rope tied to its stem that hung outside the window. It appeared to be carrying something quite heavy. Quickly, Ember led the pumpkin to the desk, which was bolted to the floor, and they worked together to secure the rope to its leg.

Fog, thick and white, spilled into the room, and Jack took shape, hauling on the rope. His greatcoat was soaked and his blond hair was plastered against his head. She'd never been so relieved to see someone in her entire life.

"Jack!" Ember cried, and threw her arms around him.

He gave her a half smile in return but strained to pull the rope. "Help me, Ember."

"But I don't understand. If you're here, then who's out there?"

"Finney."

"Finney? Finney!" she cried.

Ember grabbed on to the rope as well and leaned a bit too far out of the broken window. She nearly lost her hat as well as her balance. Jack yanked her back, tearing the sleeve of the beautiful dress. "Careful!" he shouted. "Don't want to lose you too."

Nodding, rain running down her nose, and wet strands of fallen hair sticking to her face, Ember took hold of the slick rope and pulled. Her arms were shaking by the time Finney's red mass of hair popped up over the sill of the window. Together, they hauled him in and once the three of them were safely aboard the skyship, they all fell back on the wet carpet, breathing heavily.

Jack was the first to recover. He gently removed the rope from Finney's chest and freed his pumpkin. Somehow, Finney had kept hold of his bag as well as his spectacles. The rope that had been lashed beneath the boy's arms had torn his shirt and given him a terrible burn, but he was alive.

"You've certainly got gumption, Finney," Jack said, admiring both the boy's ingenuity and bravery as he lifted the heavy bag from

Finney's arm. "Tying yourself to my pumpkin. I honestly didn't think you were going to make it."

"Your pumpkin likes me," Finney said with a grin as the smiling orb floated over to him and settled beneath his hand. "He wouldn't have let me fall."

Jack looked at the blinking gourd. He would not at all be surprised if it had thoughts independent of his own.

Ember, tripping on her sodden skirts, ran to the water closet and picked up the entire stack of towels. She handed one to Jack and then gave one to Finney. He started rubbing his chest dry but then winced at the pain.

"I think I've got something for that," Ember said. "I'll be right back." Riffling through her belongings, she threw items every which way until she found a tube of healing ointment she'd made before she entered the Otherworld. Wetting a towel with the stuff, she pressed it against Finney's burns.

He howled each time she moved it, but it was plain to see the potion worked. Finney's skin healed before their eyes. When she was finished, he said, "Thanks, Em. That's a handy one. Glad you saved it for me." Jack glowered a little. He was happy to see Ember, but he didn't at all like the way Finney gave her a nickname, or how he was looking at her all moony-eyed, or how his breathing fogged his glasses as she leaned over him.

"I'm so happy you're here!" she said, and hugged Finney gently, careful not to cause him more hurt.

"Me too. This place is amazing!" Finney said. "Can we meet the captain? How does the ship stay aloft? Do you think you could get me in to see the engines?"

"This is what he's been like the entire time," Jack said. "Nonstop questions. How do you stand it?"

Ember shrugged. "Finney's brilliant. Talking excessively is how he thinks things through. Most of the time you don't need to even listen." She winked at Finney and his entire face turned as red as a beet.

"But, Ember," Finney began, "why are you here? Were you abducted? Did that vampire put you under his thrall?"

"How did you know there was a vampire?" she asked, then looked at Jack. "Oh, you told him."

"Yes, I told him. Finney was the only way I could track you. You should have told me you were coming here."

"If I had, you wouldn't have let me leave. And I . . . I had to come here, Jack. You don't understand. Since I've been here I've felt right. Like this is where I belong. Like I'm moving toward something important. I've never been so sure of anything."

Except that now, staring at Jack, Ember realized she had been sure of something else in her life: Jack. She gave him a drunken sort of smile. It was ever so nice having Jack near her again.

Jack ruffled his hair worriedly. He didn't understand why she'd be drawn to the Otherworld, but he could see that she was, as surely as she'd been drawn to his crossroad. He'd hoped it was that she'd felt a connection to him, but maybe it was more complicated than that. "But it's dangerous for you here in the Otherworld, Ember. Surely you've seen that by now. There are all kinds of terrible creatures who live in this place. Probably even on this ship."

"I know. I've met several of them. But there are many nice people here too, and there's something here, something that calls to me. Oh, Finney, wait until you meet Delia, the captain. She's a bit intimidating, I'll admit, but I'm sure you'll hit it off. Then there's Frank. He was, um, reassembled, so to speak, but he's absolutely lovely once you get past the mismatched limbs."

"Mismatched limbs?" Finney said, his eyes wide as he wiped water from the lenses and pushed his normal spectacles over the bridge of his nose. "Can we meet him?"

"Of course. Why don't we—"

"No," Jack said, drawing his legs up and wrapping his arms around them. "Absolutely not. No one is going to meet anyone. We're getting out of here, all three of us."

"And how do you propose we do that?" Ember asked, her brow furrowing. "We're sky high over an ocean filled with monsters, and I'm assuming you can't fog us out of here; otherwise Finney wouldn't have been tied to a rope."

Jack bit his lip and glared at Ember. She was right, of course. But he didn't like that she was right. Instead of answering her question, he posed one of his own. "And how is it that you've remained hidden from the masses?" he asked grumpily. As he said it, he realized something was wrong with her aura. Jack looked beneath Ember's skin. His eyes gleamed silver as he looked her over from top to bottom. Her aura was fully intact, but it was terribly dim. He'd wring the vampire's neck if she was permanently damaged. Jack blinked twice, and his eyesight went back to normal. "Has the bloodsucker been drinking from you daily?"

The way he said it made Ember feel guilty, like she'd been purposely walking around in front of the window wearing only her chemise. "Not that it's any of your business," she said, "but Dev only did that the once. There wasn't a choice at the time."

"Ha! I'll bet there wasn't. So your debonair vampire—Dev, is it? What's his plan, then? Is he going to sell you at auction? Take you directly to the Lord of the Otherworld? Hook you up to a machine and drain you of all your light?"

Ember swallowed. "No," she replied, flustered at his questioning tone. "Dev's been the perfect gentleman. He's taking me on a tour of the Otherworld. We're to have an audience with the high witch herself. But first, we're meeting an inventor. Oh, I'm so glad you're here, Finney. You'll be able to explain all his creations!"

"The high witch?" Jack shook his head. "I knew you were stubborn, Ember, and prone to act before thinking. Until now, I'd chalked it up to youthful mettle. But this whole adventure has been just plain senseless. Why didn't you just talk to me about this feeling you had? Instead, you've endangered yourself, probably gotten me an extra fifty years added to my contract, and you've put Finney in harm's way." Jack ran his hands down his sodden vest and pulled out one of his watches. "And what's worse, my human-made watch has stopped working."

"I don't care about your bleeding pocket watch. Besides, bringing Finney along was entirely your idea," Ember spat. Angrily, she unpinned her hat, since it was barely hanging on her head, and tossed it aside before storming into her room and slamming the door.

Finney took Jack's watch, dried it off, and held it up to his ear. "I can probably fix this for you," he said. "You're going to have to patch things up with Ember on your own, though. In my experience, Ember just wants a bloke to believe in her. I think if you'd given her any indication that you were going to help her see the Otherworld at some point, in a more careful and proper sort of way, she would have waited for you. I've found her to be a very loyal friend. One worth keeping, and one worth being honest with."

Jack mumbled something indiscernible, stood up, and tossed off his greatcoat. "Do you have any extra clothing in your bag?" he asked Finney.

"Nothing dry."

"I can fix that. Hand over what you want to wear."

Finney did and Jack laid out the sodden clothing including his own greatcoat, boots, vest, and shirt, over the back of the couch. He summoned the pumpkin and turned its light on the fabric, and the heat from its gaze dried the clothes in an instant. While Finney changed in the washroom, Jack allowed his light to envelop him and removed the rest of his clothes.

His body and hair dried quickly. With his light still shining, he donned his newly dried pants and then spun when he heard a sound. Ember stood in her open door, staring at him. She'd changed into her usual attire: a pair of leggings, a corset, a comfortable blouse, short skirt, boots, and her gun holsters, weapons included. He preferred Ember dressed this way. It was more her than the showy, expensive gown she'd been wearing before.

When she didn't move, Jack realized he was staring at her and that he was barely clothed, with his unbuttoned trousers slowly sliding down his hips. Irritated, he yanked them up and picked up his now-dry shirt. It wasn't like she could see him. Most people were so blinded by his light, they couldn't even keep their eyes on it, let alone peer through its depths to find the man within.

What he didn't realize was that Ember had a very fine view of Jack. She'd never seen a man in such a state of undress before, and she was fascinated with the way the light kissed his skin. There were all sorts of interesting little dips and hollows on his body, some shadowed and some gleaming. The trousers were loose at his waist but hugged the muscles of his thighs. She swallowed as she watched the ridges of his abdomen disappear while he buttoned his shirt, and then her eyes fixed on his long fingers.

It wasn't until Finney emerged from the washroom that Ember

stirred. She busied herself examining her weapons. By then, Jack was buttoning his vest. "Thanks for that, Jack," Finney said. "It feels much better to be out of those wet clothes."

"Any time," Jack replied, dimming his light to a comfortable level. As he perched on the settee to pull on his boots, he tilted his head toward the broken window and the storm outside. "Going to fix that, Ember?" he asked.

"Fix what?" She frowned. "Do you mean the glass?"

"Of course I mean the glass. What else is in here that needs fixing?"

Ember put her hands on her hips. "I can think of a lantern that could use a bit of a tweak," she replied.

Jack smiled. "I'd like to see you give that a try."

Her eyes narrowed, and Ember was about to say something to put him in his place when Finney said, "She can do that? Fix windows and the like?"

"Of course."

"But I don't know how," Ember said. "Dev was going to teach me, but there hasn't been much time."

Jack raised an eyebrow and Ember did not like the places she thought his mind was going. She stiffened her back and lifted her chin, though she was too short to make the effect really sink in.

Sighing, Jack picked up a piece of glass and placed it in her hand. Carefully, he folded her fingers over it. "Now fill it with witchlight and tell it what to do."

"Just tell it? Like it's a dog?"

"Yes. If that helps you picture it."

"Fine." Ember closed her eyes and felt the bit of glass pinch her palm. She summoned the power, trying to mimic what she'd done before for Payne, but the tickle in her stomach felt more like a cramp. She blinked. "I don't think I can."

"Are you sure he only drank from you the once?" Jack said, his face a storm cloud.

"It's true. Since then he gave me some tea to dampen my powers."

"Show me."

Ember found the now-cold mug of tea and brought it to Jack. He dipped his finger in and tasted it. "That angler," he said with disgust. "This tea mutes your powers, yes, but what he didn't tell you is that there's a compound that also makes you a bit more susceptible to suggestion."

Ember stared at the tea, aghast. "Do you mean to tell me he's poisoning me?"

"No, love. It's more like he wants you intoxicated. He's got a compound in here that would incapacitate a werewolf. Luckily, your witchlight burns it off quickly." Jack took her arm. "Think back—was there a time when he tried to seduce you or convince you to see his side of things?"

Frightened to be so used, she thought back. "Not at all, actually. But . . . the tea was given to him by Payne, the tavern owner. Maybe he added something to it and Dev was entirely unaware," she said, and then grimaced, wondering if it was the tea making her say that.

Jack rolled his eyes. "Never you mind. We'll get to the bottom of it. Now, as for this tea"—Jack took the mug to the washroom and poured it down the basin, pulling the cord to flush it away—"you're no longer to drink it. As long as you're near me, I can hide your witchlight. Any excess power will be absorbed into my pumpkin."

"But what happens if you leave?"

Jack took hold of her shoulders and brought his face down to hers until their noses nearly touched. "I will never leave your side. And you," he added, shaking her a tiny bit, "will never leave mine. Now let's go."

"But, Jack," she said as he tugged her toward the door.

"Not now."

"Jack," Ember said again.

"Later, Ember."

He reached the door and tugged. It wouldn't budge.

"That's what I was trying to tell you. Dev locked me in." Ember frowned. "He should have been back by now."

Jack spun around. "The vampire locked you in here?"

"He said he was only trying to keep me safe." The words sounded wrong even as Ember said them.

"So I keep hearing."

Jack lifted his hand and light shot from it into the metal frame of the door. The thin seal around it ignited, and the area where the lock was dissolved. He kicked open the creaking door so he could keep his hand around Ember's arm. "Finney?"

"Here, Jack."

"Come along, and bring those fancy goggles of yours."

"You got it, boss."

They marched up the stairs, and Ember couldn't help but note the differences between Dev and Jack.

Had she been so wrong about the vampire? He'd been cordial, gentlemanly, regarding her. He hadn't lied; his blood oath confirmed it. Dev seemed to be a man bent on accommodating her. Jack, on the other hand, had a temper as hot as a forge. When he wanted to say something, he didn't try to charm or beguile her. He was abrupt and to the point. Much like a hammer. Yes, he might back her up against a wall, but she wouldn't hesitate to push him right back. The possibilities were interesting.

When it came to Dev, Ember was not so bold. She might get burned by being close to Jack, but such a thing was infinitely more exciting than being shown off on a man's arm, as if she were merely a fashionable accessory without a thought in her head.

As they stepped out onto the main deck, all those thoughts fled, and she barely noticed her hard-eyed vampire or her lantern, radiating power. It was the terror above them that caught her eye.

CHAPTER 19

GETTING INTO THE SPIRIT OF THINGS

Ember didn't know what she was looking at, not at first. She knew it felt dangerous. Finney, standing close by, seemingly oblivious to the danger, twisted the different lenses on his spectacles, quite enjoying the sight above and around him. Ember was certain she heard him mumble words like "beautiful" and "amazing."

Spectral shapes were swirling in the air above her. They were wispy and loosely defined, until a moment after Ember stepped on the main deck. Once she looked up, they began to coalesce and take form.

One circled overhead, lightning sparkling and crackling inside its mass. Then a ghostly sort of light twisted inside it, elongating until it became a pair of arms, legs, a face, piercing eyes, and streaming hair. The vaporous entity, now recognizable as a woman with the tatters of a dress floating around her, stretched out clawed hands and shot toward Ember, her scream shattering the night air.

Jack leapt into its path, holding his pumpkin high. The smiling orb blasted the ghost with its light and it burst apart into floating pieces of phantom energy. Before Ember could feel relieved, the pieces started to merge again, much like water droplets on a window.

"You idiot!" Jack shouted at Dev as he pulled Ember close to his body, using his light to dispel ghost after ghost. Ember wrapped her arms around Jack's waist and buried her head in his chest. "You brought a witch into a ghost storm?"

Dev didn't like the way the lantern clutched Ember or how comfortable she looked in his arms. He was also extremely irritated that the secret that Ember was a witch was now out to Delia's crew. "I thought I told you to stay below!" Dev bellowed in Ember's general direction. "How did the two of you get aboard anyway?" Understanding lit the vampire's face. "Ah, you were on the banshee we shot down. How interesting that you survived."

"Yes. Interesting," Jack spat. "Thanks for that, by the way. Now turn this blasted ship around and get us out of this storm!"

"I'll thank you not to tell me how to run my ship!" Delia yelled as she slashed at a materializing ghost with a gleaming sword and shot another with a sort of electric gun. "Dev assured me that his little witch's power was dimmed to the point of being nonexistent. We came through the storm on purpose."

"On purpose? *On purpose?*" Jack hollered above the din.

More and more spirits were taking form the longer that Ember was on deck. Dev, too, began to fight them off, using his cane, which now glowed on each end. He whirled it overhead and brought it down hard, the light on the end sliced right through a ghost. But like the others, the ghost just began to rematerialize.

"Did you know it would be this bad?" Dev shouted to his sister.

"I've never seen it like this before!" she replied. "Usually, when we dim the power, they can't take corporeal form!"

Dev cursed under his breath. He knew Ember was different, more powerful than any witch he'd ever come across, but this?

Watching the blue light that exploded from Delia's barrel, Ember realized she was cowering instead of helping them fight, which was decidedly unlike her. She attributed her momentary lack of mental clarity to the disturbingly nice feeling of being pressed against Jack's chest, and his arm holding her tight against him. The subtle scent of him—woodsmoke, fall leaves, and spice—made her think of home. Sighing deeply, she pushed against Jack's chest determined to assist the others, but he held her in an iron grip.

"Don't even think about it," Jack warned, his moonlight hair flopping over one eye.

"I'm helping, Jack, whether you like it or not. I have my pistols, and they're already loaded with spells." When she saw the worry in his eyes, she added, "I'll stay close, I promise."

After a beat, he nodded. "They're attracted to your witchlight. It draws them in." Jack told his pumpkin to stay and protect Finney and Ember.

"What are you going to do?" Ember asked, suddenly nervous about Jack leaving her side.

"I'm going to force them to turn this ship around. If they don't, this ghost storm is likely to swallow us up."

Jack seemed almost hesitant to leave them, even after he declared his intentions. He glanced at Finney and nodded; his eyes softened and turned molten when they touched on Ember. His hand caught hers and he squeezed it lightly, and then he was gone, heading to the stern of the ship where Dev and the captain had disappeared to a moment before.

The pumpkin did what it was supposed to, turning this way and that, attacking ghosts as quickly as it could spin. Finney snapped to attention and suggested Ember try the freezing spell and then the disrupted-vision spell. He loaded her second pistol while she tried the first two spells. Closing one eye, she carefully aimed at a circling ghost and fired.

Unfortunately, the freezing spell didn't affect the entity much. It slowed, splintered, and then quickly knit back together. Disrupting its vision didn't stop it either. As Ember wondered which spell to try next, a ghost chasing a crewman through the rigging stopped and turned its sights on the two of them. It opened its mouth and screamed, barreling toward them.

The pumpkin blasted away the lower half of its body, but it wasn't enough. Finney pushed Ember aside just in time, and the ghost hit him with full force, knocking the boy away. Finney's body rolled until it came to a stop near the iron door. The ghost followed, and began trying to dig its fingers into the young man's chest. The pumpkin's mouth widened in alarm, and it turned toward Finney, leaving Ember exposed.

Eerie moaning assaulted her ears as she was quickly surrounded. The manifestations howled, cried, rent their hair, and ripped their clothes. Ember covered her ears and screamed as more and more of them pressed in on her, piling on like ants over a fallen apple. She wrenched back and forth, but they held her in a firm grip. Their moans increased in volume and clarity, as if they were trying to speak to her, but water dripped from their mouths and gushed down their chests. Instead of words, their utterances sounded like the roar of the sea.

She saw white and blue lights pierce the horde of ghosts, and the specters melted away in groups. She allowed hope to bloom. But as many as were driven off, there were others jostling to take their places.

There were too many to fight. As if sensing her desperation, something pressed into her back and seemed to scrape her heart on the inside. She crouched, curling into a ball and wrapping her arms around her legs. It was then that Ember felt a familiar tug, a small burning in the pit of her stomach: Her witchlight.

She drew it up and out slowly, tending to it like she would the first spark of a fire. She took in a slow breath, and her inner power built and began filling her with warmth. Her witchlight strengthened her limbs. She straightened her back, and whatever being had been digging into her squealed and vanished.

Cold spray hit her back as she stood. It reminded her of when she'd stand beneath a tree in the winter and a wind would whip up a freezing cloud of snow that would land gently on her arms and neck. It gave her strength, woke her. She looked at the nearest ghost and pushed her power out and toward the creature. It lit up on the inside. The spectral woman smiled at her, nodded, and then burst into a cloud of ice.

Ember did the same thing again and again. As the beings crowded around her, all she had to do was stretch out her hand and touch their shoulder or arm, and they'd completely dissolve for good.

Through their transparent bodies, Ember saw Jack. He and his pumpkin were decimating ghosts, trying to tear a trail to her, but as soon as he carved out a section, the space was refilled. On the other side, she saw the blue light of Dev's cane-turned-staff and heard the blasts of Delia's pistol. They were much closer now than they had been before.

The witchlight inside her burned through whatever drug Dev had given her, gaining momentum. She allowed it to come, to surface, layer after layer, until her whole body glowed with it. Ember held out her arms and threw back her head. Ghosts came, taking hold of her hands, her arms, her hair, and when they did, they lifted their faces to the heavens, smiled, and vanished.

Ember didn't know how long she stood there, acting as a beacon to spectral oblivion, but the voices soon grew quiet. There were only a few ghosts remaining. Ember opened her eyes and saw Dev, Jack, Frank, Delia, and several crew members, their chests heaving from exertion. They all watched her with mouths open. Finney came close, holding out her pistols, Jack's pumpkin floating just behind his shoulder.

She shook her head. There were only five ghosts left. The first approached slowly. It was a young girl, maybe ten years of age. She hesitantly reached up and gripped Ember's fingers. Her mouth shaped into an O as she burst into a white cloud. The next, an old man, came forward and bowed his head. Ember held out her hand to him, and when he took it, he also disappeared.

The next two—twins—came together. The two young men looked at each other, smiled, and touched her shoulders. Then there was only one. It was eerily quiet now. The creaking of the ship and the balloon overhead was the only sound. The last ghost, an older woman, came forward. She hummed. The tune resonated sadness and salvation at the same time, and Ember realized it was the wailing song she'd heard before. The ghosts had been singing for her.

A bit of water trickled out of the ghost's mouth as she approached Ember. Leaning close without touching her, the ghost whispered something into Ember's ear and then stepped back and lowered her head.

"Yes, of course," Ember said. "Fare thee well."

The ghost's eyes glistened with damp as Ember pressed her hand to the woman's cheek. The woman sighed deeply, touched her own hand to Ember's, and then disappeared in a flurry of light snow that quickly melted away to a puddle near Ember's feet.

Jack was the first to move. He pushed between Frank and Delia and gripped Ember's shoulders. His chest heaved and he worked his jaw, but whatever it was he wanted to say, he couldn't get the words out. Instead, he swept Ember up into his arms. Ember's body shook as her witchlight drained out of her limbs and pooled in her belly. She was suddenly very, very tired. Was this what had drawn her to the Otherworld? Were the ghosts summoning her from beyond the crossroad?

"They're gone," Frank said. "All of them. Even the jumper and my own personal shadow."

Ember smiled and let her body relax against Jack's warm chest. On a railing overhead, she saw the golden eyes of Delia's cat intently watching her and twitching its tail. "I wonder how you got out," Ember said, her eyes closing.

Turning with Ember in his arms, Jack's pumpkin floated closer, bathing them in its light. "I'm going to help her get to bed," Jack said. "We're not done," he said to Dev.

With that, Jack headed back to the iron door. Finney scrambled to get there first to hold it open, and Jack carried Ember down the stairs and into the dark hall. She liked the scrape of his unshaven cheek against hers, and how languid and peaceful she felt. Ember also was vaguely aware of the shifting of fabric on her body, clean sheets in a cold room, and the press of Jack's lips on her forehead.

She fell asleep with a contented smile.

CHAPTER 20

THE WRONG SIDE OF THE BED

Once Ember was in bed, with Finney guarding her door, Jack headed back to the main deck, fury fueling his footsteps. His pumpkin appeared to prefer staying with Finney, though it had never left his side before unless he commanded it. It seemed the orb had indeed developed its own persona. He wondered how that had happened and if it was a natural progression of the ember inside it or if there was something wrong with the container itself. He'd never heard of such a thing before. Again he wondered if there was something more to it than just removing his soul and placing it inside.

When he burst through the iron door, he found the captain and Ember's vampire both hovering over a large astrolabe. Dev glanced up and summarily turned his back.

With all the asperity Jack could muster, the lantern channeled his distant pumpkin and gathered his light around him until he knew he looked like a bomb about to blow, then threw his hands out toward the two of them. Lightning shot out, blistering the deck near their feet, but the man just sighed and gave him a long-suffering look while the woman narrowed her eyes and scowled at the score marks on her ship.

"While I understand your impatience with me, I'll thank you to note that my ship has done you no harm," the captain said.

Jack retorted, "If I could carry the witch and the human lad away from this vessel, believe me, your ship would have already been riven asunder."

"Are all lanterns this insufferable?" the vampiress asked Dev.

"All that I've come across," the man replied, dusting imaginary lint from his collar.

Steaming, Jack began gathering his energy to attack, when the captain held up a hand. "We are not your enemy, lantern," she began. "Your witch will come to no harm."

"His witch?" Dev said, stiffening.

"Oh, Dev. Come now," the captain replied. "Isn't it quite obvious? The lantern didn't come all this way to *report* the girl. You saw as well as I did how comfortable they were together. That being said, lantern, it is not our intention to send her home with you."

"Then what exactly are your intentions?" Jack asked, folding his arms across his chest.

Dev struck his cane against the deck and the witchlight orb glowed menacingly as he pointed it in Jack's face. "This lantern's unbearable," Dev said. "Must we tolerate him? It's like having water in one's shoes."

Jack leaned toward the vampire. "I promise you, vampire, that I'm a lot more dangerous than water in your shoes."

The captain stepped between them. "Calm yourselves. Both of you. Dev, you know where we're heading is dangerous. The lantern's already proved a help against the ghost storm. Who knows what else we're going to come up against on this crazy path you've decided to tread."

She turned to Jack. "I believe proper introductions are in order. My name is Captain Delia Blackbourne, and this is my brother Deverell. As of this moment, I officially welcome you and the human boy aboard my ship, the *Phantom Airbus*. I'll even offer my thanks for helping us navigate the storm safely."

"That's right. You flew through a storm of ghosts on purpose!" Jack said.

"You see?" Dev said. "There's no talking to him! He's mortal born. Lanterns only understand what they're taught. Their single-mindedness makes working with them impossible."

Delia put her hands on her hips. "Clearly you're wrong about this one. The fact that he's here shows he has doubts about the establishment. I give all my crew members a chance to earn my trust. So far, he's done nothing but help. Now, if you want to be helpful, start up the nets so we can get out of here. This empty space where the storm used to be is giving me the shivers. The faster we can vacate this piece of sky, the better."

Dev threw up his arms and stomped off, hollering, "Frank! Let's get those nets back up!"

Delia noted their position on the astrolabe and adjusted their heading. Jack frowned, glancing up at the balloon high above. The nets sparked and flickered and then ignited, the power flowing through them growing brighter with each passing second.

"You were navigating the storm without witchlight," Jack said.

"It's the only way to survive such a storm. If we hadn't turned off the nets, the entities would have attacked them."

"But how did you remain aloft without the nets being active?"

Delia tapped her temple, smiled, and winked, flashing her silver fang. "We've got a backup generator. It's totally encased in a special alloy that is virtually undetectable. It doesn't last long, though."

With the storm of ghosts gone, the moon peeked out from behind the clouds, bathing the deck in cool light that glinted off the metal of the ship. "That's why you locked Ember belowdecks," Jack said.

"Yes. It was dangerous enough to navigate through the storm even if Ember hadn't been on board. Dev tamped her power, but we still knew the ghosts might sense her. Keeping her confined was the best option." Delia eyed the lantern. "She's a special witch, that one. Never seen one handle a storm like that. She didn't destroy them, she . . ." The captain's words trailed off.

"She saved them," Jack mumbled.

"Yeah, like I said, that girl of yours is special. But I can see that you already know that."

Jack's mouth tightened and Delia's suspicions were confirmed. The lantern was as sweet on the girl as Dev. Both men were puffing hot air like rival smokestacks. Delia sighed and lifted the corner of her mouth as she allowed herself, ever so briefly, to remember the heady feeling of being in love. Then she remembered how it felt to be betrayed and she sucked in a breath. Whatever the men's intentions were regarding Ember's heart, they had a job to do, the first part of which was to get her ship back up and running like clockwork.

"Her tea was laced with devil's breath," Jack said bluntly, rousing Del from her thoughts.

Delia's mouth gaped. "Dev wouldn't," she began. "He couldn't."

"Well, he or someone he knows did."

"Could it have been a mistake?"

"Devil's breath is expensive. There aren't too many who could afford such a thing, let alone make a mistake with it. And the only one I can see benefiting from it is your brother."

Delia hesitated. "So you believe your witch was coerced into coming here?"

Jack sighed. "Yes and no. She's wanted to come for as long as she's known about it. But I've kept her away. Someone powerful wants her here. That much is clear. And I think you know who it is."

Delia bit her lip, then said, "You were right to refuse her entry before. There's only suffering on this side. She'd be better off in the mortal world."

"Then let me take her back."

"Can't. I owe Dev a favor, and a pirate never reneges on a favor. It's part of the code. As is the rule of not discussing jobs or employers," she said, glancing at him meaningfully. "Besides, even if I took you back, odds are someone would find her and follow the trail back to your crossroad. Best you can do for the girl is let Dev use his connections to help her disappear. That's his true purpose. I can at least assure you of that. Letting him work the system is the only way to protect her from here on out."

Jack shook his head. "Absolutely not."

"And what are your other options, then, young Jack? Are you abandoning your duty for a girl?"

He waited a tick before answering. "I suppose the answer to that question is obvious."

Delia started, surprised that a lantern would give up so much for another human. "I suppose it is."

When Dev returned with a scowl on his face at seeing his sister engaged in polite conversation with the lantern, he said, "Nets are back up. I'm going to head down now and—"

The captain interrupted him. "Jack's taking your bunk, Dev. You'll be sleeping in the quarters adjacent to mine."

The vampire's face turned red. "Del, I don't think you under-stand the—"

"Believe me, if anyone understands, it's me." She patted her brother's chest and offered him a fond smile. "This is for the best. Trust me. Now head off to bed. I'll wake you when we pass the meridian."

Dev stared at his sister, trying to bore a hole through her with his eyes, and then, knowing he'd lost, he powered between the two, shoving Jack with his shoulder as he did. He knew there was no ar-guing with Delia on her ship.

After he was gone, Jack said, "Thank you."

"Don't thank me, lantern. The duty of protecting this particular witch is not one I'd wish on anyone, especially my brother." Her face saddened for an instant. "He's a soft-hearted sort of vampire. A rare thing among our kind. I don't want to lose him. Do you under-stand?" she asked, her eyes trained on Jack.

"I think I do."

"Then, best get below and look after your charge. Or charges, I should say. What on earth would inspire you to bring along a pet mortal?"

Jack shrugged. "The boy is clever. He was able to track Ember when I couldn't. Your brother hid her particularly well."

The captain grunted. "Sounds like the glass-eyes is a young man I should get to know."

"We won't be with you long enough for that," Jack said, turning, his mental focus already turned to Ember.

"I wouldn't count on that," Delia said.

Jack didn't reply, but headed downstairs. He found Finney, seated on the floor in front of Ember's door, asleep, his spectacles ready to fall off his nose. The poor boy was as baked as Jack was. It had been quite some time since they'd slept. Jack eyed his pumpkin, which sat underneath the boy's arm. It smiled at him, its eyes following him around the room.

He found a blanket for Finney and tucked it around the boy, then shifted him so he lay down on a pillow. The wind whipping through the broken window was calmer now, almost balmy. Changing to fog, Jack slipped beneath Ember's door and hovered over her, listening to her breathing.

She sighed in her sleep and mumbled something, then brushed her nose. Jack felt a shift of power. It hit his form, manipulating him and forcing him to transition. He resisted it at first, confused. Such a thing had never happened to him before. Ember stretched up her hand, found his half-formed arm, and tugged.

Her magic worked on him, and he materialized on the bed next to her. Now satisfied, she turned her back to him, and dragged his arm across her side, clutching his hand between hers. Jack thought he'd stay for just a moment, allow her to fall more deeply asleep, and then try to slip away again. He waited, her back pressed into his chest, his nose buried in her hair, but whatever magic she was using to keep him close didn't wane.

Jack wondered if it was part of her natural defense mechanism. Perhaps she knew that Jack's presence meant safety and as long as he was close, she could rest. He relaxed, threading his fingers through hers and closing his eyes. He was glad Ember trusted him, even if it was only on a subconscious level. He told himself that their being close was simply an extension of his duty, but deep inside, he knew that wasn't entirely true.

Lying next to Ember, her fingers entwined with his, her soft body pressed close, felt so right that Jack feared it was very wrong. He listened to her quiet breathing and slipped into a comfortable and deep sleep himself.

Jack was surprised that he slept so long next to Ember—at least double the number of hours he usually did, especially when he didn't wake naturally. The ship lurched and the two of them were tossed out of bed in a heap of sheets, pillows, and limbs.

• • •

Rune crumpled the message in his fist. The Lord of the Otherworld was growing impatient, the fact that Rune was now on the man's personal flagship proved as much. If he couldn't produce the witch the Lord of the Otherworld wanted, Rune's contract—no, his very life—might be forfeit, not to mention his dreams of ruling. Tamping down his rage, he wrote back.

> We are tracking the rogue lantern as we speak.
> I have not yet been able to ascertain who it is, but I assure you I am making every effort.
> I will keep you apprised as the search continues.

With his message finished, he sent the mechanical bird off and stared gloomily ahead at the impending storm. He hated skyships.

• • •

The Lord of the Otherworld shoved his wife's face toward the brass globe and spun it. "Tell me again," he demanded. "Scry."

"She's here," the high witch swore, pointing to the vast area of ocean known as the Saccadic Sea. "I'm certain of it. She's in the sky somewhere. But I'm so drained, it's difficult to get a more precise reading right now. Perhaps if I could just rest a bit."

"You will rest when we capture the witch!" the Lord of the Otherworld spat. The sight of his sickly, feeble wife disgusted him. Her hand shook as she wiped the drops of spittle from her cheek.

"Yes, my dear," the high witch said.

When she rose from the chair, he violently shoved it against the wall. "Apparently, my lot in life is to be surrounded by incompetents!" he shouted, then turned to the guard standing at the door. "Pack my wife's necessities. We're taking a trip. It would seem there are some things a man has to do for himself."

CHAPTER 21

BETWEEN THE DEVIL AND THE DEEP BLUE SEA

They both awoke suddenly when the ship lurched, dumping them onto the floor with a thump. Ember pushed a pillow out of the way and removed the sheet from her face, wondering what on earth was pressing down on her. Then she saw it wasn't a what, it was a who.

"Oh," she said, brushing the hair from her eyes. "It's you." Jack looked down at Ember and realized their position was entirely inappropriate.

"I . . . I do beg your pardon," Jack said, his blond hair falling in his face as he attempted awkwardly to extricate himself from the sheets that had wrapped around them.

The long shirt Ember wore from the day before shifted loosely, exposing a bare shoulder, and her unbound hair framed her face in soft curls. Jack pointed in the vague direction of her neckline and mentioned that she might wish to adjust her frock. Ember squeaked and tugged on the shirt only to pull it tight against her form. Jack sucked in a breath and moved away faster.

He'd just gotten to his feet and helped Ember to hers when a blast rocked the ship and Ember fell into his arms. He tried to ignore the swell of her hips meeting his palms and asked, "Are you all right?"

She nodded, wide-eyed. Ember's lips parted, and Jack couldn't tear his gaze away from her mouth. Their lips were just inches away from each other when the entire wall buckled and a large section of it tore away from the ship.

Ember screamed and Jack tugged her toward the door, where they found a confused Finney in the lounge. The boy took in Ember's bare legs, the long shirt not even meeting her knees, and narrowed his eyes at Jack. He pushed his glasses up and drew up his hands into fists, but just then, Jack caught a glimpse through the broken window of another ship passing by them with cannons aimed just where they stood. When Finney saw it too, his eyes widened.

"Come on!" Jack shouted to the boy, and pushed Ember out of the lounge as quickly as possible, totally ignoring her and Finney's pleas to return for their things. "Get Finney!" he shouted to his pumpkin while he herded Ember out of the decimated rooms and up to the deck, hoping for safety among the crew.

Once there, Jack despaired at the bedlam. The deck was riddled with smoking holes. The whistle of bat bombs and rocket ravens overhead made speech impossible.

Above them, a bat bomb flapped metallic wings and landed with a snap to a heavy chain attaching the ship to the nets. Then it exploded in a burst of witchlight. The rigging above followed, splitting apart with the force of the blast. Ember squeaked and grabbed for Jack's arm, as the deck they were standing on lurched downward.

Ducking as a rocket raven screeched past, Jack threw his body against Ember's and used his light as a shield while calling for his pumpkin to bring Finney quickly. Jack kept his back to the chaos and prodded Ember toward a slightly better protected alcove. Smoking debris rained around their feet. When Finney finally burst through the door, Jack waved him over, then frowned at his pumpkin when he saw Finney had retrieved not only his own bags, but Ember's as well.

Several rivets popped and a portion of the metal frame overhead buckled, rupturing a nearby pipe. Something hissed from the breach, reeking of rotting vegetation and foul sulfur, and Frank hobbled over as fast as he could, calling to Jack to use his light to smelt it. It was a stopgap effort, but it worked. Once the ship was successfully patched, gas filled the balloon again and the ship steadied.

Finney handed Ember her leggings and boots, and Jack left his pumpkin behind to watch over them while he headed over to help the captain. He stumbled when the gunners manning the carronades fired. The witchlight cannonballs found their mark, and explosions lit the clouds from the inside, but still Jack couldn't see who they were fighting.

Captain Delia moved at supernatural speed, shouting orders to her crew from every place on the deck and calling out bearings. A fusillade of shots peppered the deck where she stood and Jack threw a ball of light, pushing her quickly away as the area where she'd just been standing became a jagged wound spiked with sharp, twisted metal. Just then, a girder rocketed toward Jack. He ghosted swiftly to fog and the beam slammed down into the decking of the *Phantom Airbus* instead.

Chemical explosives—invented by unscrupulous alchemists, and very illegal—sank into the rigging and rained down noxious gases in green clouds. Those who came near them began shaking with convulsions and fell to the deck, foaming at the mouth. They were unconscious within seconds, but, Jack noted, not dead. No. Some were dead, but only the male crew members. Whoever was attacking them was trying to disable the ship but not kill its female crew or passengers. That meant they were after something, or someone. Ember.

Jack spun on his heels and ran headlong back the way he'd come.

• • •

Dev was perched in the stern swivel gun, clutching the controls, waiting for the other ship to come into range so he could fire. He was by far the most skilled marksman aboard, and as soon as Delia realized what they were facing, she sent him to that position.

To say that Delia had been surprised to see the ship on the distant horizon was an understatement. Ships didn't venture out that far on their own, especially not with a well-charted ghost storm in the area, and no one, to her knowledge, knew their destination anyway. At first Delia had cautioned Dev when he panicked, saying a captain needed to keep her head, and that he shouldn't assume that just because a ship shared their sky, it meant to swallow them up. Fear can make a shark out of a minnow when you squint at it hard enough, she'd said.

So the two of them had watched and waited. Dev desperately hoped that Delia was right and that the ship was simply passing through the same airspace. Unfortunately, it quickly became apparent that the distant minnow was indeed a shark, and a hungry one, at that. When it drew closer, they realized what they were facing was a dreadnaught, the Lord of the Otherworld's prized flagship. Deverell's heart sank.

Dreadnaughts were merciless enforcers existing to serve one function and one function only. Rarely seen, they were only sent out when the Lord of the Otherworld wanted something dealt with swiftly and brutally. The crew on such skyships obeyed orders to the letter and never, ever, returned without their prize. The bottom of the dreadnaught narrowed to a thin blade and the bow was razor-sharp. The under blade would be deadly if it crossed over the *Phantom Airbus,* and would easily slice through both net and balloon with absolutely no damage to itself. It wouldn't even need to fire. Their ship would be cleaved in two, the pieces ripped apart as easily as one might divide a piece of fruit. And that, combined with twice as many guns and a hull so thick it was nearly impenetrable, made the dreadnaught almost impossible to defeat.

To be fair, Delia's own reputation for winning was also notable, but Delia focused on robbery, not murder. Even when she won, she made every effort to leave the crews intact on the ships she plundered, taking them as prisoners or putting them off at ports or islands. She was a pirate, yes, but she was a pirate who followed a certain code. She didn't kill for killing's sake.

Dev swiveled in his chair, his waistcoat unbuttoned so he could maneuver more easily. His blue vampire eyes were trained on the sky. The glass aerodome at the stern might have frightened other gunners since it sat directly behind the ship, but Dev found he quite enjoyed the view.

Jutting out into the sky and attached only by a large circular gasket through which a gunner entered the pod, the clear bubble gave Dev over a 180-degree view of the space behind the skyship.

His palms began to sweat as he held the grips in firing position, cocked low and ready. There was an almost kinetic energy he could feel. Dev sensed the weight of the heavy ship as it moved around them. The sun burst through the clouds, effectively heating his pod like a solarium. Then, right before his eyes, the dreadnaught descended from the clouds. He sighted the hull, took aim, and clicked the witchlight transmitter that sent an electromagnetic charge to the warheads.

The first two lit. Jets bursting, they shot out from the *Phantom Airbus,* gaining velocity every second as they arced in a perfect trajectory. When they met the dreadnaught's hull there was a burst of energy, enough to rock the glass aerodome where Dev sat. The hull belched smoke like a foundry, but there were no secondary explosions. He lined up a second shot and a third, trying to hit the already-weakened hull, swiveling as the ship progressed across the sky, but the dreadnaught shook off the torpedoes as if they were mere pebbles.

He fired again and again, fully knowing that the warheads wouldn't cause enough damage. Then he heard the click that told him his guns were empty. The ship drew closer, but instead of cleaving them in two, Dev saw the grapnels soaring across the expanse between the two ships. Wheeled, metal gears spun on the dreadnaught, drawing cables tight and bringing the *Phantom Airbus* closer. They were going to be boarded.

Wriggling out of the cockpit, Dev ran back through the dark corridors of the ship so fast, a mortal would only see a blur. Flickering gasoliers cast their umber light in the rooms and passageways, but they offered no warmth. Dev felt cold, clammy. His blood rushed from his bones and invigorated his limbs, lending him strength for the upcoming fight. This would be nothing like fighting ghosts seeking to take possession of the living. This time there would be death and blood.

On deck, there were at least ten grapnel hooks now connected to the *Phantom Airbus* with dozens of armed men sliding down at exacting intervals. The *Phantom Airbus* crewmen, led by Frank, shot carbines, and the staccato sound of unloading ammunition pinged as deckhands from the other ship slid down the cables and landed on the ship.

One man released a bag of clockwork frog grenades, which hopped from the deck onto the nearest men and exploded. The boarders all had little buttons on their collars to repel their own grenades. Dev grabbed the nearest enemy; then he tore into the man's neck with his teeth and took the button, determined to put it on Ember.

The brawl began in earnest and Dev fought, forging a path to Ember, inch by bloody inch. He saw the lantern darting between and around boarders, using his light to blind them and bring them to their knees while heading in the general direction of Ember.

Dev pressed on and arrived at her side at nearly the same time as Jack, not that she noticed. Dev reached for the edges of his unbuttoned vest and tugged it sharply, then swiped his chin with his palm to remove any dribbles of blood, and grimaced at seeing the stains. The lantern, on the other hand, looked as fresh as if there were no battle happening at all.

"Here," Dev said, pressing the button into her hands and frowning. "It will protect you from the clockwork frogs."

"The frogs aren't targeting her," Jack said bluntly. "They're only going after the men. I saw one leap cleanly off Captain Delia before detonating."

Ember purposely turned and attached the pin to Finney instead.

"They're after Ember, then," Dev said.

Jack spun. "Obviously. Tell me, vampire, what do we do? How do we protect her?"

"There's only one thing we can do right now. Fight."

Jack and Dev began fighting, and, strangely, side by side. Jack used his light to blind their opponents while Dev took them out with his teeth and his witchlight-tipped cane. Soon both of them were drawn into the thick of the battle and lost sight of Ember again.

Though Dev and Jack drew off several, there were too many boarders for Ember and Finney to elude. Ember pulled out her guns, firing while Finney reloaded for her, pulling new tubes from the bag. She didn't even care which spell she used. Men fell back blinded, covered with acid, shrieking with blood trickling from their ears, dripping with slime, or electrocuted.

When Finney yelled that she was out of ammunition, Ember summoned the power inside her like she had with the ghosts. But this time when she touched a man who tried to lay hands on her, he was blasted away, his body crashing among the battered decking, a smoking hole in his chest. Steeling her mind against the carnage, Ember moved forward with Finney just behind her, taking out man after man with her witch power.

Ember got a firsthand glimpse of what happened when a clockwork frog targeted a person. One of them was hiding in a corner, and when Ember passed by, it activated, leaping on Finney. She gasped, trying to pull it off, but the button on his lapel blinked red and the frog turned and hopped off his shoulder. Within two more jumps, the frog found one of Delia's crewmen, attached itself to his leg, and then detonated.

The poor man was blown to pieces. His bloody boot landed at

Ember's feet and came to a stop. They moved on, managing to collect a few other weapons: a pair of knives, a gun that shot pellets infused with witchlight, and a short sword.

They had to squint through the smoke as they edged furtively forward, trying to distinguish between enemy and crewman, but it was difficult and they made little progress. Jack and Dev were gone, though Ember thought the screams she heard were likely those of their victims. She coughed and realized the fog wasn't entirely made up of cloud. Something was burning.

Finney pointed toward a contraption just below the main rigging. "The propulsion unit is on fire!" he said. "There'll be no saving the ship!"

"I should think you'd be more concerned with saving our lives!" Ember shouted in response as she took down a man barreling in their direction, his eyes gleaming with malice.

"Well, yeah. But that's obvious, then, isn't it? Looks like we're meant to flounder between the devil and the deep blue sea. I say the sea looks like the better option."

Ember wasn't so sure she agreed.

They heard a familiar shout. It was the captain. "Five degrees starboard!" she shouted. "I agree, Frank. There's no help for it. Drop those boarders and sound the klaxon, then prepare to accelerate to ramming speed!"

Finney and Ember turned to each other, mouthing, *Ramming speed?*

They fought their way over to Captain Delia and drew close just as an alarm sounded. It blared loudly enough that Ember wanted to press her hands over her ears. "Ember!" Delia cried when she caught sight of her. "Dev told me you have a cauldron."

"I do. It's on my hat."

"May I have it? It will likely save our lives."

Ember nodded quickly and Finney fished in the bag until he found the hat and handed it to Delia. The vampire ripped the cauldron off and tossed the hat back to Finney. Then she turned and threw the cauldron to Frank, who opened a little box at the base of the balloon. A strange glow was coming from inside. He tossed in the cauldron and shouted that it was ready.

Delia nodded and turned back to Ember and Finney. "You two stay close. Once we're in position, I'm going to lash the wheel. We'll only have a few seconds to clear before the explosion."

Squeaking, Finney echoed, "Explosion?"

"Yes. If we time it right, and if the gods of luck are on our side, they'll never see it coming."

Ember didn't know how one ship could miss another one barreling toward them at ramming speed but, then again, she wasn't the captain. Finney brandished the sword and tried his best to keep men away from the helm, but it was Ember who was able to take most of them down, protecting the captain as she worked.

Delia pushed some buttons on her control console and then threw a switch. There was a great burst of energy in the nets and they began to glow white. Finney heard the engines double, or perhaps even triple, their speed. Captain Delia cranked the wheel hard and the ship surged backward, away from the dreadnaught. The cables attaching the *Phantom Airbus* to the other ship tightened and snapped. Once the captain had taken the ship a distance away, she turned it, quickly maneuvering it so the bow faced the dreadnaught's hull.

Frank appeared. "She's ready, Captain. Crew's aboard. At least, them that remain."

"And Dev?"

"He's aware and will join us momentarily."

"Good. Right, then." Delia tossed a length of strong cable across the helm. "She's lashed. Take these two down, Frank, while I put her in gear."

"'Tis a sad occurrence indeed to lose so fine a ship, Captain," Frank said.

"It is. But take heart in knowing we'll live to plunder another day."

As Frank took them to a wall and pressed a button opening a hidden door, Ember saw Delia pat her ship fondly and say, "You'll be missed, you old rattletrap. Rest assured knowing a piece of you will live on."

As the door shut on Delia's final rites for the ship, Frank, Ember, and Finney saw the captain throw the lever to full power. The ship shivered for an instant and then started forward. The box they were in vibrated, and Ember had the strange sense that they were moving downward, like the hoist she experienced at Payne's. When the door opened, she found she was in the dark center of the ship, a part she'd never explored. Crewmen with bandaged heads and bleeding gashes sat in chairs, some even at their stations, staring at buttons and knobs and levers.

"What is this place?" Ember asked Frank.

"Backup plan in case of emergency."

"Oh, then I suppose this qualifies," she said.

"Amazing!" Finney said as he hunched over, watching a crewman. He tapped a dial. "I think this is a depth gauge."

The door opened and Dev, Jack, and Captain Delia came in, the grinning pumpkin floating behind.

"Are we ready, men?" Delia asked as she shrugged into a coat.

"Ready, Captain," Frank replied.

Delia took hold of two handles and brought down a bronze tube, then peered into the visor. She turned to the left and then to the right. "There she is," Delia said. "Brace for impact. Release on my mark. Impact in five, four, three . . . release!"

There was a wrenching and a shearing of metal. Then Ember's stomach dropped as they fell. A great explosion rocked the ship and they were tossed against machinery and gadgets of all description. Still they fell, faster and faster. Even the crewmen were grimacing, holding on to the panels for dear life.

Then they hit. Finney's feet left the ground. Jack turned to fog. Dev grabbed Ember in the air, and when they crashed down, he made sure it was his back taking the brunt of the impact. Steam gushed out from a broken pipe, and red lights pinged and flickered. Frank immediately rose to tend to the pipe.

Ember ended up with a lump on the head, a bruised elbow, and a bleeding gash on her hand. The injuries on Dev's body, which were not few, healed quickly with help from his blood stores. He wrapped Ember's hand with his tie and sat her in one of the swivel seats. Jack's pumpkin hovered over an unconscious Finney, its carved mouth gaping with worry.

Jack, disgruntled at seeing Dev tending to Ember, checked the boy. "It's just a lump on the head," he said, comforting his pumpkin. "He'll be fine."

"We came in too fast from too high a position," Frank said to his captain. "Ship's not meant to take that much pressure."

Delia patted her console. "The *Phantom Airbus* still lives, Frank. She's watching over us. We'll survive. Are we ready to dive?"

"D-dive?" Ember said, attempting to sit up.

"It's a submersible," Dev said gently, inspecting the bump on her head. "Delia had it built a few years ago. Right now, we're somewhere on the Saccadic Sea. Delia timed it so we'd look like a piece of the ship, broken and dropping to the water. It should put off whoever is following us."

"Put off all but one," Frank said, dragging a man out from the supply closet.

Ember peered around Dev and saw the man who stood proud and unafraid, even though the colossus that was Frank was certainly holding his arm in a painful grip. His eyes were a piercing storm-gray, and his brown hair, darker than Dev's, was long and drawn back in a leather tie. The strong cleft chin in a square jaw and the powerful arms and shoulders of the man told Ember he wasn't someone to cross.

The captain stepped around the viewing tube and her breath caught. The man smiled as Captain Delia, her face full of fury, stormed up to him. She raised her hand and the slap was so loud, the echoes of it rang through the bridge. Everyone froze except the man who lifted his hand to his cheek and rubbed it, then moved his jaw back and forth.

Instead of addressing the captain, the stowaway said, "It's nice to see you again, Frank."

"Nice to see you too, Captain Graydon, circumstances being what they are."

"Indeed," the man replied.

"I believe you have something that belongs to me," Delia said, her words venomous.

The man leaned closer. "More than one thing, if truth be told, darlin'."

Delia hissed and raised a finger, daring him to speak again. "Throw him in a cell and toss the key out an airlock," Delia said.

"But, Captain," Frank said, hesitating. "We don't have a cell."

"Then chain him like a dog. He deserves at least that much."

When they were gone, Ember whispered to Dev, "I don't understand. Who is that man?"

"He's not a man. He's a werewolf. The same captain, in fact, that my sister tossed overboard and is still obviously in love with."

CHAPTER 22

TRICKS AND TREATS

Ember turned shocked eyes to Dev. "You mean he's alive?" she asked. "Even though Delia threw him overboard?"

"Apparently so." Dev checked the submersible's chronometer against his own pocket watch and was irritated to see Jack doing the same thing. Dev was even more irked when the lantern pulled out a second, very lovely pocket watch and wound that one as well. Jack frowned and shook it, then put it back. *What kind of a man needs two pocket watches?* Dev wondered. He rubbed his jaw considering if he should procure a second timepiece for himself as well.

Frank marched the captive, Captain Graydon, out of the command area, and an extremely shaken Delia headed back to the periscope, not deigning to look at the rest of them until there was an unquestionable clank of the metal door signifying that her lost love, the one that had betrayed her, had disappeared from view. Even then, she only gave them a cursory glance before going back to work.

She placed her eyes against the periscope viewer, and after a moment of slow turning and scanning the skies, she slammed her hand against the bronze tube. "Blast!" she said. "The dreadnaught suffered little to no damage. I thought surely, once the smoke cleared, I'd see something. . . ."

Her words drifted off. Ember would have never believed she'd see the captain look so . . . defeated. Ember didn't know if it was losing the *Phantom Airbus,* seeing her lost love returned, or their current predicament. Whatever the case, the captain's mood affected Ember and the witch felt as if she wore a cloak of foreboding on her shoulders.

Ember was weary to the bone and thought maybe her adventure had taken her far enough, at least for this trip. As exciting as it was traveling with Deverell, she missed her aunt and the little crossroad where Jack made his home. Her potions had been completely used up, and she no longer had the cauldron charm that stored her power. With her resources drained, Ember thought it might be a good time to stop and reassess her immediate goals.

She was thrilled that Jack and Finney had joined her, of course. Having the two of them near felt right—well, righter than just being alone with Dev. And even though their situation was terribly dangerous, there was something inside telling her she was in exactly the place she needed to be. Though she was certainly appreciative of the attention Dev had bestowed upon her thus far, Ember was starting to suspect that the vampire's motives regarding her were not altogether innocent. There was the tea to consider, and then there was also the way he looked at her. It was rather territorial.

There was no question the Otherworld was a wondrous place, but maybe next time she could go at a bit of a slower pace. One where she could simply meet interesting people and not be chased by ghosts or travel on skyships. Perhaps she could meet the high witch another time. Surely there was no rush.

Ember felt something brush her hand. It was the cat. She smiled and shook her head remembering never to underestimate the instincts of a cat. She picked it up and nuzzled it, whispering, "You're lucky you got off. Maybe next time you should stay home instead of heading off on a skyship. Perhaps I should do the same."

Truthfully, the skyship traveling wasn't so bad; it was the attack she didn't like so much. Maybe, if she was a bit more world-wise or understood her power better, she'd know how to avoid such situations. Not getting on a pirate airship might be the first step; to think such an attack might be part and parcel for that lifestyle!

As she considered the idea of asking the captain to drop her, Jack, and Finney off at the nearest city, something tugged in her belly again. She'd thought her purpose, the thing calling her forward, was needing to save the ghosts, but now that she had, there was still a niggling something. Suddenly, leaving didn't seem right. The more she thought about it, the more she realized she wanted to stay on course with Dev and the captain.

Ember frowned. *No, that's not right.* She would have rather liked to shop in the town, have tea with a gargoyle, or explore a tinker's shop. Dev had rushed her past all the interesting bits and she regretted not taking her time to explore as she would have liked. Perhaps, now that he was here, Jack would be willing to escort her properly. They'd have to get off the submersible first, of course. Her stomach lurched.

Ember gritted her teeth, ignoring it. Consciously, she decided that she would indeed inquire to see if Jack might have changed his mind and was perhaps willing to take over for Dev. Finney could tag along as her chaperone. Perhaps they could locate an apothecary where she could procure ingredients to restock her potions. Suddenly, she felt sick and cupped her hand over her mouth.

Dev interrupted her thoughts. "We'd better dive as soon as possible, sister. Otherwise, they may spot us floating here intact on the water."

"That's Captain when you're aboard my ship, Deverell. Eddie!" Delia barked, her nerves on edge. "Check the hermetic seal. Are we sound? Any damage?"

"Ship looks to be in working order, Captain. We're watertight."

"Good. Then prepare for diving. If they spot us here, all they'd have to do is drop a bomb and we'd combust like oiled vellum."

"I think I'll show our guests to their cabins," Dev said. "Ember needs to rest from the fight."

Delia gave him a piercing glance and a sharp nod.

The vampire offered Ember his arm, but she'd stooped down to check on the mortal boy.

"I'll bring him," offered Jack softly, placing his hand on Ember's shoulder. The lantern then scooped up the lad in his arms, his pumpkin following along behind. Dev felt like a dolt. Of course the lantern would do the gallant thing first. Dev hadn't realized how much the boy meant to Ember.

He'd been bested by the lantern again. That much was obvious. Though Ember took Dev's arm, her eyes and grateful smile belonged to Jack. Dev tried to make up for it by holding the door for the lantern, but he knew it was too little of an effort too late.

They settled Finney in the room that Dev had wanted for Ember, as it had a connecting door to his own. If he could have thought of a tactful way to suggest moving the boy, he would have, but Ember insisted that Finney have the best and she could make do wherever there was a free spot. Jack set Finney down and the boy groaned and struggled to open his eyes.

Ember went to the washroom and wet a cloth, then perched

beside Finney, pressing it to the bump on the side of his head and then to his cheeks. The crimson-haired lad winced until he recognized Ember, and then settled back on the pillow with a contented sigh. The pumpkin floated down to the bed next to the young man and nudged his hand.

"There's my good man," Finney said as he patted the side of the orange globe; then the boy promptly fell asleep, his hand still touching the pumpkin.

Jack bent over the bed and removed Finney's spectacles, setting them on the desk, before loosening the boy's vest and shirt and removing his boots. The pumpkin swiveled on its base, blinking at Jack.

"Yes, you can stay with him," Jack said to his pumpkin; then the lantern turned to Dev. "She's going to want to stay with Finney too. Can you find her an extra blanket?" The ship angled down and Jack heard the whoosh of rushing water flowing up and over the submersible. The idea that they were now completely immersed beneath the sea set Jack's nerves on edge.

Apparently, the vampire felt the same way. "I loathe being trapped inside this metal coffin in the black depths. Especially knowing that the only thing standing between a life of leisure, and one where some sea beastie from the depths slowly digests me, is this flimsy piece of tin." To make his point, Deverell kicked the wall of the ship. There was a pinging noise afterward, as if the ship protested his abuse.

Jack tilted his head, considering the vampire with his strange gleaming eyes. It gave Deverell the shivers. He'd never liked lanterns. They saw too much. He couldn't stand knowing that the man he considered a rival could peer into his very soul and, perhaps discern all his secrets. Besides unnerving, it was also unnatural.

The man's white-blond hair was mussed and stood out around

his head at all angles. His greatcoat was nowhere near as fashionable as Dev's. The boots on the lantern's feet were scuffed and worn. And though his face was young, his eyes were very old. Older even than Dev's.

Jack was such a strange creature. He was a wayfarer, a man endowed with great power, a being whose very soul had been stripped away and placed in a container for all to see. That a man like him could capture the attention of a witch such as Ember caused Dev a great deal of consternation.

Dev gestured that Jack should follow him through the adjoining door. "Ember can have this room when she can bear to be parted from the boy," he offered, purposely disregarding the lantern's raised eyebrow. "It's mine, but it's more comfortable than anything else I could offer her." Deverell strode up to a wall, sealed over by imbricated plates of metal. "She'll be closer to the young man and the view is incredible." He pulled a lever and the plates drew back. A bubble of glass, thick, hard, and resistant to all but the most powerful witchlight, gave Dev and Jack the opportunity to stand beneath the ocean and see it as if they were creatures of the deep.

"Have you seen sea monsters, then?" Jack asked, curious, as he studied fish and plants made visible by the powerful witch lamps running along the sides of the ship. "Is that what you fear? Death in the belly of a beast?"

Truthfully, Dev's fear wasn't the ocean, or even coffins, in particular. Only half-breed vampires were forced to reside in those. No. Dev's fear was isolation. Being truly alone and shut away from everyone and everything he cared about. He didn't say as much to the lantern, preferring to keep his own weaknesses to himself. Instead, he clutched his hands behind his back and stood with Jack, staring into the vastness of the sea.

"In my experience," the lantern began, his voice soft, "places like the oceans or the heavens, an undiscovered forest, a great underground chasm, or the mystery of a woman's heart and mind are not the end of a journey, but a beginning. Do not let fear of the unknown prevent you from discovery, vampire; otherwise, the story of your life will be a dull tale indeed."

"Ironic, isn't it? A lantern advising an Otherworlder about life. I can't imagine your life story is riveting."

The lantern was quiet for too long a minute. Finally, he replied, "You're not wrong. Up until Ember, I was more of a watcher than a doer. Now I'm a firefly caught in her glass. She takes me where she will. Until she releases me, I must take this road with her."

When the vampire snorted, Jack glanced over at him and continued, "Perhaps you think you're the one in charge. That you are guiding this ship. Determining our destination. Maybe you are. But you also should consider whether perhaps, like me, you are caught in Ember's glass, and the pain and frustration you feel comes from you bumping your head against it, trying to escape."

"I assure you, the last thing I want is to escape from Ember." Deverell pulled the lever to retract the metal, hiding the glass bubble from view. Jack studied Dev's aura. His abilities were diminished slightly when his pumpkin wasn't near, but he could still see enough to know the vampire had an agenda regarding Ember.

The problem lay in the fact that Jack didn't know what that agenda might be. Perhaps Dev fancied himself in love with the girl. Jack supposed the vampire's motivations mattered little. What did matter was keeping Ember safe when dreadnaughts and who knew what else were following her. He hoped Dev's mysterious end goal would hide her, as Delia promised it would.

Taking a last look at the vampire's aura, Jack squinted, unsure of what he was seeing at first. Then it became clear. Jack's light showed him that the strength of another witch ran through Dev's blood. A witch had given Dev her heart, her everything. That it was still roiling inside his aura meant that he'd selfishly kept it, along with her blood, without returning the favor. If he had shared his heart with his witch, Jack would see the signs of his being claimed. Interesting.

It might explain why he was so interested in Ember. His blood was telling him that it was wrong to hold back his heart, to hoard the power and give nothing of himself. To be whole, for his soul to be at peace, he'd have to willingly offer his own heart.

Jack was silent as the two men went back to the room where they'd left Ember and Finney. They found both of them asleep, Ember slumped over Finney as the boy lightly snored.

Gently, Deverell picked Ember up and put her into his own bed. Jack followed, tucking the blanket around her, while Dev pulled a few very wrinkled, paper-wrapped items from a bag and left them on the nearby table. Without discussing it further, both men left the room together, separating in the corridor. Dev didn't know that when he was out of sight, Jack turned to fog and slipped back into the room where Ember slept.

This time he made sure to stay well enough away from her so she wouldn't trigger the magic to cause him to take human form. He settled in the doorway between the two rooms, the pressure from the ocean making his fog thick, heavy, and wet. Soon the doorway was coated with moisture, but he was so strangely exhausted that he didn't care. His pumpkin turned to look in his direction, but his mind was soon lost as he allowed his supernatural body to rest.

CHAPTER 23

THE SPY WHO LOVED ME

"Four degrees down," Delia said to her crew.

Once they reached her preferred cruising depth, she added, "Good. Now level off and half ahead." Delia's fingers thrummed the console and her foot tapped anxiously. It felt like a gutful of snakes squirmed in her belly, nipping at her from the inside. Frank had returned hours ago, saying he'd done as she'd requested and affixed the heaviest of chains to the arms, feet, and neck of his former captain.

Delia knew it was a difficult thing to ask of her first mate. He'd loved Graydon nearly as much as she did. In fact, Frank wouldn't be the man he was today without his former captain. Graydon had personally paid for Frank's clockwork heart from his own reserves. The witchlight battery to keep the heart ticking was more than they could both earn in a lifetime. Graydon hadn't blinked an eye. He hadn't said where he'd gotten the funds, and she hadn't asked. Delia had learned that sometimes, where piracy was concerned, it was better not to know such things.

Captain Delia paced the command deck, unseeing and distracted. Finally, Frank placed a heavy, green-tinged hand on her shoulder. "Go," he said, his black lips drawing her attention. "I've got things under control here. Get some bunk time, or . . . or do whatever else you need to do. Fulminate. Dragoon. Or, don't forget, inebriation is always an option."

"For him or me?"

"Either one would probably do the trick."

Delia looked up into the kind, strange eyes of her first mate and then felt herself relax. She gave him a grateful nod to go with her slight smile and left the bridge. Heading to her cabin, she entered and splashed water on her face and neck. When that didn't soothe her, she took out a bottle of blood, her favorite vintage, and drained it. The infusion of energy left her jittery and even more on edge.

After removing her jacket, boots, and corset, she drew back the blanket on her bunk, intending to sleep, but hesitated, clenching the fabric in her fist. She had to know. Had to understand why Graydon did what he did. Delia pulled her boots back on but left her corset off. Her long shirt billowed around her hips and breeches as she strode purposefully through the ship, headed down the stairs at a fast clip, and stopped outside the thick door to the reactor compartment.

The metal hinges creaked and she entered the dark space, shutting the heavy door behind her with a bang. Instead of finding a quiet passageway, she felt her ears assaulted with the thrumming of the engines.

The reactor section was dim, the bulbs overhead barely giving off a glow. Frank was probably trying to preserve their remaining witchlight. Steam licked her arms and face, leaving a sheen of damp as she ducked beneath the hydraulic tubing that flowed to a central unit where it split into sections that rose upward like organ pipes. Each segment powered a different part of the ship.

"I wondered if you'd come," a voice called out from the dark.

Delia followed the sound to the back and found Graydon chained to the main reactor. His clothing hung limp on his body and his dark brown hair was soaked from the steam and hanging down around his shoulders. He'd always been ruggedly handsome and was the only man she'd ever met who made her feel small and feminine. It was surprising to her how much she wanted such a thing.

It was a sad fact that most men were intimidated by Delia. Not only did she hail from one of the oldest and most respected vampiric families in the Otherworld, but she was also smart, self-assured, and looked men in the eye, considering herself as either an equal or better. Once she did that, the opportunity for romance disappeared. Captain Graydon was the exception to that rule.

She'd loved him once. Fully, unconditionally, with her whole self. It made no sense. Adding the title of "turncoat" to the man she'd known was like trying to fit a bevel gear to a spur. It just didn't mesh. Graydon had shared his blood with her, freely and often. If he planned to betray his crew, abandon his ship, she should have tasted it. But he had betrayed them; there was no doubt about that.

Delia's duty to her crew and loyalty to the pirate code warred inside her against her need to wrap her arms around her former captain, mentor, and paramour. He was a traitor. The word was bitter on her tongue, as twisted as spilled entrails, and yet she couldn't bring herself to be less than thrilled that he was alive.

Delia didn't know how long she'd been standing there, fists clenched, lost in looking at him, but it felt too long. She longed to kiss the square line of his jaw, to touch her fingertip to the cleft in his chin, to run her palms over the corded muscles in his arms and shoulders. That he had been gazing at her as well, unspeaking, was something she couldn't acknowledge.

"Who are you working with?" Delia finally asked, when what she really wanted to know was why. Why had he turned against his own crew? Against her?

Graydon worked his jaw, making the heavy chains rattle. He turned his head, dropping his gaze at last, refusing to speak. Delia stepped closer and traced the emblem on his collar. It was the same one all the men who'd boarded her ship wore, the sign of the Lord of the Otherworld—the token of the establishment they were working so hard against.

"We lost Harry," she said softly. "Vic too. Rufus is alive, but he lost a leg."

She'd taken on new crewmen since Graydon had disappeared. Some retired. Some moved on to other ships. But Frank had stayed, along with a dozen or so others.

He turned back to look at her again, his eyes regretful. "I'm sorry, Del. They were worthy men. Maybe it will help to know they died for a good reason."

"A good reason?" she echoed. "A good reason? Are you trying to tell me, Graydon, that this"—she took hold of his collar and ripped it away, thrusting the emblem in his face—"organization you serve had a good reason for killing my men? We didn't provoke you. We were carrying no cargo. How do you justify destroying my ship?"

"But you were carrying cargo, Del. The most precious cargo in the Otherworld."

Delia's mouth snapped shut and she took a step back, her arms straight at her sides, unwilling to give him any sign that she knew what he was referring to.

Graydon tilted his head and then sighed. "We know about the

witch, Del. We were supposed to retrieve her. Once we had her, we would have let you go."

"And who is 'we'?"

The werewolf's mouth tightened in a thin line.

"Fine," Delia said tiredly. "It makes no difference. I can see plain as day that the emblem is the Lord of the Otherworld's. We scotched your plan and you failed in your task. As soon as I can put you off my ship, I will."

"You won't kill me, then? Have you gone soft, my darlin' vampire girl?"

Delia chose not to answer, especially when she saw the smile playing about his lips. "Just answer one question," Delia said. "How did you survive the fall?"

Flexing his hands, he jostled the heavy chains attached to his wrists. There was no escape for him, and he knew it. "I'll answer yours if you answer one of mine," he said. Delia gave no sign that she would accept his offer, but he'd answer anyway. "My . . . benefactor provided me with some highly advanced technology. It's called a manta device. I was to use it to gain access to the other skyship.

"When I slipped over the side, I clicked my boots and activated jets in the heels, along with a thin pair of flexible wings that look a bit like those of a manta ray, which were hidden inside my cloak. The metal extensions are etched with witchlight nets. I flew across the expanse, caught hold of a cable, and dragged myself into the other skyship." He hesitated for a moment, and then added, "I'm sorry that you had to mourn my death."

"It's more than your death I mourn now," Delia said, her eyes flinty. "What's your question?"

"What is it you think I have that belongs to you?"

Delia's brow furrowed. That wasn't the question she'd been expecting. She glanced down at his fingers, remembering how they'd brushed through her hair, massaged the nape of her neck, and stroked her face. To her dismay, she felt the sting of tears behind her eyes. Blinking rapidly, she answered, "The ring I gave you. The one you said you'd never take off. I can see that that promise was as easily breakable to you as your commitment to your crew, since it's no longer on your finger."

"You're right. It's not," Graydon admitted. "Come here, darlin'."

"I don't think so."

"Look closer at my neck where you tore my shirt away."

Staying where she was, Delia glanced down at his neck. She spied a flash of gold.

Ignoring the throb of his pulse at the base and the little white scars her teeth had left behind, she pulled out a chain. Standing that close to him was almost dizzying. She was so aware of his scent, the warmth of his body, the racing of her heartbeat, and the thrum of her fury that at first she didn't know what she was looking at.

Then her vision focused. Hanging on the chain was her ring. The one she'd given to him when he carved their initials on the dead oak tree on her family estate. He'd told her that he'd give up piracy and find work as a cooper, a baker, or a clockmaker if she would agree to marry him. The air had been warm and sticky, and insects were chirruping a drowsy, drunken song.

She'd kissed him sweetly. Refusing him was like trying to hold off a hurricane with a broken parasol, but refuse him she did. She'd told him she wasn't ready to abandon a pirate's life and become a baker's wife, though the thought of his bronze arms covered with flour, his hand sunken into a mound of soft dough, gave her a certain amount of pleasure.

When she saw his crestfallen expression, she pulled off her family ring and gave it to him as a token, promising that she would marry him that very day if they could stay on the ship together, or, if he insisted on domesticating her, he could wait until the sky no longer had the same pull.

He took the ring, kissed it and then her, pulling her tightly against him. When he drew back, he seemed melancholy, but he slid the ring onto his finger and said huskily, "We'll wait a while, then." Graydon placed his hands on her cheeks, cupping her face. "I just want you to know, Delia, that no matter what happens, regardless of where the wind blows us, or what future chases us down and corners us, I'll be cherishing every moment we have together."

Now, seeing her ring, the symbol of their love, hanging there on the chain, all those emotions came back and flooded through her. Her eyes darted to his, and in them she saw those lost, lingering promises, but there was something else there too, something he guarded, something that, even now, stood as a wall between them.

She was about to yank the chain from his neck when she spied an object hidden just behind the ring. Frowning, she pushed the ring to the side and then gasped. Tucked away behind her family heirloom, a hole drilled through it, was her broken fang.

CHAPTER 24

BLEEDING HEARTS

Finney woke when he heard a pinging sound, then reached blindly for his glasses. His hand brushed a nearby table and found his delicate pair of lenticular lenses instead of his regular spectacles. "Bother," he said. "Where are they?"

Something jostled the bed next to him, and he froze. Winking light flickered across his face, and he tried to make out who was shining a light in his face and why they might be in his bedroom.

"Hello?" he said fearfully.

Something touched his hand, and a cold shiver shot from his toes all the way to the tips of his ears. Then another thought occurred to him.

"Ember?" he whispered, and sighed, thinking of the girl he was hopelessly head over heels for. Her confidence and friendship made him feel less awkward, and her delight at his inventions gave him a sense of pride.

He shifted and felt something pinch his elbow. "Ah, there they are." He pushed his spectacles up his nose, and the light near him finally came into focus. It was the blinking pumpkin. Suddenly, everything came back. All the incredible mixed with all the terrifying. "Nice to see you, old chap," Finney said, patting the globe. Glancing around and finding himself alone, he called out, "Ember? Are you here?"

There was a muffled groan coming from the open doorway. He leapt out of bed and then staggered.

Maybe his clumsiness was due to his head injury. Regardless, chivalry demanded that he check on his one and only friend and confidante, and, if he was extremely lucky and blessed indeed, the girl who'd someday agree to be his wife.

Stumbling to the door, he paused, trying to quell the storm raging in his belly. It wouldn't do to show up with the intention of saving the damsel in distress only to soil her shoes with the contents of his stomach. "Ember?" he murmured quietly, and heard her soft sigh.

A hand touched his shoulder and he spun around too quickly, losing his balance. "She's still resting."

Finney peered up into the face of the lantern and noted with jealousy how put-together he looked. He was already dressed and his white-blond hair was slicked back. It didn't take a genius to see that the lantern had feelings for Ember and that they were a bit more than brotherly or that of a well-wisher and guardian. It made Finney want to despise him, but he didn't. He liked the man. Maybe it had something to do with the pumpkin, but Finney trusted him, admired him even.

This was a very different feeling from the one he had concerning the male vampire. Finney had a distinct lack of good feelings regarding that man. Though he'd only seen him once or twice, Finney thought the creature was too slick. Too self-assured. Too much of a dandy. The captain wasn't bad, even though she was a vampire too, so Finney determined he wasn't biased against vampires in general, just that one specifically. The one that kidnapped his . . . his Ember.

He lifted his glasses and rubbed his eyes. So much had happened in such a short time, and all of it too quickly. Even a person with a gifted mind like Finney was having difficulty keeping up.

"Where are we?" Finney asked Jack.

"Deep under the sea."

"A submersible?" Finney gaped. "I've only heard fanciful stories of such things."

"Shhh. Let Ember sleep some more."

Jack closed the door, leaving it just a crack open so he could hear Ember if she needed him. While Finney washed up, Jack told him, to the best of his knowledge, what was going on.

"So," Finney said, "this vampire, Deverell, has designs of a sort on Ember, either in a romantic way or for his own personal gain, and he's taking us where?"

"That's just it. All I know is we're headed to see some sort of inventor. Delia assures me Dev's intention is to hide Ember, but it's obvious to me that there are things happening in the Otherworld that I'm not privy to, and I'm suspicious that there's more to it. My plan was to get the two of you out of here and back in your world as soon as possible. Your role is to help Ember understand that this is necessary."

Finney, who'd just washed his face, paused with his towel pressed against it. "And we absolutely must return, I suppose," he said.

Jack's brow furrowed. "Don't you wish to return?"

"Oh, I do. Don't get me wrong. It's just that—" He sighed. "There's so much I want to learn and study. So many questions. Do you realize that based on what I've seen so far, I have added over one hundred new ideas to my notebook? Heaven knows what I'd come up with if I had time."

Jack nodded. "I understand the pull. Your mind was already gifted, but spending so much time around Ember, well, it does things to broaden the reaches of your mind and further your curiosity."

Finney dropped the towel. "Yes. You mentioned that before. I wonder how it is that Ember is the spark that lights my imagination. Is there a physical or, perhaps, chemical exchange that acts as a trigger toward invention?"

"There is. I'm not sure how it works exactly." Jack tilted his head and asked, "Have you ever heard the term 'vanishing twin'?"

Finney shook his head.

"It's the reason the witches left the Otherworld in the first place, supposedly. Before, there was balance. Our worlds progressed at close to the same rate, but now the Otherworld has pulled far ahead. Think of our two realms like twins residing in a mother's womb. If one grows too powerful or something happens to cause damage to the other, then, on occasion, the weaker is absorbed into the stronger and the mother gives birth only to the healthy child. But if the feebler babe is rejected by the womb or miscarried, there is a risk that the other baby, no matter how strong and well nourished, might be lost as well."

"And you think this is happening to our two worlds?"

"It's why I exist. My job is to guard the cord that connects the two worlds. By identifying the witches, the source of the power, who contain the energy to feed both worlds, lanterns can help maintain the balance. The problem is, I don't know what happens to the witches once they are found. I'd assumed they were relocated to other more vital areas, and that those who went rogue were shifting power as they willed, causing chaos in their wake; but now I'm not so certain."

Finney eyed the lantern. "You care for her, don't you?"

Jack didn't need to know who Finney was referring to. "I do."

"And you're risking your job to save her, to bring her back?"

"I am."

"Why?"

The lantern didn't answer. His pumpkin floated over and hovered between them, turning to one and then the other as if encouraging full disclosure. Jack refused to cooperate and poked the hovering orb with his finger. It bobbed away and then came right back as if it was attached to him by a springy cord. In a way it was, he supposed.

Seeing Jack's feelings flash across his face, Finney's heart tightened. He knew he was a better choice for Ember than the vampire, but was he better than Jack? Trying to swallow the lump in his throat and speak bravely, though his heart felt crushed, Finney said, "Then you should tell her how you feel."

Jack looked up. "It doesn't matter." He paused, then continued, "I can't love her. I won't. It's not my place. Ember belongs to the human world. She should be with someone like you. Someone she can inspire and help. Someone who's not . . ."

"Already dead?" Finney said softly.

Jack nodded, and his pumpkin slowly lowered until it touched his shoulder, bumping against it as if to offer comfort.

"I have no future," Jack said. "My mortal life was sacrificed long ago. What I feel and what I wish are irrelevant."

. . .

Ember had woken to the sound of voices, and she slid the covers aside and padded across the thick carpet to the door. She was about to say good morning when she heard what Jack said.

I can't love her.

I won't.

Quickly, she backed away from the door, pain and confusion muddying her thoughts. Had Finney been asking Jack if he would take care of her? It was just like her friend to consider her safety and comfort. But Finney hadn't just asked for Jack to keep her safe. He'd asked if Jack could love her, and Jack had said no.

Ember knew that she shouldn't care. She'd told both of them that her intentions were to see the world, not settle down. But that didn't mean she didn't daydream of a boy who would hold her with tenderness and listen to her occasionally nonsensical ideas without laughing. One who would give her drowsy kisses, and, most important, look her in the eye instead of ogling her chest. She'd only known two men who'd ever been able to prevent themselves from doing the latter, and both of them were in the room next door.

True, Dev hadn't appeared to be overly fascinated with her bosom either, but he looked at her hungrily, and he was certainly interested in her power. Wasn't she involved with Dev for the same reason? Taking advantage of his knowledge and ability to guide her through the mysteries of the Otherworld?

Since she wasn't looking for love anyway, what did it matter how Jack felt?

But deep down, there was a secret part of her that cared very much indeed about the feelings the lantern might have for her, and that part mourned.

CHAPTER 25

A DARING PROPOSAL

Ember wondered if there was a spell to soothe the distress of heartbreak. But with no ingredients to make up a tonic, she decided to simply hold together the pieces of her heart by tightening her corset around it and finishing the bag of chocolates.

Dressing as quietly as she could and concealing her feelings well enough by pasting a carefree smile on her face, she knocked on the door and breezed through. Jack and Finney were as affable as usual, and she was quickly distracted from her somber thoughts as Jack demonstrated the wonders of the ocean outside the hidden bubble in her stateroom.

While Finney peppered Jack with questions, she only half listened because she was hyperaware of Jack standing behind her, pointing to one outcropping here and a remarkable fish there, his breath tickling her bare neck, the length of his arm brushing against hers, and his hand on her waist. She wished she had the gumption to put some space between them, but she liked being close to the mysterious lantern too much to deny herself the pleasure of his nearness.

Then Dev stepped into the room, frowning at seeing all of them together.

"I've come to escort you to the galley," he said, giving Ember a stiff bow. "I'm sure you're famished."

"Absolutely starving!" Ember said a bit too brightly, and rushed to take his arm.

The group breakfasted on the ship's stores, which included a bowl of hot porridge mixed with dried fruits and nuts, crisp biscuits with jam, and salted fish. They were also served a rather nice tea, which reminded Ember that she had yet to confront Dev about his particular brew.

As she poured a mug for him, she said to Dev, "I believe I still have some of that tea you acquired for me. Would you prefer some of that since you're not eating anything else?"

He grimaced. "I should think not; thank you for inquiring."

"Not at all. May I ask why it is that you don't wish to sample it?"

"I don't like the flavor. Besides, it doesn't work on tamping down a vampire's abilities. Even if there was such a thing, I wouldn't want it. I like my abilities."

"And I like mine too," Ember said with a tight smile. "In addition, I like my choices to be mine. Do you not also wish to be in charge of your own mind, Deverell?"

The vampire frowned and glanced at Jack and Finney. The former was eating and the latter was stirring his porridge with a spoon, trying not to look at Dev. He hesitated before speaking. "Yes. I like to be in charge of my own mind. Where are you going with this, Ember?"

She dropped her spoon with a clatter, dribbling tea over the edge of the saucer. "That tea you gave me had devil's breath in it!" she accused him.

"Devil's breath?" Dev sat back in his chair, stunned. Then he slapped his open hand on the table. "Payne?"

Jack interjected: "You, vampire, were the only one with something to gain."

Dev scowled. "Surely you're not insinuating that I have been less than a gentleman where Ember is concerned."

"Well, surely I—" Ember started.

"I'm not insinuating," Jack answered Dev as he leaned forward, the chains of his pocket watches dangling in the air as he pressed his fingertips on the table. His pumpkin reared up behind him, grinning at Dev over Jack's crown of white-blond hair. "I'm outright accusing."

Eyes narrowing, a dangerous fire rising in them, Dev shifted just a degree closer to Jack. Ember tried to interject, only to be drowned out by Dev's growling. "Be careful when you accuse a vampire," Dev warned. "We are honor bound to defend ourselves. And I assure you, if I was after Ember's affection, which is something that is entirely outside the realm of your business, I wouldn't need a drug to convince her."

Ember gave Finney a horrified, pleading sort of look, but the young man shrank back as if trying to make himself invisible.

"Is that right?" Jack pressed.

"That's right," Deverell replied.

Ember was about to throw them *both* out of the submersible. Why couldn't Dev give her a straight answer? And why must Jack take over like she couldn't handle it herself? Then Dev rolled up a sleeve and Ember thought he meant to engage in fisticuffs with Jack right there at the breakfast table. Instead, he bit his wrist and held it out to Jack.

"Vampire's vow," he said. "Taste my blood and know that I was never aware that Ember's tea had anything in it except a suppressant for her power."

The two shiny drops of blood welled on his wrist as he held it out. Jack stared into Dev's face, ignoring the offer.

"If you won't check, I will," Ember said. Taking Dev's wrist, she touched her tongue to a droplet. Finney went pale, and Jack looked even more hot under the collar than before. Once again there was a ringing in Ember's veins and a cool confirmation of truth.

"He's not lying," Ember said. "He didn't know."

Dev pressed a napkin to his wrist and pulled down his sleeve, touching the cuff link to close the opening.

"I'll remind you, I'm a lantern," Jack said. "I knew he wasn't lying."

"Then why do you look like a vengeful angel about to rain down death and destruction?" Ember asked.

Jack ground his jaw but refused to answer.

Finney cleared his throat, his voice squeaking as he tugged on Jack's sleeve.

The lantern's brows furrowed as he finally broke eye contact with Dev and turned to Finney. "What is it?" he asked.

"Jack," Finney said, trying to distract from the current tension. "If you wouldn't mind, could you take a look at the gash on my head? I'm feeling a bit woozy. Check for suppuration. I wouldn't want anything to get infected."

"If I had the proper ingredients, I could make an embrocation for you," Ember said. "One that would soothe your headache and speed your healing."

"I'd most appreciate it," Finney replied.

"There's no need," Jack proclaimed after examining the boy's head. "It's more of a bump than a cut. He'll heal well enough on his own."

"If you'll excuse me, there's something I'd like to talk with the captain about," Dev said as he pushed back his chair.

"I'll accompany you," Ember said. "I'd like to ask her a few questions about our destination."

Dev stiffened, but nodded.

Finney and Jack rose immediately and protested, saying they should stick together and that they also had many questions.

"Nonsense," Ember replied. "There's plenty of time for you to finish your repast first. Besides, I assure you two, I can take care of myself." She turned to follow Dev but then stopped and added, "Finney, be a dear and see if the galley has any ingredients we might acquire so we can restock my potions. We brought some dried pouches, but they might have the fresh items we need."

After glancing at Jack and just seeing a glowering expression, Finney replied, "I'll take a look and bring the items to your room."

"Thanks, Finney," Ember said. She graced him with a smile, pointedly ignored Jack, and followed Dev from the room. The door shut behind them with a resounding clang.

"If you're so mad," Finney said to Jack after seeing the lantern trying to pierce the vampire with his gleaming eyes, "why'd you let her go?"

Jack sighed. "I've been watching Ember since she was a child, and if there's one thing I know about her, telling her no just makes her that much more determined to do whatever it is she wants, despite the danger to herself or the irritation it causes me."

Finney laughed. "She does have a way of getting under your skin, doesn't she?"

"She does, lad. She does." He rose from the table. "I'll help you gather her ingredients. What sort of things does she require?"

"We'll get to that, but first, do you think you could convince the cook to give me a second helping? It's been a long time since my last meal."

. . .

As they walked silently down the corridor, Dev wondered what Ember was thinking. How long had she believed that he would do something as malicious as drug her, especially after the time they'd spent together?

It was the blasted lantern's fault. Ever since he'd arrived, Dev's relationship with Ember had been strained. He wasn't a fool. He knew the lantern would try to abscond with Ember the first chance he got. Perhaps it was time to be more straightforward and lay his cards on the table. It was too early in the game, but maybe he'd get lucky and Ember would see things his way. But first he'd have to repair the damage.

"It's just through here," Dev said as he opened a door and ushered Ember inside.

"Where are we?" Ember asked. "This is a stateroom, not the bridge."

"I know." He sighed, shutting the door behind them. "I'd like to talk to you before I speak with my sister, if you're amenable," Dev said politely.

Dev had, in fact, escorted Ember to his own cabin. It was small in comparison to hers—well, in comparison to his *usual* room. The bunk was barely big enough for one.

Ember eyed him with not a small amount of suspicion, but

she perched on the chair anyway, avoiding even looking at the bed. "What would you like to talk about?" she asked.

He removed his batwing hat and set it on the bed. He'd been exceptionally fortunate that the captain's quarters on the *Phantom Airbus* were close enough to the submersible entrance for him to scoop up his meager belongings. He would have hated to lose his hat. "I . . . I wish to bare my soul, such as it is. I won't have you believe I'm the blackguard the lantern makes me out to be."

Ember's expression softened. "I've never thought you a blackguard, Deverell. Perhaps the tiniest bit selfish and a smidge secretive, but never a blackguard."

Dev paced the small room and sank to the bed across from her. He picked up his cane where it rested against his nightstand. Rolling it between his hands gave him some comfort. "I must hear you say again that you believe me when I say I had no idea the devil's breath was in the tea. If I'd known, I would not have let you drink it. I cannot abide having you believe that I am so sinister as to take advantage of a woman in such a way."

"Then devil's breath is used primarily as a means of loosening inhibitions? Making someone more . . . compliant?"

"Yes, but it's also a sort of relaxant. It's used to interrogate enemies of the state, and it works on most of the population of the Otherworld, but its most prevalent application, historically, has been on witches."

"Witches."

"Yes. When my witch was . . . was killed, she had high doses of it in her system."

Ember frowned. "How do you know?"

"I could smell it in the pyre they burned her on."

Gasping, Ember covered her mouth with her hand. "How

horrible! But that means someone gave it to her on purpose. A human wouldn't know of it."

"A few knew. There are Otherworlders living in the mortal world who would know such things. It could even have been another witch, one who frowned on vampire and witch liaisons."

"It must have been terrible for you."

"It was. The point I'm trying to make is, I am the last person who would drug someone I love."

"L-love?" Ember said.

"Well . . . yes." Deverell sank to one knee beside her, tossed his cane onto the bed, and clasped her hands. "My dearest Ember. I know we've only known each other a short while, but I feel a great deal of affection for you. My heart leaps when I think of laying it at your feet. I've been alone a long time, and I know a treasure when I see one. You are a girl deserving of boundless devotion, of the utmost loyalty. I am a man who can provide both of those."

"What . . . what are you saying?" Ember asked, astounded at his words.

"I was hoping to woo you slowly, to take my time to teach you the subtle nuances of courting, but I fear I must bare my heart quickly, lest you think me unmoved. My intention, my dove, is to win your heart fully, completely, and utterly.

"You know we are meeting with an inventor. Even now Delia's taking us to his home. He's an old friend, one who smuggles Otherworlders to places of safety, far from the reach of the leaders here. If you will trust me, I can keep us safe. I'll admit to you now that I was paid a large sum to bring you to the capital, to introduce you to the high witch, but when the meeting was postponed, I rejoiced. You see, once I got to know you, I knew I couldn't do it. Taking you there would be dangerous. She is the wife of the Lord of the Otherworld, after all. Truthfully, even before I met you, my heart wasn't in the task. I have a certain fondness for witches, you see." Dev gave her a sad smile.

She squeezed his hand as he continued, "You must understand that there is still danger here. I never lied to you about that. That's something even your lantern agrees with. Our life beyond this realm would be a simple one, without all the frippery you've seen in the Otherworld, but you're already used to that. We can find a place in a distant city, one far from any crossroad or coven, where you'll rest easy all the days of your life, knowing I'll be there to protect you."

When she didn't say a word, just gaped like a fish, Dev thought more drastic measures might work. He stood and pulled her up firmly, his arms wrapping over each other, hands locking, as if the very idea of her leaving him was impossible. With his mouth pressed against the top of her head, he continued, "You know I am a most loyal companion. The witchlight in my cane told you as much. And I will strive to become the upright man you deserve.

"Even if your affections for me aren't yet as strong, our propinquity to each other and the sharing of blood will deepen your feelings. You will come to love me to a degree where parting would seem to you like the most horrible of tortures."

He drew back, his hands moving to grasp her shoulders. "Serendipity brought you to me, and only a fool of a man would allow you simply to walk out of his life. Tell me there's a chance for us. Tell me you'll at least consider me in this panoply of suitors you've gathered to your side."

"I . . . I . . . I don't know what to say," Ember said.

"Then allow me to fashion comely words for your lips to replicate."

Dev slid one hand up to her neck and touched his mouth to hers.

It wasn't the passionate, swooning embrace that Dev anticipated, especially after the very vivid memory of drinking her blood.
Still, it was pleasant and warm. Her body was soft and pliant. He
drew away with a smile and was about to make his final point—lay
down his last card, the trump, the one that would definitively place
him in her good favor—when his head whipped to the side, a sharp
sting heating his cheek.

He turned wounded eyes to his ingénue, the girl who had just
slapped him so hard, his fangs pinched the inside of his lower lip,
making it bleed.

"How dare you!" Ember said, her expression full of fire.

Deverell's hopes for an easy win failed.

But Deverell Christopher Blackbourne never gave up easily.

CHAPTER 26

WAITING FOR THE OTHER SHOE TO DROP

The dreadnaught circled the ocean again, checking the flotsam for survivors. Rune stood at the bow, his firefly earring zooming back and forth, checking for signs of the captain and her crew, specifically any beings still containing the ember of life.

They'd only pulled a few dozen dead men and several body parts from the water so far, but most of those men were from their own ship. They'd accounted for all of their own men except three. The arm of one man, drawn up in a net, fishing for a macabre catch, was unmistakably theirs. If the tattered black shirt weren't enough to identify him, then his tattoo certainly was. The shoe was all they found of the other missing man; the blood smeared on it and the pulp inside meant whoever wore it had died while wearing it.

There'd been no signs of the third man, though. Not a finger or a toe had been discovered. What was more interesting, he hadn't been assigned to board the *Phantom Airbus* either, so there was no reason for him to be missing at all. He'd have to send a clockwork owl communique to his boss.

He'd been shocked when the Lord of the Otherworld had insisted that Rune commandeer his own personal dreadnaught to hunt the witch down. He'd never commanded one before, and it was a touchy mission—not even an experienced captain would fly through a ghost storm. But that was the direction the Lord of the Otherworld insisted he search. He was also told to take down any skyship he came across, with the added instruction that he was to dispense with any and all Otherworlders except those of the feminine persuasion.

Regardless of the danger to the skyship and crew, they followed the path toward the storm, each man whispering uneasy prayers for his own safety lest he end up dead and trapped in the ghost storm. Even Rune wasn't exempt from edgy feelings.

The interesting thing was, when they entered the area of sky where the ghost storm should have been, they found nothing except the empty sky, which was still humming with enough witchlight to power an entire city for a year. He immediately sent a message to the Lord of the Otherworld saying they were getting close.

The sky they passed through was eerie. It should have been aswirl with centuries' worth of Otherworlder ghosts who were unable to move on to the great beyond. The storms were a mystery, and a dangerous one, at that. It had been studied, and the most current theory had to do with the witchlight shortages. The worse the shortage got, the more ghosts gathered. But now, *poof.* The biggest storm in the Otherworld was gone.

There were no hovering specters, no groaning winds, no noisome odor, not even a cloud in the sky. Just a silent, still, dead space. It was almost worse than finding a storm. The men on the skyship became spooked. Nothing could take out a storm that size. It had never been done. Not in the history of the Otherworld.

And then they spotted the skyship. It gave them a mighty chase. Then, finally, the stubborn pirate wench had scuttled the ship rather than being taken, and it appeared all hands were lost at sea. "Appeared" being the key term. It was highly unlikely that a ship of that size would only lose a handful of men. There should have been floaters spread over a vast range. The numbers just didn't add up. He was missing something.

With his task thwarted, Rune gave the order to head back to circle the area and await further orders. He had a hunch that the ones he was looking for were still alive. Also, there was the fact that there had been traces of a lantern once again on some of the recovered pieces of ship.

Rune didn't understand it. If a lantern had been on board, fighting, he should have sensed it. He was the head lantern for all their kind. He controlled their embers. Something or someone was blocking him, hiding the lantern's identity or scrambling his signature somehow. Never in his long life had a lantern betrayed him. It wasn't just that he was confident they wouldn't; he knew that they *couldn't*.

But Rune had a hunch.

He twisted his earring as he thought and then leaned over the railing scanning the water and looking into the distance. If he was right, then the balance was shifting. The only way to be sure was to check the crossroads. Pennyport wasn't an accident. There was only one crossroad connected to that town and it just happened to be that the mortal village that lay on the other side was the one rumored to be kissed by a powerful witch wind. It couldn't be a coincidence.

He just wished it was.

It was time to check in on Jack.

• • •

Dev rubbed his cheek. "What was that for?"

"For kissing me without permission. How dare you assume I wanted you to be my first kiss? That's something a girl should choose for herself, don't you think?"

"Well, yes, I suppose it is."

"I assure you it is. As much as I appreciate your full disclosure and your amorous attentions, I'll have you know that I'm not ready to settle down yet. I'd like to determine for myself where and how I wish to live in the future. Heed my words, Dev: I'll not be forced into anything, especially romance, and I'll thank you not to beleaguer the point."

Ember adjusted her tiny hat, repinning it to her chignon and tucking in the curls loosened by Dev's agile fingers. Truth be told, kissing Dev wasn't entirely awful. It was rather nice, in fact. But she didn't want him to know that. He was cocky enough as it was, and he needed to understand how she felt, or didn't feel, or should have felt.

And she was scandalized further by the fact that the face she envisioned on the other side of those lips was entirely different. Ember had imagined a man with piercing eyes and mussed blond hair. If he had been the one who attempted to kiss her, Ember didn't think she'd find it quite so easy to push him away. And the idea of slapping him just made the breath catch in her lungs. Or perhaps that was the corset. Yes. Definitely the corset.

"Ember, don't make a great harvest of a little corn. I am a patient man," Dev said. "I don't mind waiting for you. Like I said, I'm only putting everything on the page for you to read and ponder. But, please, my dove, I beg you not to dismiss my suit out of hand. Let me at least believe you might consider me."

Ember pursed her lips and gave Dev a piercing stare. Finally, she said, "Very well. I'll consider your, er, proposal, but I'll make you no promises at this time other than that. It's all I can offer at the moment."

"Then, that's enough." Dev stood, picked up his hat, dusted the brim, and settled it on his head. "Now, I understand you have some questions about our destination. Perhaps we can talk further on the subject as I escort you to the bridge."

Ember nodded and followed him out the door. Instead of offering his arm, he simply walked beside her, his cane tapping the metal-floored passageway.

"Can you tell me more about where we're going?" Ember asked.

"Yes. It's a hidden island that was, at one time, surrounded by a very wide, and very extensive ghost storm. The same one, in fact, that you just dissolved."

"Oh."

"It's a strange phenomenon, to be sure. It appears there is a certain imbalance around the island that causes this area to become a magnet for ghosts. I'm sure the spectral barrier will replenish itself at some point, but let's hope for clear skies during our sojourn."

Ember didn't know how she felt about that. The ghosts had seemed like they were reaching out to her not to hurt, but in a supplication for help. She was happy that she'd been able to offer them relief, and the idea that more would gather in the space she'd just cleared left her feeling uneasy.

Dev went on, "A great genius lives on the island; one I count as a friend. Once he was the head inventor and metallurgist of the

Otherworld. His technology was, and still is, used far and wide. But he gave it all up. He didn't like how his inventions were being used as weapons. He was the one who invented the clockwork mechanism that makes the frog bombs target enemies. Of course, that was never the original intention. They were supposed to be used as a sort of security system. The frogs would leap onto interlopers and identify strangers."

"That seems useful," Ember said.

"Yes. There are many other gadgets we owe to him. He worked very closely with witches for years and developed the means where a witch can store her power outside herself. He also discovered a way to imbue certain metals with magic and mold them to suit his purposes."

"But he left all that behind?"

"He did. He still has a large laboratory on his island, of course. His work hasn't stopped, only moved. Delia has worked for him from time to time, taking his latest inventions to the black market, trading them for the goods and supplies that he needs.

"The last time I was here, he was working on something he called a snapshot that created a perfect portrait of his intended subject."

"Does it hurt?"

Dev chuckled. "There's no projectile, though there is a trigger. I'm not sure exactly how it works but I've seen the results and they are amazing. What's most interesting, though, is what happens when he uses lantern light instead of witchlight. Seeing as you are somewhat familiar with lanterns, can you guess what happened?"

Ember shook her head. "Does it have something to do with their ability to see inside people?"

"Yes. The silver recorded not a person at all, but a colored aura around the heart. Interesting, don't you think?"

"Fascinating." Ember immediately thought of Jack and what he might feel regarding such a prospect. Then she wondered where this secretive inventor even got lantern light. Ember shivered thinking about Jack and his pumpkin being separated.

Dev stepped through a bulkhead opening, still talking about the inventor. "In his spare time, he smuggles Otherworlders into mortal towns and occasionally brings mortals over here. I've used his services countless times. It's a way to avoid traveling under the piercing glare of a lantern's gaze."

Dev opened the heavy door and they stepped into the command center of the submersible. He could tell immediately that something was wrong with his sister. Ember reached Delia's side before he could.

"You look like death chewed you up and spit you out," Ember said bluntly.

"That's about how I feel."

"Is it the imbroglio with your captain?"

"You could say that. I spoke with him briefly last night. Nothing has changed. He's a spy. One who, somehow, snuck aboard my ship."

"Yes, and exactly how did he do that?" Dev asked. "I thought the entrances to the submersible were coded and only you and Frank could enter."

Delia glanced up at her brother, her face haggard. "I never changed the codes. I thought he was dead, you see. It didn't seem important."

The weight of her past hung on Delia like a mantle of lead. She didn't know what she hoped to accomplish by seeing Graydon. What did she expect? That he'd empty the bag and tell her everything? She supposed a part of her hoped he'd deny it all. Tell her it was just a misunderstanding. That he hadn't abandoned her.

Then there was the ring. She'd wanted to tear the emblem from his neck. She'd wanted to hurt him. Wanted to rend it from his throat just as he'd rent her heart. In the end, standing there, close, breathing in the heat and familiarity of him, broke her instead. She turned away then, leaving the chain intact, the ring and tooth still dangling from it.

Delia hadn't slept at all that night. She tossed and turned, too cold and then too hot. Her skin felt as tight as a waterlogged pair of boots.

A few restless hours later, she was back at work. She asked for a depth measure and when it was reported, she called, "Take us up to six fathoms, heading . . ." Delia bent over the gyrocompass. "Heading fifteen degrees starboard."

"Aye, Captain, fifteen degrees starboard."

"We should be getting close, De—I mean, Captain. Could we take a look?" Dev asked.

Delia sighed. "Very well. Crewman Caspar, open the viewing window."

The crewman rose, torquing a lever that opened up a section of plates at the front of the command station. When the steel peeled back, Ember saw behind it a thick, glass dome, much like the stateroom where Ember had slept. She gasped and wandered forward.

Dev followed, his hands clasped behind his back and a pleased look on his face as he watched Ember. He glanced in Delia's direction and she shook her head, the hint of a smile on her mouth as she lifted a finger to a crewman, who threw another switch before returning to his station.

CHAPTER 27

THINGS THAT GO BUMP IN THE NIGHT

Ember gaped. The view was incredible.

The witch lamps inside the ship dimmed and powerful beams located on the outside of the ship turned on, illuminating the area around them. With the lights on, Ember could easily make out the sea and everything in it. Tall rock formations jutted up from the ocean floor on either side of the ship, but Delia guided the *Phantom Airbus* easily enough between them without even looking out the dome.

When she asked how it was accomplished, Delia explained they used various scopes and a detection device that emitted short pulses of witchlight in every direction. If the witchlight hit something, there was a small burst that made a nearly undetectable sound. One of her men sat at a station with a large cone pressed to the side of the ship. At the tip of the cone were thick copper wires that connected to some kind of earpiece. The young man had one in each ear and appeared to be listening to both sides of the ship at the same time.

As she watched, Ember saw the crewman giving Delia hand

signals every so often and when he did, she invariably announced a slight change in direction. "But what if the witchlight hits a fish?" Ember whispered to Dev.

"Any fish who gets hit by the burst would scurry away immediately," he said. "In fact, the witchlight levels can be raised to a degree that would drive off even the largest curious creature that might come across us. I once heard a tale of a kraken attacking a ship. Once the suckers attach, it's very difficult to remove the beast. Witchlight in vast quantities seemed to do the trick though. The creature hasn't been seen in our oceans since. Perhaps it's crossed over and made a new home in your world."

"Oh dear, I hope not," Ember said, aghast at the idea of such an animal. It wasn't that she disliked animals. She quite appreciated them in all their varieties. But she didn't think mortals were a good enough match for a sea monster such as Dev described. Perhaps it had found a nice cave somewhere. A place where humans wouldn't bother it too much.

Ember took great delight in seeing the fish of all types; some had fins so delicate, they fluttered like lace, while others looked like giant bats with wingspans to rival the greatest of birds. She spied several sporting large, sharp teeth. They moved fast and powerfully through the water while other fish followed them, some clinging to their backs and bellies.

Ember felt like she could stand there forever, just watching the magical scene before her. It was peaceful and serene. That is, until she saw a fish so monstrous in size that it could surely swallow their ship. She gasped and turned to Dev, her face full of alarm. The vampire shook his head and said, "Don't worry about that one. He's harmless. His teeth are so small only the tiniest sea life can fit between them. He's more frightened of us, I assure you."

Dev was right. As soon as the massive creature spotted them, he flicked his giant tail and disappeared down into the black depths.

Jack and Finney soon joined them on the bridge, the pumpkin's light making it so Ember saw more of their reflection instead.

"We found several items you might deem useful," Finney said. "We put them in your room."

"I appreciate it," Ember said. "As soon as you're ready, I'll start brewing up some more potion vials. We'll have to heat it with witch-light instead of fire but I think I can manage that. Dev?" she said, turning to the vampire. "You promised to give me some lessons in controlling my witch power."

"So I did," he said, boldly lifting her gloved hand to his lips and kissing it. "But that will have to wait for another time." He cleared his throat and looked at Jack and Finney. "And now that you have an escort," Dev added, "perhaps you will excuse me so that I might speak with my sister."

"Yes, of course," Ember said. Dev and Delia disappeared, leaving Frank to navigate the ship. Ember frowned, watching them leave. "I wonder what all that's about?" she said and glanced up into Jack's deep-set eyes. There was a sparkle in them. The one she saw when he was trying to look inside her. She knew it was a lantern thing and he probably meant nothing by it. But at that moment, it felt much more intimate.

Jack was standing very close to her. The warmth of his body was at once soothing and electrifying. She found her own eyes wanted to linger on him too. Jack's face was very pleasing to her, even though, at the moment, he was frowning. There were sharp, brooding an-gles she wanted to smooth into smiles.

Her fingers itched to brush against his and take his hand, press-ing palm against palm. The very idea of such a thing made her draw in a sharp breath. Blushing furiously, she deliberately turned away. She knew she couldn't blame the tightness in her chest on the corset this time.

"What the devil is that?" Finney asked, pointing out the window, oblivious to the tension between his two companions.

Jack leaned forward and spotted the flash of silver. Soon a school of fish darted toward them, their long bodies sparkling with their own light. Intrigued, Jack whispered to his pumpkin, which shined its light out the window. If Ember thought the sea bright before, it was doubly so with Jack's pumpkin lighting the water.

Several fish swam closer and the school broke up, as if confused. A few of them bumped against the glass dome, their bodies hitting with clinks. "Are they . . . are they metal?" Ember asked.

Finney lowered his goggles over his normal spectacles and flipped the lenses up and down. "Fascinating," he said. "It would appear that at least a portion of their bodies are indeed encased in metal." He pointed to one flash. "That one looks to be armored in bronze. Two over there, in silver."

Soon they saw other creatures, some of them the very same type Ember had gazed upon before, but now they were all covered with a thin coat of metal across their spines. One larger animal blew bubbles at their dome and peered at them with an open, laughing mouth. It was missing a conventional tail, but a new one had been fashioned for it from silver. Flipping in the water, it knocked against the dome with its tail and followed them. It was joined by others, almost as if they were escorting the ship.

In a quiet, murmuring voice, his eyes shining in the dimness of the command center, Jack said, "They are alive, but they've been fused with . . . with clockwork parts made of . . . made of . . ."

"Magical metal. Witch-infused," Ember added softly. "Dev told me the man we're going to see was once the head metallurgist in the Otherworld."

Jack looked at her, then at Frank, who sat working his controls in an unhurried, desultory manner. Jack asked him, "Are we visiting the man who did this to the fish?"

Frank stood and turned his body stiffly, his short, booted leg stomping while his longer one dragged behind. He squinted out the dome to see what Jack was referring to. "Oh, yeah. If you're meaning the enhanced specimens, that is."

"And you . . . trust such a man?"

"Have to, don't I? Dr. Farragut's the one that put me back together. Gave me a new heart. He's a smart one. Promised to give me a tune-up on my next visit. Getting a bit out of sorts in my amidships area, and my ticker's getting a bit slow."

Ember didn't know what a ticker or an amidships area was and didn't want to know, but she did give Frank a long look and then turned to the friendly creature swimming alongside them.

Jack worked his jaw and said, "I see."

Just then, the ship rocked. Frank turned to the crewman with wires attached to his ears. "What do ya hear, man? Did we strike a ridge?"

"I'm not sure," the man called out. "Whatever it is, it's moving."

"Turn up the witchlight. Give it a full blast."

Another crewman spun a crank until the red bar on his panel rose to the top. "Ready, sir."

"Incoming!" the other man shouted.

The crash shook the ship wildly, and they listed to one side sharply before straightening again. Jack caught Ember before she hit her head on the corner of a console and held her tightly.

Steam hissed up from the floor and the glass cracked; then

something huge, so large they couldn't even see what it was, passed the viewing window. Ember screamed. Frank's eyes widened at the sight. A moment later, a crewman shouted, "The witchlight is having no effect!"

Gauges whirled and hit the maximum limit. The entire craft shook as a man cried, "It's crushing the ship!"

Thoughts of the giant kraken Dev had mentioned filled Ember's mind. She grabbed Jack tightly, burying her head in his chest, just as Frank gave the command, "Emergency blow!"

CHAPTER 28

THE ISLAND OF DR. FARRAGUT

Jack grabbed a handle as the ship wrenched upward. Ember still clung to him, but her arms trembled. He wrapped his other arm around her and told Finney to hold on to something. The boy took hold of his pumpkin. Jack was about to tell him to find something *attached* to the ship instead, but thought better of it. His pumpkin had its own ability to right itself and would likely keep the boy safer than anything else.

A gaping maw swam toward them from the depths, far too quickly for Jack to determine what it was. The mouth locked on to the viewing dome of the rising ship and followed it upward. All Jack could see was the flash of metal and a large tongue pressed against the glass. It pulsed and moved over the surface like a suction tube.

Then the submersible breached the water, and they were airborne for just a few seconds. Ember's skirts shifted around her legs, weightless, but when they reached the zenith, the creature gripping them fell away. The sun pierced the window, bathing them all in its warm light before they dropped.

They got a good view of the beast's face now that they were above water. Its long snout was filled with sharp teeth, but its neck was long and snakelike. The skin, as far as she could see, was a mottled green and gray. She marveled at the view since she could now see half above and half beneath the water.

She'd originally thought that the beast was a giant sea snake, but now she saw that its torso was not narrow and small at all. It was thick and broad, with four flippers that propelled it quickly through the water. The tail, short in comparison to the neck, acted as a sort of rudder.

What she'd believed were coils was actually the animal's long neck, which stretched out farther than its entire body, tail included. It darted through the water with the ease of a fish, which was an incredible feat when she considered its size.

The body and tail banged against the side of the ship, and she heard a low moan and a hiss as a flipper splashed water over the viewing bubble, obscuring her view. A thought occurred to her: "It doesn't seem to be angry as much as it appears to be trying to get our attention, does it?"

Jack looked outside as the beast swam by again. Its head came close, and the dark eye peered at them briefly before it drew back, blowing a giant air bubble that popped when it hit the glass. Now that they were floating on the surface of the sea, the creature seemed to be content to swim around them and simply nudge them from time to time.

"Perhaps you're right," Jack said. He loosened his grip on Ember, though it pained him somewhat to do so. He rather liked the way she clung to him.

"Look," she said, drawing close to the window. The creature had turned on its side, flashing them its belly. Ember saw veins of blue light flicker on the beast's underside. "I think . . . I think it's courting us." Her statement was followed by another burst of bubbles and a series of clicks that pinged against the ship and echoed back.

Finney, who had been scribbling notes like mad since they'd stabilized, paused to look up. "I concur, Ember," he said. "I believe it's—oh, what's the fish term? Ah, yes. Flashing. Though now that I look closer, I believe it is more reptilian in nature, since I see no sign of gills. I'd want to see another of the species before I'd deign to make any sort of conclusion one way or another." Finney tugged on a lock of his red hair, wet the tip of his pencil on his tongue, and continued scribbling. When Ember peeked at his notebook, she saw a crude drawing of the creature. On the next pass, they got a good view of its back and vestigial tail. They saw the same metallic plates running down its spine that they'd seen on the other fish.

Just then, Del and Dev crashed into the command center.

"Status report!" Delia shouted as Frank gave up the controls.

"We've done an emergency blow," Frank said. "Seems a wee beastie has become smitten with our ship."

Delia peered out the viewing bubble. When she saw the creature, the concern on her face melted away. "Oh, it's just Nestor. And yes"—she tapped the crack on the screen—"it looks like he's been lonely for a bit too long. Dev? Do you think we should be worried?"

Dev rubbed his jaw and glanced at Ember, who was standing much too close to Jack for his liking. "No. Nestor's usually friendly and gentle; I think showing his belly means that he knows he's been a bit too aggressive with us. If he wants our amorous attention, he's going to have to earn it. I say we dim the lights, move slowly, and dive again. He's likely to follow along behind like a slightly too-exuberant lemming."

"Agreed," Del said. "Helm, take us back down. Slowly."

Evanescent bubbles hissed around the viewing window and they were soon swallowed in the cerulean waters once again. Ember nervously stepped closer to Jack. Their fingers brushed, and Jack wrapped his hand around hers. Ember glanced up but saw that Jack was still staring out at the sea, his eyes gleaming. If he had looked back at her then, he might have noticed the ebullient lights dancing around her heart.

As for Dev, he stood there watching the two of them, jealousy running through his veins. She was so at ease with Jack. Though their locked hands were hidden behind her skirts, his blue vampire eyes easily caught their reflection in the glass.

On the surface, Dev was a halcyon sea, as smooth as glass. But beneath the skin, a monster roared and demanded he stake his claim. The untapped power roiling in his blood and the pangs in his heart demanded he find someone to share his life with. *Ember*. Over the last few days, his mind had teased him with dreams of walking through a park, his fetching witch on his arm, as they greeted passersby. On long autumn nights, they'd relax together near an inglenook as she practiced a spell or brewed a potion. She would dote on her vampire husband, for he would make her his bride, if for no other reason than to signify to all others that she belonged exclusively to him. He would pet her and spoil her and give her everything her heart wished for.

For a vampire who was much too sinful for heaven and much too good for hell, a man doomed to live far too many years as a lonely wanderer, a life with a witch he could love seemed like a rare blessing indeed. As rare as finding a will-o'-the-wisp. And Dev had no intention of allowing a mere Jack o' the Lantern, a poor, doomed pastiche with one foot bound to each world and no possible hope of a future, to steal his dream away.

But Jack wasn't Dev's main concern. His real enemies were all those who would invariably try to take away his little witch by force. He knew that stifling her powers wasn't a long-term solution, which was why he wanted to go to Dr. Farragut's island. If anyone in the Otherworld could help him hide his witch, or at least help him figure out a way to prevent those in power from accessing hers, it was the good doctor.

Outside the *Phantom Airbus*, Nestor swam next to the ship, his body brushing against protruding rocks that stained his scales with chalky efflorescence. The sea monster moved almost languorously through the sea, turning his long neck from time to time to check on them, making sure they still followed. The beast probably thought it was escorting the submersible home to nest.

If only women were that easy, Nestor, Dev thought with a twitch of his lips. Then he paused, worrying about what it meant to watch the giant sea beast trying to woo the ship as a mate as he thought about his prospects with Ember. Was he as doomed as Nestor?

They finally reached the landmass at the coordinates Delia had given to her helmsman. "There!" she called, pointing at a shadow hidden among the coral, waving grasses, and starfish. "Behind that penumbra of seaweed. Take us in gently."

One of the crewmen turned on the outside lights, and they could clearly see a dark passageway, a tunnel into the island.

"Are you certain, Del? What if we get stuck?"

"That's Captain, Dev. And who do you think gave Frank the specs to build the submersible in the first place?" she asked. "Of course we'll fit."

As the nose of the ship disappeared into the black cavern, their protruding rear was thumped by Nestor. They all heard his disappointed groan and series of clicks. But then there was a whoosh of water propelling them forward, as if the massive sea creature had moved away.

Del said, "He'll probably be waiting for us up top. Not sure the doc anticipated his favorite pet's reaction to the submersible."

They continued, Delia giving minute-by-minute directions, and then finally the cavern opened up and light shone down on them through the water.

"Want to take a look?" Delia asked with a smile as they breached the surface.

"Could we?" Ember replied.

Delia nodded and guided them to an opening in the top of the submersible. She climbed the stairs, took hold of the wheel, and cranked it until the seal cracked and she could throw back the hatch.

Ember, Jack, Finney, Dev, and Delia stepped out onto the surface of what remained of the old *Phantom Airbus* and looked around. They appeared to be in a lagoon in the middle of a mountain.

Dev took the liberty of placing his arm around Ember's shoulder and pointed upward. "It used to be a volcano," he said. "The doctor discovered and claimed this island demesne. There's actually a chain of them. Most Otherworlders consider them uninhabitable, but the doctor has made quite a home for himself.

"When he set up his laboratory, he discovered that there is a peculiar aetheric energy here. Whatever it is not only enhances witch power, but also lures ghosts to certain pockets. The ghosts served as a natural airspace barrier, preventing all but the boldest from crossing into his territory."

They drew closer to the small beach and the dock, where a boat was moored. "Is that a steamboat?" Ember asked. "I've heard of those at home, but I've never seen one!"

"Close," Dev said. "Instead of steam or witch power, the doctor's modified it to run on aether fumes. His hopes are that the Otherworld might be able to tap into this aether and solve the energy shortages, making witch power completely unnecessary as a fuel."

Delia went below to orchestrate the docking procedure for their submersible, and Dev took the opportunity to elbow Jack aside, asking Ember if she'd like to gather her belongings.

Ember said yes and asked, "Will you be joining us, Jack?"

The lantern gave her a long look and a small smile. "You two go ahead," he said. "I'd like to get my bearings."

With that, Jack's pumpkin rose high above them and began slowly circling the lagoon, the light from its eyes and open mouth chasing away every shadow it touched. Jack's own eyes took on their familiar sheen, and Ember knew he was seeing something very different from what she saw.

Ember headed down with Finney and Dev. When she got to her stateroom, she found the observation glass lit by an unusual plethora of fish, moving in a strange synchronization. Not only were they covered with metal, but their fleshy parts glowed like the belly of the sea monster, casting an eerie light as they moved past the window.

As she began to step away, she noticed that the moving shadows and lights created by the fish made a haunting, devilish image on the rug, like a skull with hollow eyes. It might have been a trick of her imagination, but she thought the shadowed eyes were watching her.

Dev took her bag, and she followed him and Finney back to the top of the ship. It was nearing the dock, and now that they were closer, Ember could see the large home carved into the mountain. It sat like a castle made of sand, complete with minarets, sparkling windows, and balconies. A series of steps, also carved into the stone of the mountain, led from the dock up to the gate.

Jack was the first to jump off. *Jump* was probably the wrong word, since the lantern turned to fog and skimmed over the surface of the water, taking human form on the dock. His pumpkin must have been high overhead, so distant that Ember couldn't make it out, even when she shaded her eyes.

Ember took Dev's hand, and he lifted her off the ship and set her down on the dock. The moment her feet touched ground, she swooned, nearly fainting.

"What is it, my dear?" Dev asked, concerned.

"I . . . I don't know." She truly didn't. Now that she was on the island, it was almost as if that thing that called to her stilled. It curled up in a contented ball inside her and purred. Ember wasn't sure if that was a good or a bad thing, but something, or someone, wanted her here—and had, since long before she began this journey.

The group gathered on the dock, and Delia sent a crewman ahead to make their presence known while they waited for Dr. Farragut. They had been expected to arrive on the mountain peak via the skyship, not on the dock by submersible, and they knew better than to assume they were welcome.

The doctor was something of a recluse and strictly prohibited guests from entering his home without his consent, preferring to handle his business at the skyship dock. Frank had seen the inside of only the laboratory and the surgical and recovery wings. Though Delia and Dev were considered friendly associates, they'd never imposed on the doctor without invitation or strayed beyond the skyship dock.

Delia deliberately turned her back when Graydon was brought out. He was still chained and looked as haggard as she felt. He'd been given only water, and she doubted he'd slept at all, considering he'd spent the night shackled next to the reactor.

Truthfully, Delia felt about as hollowed-out as Jack's pumpkin. She didn't know how to process Graydon's sudden return, but she knew she couldn't get back to normal with him nearby. Her plan was to turn him over to the doctor and wash her hands of him, hopefully not looking back as she left him far, far behind.

Her crewman returned with one of the doctor's servants. Despite the heat, he wore thick gloves, boots, and a hooded black cloak that kept his face in shadow. All they could see was his wide jaw, covered with white powder, and a pair of fangs that hung down almost to his chin. Delia frowned. She'd never seen a vampire or a werewolf with such prominent fangs.

The servant spoke, his voice emollient and unexpected, with a strange lilt. "Was the submersible gas-tight?"

"It was," Delia replied.

"Wonderful. The master will be so pleased."

The servant raised a hand in greeting, gesturing to the group. "You are all, of course, welcome. The master is delighted to have such a fine assortment of guests ready to regale him with wondrous tales of their adventures."

"Speaking of adventures," Delia said. "I believe Nestor is rather enamored of our ship. He's been quite, er, persistent since he spotted us."

"Ah."

Ember saw the servant's jaw working, and his thick, stained tongue licked his bulbous lower lip.

"Nestor has been rather fugacious as of late, but never fear: adjustments can be made." "Adjustments" seemed an odd word to Ember.

"How delightful to see you are functioning well," the servant said to Frank.

"I'm doing all right," the green-skinned man replied. "Could use a bit of a tune-up, though."

"Indeed? I'm sure the doctor would love to tinker around in that chest of yours." He clapped Frank stiffly on the arm, his gloved fingers unbending, and then turned back to the group. "My name is Yegor. I will serve as your contact should you need to speak with the master. I have been asked to give you a short, somewhat limited tour of our island home and set you up in our most comfortable accommodations."

"Thank you, Yegor," Delia said. "That is most appreciated. I'm afraid much of our witchlight has been exhausted in battle." She nodded toward Graydon without making eye contact. "In addition, I wanted to make you aware that we have a prisoner. I should—"

Yegor cut her off. "Yes. We are aware of your prisoner. I can assure you we will house him in a manner befitting his crimes."

No one else seemed to be suffering the same level of mistrust Ember was experiencing, and she longed for her pistols. It wasn't that the servant was acting sinister, exactly, but her gut told her something was wrong.

At last, Jack's pumpkin returned, interested in the servant now that the mountain had been fully surveyed. Yegor stiffened and lifted his head to peer at the floating orb.

Ember's lips parted as she took in the gleaming, whiskey-colored eyes. They were too close-set and round to be human. They disappeared completely when the light of the pumpkin shifted away. She wondered what Yegor was. He didn't look like a goblin or a vampire. She didn't sense any magic in the man, so she doubted he was a warlock, but there was a tiny tickle of apprehension in her belly. She stepped a bit behind Jack. Dev narrowed the distance too, so he and Jack stood like knights protecting their lady.

The servant finally ducked his head again, obscuring his face. He turned and said, "Come along, then. The master is resting at the moment, so your forbearance will be most appreciated."

They followed Yegor up and up the stone steps and entered a wide gate. An effervescent fountain bubbled in a courtyard filled with all manner of trees. Interestingly, though well-tended and healthy, the plants and trees appeared to be placed randomly: fruit trees next to conifers and chestnut trees near beeches. The flowers and plants were mixed in a similar fashion.

Upon closer inspection, Ember found that all the flora were carefully labeled with engraved metal plates either staked into the soil nearby or screwed into a trunk. She wondered why a metallurgist would play at botany.

One area seemed to be plagued by desuetude. The plants were either dead or rapidly dying. "What happened here?" she asked. "Not enough water? Blight?"

The servant turned back to look at the place she indicated. "Oh, that. Unfortunately, those particular cuttings proved unsuccessful. They had to be expunged. I'm afraid when it comes to the master's disappointments, vengeance cometh speedily."

Ember frowned and paused, staring at the scraped dirt. For a moment, it reminded her of a graveyard. She almost expected bony fingers to push up through the soil. Jack took her arm and gave her a reassuring smile. With him at her side, her fears seemed somewhat silly. She wrapped both hands around his elbow and followed along.

Yegor took them into the house, throwing wide the heavy doors, and Ember was surprised to see cats draped over every table, chair, rug, and mantel. "Oh, my!" she said. She had always adored the creatures, and they her.

Clearing his throat, the man said, "My master is somewhat of an ailurophile. He finds felines quite beneficial. They keep out harmful spirits, you know. And this island chain attracts quite a lot of them."

A lovely slate-gray cat with onyx eyes rubbed his head against Ember's leg. She stretched out her gloved hand to scratch it behind the ears. Others meowed and rose from their positions of leisure. Soon Ember had at least a dozen surrounding her, all meowing and begging for attention. Their bluster soon rose so much that Ember lost her balance, reaching out to Jack to steady her.

Yegor hissed, and the cats screeched and darted from the room. "That's quite enough," he warned, though the room now appeared empty.

They passed by a few rooms—a dining room, a solar, a great hall, and a set of stairs leading to an observatory and the airship dock. The next set of doors led to the surgery and laboratory, but Yegor was firm that they were off-limits unless they were escorted personally at the doctor's orders.

"Here we are," he said. "This is the seraglio, where the ladies will stay. Men are not allowed in these chambers, so you are certain to feel entirely safe and comfortable."

He told the women to rest and recuperate and they would be fetched for dinner at precisely eight o'clock by the clockwork timepiece, or, if they preferred, after four turns of the hourglass, a relic the doctor had picked up and used as a decoration for those ladies who spurned modern technology.

Once the door was closed, both Dev and Jack frowned as Yegor locked it with a key kept on a chain around his neck.

"Why have you locked them in?" Dev asked.

"I assure you, it's for their own protection. I shall show you gentlemen to your rooms now."

Jack, Finney, and Dev all looked at one another, a silent message passing between them, but they said nothing in the presence of their guide. They quietly followed Yegor up a flight of stairs to the gentlemen's quarters, where they too were locked inside and given the same invitation to dinner.

"What do we do?" Finney asked.

"We wait," Dev said. "And watch. The doctor is doing us a kindness to allow us to stay—he's never extended this courtesy to anyone I've known. I'm sure this is simply a part of his eccentricity. Besides, Frank has spent many days in the doctor's care and he's no worse for wear."

Jack's eyebrow shot up, especially when he noticed that the windows in their rooms all had bars. It didn't matter to Jack; he and his pumpkin could squeeze out easily enough. It was the boy he was worried about.

Delia and Ember didn't even notice that their doors were locked, the rooms were so sumptuous. When the invitations to dinner arrived, along with large boxes full of clothing, they were happily surprised. Ember pulled the card from the gilt-edged envelope and read:

> *Welcome, most honored guests!*
>
> *Please join me for an intimate dinner on the Neptune deck.*
> *I've arranged for extra clothing, as I imagine much of yours was lost at sea.*
> *Please inform me if you need anything else during your stay.*
>
> *Sincerely,*
> *Dr. Monroe Farragut*

CHAPTER 29

DRESSED TO THE NINES

Jack stared at the clothing lying across the bed with a frown. Since he didn't need clothes to keep him warm or even boots to protect his feet, he usually gave his attire very little attention. New clothing appeared at the crossroad when he desired it. The fabric was often simple and, for the most part, mimicked the styles of the area where he was assigned to work. He shunned wigs when they were in fashion, and if he found something unappealing, he simply left it at the crossroad breach and eventually it disappeared.

The only items he insisted on acquiring for himself were his pocket watches, his greatcoats, and his boots. He loved his boots, and no footwear he'd tried on as replacements felt quite right.

His greatcoat was the one item he'd had specially made. The buttons and fasteners were one of a kind, and he'd been inordinately pleased when Ember had noticed them. He wasn't one to really care about style or fashion like the vampire, but the coat was a symbol of who he was, and his memory of sharing it with Ember was one he cherished. Jack took comfort in the idea that even after the fabric became moth-eaten and threadbare, the buttons would survive the passage of time. It would be the only sign of his having lived, of what had become of the erstwhile mortal boy called Jack, consigned to a life of roaming the countryside with his lit pumpkin.

Picking out only the simplest choices of the garb their host had sent up to them, Jack set aside his other well-used items and hoped they would be cleaned rather than tossed aside. Deverell seized upon the flashier items, which left Finney with choices that fell somewhere in between.

While the other two men bathed and dressed, Jack took the opportunity to snoop.

Finney's notebook was something he found deeply fascinating. He leafed through pages and pages of notes and found quite a few pertaining to him personally, beginning back when Ember had first told him about her guardian. He laughed at some of the young lad's observations and was so enthralled with Finney's plans for new gadgets that he didn't notice the boy's return.

"Like what you're reading, then?" Finney asked as he toweled his shock of red hair dry.

"You're quite inventive, you know. I looked among Dev's things too, but found nothing as interesting as this. Your thoughts on the skyship nets are noteworthy."

"Yeah. It's easy to have an epiphany when ghosts are trying to eat your face off."

"I wonder if it would work." Finney had postured the idea of using a retractable net lit with witchlight to scoop up the ghosts like fish rather than trying to plow through them. "The question I would ask," Jack said, "is what would you do with the ghosts once you had them?"

Finney shrugged. "Take them to Ember, I suppose. Then she can help them move on when she has enough energy to do so. Working in small batches would be less draining."

"How litigious," Dev said, emerging from the washroom and knotting his cravat. "What Jack isn't telling you is that Ember's ability is entirely unique. Even so, no witch worth her salt would ever waste her days in the stygian clouds helping those beyond help."

"Ember would," Finney said quickly.

"Perhaps," Dev acquiesced. "But tell me, young lad, why Ember should. Don't you think there are many more important things or, dare I say, people—living people—that Ember might devote her days to?"

Frowning, Jack stared into Deverell's arctic-blue eyes and said, "Ember should be able to carve out a life of her own design."

Dev gave the lantern a wide smile, the tips of his fangs protruding. "Yes," he agreed. "She should."

The vampire smoothed his hair back, carefully tied it, and placed his hat atop his head. His suit was impeccable. Every detail from the waistcoat and cape to the chain of his pocket watch and the cuff links at his wrists spoke of elegance, sophistication, and privilege. The man was also tall, handsome, and well spoken.

Jack wasn't so taken in by Dev's outward show of poise. He could read the vampire's heart. See all the way through him to his blood-filled bones. The vampire was all bluster and show. Dev's heart held a secret despair, something he believed Ember could fix. They weren't suited for each other, in Jack's opinion. Ember deserved more than to be tied to a man who thought he needed her to fix him. Even if Dev believed he could make her happy—which, to be fair, Jack had read the truth of in Dev's aura—the lantern didn't think it would last for long.

The knock on the door signified it was finally time for dinner.

They followed Yegor down to the drawing room, and then the manservant left them alone there while he escorted the women.

There was a sound at the door, and all the men turned to see Delia and Ember come into the room. Delia was a beautiful woman in her own right. Her long black hair was drawn up into a comely arrangement, with curled tendrils brushing her bare shoulders. She wore a red dress trimmed in black with a pleated ruffle and a black outer corset.

The black bustle was something Dev had not seen her wear before. Her blue eyes, just a shade sunnier than Dev's, flashed as if she knew what he was thinking: she loathed bustles. But Dev's eyes didn't linger on his sister overlong; instead, they sought out the petite, curvy girl entering behind her.

Ember's dress was a bit simpler in design than Delia's but it was no less appealing. The sea-green blouse wrapped around her neck in a halter style, twisting in such a way that it accentuated her figure without revealing even an inch of décolletage. Her waist was cinched tightly with a corset of the same color, embroidered with starfish, seashells, and other underwater creatures. The skirt was simple and straight, so the eyes were drawn to the corset and the skin of her arms, bare from the top of her long golden gloves all the way to the neck. The green hat that sat jauntily on her head was trimmed in black, gold, and peacock feathers.

When Ember greeted the gentlemen, Finney's Adam's apple bobbed so vigorously as he sputtered and wet his lips that she just laughed. Dev's eyes roved over her form like she was sitting atop a platter of desserts and he couldn't wait to pluck her off the tray and taste her. She flushed red.

Jack's eyes, however, were warm—a dove-gray that looked at her as softly as the cooing bird's feathers. He held out his hand, and when she placed her gloved hand in his, he bent over it, pressing a kiss to her fingers. She cursed the glove then, wishing his lips had touched her bare skin instead. "You look lovely," he said simply.

"'Lovely' is too poor a word," Dev chimed in. "She's ineffable."

Ember's eyes darted between the two men when they both offered their arms. Instead of choosing one over the other, she said, "Finney? Would you mind? I wanted to talk to you about something."

Straightening immediately and grinning as widely as the pumpkin floating just behind his head, Finney held out his arm, and Ember slid her hand through it. Dev's dark expression made Delia laugh. She was still laughing when Jack offered to escort her. She happily accepted, and the group made their way outside.

Yegor took them down to a wide glass deck sitting on top of the lagoon. Tall columns sparkled with pale witchlight that warmed the deck and lit the area. What they could see of the night sky was obsidian and full of stars. When Ember looked up, she gasped. Flickering fields of purple, blue, and pink spilled across the canopy, advancing and receding like water. Then she noticed the same thing happening in the lagoon.

Through the glass floor of the deck, she could see the metallic fish swimming. They flickered with a luminescence powerful enough to be seen through the dark water. Dr. Farragut's cats lurked in shadowy corners, alert and watchful, and when fish came close enough to the surface, a paw would lash out and pat the water. They sat and waited for their mysterious host.

CHAPTER 30

WEREWOLFING IT DOWN

They took their seats, and a moment later the doors were thrown open to reveal their host. The doctor's slate-blue waistcoat strained at the buttons as it tried to encompass his portly belly, and when he handed his top hat and gloves to his servant, his thick crop of charcoal-gray hair, muttonchops, and long, tapered fingers were revealed.

The doctor flashed the group a welcoming smile and approached the table. "How very good to see you all," he said jovially. "You cannot guess how delighted I am to have such a variety of dining companions this evening."

He walked up to each person in turn, taking their hand and peering into their eyes as he greeted them.

"Deverell Blackbourne," he said when he reached the vampire. "I would imagine you living a life of bliss far from here in the mortal world."

"Yes. I suppose the last time I saw you, I was escaping with my witch. Thanks to your timely assistance, we made it."

"And where is your lovelier half?"

"She . . . she's dead," Deverell said slowly. "Burned at the stake."

The doctor clucked his tongue sorrowfully. "Oh, my. My, my, my, my, my. How vastly unfortunate." The man clapped Dev on the back a bit too vigorously for someone who'd just heard something that unpleasant and moved on to Delia.

He clicked his boots together, took her hand, and bent over it, touching his lips briefly to her skin. "My dear captain. How beguiling you look this evening. I'm so glad to hear the hidden submersible was a success."

"Yes, it was. We wouldn't be here talking to you if it hadn't been for the designs you put in Frank's head."

The doctor looked around dramatically. "And where is the old boy?" he asked. "I should very much like to see him."

"He's working repairs tonight. You're meeting with him in the morning. Isn't that right?"

The man's brow furrowed, but then he smiled distractedly. "Oh, indeed. Yes, yes. I'd be happy to hook him up to the machines and see how everything's functioning." He turned next to Finney. "Hello, young man. I say, that's quite a color of hair. Haven't seen hair like that since . . ."

Pursing his lips, the doctor took a pair of spectacles from his pocket and slid them up his nose. He looked Finney up and down. "Are you a mortal, then, boy?"

"I'm human, if that's what you're asking," Finney replied, taking his own glasses off and replacing them with his goggles. He flipped lenses up and down, studying the doctor as much as he was being studied.

"Fascinating," they both said at the same time.

The doctor chuckled and gestured to Finney's invention. "May I?"

Finney handed him his goggles and the doctor slipped them on, putting his own back in his pocket, before quickly adjusting the various knobs. "How interesting!" the doctor said. "If I'm not mistaken, you were trying to see my aura."

"I was," Finney answered.

"And did you see it?"

Finney frowned. "No. Not exactly. It was a bit . . . indistinct."

"What a marvelous contraption," he said, handing back the goggles. "It's quite a feat for a mortal man. Especially one of your age. Tell me, are you at all interested in metallurgy?"

"I'm interested in a variety of things. Though I've heard my world is considerably behind yours technologically, as of late I've been working on an automaton to harvest crops."

"Have you, now?" the doctor replied, a delighted smile on his face.

"I'm sure it's crude compared to what you have here in the Otherworld."

"Oh, to be sure, to be sure. But still, to do that on your own? I sense a lot of promise in you, young man." The doctor glanced over at Ember, giving her a discerning look before cutting his eyes back to Finney. "A lot of promise."

"I should very much like to visit your laboratory," Finney added.

"Absolutely. Yegor will arrange it. Yegor," he called loudly as if the man was hard of hearing. "You must give the boy a tour of the lab."

"Yes, master," Yegor replied.

The doctor stopped and turned to his servant. "Yegor, how many times must I say it? You are to call me Doctor, not master."

"Of course, Doctor Master."

Sighing, the doctor approached Jack. "Ah, now here is the man of the hour. Good heavens, I haven't had a lantern at my table in . . . well, in far too long. You are welcome, good sir." The doctor reached out his hand and left it there awkwardly until Jack surrendered his. "If it's not too impolite, might I ask where you keep your ember?"

"Oh," Ember chirped. "I'm right here."

The doctor looked startled. "You . . . you keep your ember inside a witch?" he asked. "How . . . unique."

"No," Jack said as the pumpkin floated in the air behind the doctor. "Her name is Ember. My lantern light resides in my pumpkin."

"A pumpkin, you say?" When the doctor turned, he squeaked in fright but quickly recovered and pulled his spectacles from his pocket once more. "Ah, how curious."

He tried to look on either side of the pumpkin, but the globe turned so its smiling face was always facing him. It blinked rapidly when he drew closer and almost looked as if it was going to sneeze. "Er, yes. Well . . . I suppose there's plenty of time to explore your light at a later time. Now, I'm sure you're all famished, yes?"

"You forgot me," Ember said, rising and curtsying to the doctor.

"Indeed, I have," the doctor said, taking her hand and kissing it.

Ember noticed that the doctor had a crooked tooth, but otherwise his skin and face looked flawless. Too flawless for a man his age. There was a meow and the doctor looked down. He leaned over and picked up a large tabby cat.

"Why are you such a needy girl, Brunhilda?" the doctor asked. "Can't you see I'm busy talking to this lovely little witch?" The cat began purring and soon others came close, rubbing against both the doctor and Ember. "I'm so sorry, my dear. The cats have a natural affinity for witches. I'm afraid you're like catnip to them. They like the little static shock of witch power they get when they touch you."

"I don't mind," Ember said, reaching down to scratch the head of a black cat with a white streak. "What's the name of this one?"

"Nicodemus," he replied distractedly as the cat mewed loudly and scratched at Ember's skirts. Another jumped directly into her arms. Ember barely caught it. The doctor quickly dropped the one he held and pulled the new one from her arms. "Hazel, you little hoyden," he said, tapping the creature on the nose. He set her down as well, shooing the beast away. But she was replaced quickly by others. "Oh, my," he said as a dozen cats began circling. "They are indeed proving an annoyance. Yegor, have the cats removed from the immediate vicinity."

"As you wish, mas—Doctor."

He clapped his hands and the cats hissed and meowed loudly, all of them turning their attention to Yegor. After he slipped one hand in his pocket they vanished from sight far too quickly for Ember to see where they went.

"How . . . how did you do that?" Ember asked.

"Do what, my dear?"

"Get the cats to follow your commands."

"Oh, that's easy enough. They're all implanted with a tiny chip as big as your smallest fingernail. It gives them a wee little shock. It doesn't hurt them, merely irritates them enough to make them leave the room."

Ember glanced at Finney. His eyes were wide, and he began scratching furiously on his notebook.

"Now," the doctor said. "Where were we? Ah, yes. You were about to introduce yourself."

Ember was not quite so enamored of the doctor as she'd been before he sent the cats away. "I believe it would be more appropriate for you to introduce yourself first."

"Me?" The doctor looked around the table. "Haven't I already?" Ember shook her head.

"Well then," the doctor said. "I'm afraid it is a terrible habit of doctors and men of philosophy to often forget the social niceties. Do forgive me, won't you, my dear?" When Ember inclined her head, he bowed his and said, "Allow me to introduce myself properly, then. My name is Dr. Monroe Farragut, and this is my home here on Deadman's Island."

Swallowing, Ember said, "What a . . . what a charming name. Did you come up with it yourself?"

"The pirates named it," a man's deep voice called out from the darkness, just beyond their lit, intimate setting.

"Ah, I forgot to introduce my other guest. I knew we were missing someone. Come on in," the doctor said gleefully. "Don't be shy. We're all friends here."

Ember didn't recognize the handsome man who stepped from the shadows, not at first, but then she heard Delia's gasp as the captain rose abruptly from the table.

"What's he doing here?" she demanded. "He should be locked up in whatever passes for a dungeon here and the key thrown into the lagoon."

"I'll thank you to treat my guests respectfully," the doctor said sharply. "Captain Graydon, you'll be sitting between the young witch and myself."

The man who came forward was dressed as impeccably as Dev, though as soon as he sat down, he pulled at the sash around his neck, slipping it off, and unbuttoned the top two buttons on his shirt, exposing his tanned throat.

Dinner was served, beginning with a warm fish soup accompanied by pumpkin-buttered toast. When Finney took a bite of the toast, Jack's pumpkin flickered franticly. Finney looked at the pumpkin, then at the bread, and mumbled his apologies, before setting down the toast and picking up his spoon.

Next were courses of pheasant; salty, green sea beans; and something Ember thought tasted like boar. Then a large platter holding a beast with multiple arms and a bulbous head was presented. The purple-pink meat delicately carved and placed on her plate made Ember hesitate. "Is it a fish?"

"Octopus," Dev said, grinning. "The little cousin of the kraken."

Ember and Jack were cautious, especially when the doctor bragged that the various cheeses Dev was enjoying had been made from the milk harvested from a wide assortment of marine mammals. The werewolf captain devoured everything set in front of him, almost without tasting.

When he wasn't eating, or swallowing his beverage in great gulps, Graydon's burning eyes invariably drifted to a disinterested Delia.

Ember tried to break the tension. "Doctor, please tell us about your work."

"Oh, are you an aspiring student like your young friend?" he asked genially. "Perhaps you could join in the laboratory tomorrow as well."

"That sounds delightful."

"Wonderful!" He gave Ember a beatific smile. "As for my work, you must have seen many of my creations on the way to the island."

"Yes," Ember replied. "All those fish. They're your doing?"

"They are. I've been trying to fuse the animate with the inanimate."

"Are you attempting to protect them?" she asked. "Like dressing them in a suit of armor?"

"Not at all. Though that is a happy side effect." He lifted his fork to his mouth and chewed thoughtfully, then set it down and continued, "Oh, dear. To abridge a lifetime of research and experimentation into one simple concept is a most frustrating task." He pinched the bridge of his nose and then explained, "All sentient life has a common nemesis, a villain that murmurs softly in the beginning but whose voice becomes more powerful as the days pass, until all you can hear is his cry. It is a seed of evil that I've sought to eradicate."

"I'm not sure I understand," Ember said, setting down her goblet.

"The enemy I speak of is death," the doctor said. "Let me ask you: If there was a way to capture the essence of life, to hold it in one's hand, and then to give it the gift of eternity, would you do it?"

"I—I don't know," Ember stammered. "I suppose I'm not the most qualified at this table to answer your question."

"Indeed? How about you, Jack. Of us all, you have benefited the most from my research."

"Have I?"

"Why, it was my research that made being a lantern possible."

Jack's knife clattered to the table. "You must be mistaken," Jack said. "My mentor, Rune, conscripted me many of your lifetimes ago."

"Ah, that's where *you* are mistaken, young man. I am four-thousand, nine-hundred and ninety-nine years old, give or take a few days."

"Surely you jest," Ember said.

"I do not."

She frowned. "Then you must not be human, though you certainly look it."

He ignored that comment. "Let me direct you all back to my

original question. If you held the very key to everlasting life in your hand and the door stood before you, ready to open and reveal all the secrets of the eternities, would you be brave enough to unlock it and step through?"

"No," Jack said abruptly, tossing down his napkin. "There are some things we aren't meant to know; some people so villainous, the world is better for their deaths."

"But what if you could select those to give the gift of immortality, determining it by, say, what you see in their hearts?"

Jack froze. He *could* do exactly that. "It wouldn't matter," he said. "The so-called gift of your research has set me up in a life of servitude."

"It's remarkable to me that you resent this. Would you have preferred death by disease, by gibbet, by war? You've been held apart from these things, become a watcher. You are much, much more than the sum of what you would have been."

"Perhaps. But maybe the purpose of life is to experience those things, however fleeting. I'll never know now what my life might have been."

"Well then." The doctor smiled. "I can understand your feelings. When I first performed a ramification, I myself was hesitant and wondered the same things you did. But a man of my station must maintain a certain insouciance regarding his creations; otherwise he'd go mad."

Ember wondered if perhaps the good doctor was already mad.

"All I ask," the doctor said, "is that you keep in mind that all creations, all advances, all inventions, come with a price. They can be used for good or they can be used for evil. But in my philosophy, mine is not to determine politics or to decide if a certain advance *should* be created. Mine is to determine if it *could* be created. There's no use in debating the morals when I don't even know if something will work."

The doctor sat back in his chair, his fingers threaded together over his broad belly. "Now, enough talk of serious things," he said jovially. "Yegor? Bring out the after-dinner tea."

Once the servants cleared away the dinner plates, the doctor leaned on the table with his elbows, cupped his hands together, and rested his weak chin upon them. He glanced first at Delia and then at Graydon. "I think it's time we cleared the air a bit, don't you?" The doctor paused, dressing his tea. When he was satisfied with his brew, he said, "The good captain has been playing the double agent as of late."

"Double agent?" Delia's eyes jerked up. "For whom?"

Scooping up a flaky tart, the doctor popped it into his mouth and chewed slowly while everyone waited. "The lemon tarts are excellent!" He nudged the plate over to Ember. "Do try one. The secret ingredient is an egg harvested from Nestor's former mate. They make the fluffiest curd, the most delicate meringue. Of course, she died recently, of a vivisection gone wrong. Ah, well."

Ember's face turned pale and she shook her head; the doctor took another tart. "Where was I? Oh, yes. Captain Graydon. Our good captain has been playing the part of a spy for the Lord of the Otherworld, when in fact he is *my* emissary and has been feeding the man false information for me."

"B-but," Delia sputtered. "But why?"

Captain Graydon sighed, worked his jaw, and said the one word the doctor wanted him to say. Looking up at Delia with red-rimmed eyes, he muttered, "Frank."

CHAPTER 31

DEATH BECOMES HER

"Frank?" Delia repeated. "What does he have to do with anything?"

Tossing his napkin on the table, Graydon sat back in his chair, clearly uncomfortable with the turn in the conversation. "The good doctor is the one responsible for saving Frank's life on more than one occasion," he said.

"Yes, of course, but we traded for that."

Graydon shook his head. "The cost was much more than you knew. Frank's heart alone was worth more than the *Phantom Airbus*. There was no way to repay him, especially after . . ." His words trailed off.

Moving on to his second dessert, the doctor popped a spoonful of thick pudding into his mouth, the spoon upside down as he watched the interchange gleefully. "Go on. Tell her the rest."

"Frank . . . wasn't the only one the doctor fixed."

"But who . . . ?"

The doctor laughed.

The werewolf's eyes turned silver and he growled sharply at Farragut. When he looked back at Delia, the light in his eyes dimmed.

Delia stopped, then said, "No. Tell me it's not true."

"It is. Do you recall the encounter with the frigate carrying a cargo of nets and power cells? You were injured." Graydon paused. "I never told you that the doctor saved you."

"Yes. It was a rather brilliant surgical maneuver on my part, if you don't mind my boasting. If you feel carefully around the scar tissue at the base of your skull, my dear, you'll feel the edges of a small metal plate about the size of a coin."

Delia's hand crept up beneath her hairline, and she gasped when her fingers discovered the plate the doctor described. "What . . . what did you do to me?" she demanded.

"Well, that's a rather complicated answer. In brief, I revived your dead brain."

"I . . . I died?"

"Oh yes, very much so. To summarize, I managed to capture the spark of your life left in your healing vampiric bones with an ember before it departed. Then I used my research with Frank and the skills I've gained in creating lanterns, and now, my lovely vampiress, you are the first truly immortal creature I've ever fashioned. Congratulations!"

The doctor began clapping and the servants standing around clapped with him. His enthusiasm waned as the rest of the party sat there dumbfounded.

"I don't understand," the doctor said. "I would think you'd find this a cause for celebration."

"I . . . I'm a monster!" Delia said.

The doctor dropped his napkin as Dev put his arm around his sister.

"No, dear. Not at all," the doctor replied. "You are a miracle. A merging of animate and inanimate." He pounded the table. "Besides, I despise the term 'monster.' Are we not all monsters at heart? Who are we to judge others so harshly? What you are is a rare creature indeed, and one close to my heart."

"Yes. So close you put in a fail-safe," Graydon accused with a snarl.

The doctor pursed his lips with irritation. "It's nothing, I assure you. Just a little switch in case something went wrong."

"Something could go wrong?" Delia murmured with renewed alarm.

At the same time, Dev cried, "What switch?"

Graydon answered, his face miserable. "If I didn't cooperate, he threatened to throw the circuit breaker, effectively turning her brain off. She'd die instantly."

Dev stood abruptly, throwing back his chair. "You are the monster! How dare you play with people's lives this way!"

"Well, technically, she wasn't really 'people' any longer, was she? Your dear sister was a corpse. Perhaps you should consider that fact before you go around throwing querulous accusations."

Delia sat back in her chair, her face slack. Her eyes met Graydon's, and in them she saw all his self-hatred, all the compromises he'd had to make just to keep her alive.

The doctor scooted back his chair. "I'm afraid this accusatory turn in the conversation isn't quite what I was hoping for. As such, my appetite has soured. If you'll excuse me, I believe I'll turn in for the night. I suggest you all do the same."

"And if we leave?" Dev threatened.

"Oh, your cooperation is assured one way or another. As Captain Graydon so eloquently averred, my thumb literally rests on the pulse point of the lovely Delia's life. Now that all the cards have been laid upon the table, as it were, it's up to all of you to determine if you will enjoy your time here or consider it an incarceration."

He drew his mouth up into a cupid's bow. "I've found in the many, many, many years I've been alive, that happiness often depends on one's attitude. You'll have until the morning to think about it. Please do finish your tea. Yegor and the others will escort you back to your rooms when you are done." He patted his neatly combed hair, turned, and exited, leaving the group at the table astonished and unmoving.

Strangely enough, it was Finney who was the first to speak. He scratched his thin nose and pronounced, "I say we cooperate. We've got nothing to lose and everything to gain."

Ember held her teacup in her hands, the drink had long since gone cold. "Can . . . can we go home, Jack?"

Dev couldn't abandon his sister, but he could help Jack escape with Ember. It would give him some comfort to know that at least she'd gotten out alive. He waited to hear Jack's answer too, hoping the lantern had some ideas.

The lantern shook his head. "I have no way to get us off the island. My pumpkin can float, but as you saw before, it could barely hold Finney's weight." He turned to Delia. "What about repairs to the submersible?"

Graydon replied when she looked too stunned to do so. "I'm afraid we wouldn't get too far. The doctor has complete control of Nestor. If the doctor doesn't want you leaving the island, you won't."

"You . . . you did all this, turned spy, for me?" Delia said to Graydon.

The werewolf got up and knelt next to Delia's chair, gripping the armrest. "It started with Frank," he said. "I already owed the doctor so much, and all he asked in return was that I run little errands, gather some things he wanted. But he kept upping the game, and after he fixed you, I knew we'd be doing his bidding for the rest of our days. I thought I could at least save you from my fate if you thought I was dead. I would have told you on the submersible but he . . . he listens."

"Oh, Graydon," Delia said, tears welling up in her eyes.

"I'm sorry about everything that's happened," he continued. "He didn't tell me about the kill switch until it was too late. I had no idea the doctor was capable of doing such a thing. If I had known . . ." The man ran a hand through his long brown hair. "If I had known, I can't say I would have done any differently. I couldn't lose you then, and I refuse to lose you now. I'd do anything for you, Del."

Delia reached out and smoothed her thumbs across his broad forehead, trying to even out the lines. Strangely, in that moment, all she could think about was how those lines were a sign that he would someday die and she wouldn't.

Meanwhile, Dev tried to rack his mind and figure a way out of the situation he'd put them all in. How had he missed the doctor's break with sanity? "I agree with the mortal boy," Dev declared, raising his head wearily as if it weighed a hundred pounds. "We will work with the doctor. It seems we have no other recourse." He rose from his seat. "Gentlemen, let us walk the ladies back to their rooms."

• • •

In their rooms, Jack and Dev heard Graydon's full side of the story. He told them about some of the strange things the doctor had asked him to retrieve, items such as tonics and elixirs, unusual plant clippings from the mortal world as well as the Otherworld, metals of all description, several boxes of kittens. His hope had been that the doctor wouldn't ask too much more. Then, finally, he did.

"He sent us on a suicide mission," Graydon said. "The Lord of the Otherworld had stolen some technology from the doctor, and used it to create a doomsday device. The *Phantom Airbus* was to distract the Lord's skyship, which was carrying the device, while one of the doctor's own would take advantage of the distraction and steal the cargo."

"Delia told me about this," Dev said. "She believed that the device could separate the mortal world from the Otherworld. Is this really possible?"

"That's what I was told, but I don't know if it's true. After the doctor's ship decimated the Lord's skyship, the doctor had me swap clothing with one of the officers and left me floating in the debris. When rescue came, they found me and hauled me out of the water. With a new identity, I was able to insert myself as a spy on board the flagship dreadnaught." Graydon turned to Jack. "Strangely, another lantern led the charge when we attacked the *Phantom Airbus*."

"What did he look like?" Jack asked, suspicion already making his pulse tick.

"His name was never given to us, but his ember was kept in his earring."

"Rune," Jack said. "I knew he worked for the Lord of the Otherworld. I just didn't know he did more than recruit new lanterns or check on crossroads. It sounds like he's even more enmeshed than I thought." He paused. "Don't you work for the Lord of the Otherworld too?" Jack accused Dev. "Aren't you a bounty hunter looking for witches?"

"I did accept the assignment to find a witch in your territory, but it wasn't the Lord of the Otherworld who sent me."

"Then who did?" Jack asked.

"The high witch."

"Isn't that the same thing?" Jack accused.

"I'll admit I'm not entirely certain," Dev said. "But I don't believe it is. She appears to be interested in Ember on her own terms. But that no longer matters. I abandoned my plan to turn in Ember shortly after I met her. I'd hoped to convince her to escape back to the mortal world with me."

"Right," Jack said, folding his arms across his chest. "So you can spend the rest of her life draining her?"

"I have no intention of hurting her," Dev said. "I care for her a great deal, and I believe that she would come to feel the same for me."

"Not bloody likely," Finney muttered.

Just then, the echo of violin music filled the house. It was quiet at first. Then it crescendoed, becoming haunted and then, finally, mad. Captain Graydon's face whitened. "He plays every evening before a surgery." All the men swallowed. "He believes it helps steady him for the task ahead."

Finney picked up his notebook. "Right. Come on, lads. It's no time to act like sheep before a slaughter. Whether an escape is in the offing or no, we need to focus on tomorrow first. I say we play along. The doctor clearly likes to talk about himself and his work. We can learn more by listening than by fighting. If we're going to save Delia, we need to find out more about the trigger he planted in her brain."

"Agreed," Dev and Graydon said at the same time.

"Jack?" Finney asked.

"I don't see that we have any other choice. But there's something more you should know about the doctor," Jack added.

"What's that?" Graydon said.

"There's something off about his inner light. Finney noticed it too. When the pumpkin shone on his face, the light revealed nothing—no aura or reflection of his soul."

"What does that mean?" Dev asked.

"It means that either he has a way to block a lantern light or . . ."

"Or he doesn't have a soul," Finney finished.

CHAPTER 32

THE KISS OF DEATH

When they were all asleep, Jack left his pumpkin to guard Finney and turned to fog. He streamed down the stairs and through the halls until he found the locked door where the girls were staying. Slipping through the crack beneath the door, Jack materialized when he found the sleeping Ember.

"Ember?" Jack whispered softly. "Ember, are you all right?"

"Hmm?" Ember opened sleepy eyes and then smiled. "Jack." Suddenly, she sat up. "Jack?" She leapt out of bed and wrapped her arms around him. "I'm so glad you're here," she said, her cheek pressed against his chest. "Oh, Jack, I'm so sorry. I should have listened to you. The Otherworld is dangerous. Extremely! My curiosity just got the better of me. . . ." Her voice trailed off and she paced away from him and then returned. "I thought I was ready. That I'd prepared well enough. Instead, I've proven just how foolish and ignorant I am. I wish I could explain why I had to come when I did, but I just can't. Whatever it was tugging me here seems to have gone away. And now I'm just left with self-doubt and recrimination. Not to mention I've also dragged Finney into this mess."

Jack touched his finger to a corkscrew curl near her temple. "Technically, I was the one who dragged Finney into this. And truthfully, I don't think he minds so much."

Ember looked up at him with her bright eyes. "But you had to abandon your post to come after me. If it wasn't for my willfulness, you'd be back at home right now, sitting on top of your bridge and napping in the sunshine."

Laughing softly, a sound that made Ember's stomach flip, Jack said, "Believe it or not, my life wasn't all about sunshine naps."

"Oh, I know. Your work is very important."

"I'm not so sure about that anymore."

His platinum hair shone although the room was dark; the only other light emanated from a tiny flickering gas lamp. Ember wanted to touch his hair, to feel the soft waves of it against her palm and fingertips. She licked her lips and said, "Part of your job was important, Jack. At least to me."

"Which part?"

"All my life, you've watched over me. Even when I was a little girl." She turned away. "When I was young, I drew your picture with a prominent brow, a hawk nose, and a craggy face—a man intimidating enough to scare off the monsters that haunted my nightmares. But then the picture changed. Over the years, you morphed into someone quite different."

"Someone with a protruding brow, an underbite, and a bulbous nose, perhaps?" he teased. "If so, I can understand your disappointment upon seeing me for the first time as a young lady."

Ember turned. "That's just it. When I saw you in the mirror, when you finally showed yourself, I knew it wasn't my imagination.

That you were real. And you were more beautiful than I dreamed. Even in the private wishes of my heart. You were my friend all those years, as important to me as Finney, but you were different. You were secret. And you belonged to only me. You can't know how much I needed that."

"I knew. You were alone. I could see the ache in your heart."

"But don't you see, Jack?" Ember said, stepping closer. "The ache is still there. It's different, though. I thought it was just a longing to find out who I was and where I came from and that coming to the Otherworld would fix that. But the pangs of my heart have only intensified. The more I've learned of what it means to be a witch, the more I tap into my power, the more I realize what it is that revitalizes me."

"And what is it, Ember? What cures your lassitude?" he asked with a turned-up mouth.

She tilted her head to look up into his pewter eyes. "Can't you see, Jack? Of all people, you know me best. You can see into my soul, if you would just . . . look."

Taking a small step back, she dropped her hands at her sides, closed her eyes, and stood very still. Jack took in her small, hourglass stature, the heart-shaped face, lips drawn up in a russet bow, and her cocoa-brown curls. Then he looked deeper. Behind the crisp white nightdress and layers of skin, muscle, and bone, he found her inner light. The warm goldenrod soul was as familiar to him as her form. He sought out her heart and was surprised for the first time to see a telltale loop around it.

The ring encircling it was nearly complete. Such a phenomenon spoke to a soul's connection to another being. When Jack looked at Graydon, it was quite obvious that his heart belonged to Delia. The ring was thick and red, the color representing the vampire captain.

But when he'd looked into Delia's heart, the gray ring was thin and broken.

"You . . . you love someone," Jack said, his own heart thumping like a bird trapped in the rafters of his bridge.

Her eyes fluttered open. "Yes. I think I do," she said softly.

"And it's not the vampire," he said.

"No," Ember admitted. "It's not."

Jack felt like his mind was floating in a barrel of whiskey. He felt useless and drunk and not quite right. "F-Finney will be happy to hear of your budding affection," Jack said finally.

"But Jack, it's not Finney I have feelings for either. Look again. Can't you see it?"

Taking Jack's hand, Ember nervously pressed his palm against her chest. His fingertips grazed her collarbone and he felt the hummingbird clip of her pulse. His eyes glowed silver as he looked again. This time his eyes stayed focused as he spoke. Lips parting, he studied her golden gleam and the band circling her heart. It was . . . it was white. He'd never seen a band like that before. It looked almost like . . . like a lantern light.

His eyes flew to hers, and the gleam in them dimmed. "What does this mean?" he asked.

"It means," Ember said, "that I'm falling for my guardian."

Jack's mouth snapped shut, his jaw tightened making the angles of his cheekbones that much more prominent. "That's not possible, Ember," he said, though everything inside him wished it was.

"Why not? Is it because you can't see me as a woman?"

Turning away, Jack said, "Believe me, that's not the problem."

"Then why did you tell Finney that you couldn't love me back?"

Jack froze. "You heard that conversation?"

"Some of it."

"Ember." When Jack turned back, her eyes wouldn't meet his.

Hearing him say her name in such a disappointed way was a sharp enough blow to slash Ember's heart. She couldn't stop the tears that filled her eyes. "Then . . . then just forget we had this conversation," Ember said. "We have more important things to think about right now anyway."

He took hold of her arms and shook her lightly until she looked at him. When he noticed the wet sparkle in her eyes and a fat tear rolling down her face, his heart melted. He swiped the tear with his thumb and then stroked her satin cheekbones. "My stubborn little witch," he said softly. "Don't believe for a clockwork minute that you are unlovable. You are not at fault. Not at all. If I were a mortal, a man not doomed to walk the earth as a haunted specter, I would be the first suitor in line. Please believe that."

She hiccupped. "You . . . you'd want to court me?"

Jack laughed. "Court you? I'd follow you around like Finney and stare at you all moony-eyed. I'd spend my days fending off your other would-be suitors, my evenings charming Flossie, and my nights stealing kisses at your window."

Ember had stepped closer and boldly touched her palms to his muscled stomach, bunching the fabric of his loose shirt in her fists. Jack sucked in a breath.

"You would?" she asked. The dark lashes framing her wide eyes were full of wanting.

Her hands were like hot brands on his abdomen, which, technically, shouldn't have been possible. Jack felt the fire that lived inside him spark to life. It meant his skeleton was becoming visible through his skin. He looked down at his little witch, expecting to see fear.

What he saw was much, much worse. She lifted her chin, gazing up at him with all the wonder and want of a woman caught in the throes of first love. It was heady and addictive. Ember's rosebud mouth was the devil's own temptation. His fingers slipped into her glossy hair before he could stop himself.

"I would," Jack replied finally. Giving in just the tiniest bit, Jack kissed her eyes. The thin, translucent lids were baby-soft. Her lashes fluttered, tickling his lips. She sighed, and in that breath, he could hear satisfaction and deep pleasure. He longed to give her just a bit more and kissed her cheeks, softly, slowly.

Ember had never imagined a kiss to be so innocent and so wanton at the same time. Her whole body trembled, and she felt as if she stood on the cusp of something wonderful. That if she was just brave enough to step over the edge, she'd experience the most exhilarating moment of her life.

Her witchlight flowed to every cell of her body, igniting and making her senses hyperaware. The rasp of his unshaven cheek, the texture of his lips, the silky feel of his hair where it touched her skin, the warmth of his body, and the grip of his hands on her arms, were like tiny explosions of knowing.

Jack was about to draw away when he felt the whisper of her breath on his face. She reached up and held his face still, pressing reciprocating kisses on his own angular cheekbones. Jack smiled at the gesture but before he could pull back, her sweetly open mouth was on his. For what felt like a long moment, he froze with indecision, unable to either pull away or return the gesture.

Then something in him broke and he folded her in his arms, kissing her back with an equal measure of passion. When her fingers dug into his arms, kneading impatiently, and her searching mouth moved too quickly, he captured her hands and pressed them against his chest. Then he cupped her face and kissed her deliberately, languidly, as if they had thousands of such moments to experience and enjoy.

He stroked the soft skin just beneath her ear, and his mouth trailed down the arch of her neck. When his hand circled her waist, drawing her closer, she groaned and sought out his lips again. They were melting together like butter and sugar in a hot pan, and Ember could feel the sweet effervescence lick her skin from the inside out.

Ember's hands finally knew the texture of his hair and the feel of the stubble on his cheek as she touched his face. It tickled her fingertips, and she found she quite enjoyed the contrast between the tiny, prickly hairs and his oh-so-soft mouth. She never wanted to stop kissing him. Jack was addictive. The more she caressed him, the more she wanted to. Suddenly, his hand caught hers, stopping her progress.

Lifting her head, Ember looked up at the man she trusted more than anyone else in the entire world, the man she'd do anything to be with, the one she'd do anything for. Both of them were panting and flushed, and Ember couldn't wait to hear what he was going to say. Maybe he wanted to express something lovely and meaningful. Maybe he wanted to know if he was moving too fast for her. Maybe he wanted to talk of their future together.

She waited for what felt like forever, gazing into his eyes with hope and burgeoning love. Finally, he spoke.

"Ember," he said, his voice husky.

She liked the way he said her name, especially at that very moment. "Yes, Jack?" she answered; her own words sounded throaty and thick and full of longing.

"This was a mistake."

CHAPTER 33

A WITCH'S SCREAM

Ember sputtered. "What . . . what . . . what do you mean 'a mistake'?"

"I mean that we can't be together like this." He took her hands and stepped back from her. "Look at me, Ember. What do you see?"

"I see a man. A very handsome one. A man I . . ."

He shook his head. "No. You're not seeing everything. Look again."

This time Jack called upon all the strange and different light that lived inside him. His entire body filled with a pulsing force and it lit his bones until his outer layer nearly vanished. When he spoke, his skeleton moved, clacking his teeth together in a frightening way. The hands that held Ember's were white bones and his pale heart beat inside his rib cage.

Stepping back, Ember took in his appearance. He wasn't hiding it from her; he held nothing back. Arms wide, he released her hands and turned in a slow circle. With fascination, she watched his boney hips and legs shift and move beneath his skin. When he was finished, he dropped his arms and waited for her verdict. Now she could see what he truly was. Now she would know their being together was impossible.

"Interesting," Ember said.

Jack was so shocked at her steady, slightly curious tone, that he felt the light fade.

"Can you control it?" she asked, walking around him. "Finney would love to study the internal bone structure of a person without, you know, killing him."

"What?" he mumbled, shocked and confused. "No, Ember. You're missing the point."

"Then what is your point? You think this"—she waved a hand, gesturing to his body—"is a reason for us to remain apart? It's just light and a skeleton, Jack. I have those in me too, or are you forgetting that?"

"No, I know that. But I'm different, Ember. I have no soul. It was removed and placed in a pumpkin."

"But didn't the doctor say he was the one who invented lanterns in the first place? If the pumpkin does hold your soul, then we'll bargain with him to put it back."

"I'm dead, Ember," he said flatly. "What kind of a life can you have with a dead man?"

"Isn't Delia technically dead? You can see Graydon doesn't care a whit. Do you judge me to be more fickle in my affections than he is?"

Jack sighed. "No. You are the most immutable, obdurate girl I've ever met." He glanced at her lips again. Ember tasted like escape, and he wanted to lose himself in her arms and never look back. The tiny seed of possibility grew in his heart, taking root and extending its tender, frail foliage. He took her hands in his and kissed her fingers. "We will speak more of this at another time, agreed?"

"Agreed," she answered. Her smile was as bright and wild as a bonfire. "So I'm assuming you didn't come here just to check in on me or kiss me until my toes curled, which they did, by the way. Best tell me the plan, then."

. . .

Jack slipped back into the room with the men a few hours later and settled into a corner as a small cloud of fog to sleep. When he dreamed, it was of surreptitious encounters in the sleepy little hollow and long, drugging kisses beneath his bridge. But then the nightmares came. Instead of kissing Ember, her back pressed up against the bridge railing, she hung dead from the rafters, a rope tight about her bruised neck as he howled his sorrow at the moon.

Then he was chasing Ember on horseback as she raced across a meadow, Jack summoned his inner light and his skeleton face gleamed. The grinning skull crowed with delight as he lifted his sword and sliced off Ember's head. Then he removed his own head and replaced it with his pumpkin. The light inside it was no longer white but red, lit by the flames of Hades.

He heard a cackle and entered the trees to find a coven. Crooked, hunchbacked witches, half living, half dead, with clockwork eyes and metal mouths, stirred their hell broth as they poured the souls of the dead into their cauldrons and chanted.

> *Chapped rats and bats' wings,*
> *Brandied worms and adders' stings,*
> *Goat's wool and owl's hoot,*
> *Fish's tongue and dog's foot.*
> *Into the potion, all you go,*

Add clockwork hearts, positioned so.
A touch of hyssop, a cat's meow,
A pinch of hemlock, a lover's vow,
A snip of time, a dewy toad,
A goblin's thumb, all tightly sewed.
Now let the brew bubble, cook, and settle,
Then watch the brew quicken in the kettle.
When the draught is weighed
'Neath a pale moonbeam,
And a doctor's blade
Cuts a shroud of steam,
When a graveyard kiss
Lights a dead man's dream,
And a devil's trick
Snares a witch's scream,
Then the potion's done, a flawless spell.
And you'll hear the peal of a burial bell.
Then it's time to harvest a lantern's gleam,
And you've got the beginnings of Halloween.

Jack watched as Dr. Farragut stepped into the glen. He took the potion from the witches, then bade Jack follow to his laboratory, where a long table was draped with a white sheet. When he removed it with a flourish, he saw Ember's headless body. Pieces of metal were grafted onto her skin like armor—bracers and gauntlets on her arms, pauldrons crossing over her chest and shoulders.

The doctor pulled open her breastplate, displaying her peeled-back skin and internal organs. He took a knife and carefully continued his vivisection, saying jovially, "Come closer, young man, you'll want to see this."

When the girl's heart was exposed, the lantern saw that the white light encircling it had turned brittle. The fragments shattered as the doctor removed the organ and then replaced the heart with a new clockwork version. Once it was in place, he poured in the witch's brew, then closed the breastplate.

"Excellent!" the doctor said, wiping his hands on his apron and smiling. "She's ready!"

The horseman pointed to the stump of the neck where the head had been severed.

The doctor's smile twitched and fell. "Ah, yes. How could I forget?"

The doctor pulled a new, smaller table close to the body and removed the cloth covering it. There was Ember's head. But it had been altered. The chocolate-brown hair was now jet-black with a white streak running through it that looked like Rune's. The curls were stiff and wiry, and they stood straight up from the crown of her head.

The doctor picked up the head and attached it to the body, tightening it in place with heavy screws at the neck; then he snapped thick gorgets in place to hold it on. "There now," the doctor said, finishing up. "I believe she's finished at last. Shall we try a test run?"

The doctor headed over to a wall of knobs and threw a lever. Witchlight sparked and crackled in the lights over the table, the metallic bindings holding her limbs, the screws at her neck, and in the doctor's control panel. The woman's eyes opened. Electric lights buzzed in aftershocks, arcing between the metal plates of her body.

Her exposed skin was chalky and green-tinged. Gone was the soft, sweet witch. In her place was a manicured figurine, made a half foot taller by new, longer legs and heavy boots. She sat up, the sheet falling away, and lifted robotic hands to the lantern.

Tilting her head, her rounded mouth moved over straight, white teeth and she said, "For me?"

"Yes," the doctor replied with a too-enthusiastic nod. "He's for you."

The girl stumbled closer to Jack and reached for his pumpkin head, bumping against it clumsily. The pumpkin rolled off the neck stump and fell hard to the tiled floor, splitting open and spilling seeds and mashed orange flesh.

"Oh dear." The doctor eyed the scene. "What a terrible mess." He turned back to the girl, who now hung her head in shame. "Not to worry, my pet. I'll simply have to make you another one. Yegor!" the doctor called.

The servant entered. "Yes, Doctor?" he asked.

"Bring in the next subject, won't you?"

He disappeared momentarily and then returned, dragging in a kicking and screaming boy with a shock of red hair. When the boy saw the smashed pumpkin, he screamed.

CHAPTER 34

BLINDED BY SCIENCE

Jack woke up, surprised to see he was in human form. His skin was covered with dew, and he breathed rapidly. It was rare for him to dream at all and nightmares never plagued him. *He* was the thing that haunted others. It was unnerving after all these years to experience a dream so disturbing and so vivid.

Yegor knocked, bringing in their breakfast trays on a rumbling cart that rolled in by itself. Dev was quick to explain to him that they would prefer to remain Dr. Farragut's guests rather than his prisoners. Finney asked if the doctor's offer to tour his laboratory was still on the table.

It wasn't long until Yegor returned. They were to be shown all the doctor's hospitality, with the understanding that they were not to attempt to enter locked rooms or try to escape. Both Finney and Ember were to be escorted to the doctor's lab just before luncheon for a brief tour.

When the servant departed, Dev turned to Jack. "You look like the very devil."

"I had a nightmare," Jack replied.

"Strange. A lantern haunted by the specter of sleep." He eyed Jack. "Well, since the traces of your demons still mark your face, I'd suggest a vigorous scrubbing."

Deverell, of course, was already dressed in a riding jacket, boots, and breeches. As far as Jack knew, there wasn't a horse anywhere on the island. Dev pulled his pocket watch out of his waistcoat and consulted the dial. "Best you get a move on, then. If we're going to get out of this mess, I'll need the abilities of a lantern."

Jack frowned, wondering who had put the too-handsome vampire in charge. When he headed to the washroom, Jack wrinkled his nose in distaste. The room was as florid as Dev, more suited to design than function.

He could still hear the witches singing in his mind. Deeper and deeper the melody wormed, twisting and writhing, burrowing and nibbling. *Trouble, rubble, double, stubble,* they chanted as he shaved. The intonation grew louder, until he felt the walls around him tremble in time with the song.

When it became overwhelming, he summoned all the light within him and sent it out in a burst, shouting, "Stop!"

Abruptly, the pain vanished, along with the lurid sound of the witches. He wondered if kissing Ember and daring to think they might find a way to be together was causing a wrinkle in the order of things.

Once he was presentable, he emerged to discover that Finney had already been collected and Graydon had left before that. Dev seemed content to wait for Jack, and together the two of them left their room, heading down to the library.

Once there, Dev pulled out a book, and examining the title,

he murmured softly, "Best use your prodigious talent to check the locked rooms while you can. I'll cover for you."

Jack grunted and glanced around. He was about to turn to fog when Dev added, "And don't think I missed your departure last night, or the duration of your absence."

Choosing not to respond, Jack simply melted into fog and crept through the quiet-as-a-tombstone house looking for an escape for all of them.

• • •

Finney and Ember were escorted down to Dr. Farragut's laboratory. It was down many flights, and the deeper they descended, the more mottled and uneven the steps.

Finally, they came upon an iron door and Yegor inserted a key with an interesting series of gaps in the teeth that looked like the pumpkin's carved face. The orb had stayed with Finney, a thing Jack didn't mind, especially knowing that Ember would be with him.

The lab was as different from the pitted stone steps as sunlight was from a smoking torch. The doctor's workplace was as pristine and orderly a sight as Ember had ever seen. The first room held rows and rows of plants, all growing under different colors of light. Ember recognized one with the icy blue glow of witchlight. She guessed the white light must be lantern light. Then there were purple, green, and even red.

She wrinkled her nose. "What's that smell, Finney?"

His nostrils flared as he paused from scratching notes. "I cannot be certain," he said, "but the odor is reminiscent of petrichor. Petrichor and . . . and coffee."

"That's mocha, to be exact," a voice behind them said. The

doctor emerged from behind a curtain. He wore thick leather gloves, polished to a sheen. He lifted his goggles onto his forehead and adjusted his white coat. "Salutations, my young friends," the doctor said as a second, large man parted the curtain behind him.

Ember's face brightened. "Frank!" she said. "How lovely to see you."

The big man's oblong face colored, his cheeks turning a darker shade of green. He inclined his head politely. "Miss," he said, and touched his fingertips to the bolts at his neck. They came away greasy with black oil. Frank rubbed his stubby fingers together and the doctor handed him a towel.

"Frank's just been in for a checkup. I'm happy to report he is in top working order. Though you shouldn't forget my offer to switch in some upgrades when you're ready," the doctor said amiably. He turned to Finney and Ember. "I'm just obsessed with what makes him tick." He then giggled gleefully at his own joke.

"Dr. Farragut," Ember began.

"Please, call me Monroe," the doctor said, removing his gloves.

She waved her hand at the wide variety of plants. "Are you an herbalist as well?" she asked. "You certainly have a lot of plants used in witches' spells."

"Ah, I dabble, I dabble. But, practically speaking, I'm actually more of a horologist." He stepped closer and dug around the base of the plants they'd just been looking at, then clucked his tongue. "Oh dear. These lovely tattooed goutweed plants were thriving with vitality yesterday. I'm afraid they're now sunburned."

"Sunburned?" Finney said. "How can that be, seeing they're growing underground?"

"Things are not always as they seem, are they, young man?" He clapped his hands together, suddenly distracted. "Now, where should we begin? What are your interests? Canine? Fauna? Flora? Spells? Automaton? Clockwork?"

"I don't know about canine," Finney said. "Unless by canine you mean werewolves. I'm wildly curious about that species—er, race. Ember is learning about spells and witch power and I'm building an automaton of my own."

"Yes," the doctor said. "You mentioned that. I'd love to take a look at your sketches, primitive as they may be."

Finney opened a page in his notebook, and the doctor pushed up his glasses and peered at it, then wet his thumb and turned to the next one.

"Promising, promising," he said.

"I've also dabbled in weapons-making," Finney said, barely containing his enthusiasm. "I've an idea for a tiny gun you hide in your waistcoat. You disguise it as a flower, and it fires a spell when you touch a button."

"Fires a *spell,* you say?"

"Oh, yes," Ember quickly added. "He's made me a lovely pair of guns. Unfortunately, we used up all our spells during the ghost storm."

"Are you saying you disabled the ghosts using your weapons?"

"No. It wasn't as effective as we'd hoped," Finney explained. "We ran out of ammunition, and Ember ended up taking care of them herself with her witch power."

"All of them?" The doctor's eyebrows shot up.

"Mostly," Ember said.

"You will have to tell me all about that, dear. I've never heard of a witch obliterating that many ghosts."

"I didn't obliterate them, *exactly,*" Ember said.

"My, my," the doctor said. "We are full of surprises then, aren't we? Tell me . . . Finney, is it?" The boy nodded. "Have you heard of the Prague astronomical clock?"

Finney shook his head, his ginger hair falling over his eyes.

"It exists in your world. Once I came upon a brilliant clockmaker, and we spent many long weeks together discussing the origins of the universe, the fundamentals of time, and the movement of the planets. He determined that a clock could be made that would show these functions.

"I stayed on for a time to help him in his work. It took him many years of his too-short life, and when he was done, I returned to celebrate its revealing. It was a masterpiece. The device was way ahead of its time, but there was something missing—the Otherworld. I added a small ring, a countdown, if you will."

"A countdown to what?" Finney asked.

"Ah, you do ask the right questions. Unfortunately, the clockmaker was not at all happy once he figured out what it meant. My name was maligned, and the next time I visited, they'd added statues of apostles and depicted me as the devil. Me! Can you imagine?"

Ember swallowed and glanced at Finney, whose mouth was hanging open.

"The point of my story, lad," he said as he put his arm around Finney, "is that often those who are the most brilliant—men who wish to help others and make the world a better place to live for the sad, little beings that inhabit it—are often those who either toil unseen or are branded as diabolical. The line between greatness and villainy is as thin as a garrote wire. Men like you and I are anvils. Other men are shaped and sharpened on our sturdy backs. We don't break beneath the blacksmith's hammer, and we don't bend beneath the forge fire's breath. Will you remember that, Finney?"

"Y-yes, sir," Finney said.

"Very good." The doctor grinned. "Now let me show you the most extraordinary plant. I'm quite proud of this one."

"It's a fern," Ember said.

"Precisely," the doctor said. "But consider, if you will, the profusion of seeds growing in clusters beneath the leaves."

Ember reacted with skepticism. "But ferns don't have seeds."

"This one does." The doctor's enthusiasm was almost infectious. "What's more, its seeds grant invisibility. Isn't that miraculous?" he asked.

"Are you certain?" Finney asked. "Have you done trials?"

"Oh, yes. Yegor was my first triumph. Of course, there were many gruesome failures before him. I'm afraid I'm quite impulsive when it comes to experimentation."

"Wait. Are you saying Yegor is . . ."

The doctor nodded. "He's an invisible man! That's the reason he wears so many layers."

"But I've seen part of his face and his eyes," Ember said.

"He coats his face with a special powder when he must meet the public. He's rather grim-faced about it, if you'll pardon the phrase. It flakes terribly, and his pores become inflamed as a result. I'm afraid his vision loss was a side effect of the elixir, so his eyes are clockwork. But he does still bear the semblance of a man, which is the least I could do for him in exchange for his cooperation."

Ember reached for Finney's hand and the boy took it, needing as much comfort from her as she did from him. There was a crazed light in the doctor's face, a barbarous mendacity. They would have to proceed very, very carefully.

"Doctor?" Ember started. "I mean, Monroe?"

"Yes, my dear?"

"Might Finney and I collect some of your herbs and brew spells to replace what we lost?"

"Of course you may," he replied courteously. "In fact . . ." He went to a corner and opened a closet. Several brooms and mops fell to the floor. He shoved them aside and pulled out a witch's cauldron, setting it atop a panel. "Just flip this switch here and the witch-light running through it will heat the contents of your potions." He glanced around. "Do be careful of the plants beneath the red light," he said. "They're not thriving as I'd like."

"We'll be careful," Ember said.

"Now would you like the rest of the tour?"

"Indeed," Finney said.

He showed them the area where he'd worked on Frank. Though Finney headed right to the half-built automatons and began a lively conversation with the doctor, Ember winced at seeing rats floating in pink brine, twitching human hands connected to wires, and a table full of polished surgical tools.

Dr. Farragut approached Ember as she studied various objects on a table, stopping at a tall, conical hat. "It makes sense for you to be interested in that," he said.

"What? The hat? I'm not so much interested as I am curious. Just how would you use such a thing when doctoring?"

"Don't you recognize it?" When Ember shook her head, he said, "My, you are a novice. It's a witch hat. The point at the top channels a witch's power. It draws her energy upward and out like a siphon. It's a bit archaic nowadays. We've replaced it with clockwork technology that works much better, but I spent many years examining it, trying to learn how the witches used it in crafting spells and summoning their power. Here, give it a try."

Ember put the hat on, then said, "Now what?"

The doctor pursed his lips, "Hmm, why not try a basic teleportation."

"I'm afraid I don't know how."

"Don't know how? Dear me. Then I shall guide you. First, choose something in the room you'd like to move. Size doesn't matter, though I'd caution you in moving a living object, as they are quite tricky to manage without injuring them."

After choosing something that looked like it was either a dried mushroom or a piece of the underwater reef, the doctor said, "Now think about the object. Wrap your witch power around it."

"Like a bubble?"

"Why, yes. If that works. Wrap your power around it and then give it a nudge. Make it as light as air in your mind."

The item shifted, wiggling back and forth. Ember imagined she was holding it in an invisible hand, and it rose in the air. The tickle in her stomach felt more like a tugging sensation, almost like there was a fishing line attached to the object.

"Good! Now push it to where you want it to go."

Ember held it with her mind and then tugged on the line connecting her to the object, and a moment later, had set it down on top of a book.

"Excellent!" the doctor said. "You're a natural."

Walking up to the object, Ember peered down at it, amazed that she'd been able to move it with her mind. "What is it?" she asked.

"Oh, that? A dried brain."

Ember swallowed. "Oh." Taking off the hat, she handed it back to the doctor.

"I have no further need of it. It's yours, if you would like to keep it," he said.

"Really?" Ember asked. "Are you sure?"

"Absolutely. Consider it a lagniappe. Test it out for yourself. I think you'll be pleasantly surprised at what you can do."

Ember took the hat and was tracing her fingertip along the brim when the doctor proclaimed, "Ah, it must be time for lunch."

She turned too quickly, not looking where she stepped, and tripped over a thick cable connected to the doctor's instrument board. A pair of hands caught her, but when she righted herself, she saw no one. Ember swallowed. She was being held by the invisible man.

CHAPTER 35

PORTRAIT OF A VAMPIRE

"I didn't mean to frighten you," Yegor said. "I was . . . er . . . securing the grounds, and someone ran off with my stack of clothing. I wasn't planning to alert you to my presence until I was properly attired, but then the doctor always knows when I am near. Should I have let you fall? You might have been less disturbed."

"Yes. I mean, no," Ember said, staring at his clockwork eyes, the only part of him that was visible. "I appreciate your timely assistance."

The frowning doctor said, "She'd be much less disturbed if you let her go and put something on." He grabbed a white coat hanging from a hook and tossed it in Ember's general direction. An invisible hand grabbed it out of the air, and the floating coat quickly took the shape of a man.

Finney was circling the space occupied by Yegor, his mouth open and his eyes wide. "The wonders of your world never cease, do they, Doctor?"

"If they did, that would be my cue to move," the doctor replied dryly. "Well then. Shall we, my dear?" he asked, holding out his arm to Ember. "Yegor, arrange a workstation so that the two young people may return at their leisure to brew their spells."

"But, Doctor," Yegor said from behind them. "We don't want them poking around in certain places. You know it could be dangerous to allow—"

Enraged, the doctor spun. "I'll thank you to leave such matters to me, Yegor. Do as I say or you won't like the consequences, I assure you."

Silence fell then, impalpable and intense. Finally, Yegor replied quietly, "Yes, master."

When they started up the steps, the doctor said, "I do apologize for my coarse behavior. I keep a cabinet stocked with cognac specifically because of him. I swore off imbibing spirits long ago, but I am comforted just by knowing it's there, should I have no other recourse. If there is one man in the world who could drive the very devil to drink, it is Yegor."

He escorted them to the dining room and then begged his leave, saying they should begin without him. "I have something to attend to, but I promise to be along momentarily."

Ember gave him a graceful curtsy and entered the room with Finney. She found all the other members of their party already seated in a stiflingly hot room. A crackling fire burned, and she noticed the doors were shut on both ends, making the room even hotter. Everyone appeared uncomfortable with the temperature except Jack.

As Ember took her seat between Jack and Dev, she noticed that Graydon and Delia were holding hands. She'd never seen Delia so at ease. Even though the hair near her temple was damp with perspiration, the vampiress looked almost . . . happy.

As for Graydon, he sat stiffly, his fingers constantly twitching and rubbing Delia's knuckles. Ember was about to ask him if everything was well with him, when the doctor entered, followed by two man-servants carrying a large object wrapped in paper. After a signal was given, they grasped the edges and peeled back the paper to reveal a lovely painting of the *Phantom Airbus* sailing into the clouds.

"How lovely!" Delia exclaimed as she rose to inspect it.

"Do you like it?" the doctor asked. "I'm so glad. I had it com-missioned just for you the last time the ship was docked. Well, you and Captain Graydon, that is. It ties in to a new experiment I'm con-ducting."

"That's so very generous," Delia said.

"Yes," Graydon added, his lips cracking into the barest of smiles. "It is."

"It looks so stately," Delia said sadly. "I'm afraid I'll miss her terribly."

"Then you must accept this painting as a gift when you depart," the doctor said. "Whenever the two of you look upon it, it will re-mind you of your affection for each other and what the two of you were able to accomplish together. My greatest wish is that it will serve as an inspiration for you both."

After it was set on the sideboard so all could see it, the doctor nodded and their lunch trays were brought in. Finney and the doctor carried most of the conversation, continuing where they'd left off in the laboratory. They dined on cider-scalloped potatoes, spicy bat wings, squash leaf–wrapped eel, and witch's purse canapés.

When tea was brought out, it was accompanied by a puffy white confection the doctor said were "marshmallows" and something he called graveyard cakes. He said they were made with the skins and juice of fruits called oranges and a dark powder called cocoa, the basic ingredient in chocolate. Ember was immediately interested.

Finney was just glad there wasn't any pumpkin to be found. He loved sweets above all, and he didn't want to have to skip out on anything Jack's pumpkin frowned upon. As for Ember, she ate six of the marshmallows and four of the little cakes, including Jack's, making the doctor promise to give her a bag of cocoa and a recipe.

"Oh my," she said, sitting back in her chair and slightly loosening the stays of her corset by running her fingertip just down the top center. "I do so love chocolate. It's one of my absolute favorite things about the Otherworld." Ember blew out a breath. "This entire world is a bit of butter on bacon, isn't it?"

The doctor smiled almost sadly. "Indeed it is."

When they were satiated and the tea settings had been removed, another man entered, carrying a covered tray. He pulled off the lid and they saw a plate filled with papers. There was a tiny gear affixed to the side of the paper. When Ember removed a paper, the gears unlocked at her touch and the paper separated enough for her to slide in her finger. "A ball?" she asked.

"Yes," the doctor said. "A costume ball, to be precise. I want you all to make the most of the time you have left here on my lovely island. I'm simply replete with joy at your arrival, and I feel the only way to properly express my excitement is in the company of those who might share in it."

Dev checked his pocket watch and smoothed back his hair. "And who will be in attendance?" he asked.

"Oh, I think we'll have quite a group. I have so many guests practically dying to meet you. We wouldn't want to spoil it, now, would we? Of course, every accommodation will be made. You'll all have nothing to do except dress for the occasion. Costumes will be sent to your rooms." He leaned closer to Ember, waggling his eyebrows. "There will be an entire dessert table of those chocolate sweets you enjoy. I think you'll find all the treats made from cocoa to be much to your liking."

Threading his fingers on his stout belly, he said, "Now that the pleasantness has been revealed, I'm afraid I have a bit of bad news as well."

"Oh?" Dev asked, leaning forward.

"Yes. Unfortunately, it seems not all of you are remaining true to your promise to not try to escape." Everyone at the table stiffened. Pushing back his chair, the doctor stood and walked behind Ember to where the painting sat on display.

The doctor's eyes sparkled a touch too brightly, and his too-tight face seemed unnatural, as if he could lift his hand and peel away the skin to reveal the true man wearing a doctor's face.

"It is lovely." The doctor sighed, indicating the painting. "I knew I would need it someday," he continued. "Unfortunately, that day is today."

The group looked at one another uncertainly.

"Ah, as you are aware, I have many animals of the feline persuasion in my home. They may not look as if they are paying attention, but I assure you, they are. I have equipped all my cats with a tiny device that captures the images they see, and routes it back to a gemstone that displays them for me.

"In addition, I've come to rely on clockwork spy-ders. Much like real arachnids, they fashion a tiny web for themselves in the corners of the desired rooms and perch there, never eating, only watching. They collect these images and embed them into tiny balls of witchlight I call eggs. Every few seconds, the eggs are sent via a thread of their metallic webbing to a different facet of the gemstone."

Jack sank lower in his chair, while Dev sat ramrod straight, and Delia and Graydon looked at each other with hopeless eyes.

"As such," the doctor went on, "I have determined that a punishment is in order."

Slipping a small wand from the side of the frame, the doctor touched the glowing tip of the wand to the painting and then turned and pointed it straight at Delia. Energy shot out toward her, wrapping her in a net of light. Delia evaporated in a puff of smoke. Ember screamed, and both Graydon and Deverell sprang to their feet.

Holding up the wand threateningly, he said, "Now, now, allow me to explain. Your good captain Delia is unharmed."

"Unharmed!" Graydon growled. "You killed her!"

"I have not," the doctor insisted, his bearing imperious. "If you'll grant me but a moment, I'll prove it to you. Look closely at the picture. Tell me, young Ember, what do you see?"

Ember got up and examined the painting, careful to stay far away from the wand. The *Phantom Airbus* looked exactly the same as it did before, with one tiny exception. Now a diminutive woman stood at the helm. "Is . . . is that . . . ?"

"It is," the doctor said proudly. "Captain Delia is steering her vessel in the clouds."

"Let me see that," Graydon said, and pushed through the others. His eyes softened when he saw her. "Del? Can you hear me? I'm going to get you out."

"She cannot hear you," the doctor said. "She's trapped in a sort of mirror prison. It's like an alternate reality, a bubble that sits on the edge of time, waiting to burst. All it will take to free her is to reverse the polarity of my wand." He tucked the wand into his jacket pocket.

"Is she in pain?" Dev asked.

"No. At least, I don't believe so."

"You don't *believe* so?" the vampire hissed.

"Admittedly, this experiment is in its last rounds of testing. I thought it best to try it out on a person who was, for the most part, indestructible, before I attempt to use it on someone more delicate," the doctor said.

The air in Graydon's lungs seized and sat inside him like molten lead. It slowly filled all the open spaces until he was choking with fear. "Let her out. Now!" he insisted, a snarl escaping through his bared teeth, which were lengthening into fangs. Fur sprouted on his hands and his nails became sharp claws.

"Now, now, Captain Graydon. You know I can't do that. You also know who's to blame for her being trapped. It was you making plans with Frank to sneak everyone out on the submersible. I *also* see everything Frank sees."

Graydon stepped back, the shock obvious on his face as his body slowly shifted back to his human form. "You made Frank an unwitting spy?" he asked.

With a sour look, the doctor replied, "It was part of the contract—which you signed, by the way. There's no cause for malice simply because you couldn't bother yourself to read the fine print."

"But he was dying!"

"A contract is a contract. It is not wise, captain, to snub the man your loved ones depend upon for survival."

"Dr. Farragut," Dev said, "I do believe you could convince a condemned man to place the noose around his own neck and then express his undying gratitude to you for providing the rope and step stool."

"Why, thank you, my good vampire."

"It wasn't a compliment," Dev said with repulsion.

Ember put her hand on Captain Graydon's arm. He comported himself before responding to Farragut. "We'll stay. I promise. Just . . . just bring her back," he pleaded, his voice cracking and rough.

"Well, unfortunately, your promises don't mean as much to me now as they once did. But of course, once I have your full cooperation, I'll let her go. I'll even give you my personal skyship as compensation for your troubles. She's a beauty. Even better than your *Phantom Airbus*, I'd warrant."

"I don't understand, Doctor," Ember said. "What do you want from him? From us?" she added, indicating the group. "Why do you keep us here?"

"All will be revealed in good time, my dear. Now then, I have some business to attend to. The lab is yours so that you and Finney might brew more of your spells. I must confess, I'm extremely curious to see this weapon you've made and how you transform spells to ammunition. I'm not over fond of weapons personally, but I certainly admire innovation."

"We'd be happy to show them to you at your convenience, Doctor," Finney said affably. Clearly, Finney was the most accomplished actor in the room.

"Wonderful. Just make sure to leave yourselves enough time to dress for the party. Since there will be plenty of food there, I believe we'll forgo the formal dinner hour. Carry on as you will. I expect to see all of you at the ball, with the exception of Captain Delia, of course."

With that, he and his servants exited the room, leaving all of them sitting in stunned silence, apart from the werewolf, who stood at the painting murmuring softly, his strong shoulders hunched in defeat.

Ember turned to Jack and opened her mouth to ask a question, when Jack surprised her by pressing his finger to her lips. "There's a spy-der in the corner," he said, his voice as smooth as butterscotch. "You and Finney go ahead and brew your potions. We can talk more later."

"But, Jack—" Ember began.

"Nothing's changed," he said. "Just . . . just be careful."

"You too," she said.

Finney stood. "I'll meet you there, Ember. I need to gather a few things from the bag in my room. You'll bring the weapons?"

"I will."

"Then I will escort you, if you don't mind," Dev said gallantly. "It can't hurt to be cautious."

"That's a good idea," Jack said, surprising the vampire. He then whispered to his pumpkin, who trailed after Finney as Jack abruptly left.

As Ember and Dev headed back to her rooms, she looked back at Graydon. Dev patted her arm. "He's better left alone."

In her rooms, Ember said, "I'm so sorry about your sister, Dev. You must be terribly worried."

"I am. But I'm confident we'll find a way to get her out of the picture. We must." He gave her a grateful smile and then changed the subject. "You certainly have made yourself comfortable with Stingy Jack."

"Why do you call him that?" Ember asked. "He doesn't appear to me to be even remotely stingy."

"Jack has somewhat of a reputation in the Otherworld for being . . . unbending."

"Oh?"

"Yes. He's too good, actually. You're aware that they do much more than simply guard the crossroads; they are enforcers."

"I know," Ember said. "But Jack isn't cruel."

"I never said he was cruel. I said he was unbending. Now, if I may continue. Even those who are native born to the mortal world are warned from a young age to avoid all lanterns, but Jack in particular. Rumor has it he hunts down any who wander into his territory and returns them to the Otherworld. He doesn't listen to their side of the story. He doesn't judge them and decide. He's uncompromising. Jack simply sends every creature that is not purely animal or mortal to the Otherworld. Even the young who've never known any other life are afforded no mercy."

Ember frowned. "That's not the Jack I know. He could have turned me in and he didn't. He watched over me all those years and never said a word."

Dev rubbed his jaw. "Yes. Well, it's easy to understand why he would keep the knowledge of you to himself. I'm sure you were lovely even as a child."

"Is that such a bad thing?"

"Just keep in mind, Ember, that the life of a lantern is unnatural. If even the most frightening creatures of the Otherworld are nervous around lanterns, there's a good reason. I have personally witnessed the atrocities that occur when lanterns banish mortal-world-born, half-breed vampires to the Otherworld. In the Otherworld, full vampires exterminate them as if they were vermin."

"But surely Jack doesn't know."

"They all know. How could they not? The irony is, lanterns were once mortal themselves. Perhaps if they weren't, they'd show more tolerance for our kind." He boldly lifted his hand to her loose ringlets. "Just promise me you'll be careful, Ember."

Ember couldn't help but recall that Jack had just left her side with the same words. She gave the handsome vampire a small smile. "I will," she said. "May I borrow your cane? I have an idea I want to try out."

Dev hefted his steel-gray cane and handed it to her, raising his eyebrows.

"I'll take care of it," she said. "I promise."

"You'd better not return it to me blemished," he said.

"I'll have it back to you before the ball."

"Yes. About that . . . I do hope you'll save me at least one dance. That is, if you can still bear to look upon me after all this." He gestured his hand at the house around them.

"I don't blame you for anything," Ember said. "It's not your fault, Dev. I'm glad I came to the Otherworld. Truly I am. I've met so many interesting people and seen such amazing things. I'd be happy to save you a dance at the ball, but, Dev, I . . . I think you should know that I could never be the person you want me to be, or live with you in the way you hope. I'm sorry."

He sighed unhappily. "It's my own fault," he said. "I pushed you too quickly, behaved badly. I suppose I can hardly blame you for having a low opinion of me."

"I don't have a low opinion of you. In fact, my regard for you is still quite positive."

Dev gave her a tight smile. "I'd hoped for a bit more than a positive regard, Ember."

"Still, I hope we can remain friends."

She extended her hand. He took it and pressed it to his lips. "Always," he said, and his eyes still promised much more than simply friendship.

Ember quickly withdrew her hand and left him at the door, closing it solidly behind her. Taking a deep breath, she headed over to her bag, checked the contents, and hefted it over her shoulder. She and Finney were going to have to be quick if they were going to do all she wanted to before the ball.

Once they were back in the lab and had thoroughly checked the area for spy-ders, finding none, Finney set up the cauldron and opened her spell book.

"What's first on the agenda?" he asked.

"You're going to make our four most potent spells. It shouldn't take more than two hours."

"What are you going to do?"

Ember headed over to the closet and yanked it open. The brooms and mops inside fell to the floor once again. Sucking in a breath, she grinned widely. "I'm going to figure out a way to make these broomsticks fly."

CHAPTER 36

A NEW BROOM SWEEPS CLEAN

"Fly? Oh!" Finney's face brightened. Then he whispered excitedly, "You mean you want them to levitate so we can follow Jack and his pumpkin out of this place!"

"Exactly," she said quietly.

"But . . . why brooms?"

"Well, they're the only thing in this room that won't be missed, I suppose. And they're big enough to sit on. They'll have to do," she whispered back, then added in a normal voice, "Can you manage the spells?"

"Yes. I can follow your recipes. You'll just have to add your witch's spark at the proper times."

"Great. Let's get started, then."

She helped Finney gather all the ingredients, taking the fresh herbs from the doctor's plants only when absolutely necessary.

Finney began creating their four most potent elixirs—the acid spell, which they made stronger since Dev recovered from it so quickly; the immobilization spell; a sleeping spell; and a spell that rendered its victim temporarily sightless. Then Ember asked if he could work a new one. In light of the doctor's invisible companion, Ember thumbed through her book and found one that helped "reveal that which is hidden in darkness."

Saying he'd try, Finney bent over the cauldron and proceeded to combine ingredients. His goggles quickly fogged and his copper hair frizzed in the steam. The work was slow but steady, and in just thirty minutes, Finney already had three dozen stoppered pipettes full of a sleeping spell. He moved on to the next one while Ember blew out a frustrated puff of air.

"What are you trying to do, exactly?" Finney asked, watching her study Dev's cane and riffle through the spell book.

"I need to figure out how the witch who gave it to him infused her energy into the gemstone on the top. I don't know if it needs to be a gemstone or if it could be any inanimate object. There's nothing about storing a witch's energy in the spell book."

"Sometimes the only way to know is to test out your theory and then slowly eliminate the variables. What have you seen so far that holds and/or channels witch power?"

"My cauldron charm held a great deal of energy."

"What was it made of?"

"Metal."

"Hmm. What else?"

"Lights. The strange box that collected my energy so Dev could trade it for funds. The nets on the skyships. The signposts in town."

"What do they all have in common?" Finney asked.

Ember snapped her fingers. "Conductors. They all have some kind of metal."

"Good. Now figure out what kind of metal it is, or if any metal will work."

Wandering through the doctor's lab, she gathered up metal of various types and tried filling them with her energy. She quickly found copper to be the best conductor of witchlight. "Now I just need to work out a way to fasten copper wire to a broom." Finding lengths of thin copper wire and a bolt cutter, she wrapped the wire around the base of the broom where the straw was tied on, and then, for good measure, she added copper strands to the straw base as well.

When she was done, she wrapped her hands around it and drew out her power like Dev had taught her. Once the copper was filled with energy, she put on the witch hat and told it she wanted the object to levitate. The broom shot straight up until it hit the ceiling, brush end up. "That will never do," Ember said while Finney laughed and moved on to the next potion.

Searching again, Ember found a roll of copper netting, a finer, thinner version of the nets used on the *Phantom Airbus*. Carefully, she wound it around the length of the broom, infused it with energy, and gave it the same command as before. This time the entire broom lifted off the ground and stayed level. Standing, she pushed down on it using just the power of her arms, and it didn't budge. When she used her mind, however, the broom lowered.

"Guess it's time to try it with my weight," Ember said. Awkwardly, she tried to find a good position to sit and found that the straw section in the back was the most comfortable. It was either that or lie across it.

The broom lifted her easily enough, but she felt like she was going to fall off at any moment. She gave the command to lower back down again, and the broom set her on her feet.

As Finney began on the third batch of potion, he said, "How about adding a saddle? Are you sure brooms are our best option?"

"Probably not, but it's not like we can ride cats around, can we?"

"Shhh!" Finney said. "Remember to keep your voice down. You never know when one is nearby."

Ember bit her lip and searched the corners for gleaming eyes. "You're right."

She walked around the broom, examining it from every angle. It glowed witchlight blue as it hovered, making her think of the *Phantom Airbus*. If only she had a balloon to sit on. Clutching her hands behind her back, she paced, thinking, and spied the doctor's extra lab coat hanging from a hook. She remembered when Yegor put it on and it had suddenly filled out.

Running her hand down the sleeve, she considered for a moment and then pulled it off the hook and tied it to the broom, making sure it was buttoned and the sleeves tied off. "How did the witch power fill the balloon on the ship?" Ember asked Finney.

"That wasn't magic. It was just hot air. The witch power heated the air and fans blew it inside the balloon."

"Oh!" She grabbed a bellows, opened one sleeve, and told the net full of witchlight to heat the air; then she began pumping. The coat started to inflate. "I think it's working!" Ember said. When the coat had become as puffy as one of the doctor's marshmallows, she tied off the end and clambered on top. "It's much more comfortable this way," she called down to Finney as she soared around the room. "The only problem is that we only have one coat."

"I'm sure we can get more," he said.

Once Ember was satisfied, she quickly went to work fashioning a broom or a mop for each of them. Escaping an island in the middle of the ocean on a mere broom was risky, but so was staying and playing the doctor's games. Who knew how long it would be before they too were imprisoned in paintings? Once she was done, she stored the mops and brooms in the closet again, all of them tied together in a bundle.

The doctor and Yegor entered the lab when Finney was preparing the final potion.

"What's this?" the doctor asked, leaning over the cauldron and sniffing the fumes.

"I wouldn't, if I were you," Finney warned. "It's a sleeping potion."

"Ah, and it must work well, because I'm feeling a bit sluggish now."

"It's not quite done yet," Finney said.

"Lucky for me. And your weapons? Might I have an opportunity to examine them?" the doctor asked.

Finney shrugged. "I have to keep stirring, but the guns are on the table."

The doctor picked one up and sighted down the barrel, then spent time loading a cartridge, locking it in place, and then taking it out. "Ingenious," he said, his smile genuine. "And quite uncanny. I'm frankly very impressed with you, lad. For a mortal, you've made great strides."

"Thank you."

"Would you consider staying on here as my apprentice when all this is said and done?"

Finney blinked, his eyes three times their normal size behind his goggles. "What . . . what about Yegor?" he asked.

"Oh, Yegor assists. It's true. But he has no mind for tinkering. Truthfully, he's more of a bodyguard than a true apprentice. With you I could bequeath my stores of knowledge, my legacy."

"I-I'm honored that you would consider me," Finney said.

The doctor smiled. "Then we'll speak of it later. Tonight all will be revealed, and you'll have your chance then to determine your future. I do hope you'll consider my offer. I'd hate to waste a mind such as yours." When Finney merely nodded, the doctor asked, "Are the two of you nearly finished? I can't have you missing the ball."

"Nearly," Ember said, blowing back a strand of her tousled hair as she stoppered several pipettes and then reached for the cauldron with a towel. "We're just letting this last one cool before bottling it, but it shouldn't take more than a half hour."

"Excellent. Well then, I'll leave you to it. Your costumes are waiting for you in your rooms."

Ember and Finney finished up and carefully loaded their bags to bursting with the new spells. "I might suggest you wear your guns tonight, Ember," Finney said. "Even if they don't go with your costume."

She looked at Finney's sincere face and smiled at seeing the freckles on his cheeks and nose. Stepping forward, she wrapped her arms around him in a tight hug. "No matter what happens, I want you to know how important you are to me. Your friendship means everything."

Finney hugged her back and sighed into her hair. He knew she didn't feel the same way about him that he felt about her. Any fool could see how she lit up around the lantern. He also knew that Dev regarded Ember with a sense of avidity. How was a simple human boy to compete with two such eldritch, uncanny men? Even he had to admit he was a carrot while they were chocolate truffles.

"Your companionship is dear to me as well," Finney said. Drawing back, he continued, "Let's head upstairs." They'd left one bag, filled with the brooms, hidden in the closet. Finney hefted the other, filled with potions, on his slight shoulders. He staggered under the weight but managed somehow to escort Ember back to her room, where she asked him to return Dev's cane to him.

"I'll see you at the ball," Ember said, offering Finney a small smile. "Save me a dance?"

"I'm sure my dance card will be empty," Finney said in a slight tone of self-mockery.

Ember looked back at him, noting the sloped shoulders and the lanky frame. "Thanks for coming for me, Finney," she said, and kissed his cheek.

His oval face reddened until his cheeks resembled polished apples. He nodded and turned after she closed the door, thinking perhaps his daunted heart might still have reason to beat after all.

CHAPTER 37

COSTUMES MANDATORY

Finney was in good spirits as he strode into the room he shared with the other men. Dev was already dressed in his costume, which wasn't much different from what he normally wore.

"What are you supposed to be?" Finney asked.

"I am apparently a count," he said, playing with the lace cravat and adjusting the high, red-velvet-lined collar of his dramatic cape. His shoulder-length brown hair was loose. It fell sleek and luminous, framing his face and making the already-handsome vampire look even more striking.

Finney returned Dev's cane and picked up his own costume. Apparently, Finney was supposed to be some sort of jester or clown. His top hat had a red band with black feathers, and his vest was a whimsical combination of red, black, and white fabrics with varying stripes and patterns. His polished shoes were red, and the cane given to him was topped with a face covered by a mask. He also had jars of white, black, and red paint.

"What am I to do with these?" he asked Dev, holding up a jar.

"I assume they are to be used to disguise your face," Dev said. Finney grimaced and was about to head into the washroom when Graydon emerged. He wore a blue naval jacket with gold epaulets and a tricorn hat. The gold buttons were tiny gears, and the trim that fastened across the chest made it look like he wore thin plates of armor. His hair was pulled back in a queue, and his steel-gray eyes flashed as he placed the hat on his head and sat to pull on a polished pair of boots.

He hadn't spoken since Dev had collected him from the dining room, and only the insistence that something worse might happen if he was to disobey the doctor's orders again made Graydon leave the painting with Delia trapped inside.

Watching Graydon contemplate a world without Delia was difficult. Such thoughts cast a pall over Dev's heart. He didn't want to think about a life with anyone but Ember either.

Glancing over at Jack and not even attempting to quell his antipathy toward the lantern, he said, "You'd better get dressed. They'll be collecting us soon."

Jack ran a hand through his blond hair and then went to attach his pocket watches. He was pleased to see that the human-made watch was working once again. Finney had done him a kindness, even though he also had strong feelings for Ember. When Jack snapped it shut, he caught Finney watching him in the mirror. He smiled at the lad and nodded. Finney returned the gesture.

Indicating the black fabric with white stripes, Jack said, "The doctor wants me to dress as a skeleton, but that seems to me a bit redundant. There's an easier way." Summoning his light, Jack made his skin transparent, and Dev winced at the grinning skull staring back at him. The lantern looked barbarous with his bones on display.

"Yes, well, perhaps you could dial it back a bit. No one here wants to stare at your hip bones all evening."

Jack glanced down and saw his leg bones on display through the fabric of his trousers. He dimmed his light just enough that only the bones of his hands and head showed. It wasn't what the doctor had in mind for him, but it would have to do. He refused to don the skin-tight costume. Placing a helmet-shaped hat with a rounded crown on his head, he ran his fingers across the ink-black brim and pulled it low over his eyes.

"Finney, when you are satisfied with your makeup, then I believe we are ready," Dev said.

"Almost done," Finney said. He emerged from the washroom a moment later. He'd painted his face white and drawn elaborate black swirls around his eyes and lips, filling in spots with tiny red hearts.

Dev raised an ebony eyebrow, thinking perhaps the young mortal was also attempting to win Ember's affection.

The men, finally ready, headed downstairs. Yegor met them at the bottom. "If you will accompany me, gentlemen, I believe the doctor is eagerly awaiting your arrival."

They headed into the mirrored ballroom to find many color-fully dressed guests already swirling to the music, their movements as synchronous as the fish in the lagoon. Graydon found a place in the corner to stand and glower at the others, his eyes gleaming in the dim light. Finney made his way to the buffet and was happy to find Jack's pumpkin sitting as a centerpiece. It sparked happily at seeing him.

Jack and Dev both circled the room, heading in opposite di-rections looking for Ember. The lantern frowned at seeing the pugnacious determination in the vampire's eyes. He feared she had endued the vampire with more gentlemanly attributes than the man truly possessed.

Scanning the menagerie of costumed Otherworlders, Jack scowled. Not seeing Ember stirred foreboding in his mind. He searched for a petite woman with bouncy, chocolate-brown hair, one with a generous smile and an hourglass shape. Tuning out the garrulous chatter, he passed through the crowd, his lantern light falling on them.

There was something different about the people he saw. Something incongruous about their inner lights. The auras were pulsing in staccato beats that changed color. He'd never seen such a thing before. It was like a multifarious blend of not one, not two, but many different beings. One aura, a green one, shone through the crowd. He knew that one. It was Frank. He followed the man as Frank sought out the werewolf in the corner.

"Captain?" Frank said.

Graydon stood at attention. "What is it, Frank?"

"It's the submersible. She's been scuttled, sir."

"And the crew?" Graydon asked.

"Don't know," Frank said. "They were either taken off before she sank or they went down with the ship."

Graydon's shoulders fell. He studied his longtime friend and former first mate. If there was any duplicity in the man, he couldn't see it. Graydon decided Frank didn't know that he served the doctor's whims. He was as much a victim as Delia.

"It's not your fault, Frank," Graydon assured him.

"Don't matter," Frank said. "The ship was my responsibility. I take full blame."

"There's nothing to be done now."

"Where's Captain Delia?"

"She's . . . she's been detained this evening," Graydon replied.

Hearing Graydon talk about Delia increased Jack's worry over Ember tenfold. Just as he turned to look through the crowd again, he sensed she was close. His eyes landed on her immediately. She stood in the doorway, a feathered mask covering her eyes. Her purple-and-black gown draped from her tightly corseted bodice in ruffled folds of silk and taffeta. The bustle and train were so spectacular, they practically filled the doorway.

Ember stepped into the room and Jack caught sight of a conical black hat in her hand. A band of copper circled the brim. She also carried a staff of some kind that glinted in the light. Her hair was drawn up and pinned with clips of the same metal. Dev got to her first.

The tall vampire leaned over her with a conciliatory smile and soon led her onto the dance floor. She placed the hat on her head and lifted the hem of her heavy skirts, keeping the staff in the same hand. Jack realized then that it was a broom. He studied it with his lantern's perception and smiled. She'd done it.

Jack hung back, watching them and waiting for the arrival of the doctor. When their dance was finished, Dev led Ember to the buffet. The crowd parted for them as if they were royalty. Finney loaded a plate for her and she nibbled but turned her eyes away from the two men often, as if she were searching for someone. Jack hoped it was him.

When Ember set down her plate, Finney offered his arm and they danced. The gaunt boy moved awkwardly, but Ember simply laughed whenever he stepped on her feet or they bumped noses. At the end, Finney took her arm and led her over to where Jack stood. The boy grimaced, seeing Jack's skeleton beneath his skin, but Ember acted as if everything was normal.

"Will you dance with me, Jack?" she asked, lifting her dainty chin.

Jack glanced around and nodded. "Keep watch, Finney?"

"Consider me on duty," Finney said in reply, and took Ember's broom so she wouldn't have to carry it around. He wondered when she'd had time to retrieve it and didn't like the idea that she'd wandered down to the lab again by herself. It hurt to see the way Ember looked at the lantern as he led her onto the dance floor, but Finney would rather see her with Jack than with the scoundrel Dev. Even now Dev was scowling as he slowly sipped from a golden goblet by the buffet table.

Finney pulled a pimply-skinned purple fruit from his pocket and bit into it. He chewed, quite enjoying the texture and the flavor of the sour fruit, and tried to ignore the way Jack's hand curled around Ember's waist and how closely he was holding her.

Dev also took in every glance, every touch, and realized he was losing the game. How the devil could he lose Ember to a lantern? A mortal he could almost understand, or at the very least deal with. When Ember stood that close to Jack, her witchlight dimmed to the point that not even he could tell her from a human. The lantern was a natural shield for her.

The thought occurred to Dev that Jack could better take care of her than he could. The only way Dev could hide her witchlight would be to either drain her or drug her, and neither of those options was good for the long term. He gritted his teeth. There had to be a way. His blood and his heart told him to find one—insisted that he try one last time. He'd heard her say she just wanted to be friends, but he knew there could be more, that she could be happy with him.

Ember leaned close to Jack and whispered something. Her strawberry lips grazed his ear and her cheek was pressed to his.

Jack pulled her flush against his body, and Dev's fingers tightened on his cup.

Seeing the grinning skull bending down to say something in return, his bony hand clutching Ember's, gnawed on Dev's vampire heart and made his stomach skitter like little mice were racing around in it in circles.

Enough was enough, he rationalized. The road she was heading down was a dangerous one indeed; he owed it to her to save Ember from herself. Dev slammed his cup down, the contents sloshing over the rim. He'd never considered himself a sanguinary sort of vampire, prone to machinations, but if he had to help Ember see the light by incapacitating her, then so be it. He stepped away from the buffet, his eyes fixed on the prize. He would have no peace until Jack's infernal hands were off his witch. Dev was a hunter by nature, seeking blood to sustain himself. As much as he tried to use reason to guide his actions, instinct was kicking in. The power thrumming in his blood said he not only wanted her but needed her, and that power pushed his feet forward.

Jack was quite enjoying his dance with Ember. He rather liked the feel of her in his arms, and she fit against him very nicely. The scent of her hair, the rustle of her skirts, and the warmth of her affection were nearly intoxicating. Each minute in her presence made him crave more. He longed to take away the feathered mask and slip his hands into the voluminous curls of her hair, removing the pins one by one until her hair fell down her back in soft waves.

He spotted the vampire making his way toward them and sighed, knowing a confrontation was coming and wishing it wouldn't. Just then, a buzzing light sped into the room. It was one he recognized. He frowned as the firefly zipped around him and out the door. Jack stepped back just as the vampire closed in.

"Ember, I must talk with you," Dev said. "It is of dire importance."

"Oh, well, I suppose if it's fine with Jack . . ." Her words trailed
off and she looked at the lantern, hoping he'd voice a protest.

"Yes," Jack answered distractedly. "Go ahead and talk with Dev.
I'll be right back."

Jack left in a hurry, heading out the ballroom door.

Dev thanked the maker for his luck and took Ember's arm, placing her hand on his bent elbow. "Can we speak outside?" he asked.

She sighed, watching Jack depart, and then nodded. Dev escorted her out to the veranda. Finding a quiet place away from prying eyes, he pulled her into an alcove.

"What is it?" Ember asked. "Has something happened?"

Ember removed the hat she'd pinned to her head, as well as her
feathered eye mask, and set them on the stone wall.

"No, no. My sister's painting is fine, as far as I know. I want to
speak of our escape."

"Shhh!" Ember said, pressing her fingers against his mouth.
"There's a cat farther down the wall."

"Right." He hesitated and then said the only thing he knew
would work. The only thing that would truly save her from making
a mistake with the lantern would be remembering what he could
give her. Taking advantage of her soft heart, he murmured, "I know
the timing isn't right, but I need to ask your permission to take just
a bit more of your blood."

"Why?" she asked. "Is there something amiss?"

Dev shook his head. "Regarding that . . . er . . . subject we aren't
talking about, the one that might be picked up by prying ears and
watchful eyes?"

"Yes?"

"I was thinking about you and Finney making more ammunition for your weapons. If I had some witch power in my system, I'd be much stronger. As to my current status, I'm afraid I'm rather weak. All the battles on the skyship have drained me, and there aren't any donors around who are either willing or able to sustain me. I suppose I could—"

"Don't say another word," Ember said, touching her finger to his lips. "Of course you can take more of my blood. You don't even need to ask."

Ember had no idea what she'd just promised him. It was dangerous saying such a thing to a vampire. It meant that the natural witch protections Ember possessed against him were now null and void. He paused, reminding himself that this was for her own good. He was only doing this because she was so very stubborn and was being too easily swayed by the lantern.

"Oh, Ember," Dev said, taking her hand and pressing a warm kiss on her palm. "Ember, thank you."

"You're very welcome."

He kissed her wrist in a very proper sort of way at first and then slowly pulled off her long glove. His mouth softened and the kisses became slow and drugging as he trailed more up to the inside of her delicately veined elbow. "I . . . I can't stop thinking of you, Ember," Dev murmured, punctuating each word with the touch of his mouth on her lovely arm.

"Oh, Dev. We've already talked about this."

"I know. But it hurts, Ember. My heart . . . hurts."

The tips of his fangs grazed her smooth skin, scratching it. He cursed his clumsiness. Such a move caused a pleasurable, inebriating sort of effect on a donor. Such a move was typical of an untrained or desperate vampire, and Dev was neither of those. Still, Ember's whole body relaxed against him, and he couldn't deny the effect it had on him.

"Dev?" Ember said.

"Yes, love?"

"That feels nice."

He smiled, feeling a little guilty but also wanting to make her happy. "I'll try my best to see that feeling continues." Now that he had her in his arms, her blood thrumming in her veins, Dev knew he couldn't, wouldn't let her go. He moved up her arm to her shoulder, shifting the short sleeve of her dress down, revealing a wide expanse of soft flesh.

He tasted her in short little pinches of teeth against flesh until he reached her neck. She groaned in anticipation, the effects of his vampire kisses already working in her body. "Say you desire me as I desire you," he said huskily as her fingers grabbed his lapels and she tilted her head to the side, exposing the elegant length of her neck.

She licked her lips. "I want . . . I want . . ."

Dev sank his teeth into her throat and drank deeply. He cupped her head and held her steady as his other hand caressed her bare arm, the dip of her waist, and then spanned her hip. He squeezed the flesh he found there. Her body was lush and lovely, her taste exquisite. Dev lost himself in the pleasure and didn't even realize when his mouth moved across the line of her jaw and found her lips.

He picked her up and set her on top of the wall, holding her tightly as they kissed.

Just then, he was wrenched away from Ember, who almost toppled from the wall.

Finney caught her and pulled her down, her body falling hard against his thin frame as both of them crashed to the stone path.

The pumpkin floated next to him with a menacing expression on its carved face.

"Ember? Ember?" Finney said, maneuvering out from under her and slapping her cheeks lightly. When she didn't respond, he glared at Dev. "You despicable fiend!" he shouted. "What have you done to her?"

She swooned in a faint against Finney's chest. He hastily removed his necktie and dabbed her bloody neck. Dev, who was impressed that the young human boy had been able to pull him back in the first place, wiped his own mouth with the back of his hand, sighed, and was about to answer, when his head snapped to the side. He'd been punched. Hard.

He staggered a step and then lifted his eyes to an enraged lantern.

CHAPTER 38

THE CAT'S OUT OF THE BAG

Dev touched his jaw, working it back and forth as the blood surged out of his bones and began healing him instantly. He glared at Jack through the hair hanging in his face. "Why hit me?" he taunted. "Why not use your protean powers to blast me where I stand?"

"Simple," Jack said. "With Ember unconscious, I can't ask her if she desired your advances or not."

"And if she did?"

"If she did, I turn and walk away."

"And if she didn't?"

"Let's just hope for your sake she did. I've never turned the full wrath of my lantern light on anyone before, but I've been told I have the ability to make a being like you suffer for a very, very long time."

Dev's eyes were wild and glittering as he stared down the lantern. "For your information, Ember just told me I could drink from her whenever I wished."

"Like I said, I'm going to need her to confirm the truth of that."

Jack shook with the need to further pummel Dev for daring to touch Ember, but he was determined not to assume things on her behalf, even if it meant losing her to someone else.

Barking a laugh, Dev gestured to himself with a flourish. "You know how this works, lantern. If she didn't want it, didn't want me, I'd be dead right now. Now, if you'll excuse me, I'd like to check on her."

He bent over Ember and was thrust back again. Jack punched him in the gut and then jabbed him in the throat, forgetting, for the moment, his determination to rein in his emotions. He grabbed Dev's lapels, tearing them, and said, "I'm warning you again, vampire, don't touch her!"

Dev bared his teeth, shoved Jack away, and then barreled toward him at preternatural speed, thrusting him into the wall. The stones on the wall shattered, but the lantern appeared unaffected.

"So you want to fight like pathetic mortals over a woman?" Dev said. "Then you've picked the right vampire." He tossed off his jacket, unbuttoned his waistcoat, removed his cuff links to roll up his sleeves, and then carefully set aside his cane and his pocket watch.

It was all Jack needed to proceed with a clear conscience. If Dev wanted a fight, he'd give him one. Jack followed Dev's example, rolling up his shirtsleeves before lifting his fists and rolling them in the air.

"Is this really the time for you two to have a boxing match?" Finney asked. "And thanks for the slam against mortals, by the way." Dev was big and strong, even without his vampiric blood to help, but Jack was solid and sturdy. Finney didn't know who he'd bet on. They began brawling, throwing punches, jabbing, and kicking. Dev even headlocked Jack.

Finney would have enjoyed watching the fight if it hadn't been for Ember. She still hadn't woken, though the bites on her lips and neck were now healed. A firefly zipped around his head and he waved it away, but it came back persistently, even landing on Ember's nose.

Just then, he heard a man's voice. "Stop at once!" The two scuffling men shot apart. Dev smacked into the stone wall, destroying more of the doctor's home, while Jack slammed up against the house. They panted, breathing heavily, deep bruises darkening their skin, their knuckles raw and red.

They straightened, and Jack spoke first. "I wondered when you were going to show yourself."

"A good lantern watches and doesn't get involved unless it's necessary. Clearly you have not been following that code, Jack. I thought I taught you better than that. Why have you abandoned your post?"

Dev watched with disgust as Jack straightened his shoulders and began reporting like a good little soldier.

"Finney and Ember are from the town I guard. This *vampire*"—Jack practically spat the word—"entered the town and drew me away with a steam spinner. He then proceeded to abduct Ember, carrying her off to the Otherworld. I followed, bringing Finney with me to track her. Once I found her, my intention was to escort her back to the mortal realm."

Rune's eyebrows rose as he scanned Jack with his piercing eyes, reading much more than Jack was saying out loud. The firefly zoomed up to Rune, and when he snapped his fingers, it clicked into his earring. He stroked his elegant beard and circled Finney and Ember, staring at each of them for a long moment. "Why didn't you tell me about the witch?" he asked Jack. "You knew I was looking for her."

"I didn't want you to find her," Jack replied boldly. "The last time you came across a coven, both humans and witches burned at the stake."

Dev hissed, his now-straggly hair falling in his face. He looked feral in that moment. "You're a witch burner?" He spat on the ground near Rune's feet. The lantern ignored his insult.

"As much as I'm disappointed by your betrayal," Rune said to Jack, "I understand it. You were always a soft touch regarding witches and warlocks, preferring to frighten them away instead of turning them in. You, I'll deal with later. The human and the witch are easy enough to dispose of. That leaves *you*." He pointed to Dev. "Who sent you after the witch? Unless you want to pretend that you did it for yourself?" He looked Dev up and down. "You do seem like the sort."

Dev's lips tightened, and his fingers clenched into fists.

"Stubborn silence does not endear you to me, vampire," Rune warned. "Those who won't cooperate should prepare themselves for entombment. I believe the doctor has a very nice imported casket made from the wood of a maple tree stored in a closet somewhere. I think that one would suit you quite nicely."

"Why are you here?" Jack asked. "How did you find us?"

"Now, now, Jack. Let's remember who is the more powerful among us. You're already in enough trouble as it is." He glanced down at Ember. "She is a pretty one, though. A bit plump for my tastes, but that power coming off her in waves quite makes up for it, doesn't it? I can see why the two of you are fighting over her."

"It's the three of us," Finney said, standing as tall as his wiry frame allowed and pushing his glasses up his nose. "You'll have to go through all of us to get to Ember."

Rune leaned closer and flicked the lens of Finney's glasses. "As diverting as that may be, who says I want the girl?"

"Isn't that why you're here?" Jack said. "To deliver Ember to the capital or kill her?"

"Let's just say my duty is to ascertain what the good doctor is up to. The fact that you all are here is a stroke of good fortune, a recompense for the headache you've given me, making me chase you across the Otherworld and back. Now, vampire, I'll ask you one more time: Who hired you to hunt down this witch?"

Rune turned to Dev and narrowed his eyes when he maintained his silence. "Fine. If you won't cooperate, I'll make you cooperate." The light of his earring fell on Dev and turned from yellow to red. The vampire screamed as his skin began to steam and ripple.

Jack watched in horror as Dev's flesh burned. His shirt caught fire, and the black ashes of it stuck to his charcoaled skin. Never in Jack's entire life as a lantern had he seen the full power of their light. That he, too, could render so much suffering made him feel ill. He knew he could make vampires very uncomfortable, and had done so, but the waves of power Rune was sending forth were beyond his experience.

Dev collapsed to his knees. His lustrous hair fell out in clumps, and the bald spots erupted in boils. Jack could see the vampire's body trying to heal itself, but as fast as it did, Rune's destroying light did its work again.

After several agonizing minutes, Rune stopped. Studying his fingernails as if he was bored with the proceedings, he asked again, "Tell me who you work for, vampire. I can do this for weeks without tiring, but I don't think your blood will keep you alive that long. Just tell me and you can be on your merry way. I do have the authority to exculpate you, you know."

Dev writhed in agony but drew himself up on his hands and knees, though his limbs trembled with pain and exhaustion. Only burned rags hung on his body, and as much as Jack distrusted and even sometimes hated the vampire, he felt only sympathy for the man now.

Jack stepped between them just as Rune was about to rain down agony on the vampire again. "He can barely move, let alone speak," Jack said. "Give me a chance to work with him."

Smirking, Rune said, "You mean you'll work him over as you were doing before?"

"Yes. If it comes to that. It will be my way of making it up to you. I shouldn't have abandoned my post. I know that now. I was just trying to fix everything."

Rune sighed. "And doing an appalling job of it too."

Ember moaned, and Finney crouched down next to her. "What . . . what happened?" she asked, blinking her eyes open. She saw Jack and smiled drunkenly at him, then patted Finney's cheek. Next, she looked past him to Rune and her eyes widened. "Help me up, Finney."

He did, and as she straightened, she caught sight of Dev and cried out, burying her face in her hands. His body was slowly healing, but he still looked monstrous. Like something that had just crawled out of a grave. "Dev?" she said hesitantly, taking a step forward. "Who did this to him?"

"Apparently, you did, my dear," Rune said.

"I?" She swallowed. "I did this to him?"

"No, you didn't," Jack said softly, and turned to Rune. "Let me handle this."

Rune blinked, then sighed. "Very well. But keep in mind I'm only trusting you because we've known each other so long. I encourage you not to abuse my faith in you again."

Jack inclined his head stiffly and watched Rune turn to leave, saying softly, "The same to you."

"Then I have other matters to attend to." Whistling, Rune clutched his hands behind his back and turned to fog, disappearing through the doors into the party.

. . .

Rune slipped through the ballroom and found the doctor and his invisible henchman pouring drinks. He floated around their feet, listening.

"Now, after they're contained, you're to load them onto the ship. You know what to do."

"Yes, Doctor."

That sounds ominous. It had become very clear to Rune that there was much more going on here than simply harboring a runaway witch. After the battle with the other ship and hearing no word back from the Lord of the Otherworld, Rune began to search the waters. Without the ghost storm, his firefly light could see quite a distance. To his great surprise, when he came across the doctor's island, he found not only the light of a very familiar lantern, but also a very powerful witch.

He had sped across the water and was shocked to find the Lord of the Otherworld's runaway metallurgist as well. Drifting beneath doors and hiding in closets, Rune quickly learned a great deal. Jack, the vampire, and the mortal were all in love with the witch. She held no appeal for him personally—at least, not until she stepped away from Jack. Waves of her power shot out in a wide arc. He'd never felt anything like it before. No wonder the Lord of the Otherworld wanted her.

Well, that wasn't going to happen. A witch such as that one would secure the Lord of the Otherworld's reign for a long time

to come. But if Rune could keep her for himself . . . He materialized on the roof of the home after making sure there weren't any
cats up there to give him away. Stroking his beard, he considered his
options. He harbored no illusions that the young witch would be
swayed in matters of romance. It was obvious from the telltale ring
around her heart that she loved Jack.

But Rune could work with that.

Carefully, he had watched and waited for his moment. He sent
his firefly so Jack would know he was there. He didn't want to surprise the lantern, but he didn't engage with him yet either. While
Jack chased Rune's light, he followed Ember outside in fog form.

At first, he was going to intervene when the vampire bit Ember,
but then the human boy sought them out. Rune had been half hoping the vampire would kill the mortal so he wouldn't have to, but for
some reason, the vampire held back. Finally, it was time to show his
hand. Rune not only came to Jack's defense and displayed the extent
of his own power, but he also showed mercy.

Now all he had to do was figure out what the doctor was up to,
take out the Lord of the Otherworld with the help of Jack and the
witch, and act the part of a team player. Rune sighed. An ambitious
man's work was never done.

. . .

"That's your boss?" Finney asked as Rune ghosted away. "He's a lantern too?"

Jack nodded and took hold of Ember's shoulders. "Are you all
right?" he asked.

"Don't worry about me," Ember said. "Help Dev, please."

Jack threw the abandoned coat around the vampire's shoulders and drew him to his feet. Finney picked up the cane and the pocket watch and handed Jack his greatcoat.

"Give me the cane," Dev said, his voice as rough and raspy as sandpaper.

They sat him on the stone bench and he flipped open the top of his cane, extending the gemstone to its full length. Ember hadn't even known it could do that. Then he cupped the stone in his palms. The stone glowed blue, and as it did, his face relaxed. They watched in amazement as the skin on his hands and face healed quickly. Recovered somewhat, Dev buttoned his waistcoat over his bare chest, then his jacket, and ran a hand over his bald scalp, wincing. Regrowing his hair would take more time, at least a few hours.

He glanced down at Ember's hand on his arm and then up at the lantern who stood protectively beside her. What had happened to him was nothing more than what he deserved. He found he couldn't meet Ember's eyes. Not after what he'd done in his jealousy and pettiness. He'd been the very worst type of villain—one who preyed on the innocent and tenderhearted.

"I never lied to Ember. It *was* the high witch who hired me," he said softly. "She wanted me to find Ember and arrange a meeting. Make of it what you will."

Jack frowned. "But why would she do that if not to give Ember over to her husband?"

Dev pursed his lips. "I don't think that was her plan. My impression is that there is no love lost between the Lord of the Otherworld and his witch. If it had been his idea, he would have asked for me. Instead, she approached me secretly, on her own. Perhaps she trusted me. Perhaps she thought I could get close, since I'd done it before."

"Your witch," Ember said. "She healed you just now. How? I thought you were dying."

"My blood helped, but her power still sustains me. It has for decades."

"So you were lying about needing my blood," Ember said.

"Yes."

"Why?"

"Isn't it obvious?"

"You were jealous," Finney said.

"Aren't you?" Dev retorted.

Finney tugged at his collar uncomfortably. "We're tossing all our messy business out into the open now for everyone to see, then?"

"Finney?" Ember looked at him, surprised.

"Fine. I've loved Ember since we were children. There. Are you happy?"

"Oh, Finney," Ember said. "You never said anything."

"I knew how you felt about the young men following you around. I didn't want to be dismissed like them. Admittedly, coming here was my attempt at convincing you to accept me as a suitor, but, honestly, Ember, no matter what, I'll always be your friend." He clutched her small hands in his and squeezed them.

"There you all are!" The doctor's voice rang out, startling the group. He stopped when he saw the state of them. "Oh dear. I believe you took the suggestion to come in costume a bit too seriously. You all look like you've been run over by an old stagecoach drawn by wild horses." His round face glistened with sweat, making Ember wonder what he'd been doing. "Come, come," he said. "It's time for the party to begin."

CHAPTER 39

CANDY IS DANDY, BUT LIQUOR IS QUICKER

The group followed him into the ballroom. Ember retrieved her hat but had left her feathered mask outside on the wall. Her hair hung limply around her shoulders. Reaching up, she pulled out a copper clip. What on earth had happened to her? she wondered. She remembered Dev asking for her blood and then his lips on her elbow. The next thing she knew, she was waking up to see everyone in tatters.

Graydon came up to them immediately. "What happened?" he asked.

"Long story," Jack replied, looking around for Rune and noticing that both he—and his *pumpkin*—were absent. Strange. Stretching out his senses, he couldn't even locate his pumpkin, which was so alarming he could only stand there with his mouth open. Why had Rune come? Was he going to turn them over to the Lord of the Otherworld? Jack had to find him and explain.

He was about to ask Graydon and Frank to help Dev upstairs when Dr. Farragut tapped his knife against a crystal goblet. The dancing and music immediately ceased, and the partygoers moved to the edge of the dance floor en masse, leaving their group standing conspicuously in the center of the slick ballroom floor.

Raising his glass, the doctor said, "A toast to my very special guests. Gentlemen, would you be so kind as to pass around the drinks?"

Servants bustled about making sure everyone in the room had a glass.

"Settle down, settle down," he said, holding a hand in the air. "I've waited a long time to finish my most astonishing invention— over a century, in fact. Its beginnings can be traced back a thousand years, give or take. And now it is complete. Please help me celebrate by joining me in toasting the success of my project, one that will change the course of our future!"

The guests cheered mechanically and raised their glasses. The doctor drank, his thick neck exposed as his throat moved, draining his glass. Some of the liquid spilled onto his white waistcoat.

Graydon stared into his drink, then downed it quickly and slammed his empty glass on the servant's tray. Finney, Dev, and Jack were eager to leave, and tossed their drinks back out of compunction. Jack took Ember's elbow, and just before she followed them, she raised her glass to the doctor, who smiled down on her from the dais where he stood. Putting her lips to the rim, she sipped the bubbly drink gingerly. It tasted of peaches and something else, something . . . herbal.

Her thoughts became tangled as the group moved on, pulling her forward, but then she felt dizzy and her mouth went numb. The floor tilted and the other partygoers closed in on her. Lanky limbs took hold of her, jostling her body. She thought she was going to pass out for the second time in an hour, which was two times too many, in her opinion.

She tried to shove the arms away. Voices became indiscernible, and her words sounded slurred to her own ears. Finney was lying on the ground, unmoving. Ember glanced at the doctor, who was watching them with a satisfied smile. Jack and Dev had fallen too, and even Graydon was staggering. His cheeks bristled with fur, but then his face went slack and he fell. Ember tried to draw upon her witch power to clear both her thoughts and whatever drug the doctor had given them from her body, but it didn't work.

Only Frank remained standing, but he was staring blankly ahead, his Herculean body immobile. She raised a hand to him, but then her arm became too heavy and it fell to her chest. The last thought she had before she closed her eyes was that Frank's clothes looked very weather-beaten; the cuffs of his pants and his boots were dark brown with mud.

· · ·

A tiny pinprick roused her from sleep. Then she felt a cold swipe of something on her elbow. There was a plink of liquid hitting a flask, and she groaned and tried to open her eyes.

"Welcome back to the land of the living, as it were," the doctor called cheerfully. He was clad in his lab coat, a pair of goggles on top of his head, and he was bent over a contraption, carefully filling a dozen containers with the sloshing red contents of a beaker.

Ember looked down at her body. She was strapped to a bed that was inclined to almost a standing position. There was a needle in her arm, attached to a long tube. Her blood was draining into a beaker, drop by slow drop. Looking around, she saw Finney, Graydon, Jack, and Dev also lashed down. They were all beginning to come around as well, except Finney. He was still snoring slightly. The pumpkin floated near him, a worried expression on its face.

"What have you done?" Ember asked.

"Don't you mean what am I doing?" the doctor corrected her cheerfully. "I haven't done anything as yet."

Ember watched his ink-stained fingers as they ran down a formula on paper and reached for a new bottle.

"Why do you need our blood?" she asked. "Is it a spell?"

The doctor chuckled. "A spell? What I've done is so much larger in scale than one of your silly spells."

A needle rose into the air via an invisible hand and sank into Finney's arm.

"Yegor?" Ember asked.

"Yes, he's here," the doctor answered for his assistant, then added, "Don't hurt the boy. I meant it when I said I wanted him for an apprentice."

"Yes, Doctor," the invisible man replied.

"Dev? Jack?" Ember cried. The two men looked over at her dully. Dev's hair was nearly grown out to its usual length, and his body looked healthy and hale once again.

"They'll be quite unable to help you, my dear," the doctor said. "Even they can't burn through my tranquilizer so quickly, especially one I've adapted just for them."

"I don't understand," Ember said. "What do you want from us?"

"Yegor, pull the lever, if you will."

A nearby handle slammed down and a burst of steam erupted from a pipe overhead. Ember heard a grinding noise and the wall she thought was solid behind the doctor drew back, panel by panel, revealing two large cylinders.

"What are those?" she asked.

He pulled down his goggles once more, picked up a tool that shot blue fire, and welded a piece of metal over the section he'd just filled. "I believe the Lord of the Otherworld called them doomsday devices. His intent was to detonate it at a certain place, resulting in the severing of the Otherworld from the human world."

"Why would he want to do that?" Ember asked.

The doctor looked up. "I can't pretend to know. It would cut off the very resources he needs to run the Otherworld. I couldn't have that." He paused, his eyes looking dreamily at something she couldn't see. "I do so love my little uncharted island in the mortal world," he said. "So I stole them."

"Using me," Graydon said, turning his platinum eyes on the doctor. Fur bristled on his hands, his nails elongating momentarily and almost instantly receding.

"Yes. You and Delia. Don't bother trying to change," the doctor warned. "The drug I'm giving you now prevents it." He wandered over to the large weapon and patted it almost fondly. "Now that I have it, I've modified the weapon to suit my own purposes."

The lab shifted, tilting at an angle, and the doctor clutched the table, grabbing a beaker just before it toppled.

"Where are we?" Dev asked.

"In my private skyship. Thanks to Ember, I'm now able to escape the ghost storm that trapped me here."

"Trapped?" Dev said. "I thought you liked hiding behind it and wanted to use it for experimentation."

"Oh, I did, my boy. Learned quite a bit. But those pesky ghosts haunt my island for a reason. I was the one responsible for their creation, you see."

Ember swallowed. "Their creation? Do you mean you killed them?"

"Why, yes. I thought that much was obvious."

A flask of blood moved through the air. The doctor took it. "Thank you, Yegor. Now the wolf."

"What are you doing with our blood?" Graydon asked. "I understand why you'd want witch blood, but a werewolf's blood does very little, and a mortal's blood even less."

The doctor sighed. "It's so tiring for a genius to have to explain himself to those with tiny minds. I am retooling the bombs so that they will not separate the two worlds. Instead, when detonated, they will split the souls from every mortal. The vials of your blood will serve as a marker so the devices won't target your kind. You'll be able to live on as you always have. Upon consideration, you should thank me."

"Thank you for destroying an entire race of beings?"

"They won't be destroyed, technically. The disembodied souls will gather in a great storm in the Otherworld. Since they always materialize over water, they will head in that direction. It's possible they will hinder life for ocean-goers. I'm the first to admit that it's somewhat of a Pyrrhic victory, at least for the Otherworld.

"On the plus side, the mortal world will be cleansed, leaving it for me. The empty bodies the mortal souls leave behind will be easy enough to rule, especially with my clockwork technology to help. With no souls to haunt me on that side, it will be a marvelous place indeed, especially knowing I'll have my own lovely witch by my side."

"A world full of automatons bowing down to you as a king," Jack marveled, with a disgusted sneer on his face.

"Do you consider Frank an automaton?" the doctor spat, gesturing to the large green man in the corner. "You've seen him. He has a heart, a mind of his own."

"Not when you don't want him to," Graydon replied. "But you couldn't do that to Delia."

The doctor slammed down his tool. "Not because of any special strength on her part, I assure you. Delia isn't split from her soul like the lanterns. I simply put her soul back into her body, because it hadn't gone far."

"You can put a soul *back* in a body? Does that mean the lantern process is reversible?" Ember asked.

"Yes, of course. If the soul is isolated, then yes, it can be reattached."

"So you're saying you could put Jack's soul back into his body," Ember said.

The doctor glanced up quickly. He looked over at the pumpkin and then at Jack. He shrugged. "It's possible. The thing about lanterns is that their souls are tied to an ember. It holds the soul in place, keeps it from skittering away. Doesn't matter in Jack's case, though. I won't be fusing him back together. For this to work, I need a lantern's blood too. Fusing him back together would make him human again." He glanced over at Ember. "Besides, his fate won't matter much to you, my dear. Not after the device has detonated."

Ember's voice went hard. "I won't be your witch."

The doctor laughed so hard tears trickled from the corners of his eyes. "No," he said finally. "I shouldn't think so." He picked up the next vial of blood and poured it carefully into the slot fashioned for it. "It's taken time to gather everything," he said. "And you, Ember, were the most vital piece. I had to wait for you to mature, for your blood to be ripe. Finally, it is. Of all the witches hiding in the mortal world, only you were powerful enough to hear the call, and come to help me realize my dream. Why is that, I wonder?"

"It was you," Ember murmured. "You were the one drawing me to the Otherworld."

"Of course, if I hadn't bribed several unscrupulous individuals such as your good friend Payne, and suggested to him that he might want to spike your tea with devil's breath to make you more pliable, you might never have arrived. And again, if I hadn't sent Frank a message to escape the dreadnaught by using the submersible, you might have been caught then as well. It would have been very unfortunate indeed if you'd been captured by the despicable Lord of the Otherworld. Even Graydon might not have been able to rescue you in time. Having Dev bring you was a far simpler way to do things."

"But you didn't hire me," Dev protested.

"Didn't I?" The doctor lowered his goggles and waggled his eyebrows dramatically. He sealed the finished section shut. When he was done, he checked his pocket watch. "Bah. I'm getting distracted by minutiae." He pointed to Dev. "The vampire next, if you will, Yegor." A sharp needle jabbed Dev in the arm.

A tiny firefly drifted down from the ceiling when the doctor turned his back. It zapped Ember's restraints, and the belt at her waist slipped down. She looked up quickly. The doctor couldn't see her, but a black cat watched her sleepily, its tail twitching. When the cat didn't move and nothing happened, she yanked the needle from her arm and flipped her skirt up, reaching for the holster on her thigh. Relieved to find her weapons still strapped on, she pulled out both guns, aimed them at the doctor's back, and fired.

CHAPTER 40

A SKELETON IN THE CLOSET

Ember's shots—an acid spell and a sleeping potion—hit their mark. Then she picked up a scalpel with her mind and slammed it into the doctor's hand, pinning it to the wall.

Immediately, the doctor's lab coat began to dissolve, and he howled in pain. He wrenched out the blade and turned, clutching the table as the sleeping spell did its work. His eyes closed and he staggered. Before Ember could shoot a second time, the gun in her left hand was ripped away by an invisible force: Yegor.

She pointed the other gun at the empty space nearby and clicked the weapon so the new spell, the one that would reveal hidden things, locked into place. Ember fired again and again. Finally, she hit Yegor, and his naked chest and arms and half of his face materialized. It surprised him as much as her, but then the spell faded and he disappeared again. She just had time enough to think that the next batch would need to be stronger, before someone grabbed her arms.

Ember hissed and bucked, trying to draw on her witch power to stop the doctor's minion. Her skin sizzled with energy, and a burst of light shot out from her body in a wide arc. It funneled over Yegor's frame, pushing him back, and he briefly appeared again, but when the wave passed, he was gone.

The doctor straightened, his skin healing where the acid had eaten through. "Enough!" he shouted, and raised his hand in the air. Ember's second weapon was lifted out of her hands and drifted over toward him. No matter how she tried, she couldn't draw it back.

The doctor slammed the weapon down on the table. "How very clever to combine those two spells," he said. "Both at the same time proved more difficult to overcome than I bargained for. You're quite a witch indeed. So much potential." He sighed. "I thought letting you keep your weapons would make you feel more secure. Make you listen and understand. It's too bad, little witch. I even brought along a box of chocolates to give you as a sort of token gift, since you missed dessert last night. Now I've a mind to let you go without."

There was a settling of the ship and a groan. "Ah, I believe we have arrived." The doctor approached Ember and gestured to Yegor to release her. "You'll be coming with me. Frank, I'll need both you and Yegor to set up a device on either side of the crossroad. Once they're in place, you'll scuttle this ship."

"Yes, Doctor," Frank and Yegor said at the same time.

"As for the rest of you, I bid you adieu. Come along, Ember."

Desperate and just as unable to transform as Graydon, Jack summoned his errant pumpkin and bathed the doctor in a spotlight so powerful it should have destroyed him in an instant. But the doctor just gave the lantern a pointed look then flicked the orb with his finger to move it out of his way. "Trying to nip the hand that created you is poor manners."

As Ember passed the men, they all bucked and heaved in an attempt to escape and help her, but they were tightly bound. She could see a different solution draining into each man, preventing them from using their various abilities, just as the doctor had said.

Ember tried to summon her inner witch power again and blast him like she'd done with Yegor. She sent shock after shock into the doctor, but he wasn't even fazed. "Don't waste your strength, my dear," he said as he yanked her out the door and through a passageway, following Frank and Yegor, who were each carrying a cylinder. "No one—not a werewolf, not a vampire, not a lantern, not even a witch as powerful as you—can affect me. Besides, I'll need all your energy for the transfer."

• • •

As soon as Ember and the doctor disappeared, Rune sprang into action. He took his human form and freed all the others, removing their restraints and pulling the needles from their veins. Then he led the recovering men to the place where he'd hidden all of Ember's clever little bewitched brooms.

"I must leave now," he explained to Jack. "The Lord of the Otherworld is summoning me through his witch. I cannot ignore it, but know that I am on your side. The last thing I want is to have your Ember fall into his hands. I will help as I am able."

Jack clapped his mentor on the shoulder and smiled warmly. "Thank you. I always knew there was someone noble hiding beneath that rough exterior."

Rune grunted, nodded at the vampire and the human boy, and then turned to fog and headed out of the skyship. While he sped to his leader's side, he wondered if Jack had said such to him because he wished it to be true or because he'd used his ability to look into Rune's soul.

• • •

Transfer? Ember thought. "What are you?" she asked as she stumbled behind him.

"Ah, finally another good question. All will be revealed in time, young witch."

"You keep saying that," Ember said. "But you never explain anything."

"Now, that's not true," Dr. Farragut said. "I've told you far too much as it is. It's not my fault none of you are bright enough to connect the dots."

Something grazed Ember's leg and she looked down. The black cat was following her. It was soon joined by an orange cat and a white one with patchwork spots. Then she spotted six more, then another dozen. Noticing the felines, the doctor frowned. "I don't believe I invited all of you onto my ship," he said. "I have no further need of you at this time. Be off."

There was a hiss and a meow, but none obeyed. He sighed. The cats quietly padded after them as they emerged into the daylight.

The ramp had been extended, and the group headed down into a cave—a yawning black opening in the mountain of another island. "Come, girl," Dr. Farragut said to Ember. "Don't dawdle."

When they entered the cave, a series of embedded lights powered up, fueled by Ember's presence. Just as there had been at the other crossroad, there was a membranous barrier separating the Otherworld from the mortal one. The doctor turned. "Frank, set up your device on the Otherworld side of the barrier. Once it's ready, head back and destroy the ship. Save the boy, and the painting. I'd hate to waste the technology I used to trap the good captain. Yegor, you're with me."

Once they stepped through to the other side to the mortal realm, the lights disappeared; the only illumination came from an opening ahead. Soft yellow light beckoned them forward.

They moved along, the device floating eerily next to them as they made their way out of the cave. The cats, to the doctor's chagrin, still followed them, passing as easily to the other side as they had. Their eyes were trained on Ember in a way that made her nervous.

When they reached the opening, Ember saw that they were on a beach. A vast ocean stretched out before them. Yegor planted his device in the sand, wriggling it until it was steady, its pointed end angled straight up into the air. Once it was secure, he moved to hold her while the doctor fussed with the device.

He dialed a few buttons, pumped a bar, and touched his hand to a lever. Then he opened the bottom level of the tube. Dozens of little compartments popped out with a pneumatic hiss, most of them full of vials. In the empty ones, he inserted the vials containing the blood samples he'd recently collected. Ember saw that each one had been carefully labeled—*goblin, troll, gremlin,* and so on. He added the ones labeled *witch, vampire, werewolf, lantern,* and, last, *Finney.*

He pushed a nob and all the slots closed until they were flush with the weapon. "Done. Now we wait," he said with a satisfied smile on his face.

"Wait for what?" Ember asked.

"You'll see."

Soon there was a rumble underfoot. The sand shifted, and a broad rotating cone burst from the ground a hundred feet away, followed by a vehicle. When it was settled on top of the sand, the cone stopped rotating and steam shot out the sides. A hatch opened and a man stepped out, leading a thin, frail woman by the arm, followed by Jack's boss.

Rune trailed behind the couple. The woman was so emaciated she looked to be near death. Her stringy hair, which hung down to her waist, was so wispy and fine that Ember could see right through it to her scalp. Her reedy arm clutched the man as he guided her forward.

The closer they came, the more Ember noticed a gleam in the woman's toffee-brown eyes, one that said her mind was still very much alert, despite the decrepitude of her body. The doctor shifted his feet nervously in the sand.

"Monroe, you deserter, what is the meaning of this?" the man said.

"Ember, I'd like to introduce you to Melichor Lockett, otherwise known as the Lord of the Otherworld. And this lovely lady standing beside him is Loren, the high witch and . . . Melichor's wife," he finished with a grimace of distaste. "The man standing behind them is Rune. The first lantern I ever created."

The lantern's face flashed with shock, but he quickly hid his surprise. "Doctor." Rune inclined his head respectfully.

"We got your cryptic invitation," the Lord of the Otherworld said. "Why have you summoned us here, Monroe? Do you mean to worm your way back into my favor by stealing away the very witch I've been seeking?" Melichor turned feverish eyes on Ember. She took a step back, slightly behind the doctor.

"I can assure you that I have no intention of ever attempting to garner your favor again, Melichor. In fact, it is you who should be seeking mine," Farragut said.

The Lord of the Otherworld laughed. "Perhaps you've forgotten who housed you and fed you when you wandered in as a poor metal-lurgist," Melichor replied. "Stealing my device and quitting your post, not to mention kidnapping this young witch, is a shameful way to repay the kindnesses I've showed to you over the years."

"Kindnesses? The only reason your body isn't currently molder-ing in the ground is because I have been sustaining the woman who sustains you!"

Frowning, the Lord of the Otherworld glanced at his aged wife. Her eyes weren't downcast as they usually were, but were trained on the girl standing next to the metallurgist. "What does all this have to do with the high witch?" he sputtered.

"I'll tell you exactly what this has to do with her!" Monroe went on. "All these centuries, you've kept her and used her." He pointed to the high witch. "You've called her Loren Lockett, when that's not even her real name. You care nothing for her. Not even after all she's given you. At this very moment, your devious mind is plotting how you'll steal away the little witch at my side and force her into mar-riage, finally allowing you to do away with your old wife."

Ember gasped and studied the poor witch. Her thin, wrinkled mouth curled in a smile, but it wasn't one of trickery or deception, which surprised Ember, considering the high witch had sent Dev to fetch her. Instead, it was a tired smile, and full of kindness and warmth.

A cat brushed past Ember's legs, meowing, and then trotted over to the high witch and kneaded its claws into the sand next to her feet. It rolled on its side and began purring.

"Why were you looking for me?" Ember asked the witch, but the Lord of the Otherworld answered, assuming she was speaking to him.

"Monroe is right. She's growing old," the man said coldly to

Ember. "There's not much life left in her to keep me young, let alone power the Otherworld. My people have needs. Once you've taken on the duty of replenishing the stores of witchlight and everything is stable, I'll perform the spell that binds us together for as long as we both live and we'll drain the rest of her energy, allowing her to finally waste away like she's wanted all these years."

The witch shuffled closer and touched her hand to Ember's cheek. "I've waited so long to meet you," she said. Ember felt the hum of the woman's ebbing power beneath her fingertips. Waves of sadness and exhaustion burrowed beneath her skin. "You're so lovely," the woman said.

Monroe frowned, confused, as he watched the high witch and Ember.

"She's pretty enough," the Lord of the Otherworld observed, thinking his failing wife was losing what remained of her faculties. "Not that it really matters. Now hand her over, Monroe. Or do you intend to cause more problems?"

"Oh, there's no problem," the doctor said. "In fact, everything is going according to my plan. Yegor, turn the dial to level one and initiate a pulse. That should be a wide-enough band for the moment."

The machine hummed to life. Immediately, the Lord of the Otherworld began to shake. His skin turned pink, and the color deepened until his face was purple. His eyes rolled up, and he thrust out his arms and threw back his head.

"You should feel honored," the doctor mocked. "Your death will be the first of many."

"But I thought you weren't targeting Otherworlders!" Ember cried.

The doctor snorted. "He's no Otherworlder. He's a human, one whose twisted and unnaturally prolonged existence came at the cost of many Otherworlder lives. Why do you think he wanted a ban on humans coming in? He sees himself as a being above all the rest. The witches saw him for what he was, but there was no stopping him." Farragut laughed. "Humans who wander into the Otherworld are fair game, Melichor, don't you remember? I think it's about time your own law worked against you."

Ember watched in horror as the man's soul was cleaved from his body and materialized in front of her. Only then did the body relax. It stood immobile and lifeless, the eyes still open.

CHAPTER 41

THE BOOGEYMAN

Rune stepped closer to the high witch, offering a supporting arm. *Finally!* he thought. *It's done. The Lord of the Otherworld is gone.*

Dr. Farragut pulled a knife from his boot, walked up to the body, and spat at its feet while the ghost looked on. "I was a slave to you for years. Bound by the agreement we made. Only when you created the doomsday device was I able to figure out a way to free myself from our deal."

"I don't understand," Ember said. "What deal? How could a mere human hold power over you when none of us could stop you?"

"You asked me before what I am." He turned to Ember and smiled. "To answer succinctly, I am the boogeyman, the one and only of my kind, and this man—well, what used to be a man—tricked me. Now I'll have my revenge." With that, Dr. Farragut stabbed the body of the Lord of the Otherworld through the heart. "Goodbye, Melichor," he said. "And good riddance."

The body collapsed onto the sand, the open eyes unblinking as blood streamed from the wound. The ghost floating in the air screamed and tore at his hair while the doctor laughed until tears ran down his face.

"The . . . the boogeyman?" Rune said. "You . . . you were my creator?" How had Rune not known this? Had he been an experiment in the doctor's labs, like his poor invisible servant? Rune swallowed. Manipulating the others was possible, but fighting the boogeyman himself? The man could rip his soul away without a thought. He fingered his earring nervously.

"Yes," the doctor answered distractedly as he leaned down and pulled out the knife. "That was immensely satisfying." He wiped away a tear. Turning to the ghost, he added, "The irony is, I had no quarrels with the human race. But living as your slave all these years has turned my pleasantly wicked heart blackly vengeful. Now I'm going to destroy all humanity, and you can blame yourself, Melichor. Not that you'll cry over the humans. I know you care not a whit for them."

"You've got your revenge now," Ember said. "You can stop this. You can let everyone else go."

"Stop this?" The boogeyman turned to her and she drew back, seeing the spark of wild power in his eyes. "There's no stopping this. Not now. Long ago Melichor could have stopped it. He had many chances to do so, in fact. He made a deal with the devil, you see, and I was sent to collect his soul. Most men know there's no escape and they come quietly. Not Melichor.

"He agreed to come with me, but expressed his sorrow at leaving a widowed woman who cleaned his home without recompense. I've always had a soft heart when it comes to women—widows in particular—so I transformed myself into a coin so he could pay her. Once she bought her bread, I'd come back for him and we could be on our way.

"When I changed form, he picked me up and put me into a purse lined with a powder of ground onyx. He kept me prisoner for many years. Then, when he began to age, he thought to use me to preserve his life."

"He made you bring him to the Otherworld?" Ember asked.

"That he did. Not only did I have to make him a ruler, but I had to tell him the secret to maintaining longevity, which was, unfortunately, to bind himself to a witch. I was freed, but the bargain prevented me from doing him harm. The only loophole was that if he did something to injure himself, such as an accidental stabbing or drinking himself to death, then I was under no obligation to save him."

Rune mentally filed away the fact that onyx was the boogeyman's weakness.

"So how did the device make it possible for you to kill him?" Ember asked.

"He created it," the doctor answered. "Once I told him there was a way to split the mortal world from the Otherworld, he became obsessed with the idea. I designed the construct, and Graydon stole the plans from me and delivered them to the Lord of the Otherworld. Because he fashioned the device, I was able to use it against him. I just had to wait for an opportunity to steal it. That's right," he said loudly to the ghost. "It's your own fault, Melichor. I never would have been able to separate your despicable self from your body or save my lovely witch if you hadn't gotten greedy. Now that the two of you are no longer connected, I can heal her and we'll be together at last."

"W-wait a minute," Ember sputtered. "This . . . this is the witch you're going to rule the mortal world with? I assumed you were talking about me."

"Why would I be talking about you?" Dr. Farragut, the boogey-man, spun.

"Well, everyone *else* was trying to kidnap me . . . ," Ember explained.

He stiffened, raising his chin proudly. "She didn't always look like this, you know," he said. He caressed the woman's cheek. "Once, many years ago, her husband left her alone in a colony while he sailed back to England. He died at sea, unbeknownst to her, and she pleaded with me to tell her whether he was alive. I broke the news to her and held her while she wept. Her unbound hair was lush and thick, like golden honey, her skin firm and radiant. And her power . . . Her witchlight drew me to her, held me captive." The witch placed her hand on top of the doctor's and squeezed. He went on, gazing at her with obvious affection.

"Soon I'd become quite besotted with the young witch widow. Then I discovered that Melichor was looking for a fresh witch. And of all the witches in the world, he chose to target mine. I wasn't about to let him have her." The two smiled at each other, and Ember was surprised to see love in the witch's eyes.

"I did what I could to hide her," he said. "She escaped his attention for a while, thanks to my efforts and to your kindhearted yet very unlucky lantern. But Melichor was desperate. Not just any witch would do. He needed a powerful one.

"He sent Otherworlders in to raid her colony, and then he used terrible transformation spells to draw her out, draining his existing wife dry to do so. I couldn't intervene because of my deal with Melichor. When he finally found her and took her away, I chose to condescend, taking on this form and flesh, and followed her to the Otherworld. I had to give up a piece of myself, the most important piece, a secret one, in order to make it so. I—one of the greatest beings in either realm—was suddenly a nearly mortal, humble servant.

"Since then we've shared only stolen moments together. For decades, I've plotted and planned and dreamed of a way to steal her away from the true man you should call a monster. I watched him siphon away her energy drop by drop, abusing her until she could barely stand." His eyes shone with tears.

"You can't blame yourself, Monroe," the high witch said as she trembled.

Dr. Farragut took the high witch's hands in his. "I left her, though it nearly killed me to do so. To escape the Lord of the Otherworld's reach, I fled across the sea, only to find myself surrounded by ghosts wanting to destroy me. They were the accumulation of souls I'd collected over thousands of years, and my presence gave them the power they needed to coalesce. I was imprisoned in the form I'd assumed and couldn't fight them off. They'd overturned my boat, nearly drowning me, when Nestor came to my aid.

"Nestor deposited me on an island that just happened to have a few wild cats, but I was trapped there by the storm. Over time, Nestor brought me visitors and dragged in ships and technology that had been lost at sea. I tinkered and worked on the broken machines for years, always thinking of my witch and wondering how she fared."

Ember glanced at the ghost of Melichor. It was slowly drifting toward the cave. She thought of the ghost storm and how all the poor souls had just wanted to be freed. "Wait," she said to the departing ghost. "I can help you move on."

"Leave him!" Dr. Farragut cried, grabbing her arm. "He must be made to suffer for what he's done!"

"You forget, good Doctor, that the hundreds of ghosts who were floating above your island were there because you put them there. You are no more innocent than he."

"You misunderstand, little witch. I am a collector. It wasn't I who made dangerous bargains. My duty was merely to deal out the punishment those souls earned on their own."

"Be that as it may, I prefer to deal in mercy." Ember twisted out of his grasp and ran to the floating ghost, who paused, waiting for her.

Drawing from the power inside, Ember felt her limbs hum. She placed her hand on the ghost's shoulder, and his sad expression became one of contentment. He nodded to her and dissolved before her eyes. When she turned back, everyone was staring at her. The black cat jumped into her arms and meowed, nuzzling her.

"So it's true," the doctor said. "You've a strange sort of power. Witches don't have the ability to help ghosts pass. All this time I thought you had merely dissipated the ghost storm."

The high witch put her hand on the doctor's shoulder. "Monroe," she said. "The reason she can do that is because—"

Before she could finish, there was movement at the entrance to the cave, and Ember cried out in surprise. Graydon, Dev, and Finney zipped in on her brooms and mops, circled overhead, and landed next to Ember. A cloud of fog drifted over to the device, revealing the location of the invisible form of Yegor next to it.

"Thanks, Jack," Graydon said, dropping his broom. "I think I can take it from here." The werewolf's teeth and face elongated and his body erupted in fur as he sprang toward the shadowy figure of a man. Snarling, he bit Yegor's arm. Blood sprayed on the invisible man's body, and sand clung to the drops, making him partially visible. Finney shot a dozen revealing spells at the man while Graydon continued to tussle with him.

Ember watched Jack materialize and thought him such a lovely sight, she'd happily live beneath his bridge just to look at him every day and remember how close she'd come to losing him.

Jack stumbled at the sight of the Lord of the Otherworld's dead body, but he quickly recovered and lunged for the doctor. Rune and Dev followed suit, but the doctor clapped his hands and all the men, as well as Jack's pumpkin, were thrown back. Dev was the first to recover, but when he hurtled his body forward at preternatural speed, his skin steamed and grew red. He screamed and fell to his knees, clutching his head.

Finney made his way over to the device and began furiously winding levers and shifting nobs. The doctor shouted, "No!" and ran after him, pushing Finney away and quickly adjusting a switch before slamming down a lever.

"What happened?" Jack asked Ember, followed quickly by, "Are you injured?"

"No, I'm fine. But, Jack. The doctor . . . he's the boogeyman!"

"What?" Jack glanced at Rune, who confirmed it. He took a deep breath. "Then we've got to tread carefully."

A counter on the device began moving, and the machine hummed, building power. A satisfied doctor glanced at his witch as the cats nuzzled her. "It can't be stopped now," he said. "Five minutes and we'll have our peace, my dear."

"But don't they have to detonate together?" Finney asked, scrambling to his feet.

"Well, yes," Farragut answered. "This one is the trigger, and the other one blocks the signal that would affect Otherworlders."

"But Frank destroyed the other one," Finney declared.

The doctor screwed up his face in frustration but then relaxed. "Ah, well, then if you lot have destroyed the other device, I suppose everyone in the Otherworld will split from their souls too. Frank, you say? How did you manage to free him from my control?"

"Hardly seems the point at the moment, Doctor," Graydon said, shifting from werewolf to man, blood on his face, "if we're all about to die."

Ember scanned the sand and found a strange lump that she was sure was Yegor. The lump rose and fell, so she presumed the injured man was still alive.

"I figured out how to reboot Frank's heart!" Finney admitted.

"Clever. I truly like you, young man. But, Captain, you mean 'you.' *You're* all about to die. I can tie my witch to me just as a lantern is tied to his ember, and we can depart this realm—we just need your power, Ember. Come now, young witch; it's time. The device is counting down as we speak."

Both Jack and Rune stepped between them. "You'll have to go through us to get to her," Jack said boldly.

"If that is your wish," the doctor said with a smile. He waved his hand, and both lanterns were tossed aside.

"Ember!" Graydon pulled something from his broom: her other gun. He tossed it to her. She lifted the weapon.

The doctor laughed. "It didn't work on me before, and it won't work on me now."

"I'm not aiming at you," Ember said, and fired.

This time it was the spell of immobility. The doctor gasped as his fragile witch fell in his arms. She appeared dead immediately. "You shouldn't have done that," he threatened, his face turning dark.

CHAPTER 42

CAT GOT YOUR TONGUE?

Gently, the doctor laid his witch down and pounded his fist in the sand. Cats swirled around her, purring and nuzzling. It seemed they were nullifying the spell.

Interesting! Ember thought.

The doctor didn't seem to notice. When he stood, his eyes were blazing, and the air hummed. The clouds overhead scuttled away, as if they were the only ones with the sense to vacate the area. The sun sank, as if it too wanted to hide its face, and the ground vibrated with Farragut's footsteps as he approached Ember, hands raised.

She tried to fight using her power, throwing it at him in great bursts that wrenched her stomach, but they bounced off him like filmy bubbles and disintegrated. Graydon attacked too, but he hit some sort of invisible barrier that knocked him to the ground, unconscious. Clearly the doctor wasn't as feeble and mortal as he looked.

While Finney kept frantically trying to shut down the device,

Jack and his pumpkin, and Rune and his firefly, tried to use their light to blast the doctor, but he walked through their lantern light as if it was nothing to him, even though it destroyed all the vegetation around him. When Jack's pumpkin scowled and attacked the boogeyman on its own, it was thrust back. It rolled through the sand and spat out the offensive granules. Ember tried to escape, but the doctor lifted his hand and she was drawn back to him against her will.

"Enough fighting," Dr. Farragut said, pinning all the men to the ground with a thought. "I admire your spirit, Ember, but it's time to give in. You can't possibly win." He pulled out a stopwatch and checked the time. "There's less than a minute remaining, and you'll all be dead soon anyway. I'm sure you want your life to mean something. Isn't that right, young witch?"

Ember couldn't have answered even if she'd wanted to. Her body was stiff, bending to the doctor's will. He dragged her over to his witch, who was now stirring, thanks to the help of her cats. "M-Monroe?" she said.

"Shhh, dear one. The end is near. Soon we'll be together and nothing will ever keep us apart again."

Finney gave up. "The only way to stop the process is to blow up the device before the catalyst ignites the witch power and causes a chain reaction!"

Ignoring Finney, the doctor threw Ember down to the sand next to the high witch. On her other side, Jack struggled to move but was barely able to lift his arm.

The doctor placed one hand on Ember's forehead and his other on the frail witch. "No, Monroe," the high witch said, trying to shrug off his hand.

"It will be over soon," he crooned. "I promise. Just remain still." Neither Ember nor the high witch could move with Farragut controlling them.

Jack strained and managed to stretch out his fingers to touch Ember's. She looked at him with frightened eyes. Jack's pumpkin zoomed over them and cast its light on her and then on Jack.

"I . . . I love you, Ember," Jack said; then his eyes flicked up to his pumpkin. The light inside it sparked and cracked, turning red, then white, then ice blue. Finney was thrown back from the device by a thrust of magic and hit the sand hard. Suddenly, the pumpkin raced headlong toward the machine. It was still counting down, the little gears moving to five, four, three. . . . Then the pumpkin hit it and the light inside it erupted quickly.

Light encompassed the mechanism, circling it, growing brighter and brighter.

Dr. Farragut looked up. "No!" he cried as he tried to stop the pumpkin, but it was too late. The machine exploded with enough force to lift everyone off the ground and slam them back down.

Ember looked at Jack and screamed. His body was lifeless, his glassy eyes staring at her and his moonlight hair falling dully over his cheek. With shaking fingers, she touched his full lips, feeling for breath. There was none.

Ember began weeping uncontrollably. She felt she'd had her future torn from her, and all her fight left her body. She barely even noticed the feeble hand that clutched her arm. Through her tears, she saw the kind face of the high witch. "Don't despair," she said weakly.

"He saved the world," Ember said. "Both worlds."

"Jack was very brave," the high witch said. "I couldn't have chosen a better man for my daughter."

Both Ember and the doctor froze.

"D-daughter?" Ember said, swallowing.

"Daughter?" the doctor echoed, his face slackened.

The high witch nodded, her wrinkled mouth curling softly. "Do you see now, Monroe? This must stop." She had finally got his attention. She put her hand on his bulky chest as he helped her to her feet. "Didn't you wonder why Ember has the power to release ghosts— *your* ghosts? No other witch has ever had the ability to do that."

Ember stood on shaky legs, her eyes wide as she studied the high witch, trying to find herself in the woman's form. She thought her nose might be the same, but the woman's body was so broken down and her skin so wrinkled and saggy, it was hard to make out the shape of her face. Then she looked at the doctor and saw absolutely no similarity. Perhaps the witch was mistaken.

"Her power is comparable to yours," the witch said. "You have the ability to split and imprison, to doom ghosts to gather in great storms, to steal souls who have bargained away their right to one through their own evil actions." She gestured to Ember. "She chooses to use her power to unite and to heal and to send a soul to the place it belongs. Do you not see it?"

"No," the doctor said. "Frankly, I don't." He took hold of the high witch's hands. "Eleanor, are you certain of this?"

"Eleanor?" Ember said. "I thought your name was Loren."

She shook her head. "Loren is the name Melichor gave me. He called all his witches Loren. He said it was easier to remember all his wives' names if they were the same, and he liked how Loren Lockett sounded." She turned to the doctor. "While I explain, I think Ember needs to capture her lantern before he wanders off. Let her save him, Monroe. You of all people know what it's like to be separated from the one you love."

The doctor nodded distractedly.

Rune had also gotten to his feet and was staring down at Jack's body. *Well,* he thought. *This is certainly an interesting turn of events.* It explained a lot. Ember was the offspring of a powerful witch and the boogeyman. Who knew what untapped power the girl possessed? He determined that it would be the wiser course to wait and see how things unfolded.

Far away, down the beach, Ember saw a ghost floating slowly away. "Jack!" she shouted.

The ghost paused.

"Jack! Come back!" She darted past the others and ran down the beach. He turned to her and looked at her with sad eyes. When she reached him, she was afraid to touch him, fearing that he would move on like the others. "Will you please just follow me?" she begged. "You need to hear what the high witch is saying."

He lifted his hand as if to caress her face, but she swiftly moved back, not wanting him to disappear altogether. Jack's mouth curled in a miserable imitation of a smile. "I've been following you around since you were a little girl," he said. "I don't want to haunt you, Ember O'Dare. As much as I want to be with you, you deserve to have a life. I would only get in the way of that."

Turning, he began drifting again, and when she ran after him, he floated into the air, too high for her to reach. "Jack!" she shouted. "Jack, you get back here right now!" Desperate, she ran up the beach and grabbed the nearest broom. The black cat was curled in a ball on top of the straw. She tried to nudge it off, but it refused to budge. "Fine," she said. "Just don't blame me if you fall off." Hopping on the broom, she steered it using witch power and headed up into the sky, chasing her Jack o' the Lantern. The cat behind her hissed and arched its back, claws digging into the straw as it held on for dear life.

When she reached him and he still wouldn't turn around, her face grew dark as new abilities, those of a boogeyman, sprang to life. Sparks lit beneath her skin, and time sped forward around them as she drew upon powers she didn't even know she had. The setting sun was gone, and the moon rose rapidly until it framed Jack and Ember in its ghostly light. Ember cast out her hand, and slowly Jack's ghost returned, straining to get away from both her and the hissing cat on the broom.

"It's no use," he said as she spun him around in the air, tethering his soul to her own. "My pumpkin is gone. I've lost my ember."

"No," the witch said, her voice deep and resounding as she floated on her broomstick, "you haven't."

CHAPTER 43

EMBERS

As quickly as possible, Dr. Farragut—or the boogeyman, or Ember's father—rushed everyone safely back to his island. Now that he knew he wasn't the only one of his kind, that he had a daughter, he couldn't imagine destroying her, even if it meant saving his love. He hoped he could teach Ember the ways of a boogeyman quickly enough that she could help save her mother. He generously freed a rather angry Delia. Then it was time for Jack.

The doctor cleared the room of cats, and Jack's ghost drifted in through the open window. Then Farragut helped his daughter, teaching her to channel her energy so that *she* could bind Jack to his body, reversing what had been done to him, and learning in the process one of her father's greatest powers of creation. It drained both of them to do so. "It always takes more energy to join and build than to destroy, my dear," he told her afterward.

In the days that followed, Rune stayed close and observant. It was his belief that there was much to learn from the boogeyman.

He took on the role of Ember's personal bodyguard so he could be there for every lesson.

For days, Jack slept. The doctor told her he suspected it was a normal reaction. Jack was human now, after all, and hadn't slept properly in centuries. She held his hand and prayed that the boogeyman was right.

Eventually, he did begin to wake, rising only long enough to drink some water and eat a little food before falling asleep again. Meanwhile, Ember got to know her mother. She discovered that when her mother's village had been attacked, she'd saved Ember by giving her to a will-o'-the-wisp who owed her a favor. Then she sent familiars—hers were cats—to watch over Ember as the years passed.

The sprite took care of the baby, slowing her age for decades, until she could do no more for the child. Ember had grown too big to keep in the forest, and to hold her development back further would only harm the girl. So the wisp found an aging woman with no children, one with kind feelings toward witches and an affinity for cats, and cast a spell.

The cats who watched over Ember reported all this to her mother, crossing the barrier, and quietly passing on news of her daughter.

Everything was fine for Ember in the mortal world until Monroe caught wind of her, literally. He used his powers to summon her, a strong compulsion for any witch, but one undeniable to his own daughter. It was true that Eleanor sent Dev after her daughter. She'd wanted to meet Ember, but was also desperate to keep her away from Melichor, the Lord of the Otherworld. Once Ember was in the Otherworld, Melichor's spies learned of her, and Eleanor had to warn Dev to keep her away.

Meanwhile, Farragut was maneuvering events to unfold the way he wanted as well. He bribed Payne to send the vampire and his charge in the direction of his island. He hadn't known that the witch was his daughter, or that he even had one.

Ember had no memory of the decades in the forest or of the will-o'-the-wisp, but she vowed that when her mother was strong enough, they would seek her out, as well as Flossie, the sweet old woman who'd raised her, and thank them together. Eleanor smiled sadly at this, but Ember could think of no better place for her aunt to retire than on a tropical island paradise surrounded by dozens of cats.

Soon Delia, Graydon, and Dev departed in the doctor's gifted skyship. Dev had finally given up on trying to sway Ember in matters of romance, though his blood still sang for him to locate the one woman he could love and give his whole heart to. He swore with a final vampire vow that he was in earnest about leaving her to fashion her own happily-ever-after. This time Ember didn't taste his blood. She hugged him and then Delia and Graydon. They were gone before Jack got to say goodbye.

It had become obvious to all that there was no separating Ember from her lantern, though technically, Jack was no longer a lantern. He had become fully mortal again and found he didn't mind it so much, especially when he had Ember for a nursemaid. Still, he did admit, he missed his pumpkin sorely.

The power in the Otherworld was rapidly dwindling, and with the Lord of the Otherworld dead, the people looked to the high witch for help, so Ember went to the capital with her mother. Once they were ensconced, they were able to boost the fuel stores for a while, but the energy shortage appeared to be irremediable. A new solution needed to be discovered, and soon. They needed the witches back.

Finney volunteered to head back to the mortal world and send whatever witches he could find to the Otherworld. Ember was nearly devastated to see him go, and cried for a solid hour. But Finney promised to cross over every once in a while for long visits, now that she and her mother had lightened the restrictions on passing between realms.

Once he was gone and everything settled, Ember tried again to heal her mother. Years fell away from her face, but as soon as Ember's hands lifted, they piled back on. Ember wiped a tear from her cheek. "I can't do it."

"Try again," Jack answered softly.

"It's no use," Dr. Farragut said. "Her body has been taxed too much. If only I wasn't limited to this form, I could release her from these shackles and speed away with her."

Ember's mother patted the doctor's hand. "It is enough to be reunited with you and with my daughter," she said. "This time we've had together has been wonderful."

"What holds you to your form, Doctor?" Jack asked.

"My name," he said. "When I changed into this . . . this flabby body, I lost my name. I wrote it down before I condescended, giving it up so I wouldn't be discovered, but I don't remember where I left it."

Determined, Ember began again, this time pouring as much energy as she could into her mother. The lights overhead dimmed and flickered and the woman's dry, brittle hair turned from gray to sandy blond to platinum. Her skin tightened and her lips turned glossy and rosy, her cheeks shiny. Still Ember strained, her slender arms trembling as her mother became lissome and beautiful.

Jack gasped as he recognized her young face. "Eleanor?"

Ember's eyes flew open and she drew her hands back. For a

moment, Ember thought she'd won, that her mother was healed, but to her dismay, the years came back, slower this time; it was obvious that she'd failed again.

"Didn't you know Eleanor was Ember's mother?" the doctor asked Jack.

"I knew she was a witch, but you've never called her Eleanor, and Ember's last name is O'Dare, not Dare."

"I thought you'd forgotten me," the witch explained. "And I didn't want to burden your mind further. We kept the name Loren so as not to confuse the people here. You were unconscious for most of our time on the island. The 'O' in O'Dare was given to Ember by the will-o'-the-wisp." She smiled softly as her gleaming hair became spare and stringy again. "She wanted to give Ember a little piece of herself and shared the 'O.'"

"Doctor," Jack said. "Did you happen to leave your name near a skeleton?"

His eyes widened in hope. "Why, yes. It was near Eleanor's village. I fashioned myself a body from the pinky bone of a man who'd been killed."

"Then . . . then I think I know your name!" Jack said excitedly.

"What is it?" Ember asked.

"It's Croatoan."

"Croatoan," the doctor echoed, the name bouncing around the walls of the room. All at once a powerful wind whipped around the group. They heard a roar, and before their eyes, the doctor's body melted away. Sparks of energy swirled and coalesced, and then a large creature stood before them. His skin was red, his arms and chest thick and strapping.

Gone was the portly, bowlegged man with combed-back hair. In his place stood a mountain of a being with hair the color of midnight that hung in long layers of glossy curls. A widow's peak marked the center of his forehead, and his dark eyes gleamed with mischief.

Jack could see the same defiant chin on Ember, and the same hard sparkle in her eye when she was irritated. Croatoan took Eleanor by the hand, and the years fell away from her like molting feathers. She breathed in deeply and tossed her luxuriant hair over her shoulder. The couple embraced, and the boogeyman clutched the diminutive witch's hand in his. It engulfed hers completely.

Ember's father was intimidating, but he smiled at Jack, and the former lantern almost winced at the brightness of his teeth. That such a being had been trapped in the form of the doctor for so many years was quite a feat.

"You've freed me," he said in a booming voice. "In exchange, I will grant you a gift. Name your heart's desire and it's yours."

"I . . ." Jack swallowed nervously. "I suppose, then, that my heart's desire is to be with Ember always, and for the two of you to give us your blessing."

"Of course you have our blessing," Ember's lovely mother said.

"Yes," Croatoan agreed. "But as to the matter of being with her always, I'm afraid that is impossible. I told you that I am nearly five thousand years old. Ember is destined to live at least half that long. With you being a mortal, long years of loneliness stretch before her. Unless . . ."

"Unless?" Jack said.

"Unless you are willing to become a lantern again."

"I'm willing," Jack said. "But my pumpkin is gone."

"You don't need a pumpkin," Croatoan replied with a laugh. "All you need is an Ember. Fortunately for you, you already have one. And this time, you'll only be chained to her." The red-skinned man leaned forward and clapped him on the back. "Are you certain it's what you want? It could very well be that she'll be a harsher task-master than Rune and I ever were."

Jack turned to Ember with a soft smile and knelt before her. Taking her hands in his, he said, "I can't think of a better person to be shackled to for eternity."

"So be it." The boogeyman slapped his hands and a portion of Jack's soul leapt from his body, turned to a pinprick of white light, and sank into Ember's heart, where it would stay as long as they both lived.

EPILOGUE

HALLOWEEN

It was Finney who started the tradition. He'd shared many stories with the villagers about his friends, and they were welcomed with open arms.

That first year, he picked a day when the fall leaves swept the ground and the scarecrows trembled in the fields. It was always Ember's favorite time of year. Finney welcomed Dev, Delia, Graydon, Frank, Ember, and Jack to the village with a feast and a bonfire to celebrate how they'd saved the mortal world and the Otherworld from the device that had almost destroyed them.

Ember rode in on her broomstick, bringing her aunt a new kitten that trembled on the back. Jack summoned Shadow and rode him down the main street, the stallion's nostrils shooting steam. When Frank saw that he frightened the children, he gave them rides on his broad shoulders to win them over. Ember gave them some of the chocolate candies she always kept in her pockets, while Jack showed off his skeleton. Graydon changed to a wolf and howled at the moon, and Delia and Dev bared their fangs.

The next year, the children waited for them with little pails for treats and dressed up in costumes so they'd look like the Otherworlders. Ember and Jack cried when they saw that Finney had asked everyone to carve pumpkins and light them to mark the path from the crossroad to the town. The tradition caught on, and soon crossroads all over the world opened on that one night and the mortal realm was haunted by ghosts, goblins, witches, werewolves, and vampires.

Jack became known as the father of lights, though he left the job of head lantern to Rune, who had finally given up his quest to take over the Otherworld after Jack caught him trying to put an onyx ring on Ember's finger. Jack peered into his former mentor's soul and snapped his fingers. The firefly earring where Rune kept his ember flew to Jack's hand.

"The boogeyman gave me an extra gift when he made me a lantern again," Jack said. "I can read thoughts as well as souls. You know that Ember has the power to destroy you, but we have agreed that if you remain true to us, you may stay. The minute you conspire, however, I will summon your light and Ember will send it on. Do you understand?"

"I do."

Rune immediately knelt, agreeing to the terms, and became the most loyal of lanterns. At least, that was what he wanted everyone to believe.

Strangely enough, Rune was remembered as more of a pirate than a lantern. Still, he loved seeing children dressed up as swarthy pirates on the holiday. Rumors flew that Yegor had lived and escaped to the human world, but no one ever heard from him again. Delia and Graydon actually did settle down in their later years, Graydon becoming a chocolatier, much to Ember's delight.

Finney was indeed apprenticed to the boogeyman, who was happy to teach him everything he knew, though Croatoan only appeared in Finney's dreams. Together they were working on a very promising piece of technology that could capture aetheric energy from the natural stores that existed around the Otherworld island where the doctor had once made his home.

Frank became captain of the skyship Dr. Farragut bequeathed to Graydon. Finney personally created several upgrades for him and even introduced Frank to the half woman, half automaton he'd created, who eventually became his bride. Together they flew their skyship until it was no longer able to lift off the ground.

Dev eventually headed to the mortal world, searching for what he felt was missing in his life. Ember heard he finally settled in a place called Transylvania.

As for Ember, she kept her broomstick, black cat, and witch hat close, but her lantern closer.

Ember and Jack are still alive today, and every so often, they make an appearance. If you look carefully at the harvest moon on a Halloween night, you might see the shadow of a witch being chased by a rather enthusiastic pumpkin.

If you loved *The Lantern's Ember*,

turn the page for a look at the first book

in Colleen Houck's REAWAKENED series!

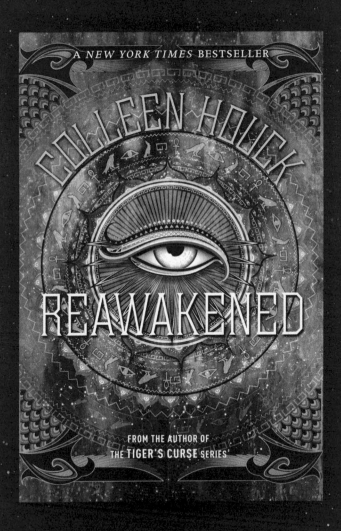

A *NEW YORK TIMES* BESTSELLER

COLLEEN HOUCK

REAWAKENED

FROM THE AUTHOR OF
THE TIGER'S CURSE SERIES

In the great city of Itjtawy, the air was thick and heavy, reflecting the mood of the men in the temple, especially the countenance of the king and the terrible burden he carried in his heart. As King Heru stood behind a pillar and looked upon the gathered people, he wondered if the answer his advisers and priests had given was their salvation or instead, their utter destruction.

Even should the offering prove successful, the people would surely suffer a terrible loss, and for him, personally, there was no way to recover from it.

Despite the simmering heat of the day, he shivered in the temple's shadow, surely a bad omen. Uneasily, he ran a hand over his smoothly shaven head and let the curtain fall. To quiet his nerves, he began to pace the temple's smooth, polished dais and ponder his choices.

King Heru knew that even should he defy the proposed demands, he needed to do something drastic to appease the fearsome god Seth. If only there was a way out, he thought. Putting the proposal to the people was something no king had ever done before.

A king held his position precisely because it was his right, his duty, to see to the needs of his people, and a king who could not make a wise decision, however difficult, was ripe for deposing. Heru knew that by allowing the people to decide, he proved himself to be a weakling, a coward, and yet there was no other outlet he could see that would allow him to live with the consequences.

Twenty years before King Heru's time, all the people of Egypt were suffering. Years of terrible drought further complicated by devastating sandstorms and plague had almost destroyed civilization. Marauders and old enemies took advantage of Egypt's weakness. Several of the oldest settlements had been wiped out completely.

In a desperate act, King Heru invited the surviving leaders of the major cities to come to his home. King Khalfani of Asyut and King Nassor of Waset agreed to a one-week summit, and the three of them, along with their most powerful priests, disappeared behind closed doors.

The results of that meeting had been a decision that tipped the balance in the pantheon of the gods. Each city worshipped a different god—the residents of Asyut, which played host to the most famous magicians, were devoted to Anubis; those of Waset, known for weaving and shipbuilding, to Khonsu; and King Heru's people, skilled in pottery and stone cutting, worshipped Amun-Ra and his son, Horus. The kings had been convinced by their priests that their patron gods had abandoned them and that they should come together as one to make offerings to appease a new god, namely, the dark god, Seth, in order to secure the safety and well-being of the people.

And so they did. That year the rains came in abundance. The Nile overflowed its banks, creating fertile lands for planting. Livestock flourished, tripling in number. Women gave birth the following year to more healthy babies than had ever been recorded. Even more astonishing was when the queens of each city, who had been the most outspoken against the deity change, were appeased when discovering that they, too, had conceived.

As the three queens each gave their husbands a healthy son, they acknowledged their blessings, especially the wife of Heru, who had never had a child and was well past her bearing years. Though in their hearts, the new mothers still paid homage to the gods of old, they agreed that from that time forward they would never speak ill of the dark one. The people rejoiced.

The people prospered.

The three kings wept with gratitude.

In an age of peace and harmony, the sons of each queen were raised as brothers in the hope that they would someday unite all of Egypt under one ruler. The worship of Seth became commonplace, and the old temples were essentially abandoned.

The sons considered each king a father and each queen a mother. Their kings loved them. Their people loved them. They were the hope of the future, and nothing could keep the three of them apart.

Now, even now, on the darkest day of their fathers' lives, the three young men stood together, waiting for the kings to make a surprise announcement.

In a moment, the three kings would ask the unthinkable. A favor that no king, no father, should ask of his son. It made King Heru's blood run cold and left him with vivid nightmarish dreams of his heart being found unworthy when weighed against the feather of truth in the final judgment. The three kings stepped into the glaring sunlight that reflected off the white stone of the temple. King Heru stood in the center while the other two men took their place at his side. King Heru was not only the tallest of the three but also the most skilled speaker. Raising his hands, he began, "My people, and visiting citizens from our dearly loved cities upriver, as you know, we, your kings, have been in conference with our priests to determine why the river, which has lapped our shores so gently for the last twenty years, does not flourish as it should in this most important season. Our chief priest, Runihura, has said that the god Seth, the one we have worshipped wholeheartedly these past years, demands a new sacrifice."

King Heru's own son took a step forward. "We will sacrifice whatever you think is necessary, Father," he said.

The king held up his hand to quiet his son and gave him a sad smile before turning back to the crowd. "The thing that Seth asks this year as a sacrifice is not a prized bull, bushels of grain, fine fabrics, or even the best of our fruits." Heru paused as he waited for the people to quiet. "No, Runihura has said that Seth has given us much, and for the things we have received we must return that which is most precious.

"The god Seth demands that three young men of royal blood be sacrificed to him and that they serve him indefinitely in the afterlife." Heru sighed heavily. "If this does not happen, he vows to rain destruction upon all of Egypt."

House of Muses

"Fifteen fifty," the driver demanded in a heavy accent.

"Do you take credit?" I responded politely.

"No. No cards. Machine's broken."

Giving a slight smile to the heavily browed eyes staring at me in the rearview mirror, I pulled out my wallet. As many times as I'd ridden in a New York City cab, I'd never gotten used to the attitude of the taxi drivers; it irked me every time. Still, it was either that or our family's personal driver, who would shadow me around, reporting every move I made to my parents. All things considered, I much preferred independence.

I handed the driver a twenty and opened the door. Almost instantly, he sped off, leaving me struggling to maintain my footing while coughing in the cloud of gray exhaust he left behind.

"Jerk," I mumbled as I smoothed my cropped trousers and then bent down to adjust a strap on my Italian leather sandals.

"Do you need help, miss?" asked a young man nearby.

Standing up, I gave him the once-over. His department store jeans, I ♥ NEW YORK tee, and scruffy boy-next-door appearance instantly told me he wasn't from the city. No self-respecting New Yorker, at least none

I knew, would be caught dead in an NYC tee. He wasn't bad-looking, but when I considered his likely determinate stay in the city coupled with the fact that he would obviously not be parental approved, I surmised that any further dialogue would be a waste of time. Not my type.

I hadn't figured out exactly what my type was yet, but I figured I'd know it when I saw it.

"No thanks." I smiled. "I'm good."

With a no-nonsense stride, I headed toward the steps of the Metropolitan Museum of Art. The girls at my school would think I was an idiot for passing up a cute boy/potential boyfriend—or at the very least, a fun distraction.

It was easier not to make any promises I didn't plan on keeping, especially with a boy who hadn't met any of my requirements for the perfect guy. The list wasn't complete yet, but I'd been adding to it for as long as I'd been old enough to be interested in boys. Above all else, I was careful and thoughtful about my choices.

Even though I was very picky, wore only designer clothes, and had a monthly allowance bigger than what most people my age earned in a year, I was by no means a snob. My parents had certain expectations of me, and the money was used as a means to fulfill them. I was always taught that the image one portrays, though certainly not one hundred percent accurate, was an indicator of the type of person you were. Despite my efforts to find evidence that this wasn't always the case, among the people I went to school and hung out with, it often was.

My father, a successful international finance lawyer, always said, "Bankers trust the suit first and the man second," his version of "Dress for success." He and my mother, who spent most of her waking hours in her skyscraper office at one of the largest media companies in the city, dictating orders to her personal assistant, had drilled into me that image was everything.

Mostly, I was left on my own as long as I did what they expected, which included attending various functions, portraying myself as a doting daughter, and getting straight As at my all-girls private school. And, of course, not dating the wrong type of boy, which I accomplished by not dating at all. In turn, I was given a generous allowance and the freedom to explore New York. A freedom I cherished, especially today, the first day of spring break.

The Met was one of my favorite hideouts. Not only did my parents approve of the institution—a definite plus—but it was a great place to people-watch. I wasn't sure what I wanted to do in the future, but this was the week I had to figure it out. I'd already been accepted to a number of parent-approved universities. Mother and Father—they hated being called Mom and Dad—wanted me to major in something that would make them proud, like medicine, business, or politics, but none of those really interested me.

What I really enjoyed was studying people. People of the past, like the ones I read about at the Met, or even just the people walking around in New York City. In fact, I kept a little book full of notes on the most interesting people I saw.

How I would turn this admittedly strange hobby into a career, I had no idea. My parents would never approve of my becoming a counselor, mostly because they believed a person should be able to take charge of their own mental health by merely willing themselves to overcome any obstacle they might face. Consorting with those they considered beneath their station wasn't something they encouraged, and yet becoming a counselor was the one career path that made the most sense to me.

Any time I thought about the future, my parents came to mind. What they had planned was a constant drumming on my consciousness, and if I entertained the idea of deviating from their plans even an iota, I was filled with guilt, which effectively choked the life out of any little seeds of rebellion.

One of those seeds was where I applied to college. Technically, it wasn't a mutiny, since they knew about it. I was allowed to apply to places that interested me as long as I sent in the paperwork to the ones my parents approved of as well. Of course they'd been thrilled when I was accepted to them all, but there was no doubt that they were pushing me in a certain direction.

Now spring break of my senior year was finally here, a time most teens loved, and I was dreading it. If only everything didn't have to be decided right now. Mother and Father had given me until the end of the week to choose my college and my major. Starting college as undecided was not an option.

Stopping at the counter, I flashed my lifetime membership card and swiftly walked through the roped entrance.

"Hello, Miss Young," said the old guard with a smile. "Here all day?"

I shook my head. "Half day, Bernie. Meeting the girls for lunch."

"Should I be watching for them?" he asked.

"No. I'll be alone today."

"Very good," he said, securing the rope behind me and returning to help with the line of tourists. There were definitely some perks to having parents who donated annually to the Met. And since I was an only child, I was lucky enough to receive the full "benefit" of their monetary donations, wisdom, and experience. They were loving, too, if love looks like a stiff upper lip of pride and approval. But I was often lonely, and at times felt trapped.

Whenever I started to feel like I needed a real mom type to bake cookies with, I asked to visit my paternal grandmother, who lived on a small farm in Iowa, a woman my parents checked in on exactly once every two months. They visited her annually, though they stayed in a nearby city hotel and worked from their room while I stayed on the farm with her overnight.

Speaking of grandmas, a very interesting-looking older woman was seated on a bench ahead of me and staring at one of my favorite pictures, *She Never Told Her Love*, by Henry Peach Robinson. The photograph was controversial. Critics said it was indecent and indelicate for a photographer to capture a dying woman in print, but I found the photo dramatically romantic. It was said that the photographer was trying to illustrate a scene from Shakespeare's *Twelfth Night*. I knew the quote on the picture's description by heart.

SHE NEVER TOLD HER LOVE,
BUT LET CONCEALMENT,
LIKE A WORM I' THE BUD,
FEED ON HER DAMASK CHEEK.
TWELFTH NIGHT, 2.4.110–12

Consumption. That was supposedly what the woman in the photograph was dying of. I reasoned it was appropriate. Dying of a broken heart must feel like a type of consumption. I imagined it to be a squeezing pain that wrapped itself around a person like a boa constrictor, tightening more and more, crushing the body until there was nothing left but a dry husk.

As fascinated as I was by the photo, I was even more fascinated by the woman who sat staring at it. Her cheeks sagged, as did her heavy body. Strands of limp gray hair hung from a messy bun. She clutched a worn cane, which meant it was well used, and she wore a floral-patterned, butterfly-collared dress (circa 1970). Her feet were planted shoulder width apart in thick-soled Velcro-closed sneakers. The woman was leaning forward, resting her hands on the edge of the cane, her chin propped on her hands as she studied the picture.

For the better part of an hour, I sat at a distance, watching her and sketching her silhouette in my notebook. At one point, a tear ran down her face and she finally moved, digging into a giant crocheted bag for a tissue. What caused her tears? I wondered. Did she have a long-lost love of her own? Someone she had never shared her feelings with? The possibilities and questions swirled in my head as I adjusted my backpack and headed down the hall, shoes clicking on the marble floor. Noticing a familiar guard, I stopped.

"Hi, Tony."

"And how are you today, Miss Young?"

"I'm well. Hey, listen. I need to do some serious work. Is there a less-trafficked place around here that I can go to before I meet my friends for lunch? The people are too distracting."

"Hmm." Tony rubbed his chin and I heard the bristly sandpaper sound that meant he hadn't shaved that morning.

"The Egyptian wing is roped off," he said. "They're adding some new pieces. But they shouldn't be in there today. The boss lady is at a conference, and nothing in this museum moves without her."

"Do you think I could go in there and sit? I promise not to touch anything. I just need a quiet spot."

After a brief frown of consideration, his brows drew apart and he smiled. "All right. Just make sure you're careful. Stay out of view of the tourists, or they might get the idea to follow you in."

"Thanks, Tony."

"You're welcome. Come back and see me again when you get a chance."

"Will do," I said, and headed toward the special-exhibitions exit, then turned back, "Hey, Tony, there's an old woman over by the photography exhibit. Can you check on her in a little while? She's been there a long time."

"I will, Miss Lilliana."

"Bye."

I sped past the wall of photographs and headed downstairs to the main floor. The Medieval Art and the Hall of Cloisters, full of tapestries, statues, carvings, swords, crosses, and jewels, led to the museum store and then, finally, to the Egyptian wing.

When no one was looking, I slipped under the fabric rope. Despite the air-conditioning, the dust from thousands of years ago had a sharp enough tang to be noticeable. Perhaps the recent remodeling of the exhibit had released centuries of dust into the air, giving the effect of old things being stirred to life.

The overhead lights were off, but sun came through the large windows and lit up displays as I continued. Tens of thousands of artifacts were housed in a couple dozen rooms, each room focusing on one era. I felt adrift in a black ocean of history, surrounded by little glass boxes that offered fading glimpses of time gone by.

Displays of cosmetics boxes, canopic jars, statues of gods and goddesses, funerary papyrus, and carved blocks from actual temples, all gleaming with hidden stories of their own, captured my attention. It was as if the artifacts were simply waiting for someone to come along and blow the sandstone grit of time from their surfaces.

A sparkling bird caught my attention. I'd never seen it before and wondered if it was part of the new display or just on rotation. The rendering, a beautifully made golden falcon that represented the Egyptian god Horus, was called *Horus the Gold*.

After finding a cozy corner lit well enough for me to see, I sat with my back against the wall, turning to a blank sheet in my notebook to list all possible majors and major/minor combinations in groupings my parents would approve of. I was matching up my top three choices with their universities when I heard a scrape.

Wondering if a tourist had followed me in, I listened carefully for a few minutes. Nothing. This wing of the museum was as silent as a tomb. Smirking at my own stupid cliché, I went back to my notes and examined a glossy college brochure.

Before I made it through the first page, there was a thumping sound, followed by the same scraping noise. Though I considered myself a rational person, not easily frightened, a chill ran from my scalp down the length of my spine, as if icy fingers were caressing my vertebrae.

I set down my pencil and notebook carefully, trying to not make any sounds of my own, and listened with increasing alarm to the scrapes, scuffs, and distinctly nonhuman groans coming from the other side of the wall. Someone or something was definitely there. Calling forth my sensible mind to dispel my fear, I considered that perhaps the sounds were being made by an animal.

An eerie moan made my hands tremble, and the sight of my shaking fingers steeled me. I was being silly.

"Hello?" I ventured quietly. "Is someone there?"

I stood and took a few steps forward. The sounds abruptly ceased and my heart stilled. Was someone hiding? A museum employee would have answered me.

Sucking in a shaky breath, I rounded the corner only to come face to face with a wall of plastic. *This must be the section they're working on,* I thought. It was too dark to make out any shapes inside the room, so I stood there for a full minute gathering my courage.

I ran my fingers along the thick plastic lining until I found an opening, gasping when I saw a figure staring back at me, not inches from where I stood. But the frightened girl clutching the plastic drape was just me: her slightly wavy, product-enhanced, long brown hair, pale skin, and white designer blouse now marked with dust. Yep, me. The tile beneath the large artifact read ANCIENT COPPER MIRROR. I shook my head as I tried to make out what else was in the room.

The polished floor was protected by a heavy drop cloth, which was covered with sawdust, and several boards, cut in various shapes, lay haphazardly on the floor. I used one to prop open the plastic curtain, taking advantage of whatever meager light I could get, and moved deeper into the room.

Dark shapes and statues filled makeshift shelves, with stacked crates blocking every path. Now that I knew this shipment was so recent, I rationalized that what I'd heard was most likely a rat or a mouse making its home in one of the boxes. That would explain the silence since I'd come in.

I saw nothing that looked out of place in a museum. A box of tools here, a circular saw there. Opened crates filled with Egyptian treasures resting on the straw. True to my word, I didn't touch any of the pieces, and moved through the space carefully and quietly until a golden light behind some boxes caught my eye. I let out a small gasp as I came upon an enormous sarcophagus.

The lid, resting at an angle on the lower half of the coffin, was breathtaking. As I focused on all the little details—the handsome carved face, with polished green stones for eyes, the crook and flail he held cross-ways on his chest, the precious gold details that meant he was likely someone of importance—my fingers itched for my pencil and notebook.

Right away I noticed the patterns of three—three birds, three gods, three sets of wings, three bands on the arms. I wondered what they signified and began coming up with possible scenarios as I continued exploring. The packing slip on the coffin-sized crate nearby read:

UNKNOWN MUMMY
DISCOVERED 1989
VALLEY OF THE KINGS
EGYPT

Despite my fascination with the upcoming exhibit, I didn't notice anything out of the ordinary. No rat tails or droppings that I could see. No squeaking mouse hiding in a corner. No grave robbers or cursed mummies. Not even any museum employees.

As I turned to leave, I looked down and suddenly realized two things: first, the straw-filled sarcophagus didn't contain a mummy, and second, there was a set of footprints other than my own in the sawdust, ones made by two bare feet, and they led *away* from the coffin.

An intense curiosity took hold of me, and ignoring strong reservations, I followed the footprints. They led me on a path between boxes and crates until I met a dead end. No climactic movie music was triggered. No rancid scents of decay or death assaulted my nose. No creepy monster leered at me from the darkness.

Recognizing I'd let my imagination get the best of me, I began making my way back toward the plastic curtain. I was passing the copper mirror when a hand shot out of the darkness and locked on my arm. My choked scream echoed, the shriek bouncing off relics. The golden gods and stony statues kept their icy eyes forward, remaining as still and dead as everything around them.

Stranger in a Strange Land

The hand, which was extremely warm and not covered in ancient mummy wrappings, let go the instant I screamed. I dashed through the plastic curtain and around the wall to grab the can of pepper spray I kept in my bag. I stood there, can aimed, finger on the trigger, as the bare feet that were poking out beneath the curtain retreated into the darkness.

The sound of rummaging soon became obvious as the mysterious person began cracking open boxes. Something, most likely a box, crashed to the floor, and a metallic ringing indicated that a precious object of some kind had also been heedlessly dropped.

"I'm warning you. I'm armed," I threatened.

Whoever was in there paused and said a few words I didn't understand before they went back to whatever it was they were doing.

"What was that? What did you say?" I asked. When they didn't respond, I tried another tack. *"Qui êtes-vous? ¿Quién es usted?"* The only response was a grunt of frustration and the unmistakable sound of a crate being tossed aside.

"Look, I don't know who you are or what you're doing in this exhibit," I said, switching back to English while I knelt and threw my papers into my bag, "but you really shouldn't be in there."

Hoisting my bag over my shoulder without taking the time to zip it, I kept my eyes trained on the sheets of plastic ahead while inching toward the entrance. I hid behind the displays until I reached the main walkway, still holding up the pepper spray in case the stranger jumped out at me. When the plastic sheet came into view, I scanned the area for a sinister shape, but nothing emerged from the closed-off section.

Was the person hiding? Was I being stalked? "Please come out and explain yourself," I called bravely. Keeping my back to the wall, I waited for an answer.

What I should have done was leave and report what was happening to the security guards, but as I stood there, curiosity overwhelmed me and I couldn't. If the person had wanted to attack me, they already had had ample opportunity.

Perhaps he or she was lost. What if it was a transient who had wandered into the exhibit and was trying to catch a nap? Maybe it was an employee. Maybe they were hurt. I lowered my aching arm and slowly walked back toward the plastic curtain.

"Hello? Do you need help?" I ventured. I didn't sound as confident as I had hoped.

I heard a sigh as someone came toward me. Even though I was no longer pointing the can of pepper spray, I was still clutching it, nervously running my forefinger in little circles over the trigger.

"Who are you?" I asked again quietly, more to express the thought out loud than because I expected an answer.

A hand grasped the curtain, pushing it aside as the object of both my fear and curiosity stepped through, mumbling an assortment of words that sounded very much like expletives in another language. Stopping just outside the curtain, he—it was most definitely a he—let the plastic fall and faced me with an irritated expression.

Though we were in the darkest part of the exhibit, I could clearly make out the pleated white skirt that ended just at his knees and the wide expanse of a tanned and very bare chest. His bare feet were covered with sawdust. He seemed young, maybe just a few years older than me, yet his head was bald.

Crossing muscular arms over his wide chest, he boldly looked me up and down and I got the feeling that he found me both surprising and disappointing. "Stay back," I said, raising the can of pepper spray and feeling like an idiot for getting into this situation. He just raised an eyebrow and smirked, seeming to taunt me.

Jabbing a finger toward me, he uttered something that sounded like a command.

"I'm sorry. I don't understand you," I answered.

Noticeably frustrated, he repeated himself, more slowly this time, as if he were talking to an imbecile.

I answered back just as slowly, first gesturing to myself, "I," then shaking my head, "don't understand," and finally pointing at him, "you."

Crying out in exasperation, he threw his hands into the air and kept them there. At that exact moment, the overhead lights came on. A little squeak escaped my mouth as I got my first real glimpse of the guy I'd assumed had been living with the relics. He was definitely *not* a transient.

Who are *you?* I wondered as I studied the person, who was not a man and yet not a teen. He seemed . . . timeless. Hooded hazel eyes, at that moment more green than brown, beneath a strong brow pinned me with a gaze that was both intelligent and almost predatory. I felt like a mouse looking up at a swooping falcon, knowing death loomed but utterly unable to look away from the beauty of it.

His physical splendor was undeniable: brooding eyes, miles of muscles beneath smooth, golden skin, and full lips that would send any girl swooning. But there was something deeper behind the beauty, something very different about him that made my fingers itch for a pencil and paper. I wasn't sure I could even capture the indescribable thing I felt when I looked at him, but I really wanted to try. As easy as I found it to put people in categories based on the things I noticed about them—

their clothes, the way they moved, the people they were with, or their patterns of communication—I thought that for him I just might have to come up with a new system. He didn't belong in any particular group. He was unique.

I blinked and realized he was smirking again. Even if the rest of him was a mystery, I could identify the expression. I'd met dozens of boys with expressions like that. International or not, they were all the same. They thought their wealth and good looks made them powerful. This guy was practically dripping with power. *Definitely not my type.*

"So what are you supposed to be?" I lashed out, heat stinging my cheeks in response to his arrogance. "Are you some international model taking photos down here and now can't find your pants?" I scoffed, indicating his costume or lack thereof. "Well, believe me," I said, using my best condescending voice and punctuating each word with a dramatic gesture for emphasis, "nobody would look twice at you, so just . . . move along."

Sighing, Model-boy mumbled a few words as he swirled his fingers in the air. Suddenly, there was a funny taste in my mouth, a kind of fizzing, like an effervescent candy had just dissolved on my tongue. The sensation quickly disappeared and I was trying to figure out what he was doing when he said a word I finally understood.

"Identify."

"Identify?" I repeated dumbly. "Are you asking my name?"

He nodded once.

Shifting my weight, I answered tersely, "Lilliana Young. What's yours?"

"Good. Come along, Young Lily, I have need of your assistance," he said, forming his lips around the words like they left a bad taste in his mouth, and effectively ignoring my question.